HE WAS DAZZLING

Katrina caught her breath. Everything about Justin bespoke strength, from the square set of his shoulders to the long determination of his stride. He walked with an air of authority, like a man who has staked his claim and has no intention of giving an inch.

His dark hair had grown longer, slightly unkempt, surprisingly attractive. He wiped his hands against his thighs as though readying himself to greet an intruder who had come upon his land.

In the time it took him to take one step, Katrina questioned every excuse she'd given herself, every argument she'd rehearsed to explain to him why she'd come. If just the sight of him could send her blood racing, how could she ever look him in the eye and calmly ask him to let her stay? Then again, how could she ever leave?

Also by Zita Christian

Band of Gold

Available from
HarperPaperbacks

Harper
Monogram

First and Forever

⋊ ZITA CHRISTIAN ⋉

HarperPaperbacks
A Division of HarperCollinsPublishers

HarperPaperbacks *A Division of* HarperCollins*Publishers*
10 East 53rd Street, New York, N.Y. 10022

Copyright © 1994 by Zita Christian
All rights reserved. No part of this book may be used or reproduced in any manner whatsoever without written permission of the publisher, except in the case of brief quotations embodied in critical articles and reviews. For information address HarperCollins*Publishers*,
10 East 53rd Street, New York, N.Y. 10022.

Cover illustration by Vittorio Dangelico

First printing: November 1994

Printed in the United States of America

HarperPaperbacks, HarperMonogram, and colophon are trademarks of HarperCollins*Publishers*

❖ 10 9 8 7 6 5 4 3 2 1

To Laurie Winterberg in Pensacola, Florida
and Eileen Gillikin in Suffolk, Virginia
my sisters

With memories both bitter and bright
that have kept us together in our hearts

Acknowledgments

The public library of Eureka, South Dakota, was closed on the only day that I would be in town. My heartfelt thanks go to the women in the town clerk's office. They listened to my plight, called the librarian at home, located the hidden key, let me in the library, directed me to the local history section, and trusted me to lock the door when I was finished. My thanks, also, to Edmund Opp, director of the Eureka Pioneer Museum, for giving me a private tour of the museum on an evening it was normally closed, and to Jim and Kathy Nelson of the Timber Lake, South Dakota, Historical Society.

With respect and gratitude I acknowledge members of my family. Though this story is fiction, their histories inspired me: Carl Dick Winterberg of Hannover, Germany, who came to America to be a farmer; his wife, Martha Ella Ryckman, an English girl who, along with her sister Annie, homesteaded adjoining quarters of Dakota land and built a soddy that spanned the boundary; Conrad

Phillip Karl Saltenberger of Frankfurt, Germany, who brought little more than his books to America, then married Elizabeth Alice Reineck of Philadelphia. The day Conrad became a citizen, he marched down the streets of Philadelphia singing "God Bless America."

Both couples settled in Missouri and raised their children. William Winterberg fell in love with the hired girl, Katherine Saltenberger. They married, left Missouri, and eventually settled in Timber Lake, South Dakota. There they rented a two-quarter homestead until they could afford to buy it, for neither wanted to go into debt. They had to wait nearly twenty years. Then they bought five quarters of land, one for each of their living children.

One of those children was my father, C. C. Winterberg of Mobridge, South Dakota. I could not have written this book without his help. Not only did he answer my long-distance questions at all hours of the day and night, he often gave me the benefit of his own instincts as a writer, offering character insights I might never have had. Most of all, he helped me understand why, after running away from the prairie at seventeen, he is so happy to be back.

Spring and Summer
1887

Merriweather, Missouri

1

Katrina Swann glanced out the bedroom window to be sure the cook was still in the garden and then rehearsed her new role again, this time louder, with more confidence, without bowing like a peasant.

"How do you do? I am Mrs. Richmond Barrison. Welcome to our home. My husband and I are delighted you could join us."

She wanted Richmond to be proud of her. She hoped he would also appreciate the dresser scarf she'd embroidered for their room. It had taken months to complete. She removed it from the basket she'd set on the green velvet chair and carefully unfolded the three-foot length of linen, thick with tiny satin stitches forming twisting green vines and creamy honeysuckle trumpets. She'd cleaned this room enough times to know the colors, but being in Richmond's room as a maid was one thing. Being here as his wife-to-be was entirely different. She brought the scarf to the cherry dresser to see how it would look. It was perfect.

Richmond's things were arranged just so, his silver tray of toiletries at one end, his black lacquer jewelry box at the other, a crystal vase of white azaleas in the middle. She didn't see any room for her. But then, other than a brush and comb and a hand-held mirror, she didn't have anything to put on a dresser.

She opened the doors of his massive wardrobe, which was cherry, to match the dresser. She would eventually need a place to put her clothes, though at the moment only one of her three dresses was good enough to warrant hanging in such a fine wardrobe. Richmond had said that outfitting her properly would be one of the first things he would do once they were married. The aroma of fine pipe tobacco scented his clothes. She once told him she thought he was too young for a pipe. After all, he was only twenty, the same age as she. He then reminded her of the importance of displaying the proper image. For the younger son of Eberhard Barrison, owner of Barrison Brewery, that image was one of success.

With the dresser scarf draped across her arm, she turned to the bed. She'd slept with Gretchen for as long as she could remember, but sleeping with a sister wouldn't be the same as sleeping with a husband. Unlike the faded quilt that covered the bed she and Gretchen shared, a thick goosedown comforter stretched over the ornate sleigh bed she would share with Richmond. Two down pillows touched each other at the head, making her think of what more they would share.

How many times had Gretchen told her that if she didn't take a man to her bed soon, she'd wind up on the shelf? Maybe so. But she wasn't marrying Richmond just to get a husband. She was marrying him because he would be the *right* husband. He was a good man. He was healthy; handsome, too. He had the respect of the community, a solid financial future, a family home on high ground. She was a lucky woman and she knew it. Besides that, she cared for him. He cared for her. Together they would have a good life. Still, the thought of what she would be expected to do between those clean white sheets troubled her. What if she didn't do it right? What if she hated it?

So intense were her thoughts, she didn't hear the front door close and a heavy satchel thud against the floor. Staring at the bed, her back to the open bedroom door, she didn't see the older Barrison son coming up the stairs. Unaware of his arrival, she straightened her posture to appear as dignified as possible and rehearsed once more. "How do you do? I am Mrs. Richmond Barrison—"

"Did I miss the wedding?"

Startled, she turned around.

"Justin!"

The tall, lanky boy had grown up. If she remembered correctly, his dark curly hair was always in need of a cut, though to see it skim the collar of his white shirt now emphasized the straight line of his shoulders and softened the square of his jaw.

"Who else?" he asked.

"But your telegram said you would arrive on Thursday. Today is Tuesday."

"I caught an early train."

She was about to say they weren't ready for him. The windows hadn't been washed. The floors hadn't been polished. Bridget hadn't prepared his homecoming meal. But of all life's desires, she understood a person's wanting to come home. "Welcome back," she said, giving him a shaky smile.

"Thank you. Where is everyone?"

She couldn't stop staring at him. He had yet to use the razor today. The effect was surprisingly pleasant.

"In town?" he asked, when she did not respond.

"Forgive me," she said. "I am just so . . . so surprised. Your father and brother have gone to the brewery. Your mother to Jefferson City. You see, we didn't expect you for another two days." She paused. "So there's no one to welcome you but Bridget and me. I'm sorry."

He didn't look at all disappointed, but rather pleased. Or at least relieved. "Jefferson City?"

"To shop for the wedding."

"So I *haven't* missed it. When I heard you—"

"Oh, no, I was just . . . I was just practicing," she stammered.

Justin had that same look—pleased, or relieved. Katrina couldn't understand why. He and Richmond had never shown the kind of bond she and Gretchen shared. She didn't think it would bother him in the least to miss his brother's wedding. Maybe she was wrong. After all, she hadn't seen them together in five years, for Justin had left for Germany soon after Katrina and her family arrived in town.

Noticing the dresser scarf, he said, "Honeysuckle, my favorite flower."

She stretched the scarf to its full length, affording him a better view. "The flower is known to summon wealth."

"All the more reason for my brother to like it."

It was also known to summon erotic dreams, but Katrina would never mention something so private to him.

Justin glanced around the room, his gaze lingering on the bed. Maybe he already knew the myth of erotic dreams. Afraid that he could somehow read her thoughts, Katrina blushed. At this moment she wanted nothing more than to get out of Richmond's room, but maybe that would draw attention to her discomfort.

"Mother wrote to me about your marriage. June first, right?"

"*Ja.* June first." Until this moment whenever anyone asked about the upcoming wedding, she answered with enthusiasm and a list of details about her dress, the flowers, the music, the food. Talking about it now made her feel uneasy.

"My brother is a lucky man."

Her cheeks grew warmer, not so much from his words, as from the way he looked at her. It was not an intimate look, of course, but one of affection. Yet even that was more than she expected from him, for the Barrisons were not given to displays of affection, not even among themselves. Besides, the last time she saw Justin he hadn't seemed the least bit interested in a skinny fifteen-year-old girl.

"Mother also wrote that you'd grown into a beauty. She was right."

A beauty? Katrina mumbled a thank-you while she fussed with her apron, suddenly aware of how ordinary she must look in her simple white blouse gathered at the neck, her white bodice laced up the front, and her dark blue skirt. Richmond was right. She did look like a peasant. Why hadn't she worn her good dress today?

Increasingly conscious of Justin's scrutiny, she looked away. He was waiting for her to say something, but the confidence she'd felt just moments ago had disappeared, leaving her confused and, worse still, troubled. Why should she care how she looked to him? He was not the man she had to please.

"Looks like we had another flood," Justin said to fill the silence. "I stopped at the livery on my way in this morning. It's still under two inches of water. Did it hurt your family?"

"We will survive."

A small spring flooding, that's what everyone called it. Still, it had ruined every sack of flour in the Swann family bakery. Katrina had left for work at the Barrisons' that morning feeling guilty that she couldn't stay and help her parents and sister clean up. Now she felt guilty for other reasons.

The sound of the back door drew their attention.

"That's Bridget," Katrina said. "Does she know you're home?"

"As soon as she sees my satchel, she will."

A shriek of pleasure came from the bottom of the stairs. Justin grinned. "Excuse me."

To Katrina's relief, he hurried down the stairs, leaving her to grab her basket and take one last look at the room she would share with Richmond. Justin's room was right next door.

Katrina heard Bridget's booming voice. "Well, well, well, will you look at what the wind blew in? A sight for me poor old eyes, now that's for sure."

"Bridget O'Malley. Beautiful as ever."

From the top of the stairs, Katrina could see Justin give Bridget a hearty embrace. She could also see the sheer happiness on the old woman's face as she held at arm's length the boy she'd watched grow to become a most attractive man.

"Look at you," Bridget said as she reached up, barely able to touch Justin's shoulders. "Tall as your da and fleshed out so fine. So handsome and" —her voice cracked— "so grown up." She grabbed the hem of her apron and wiped her eyes.

"Now don't cry," Justin said as he pulled her into his arms once again. He bent to kiss her rosy cheek. "I'm going to take my bag upstairs. Then I'll be down for a cup of your delicious tea and you can fill me in on what's happened since I've been gone. I don't suppose you have any biscuits left over from breakfast?"

Bridget beamed. "Now that I do. And a jar of just-opened grape jam. I'll stir up some ham and eggs, too. How'd that be? And some fried potatoes." She reached up and patted his cheek. "It's good to have you home, Mr. Justin. You've been gone far too long." With a smile and a sigh, she added, "Now off with you. I've got a meal to fix."

With that, Bridget waddled to the kitchen while Justin lifted his bag and headed for the stairs.

Katrina met him at the bottom, her hand gripping the railing tightly. "Your old room is all ready."

He looked at her with curiosity and asked, "Does Richmond still have the adjacent one?"

"He does."

"And the walls? Thin as ever?"

Thin enough to allow the sound of laughter? Yes. The sound of tears? Yes. She'd worked here long enough to know. Still, something told her not to discuss anything personal with this man, even the proximity of his room. To do so seemed somehow dangerous. Instead, she said, "No need to worry, Justin. I'm sure you won't disturb us."

"Come, Molly," Katrina said to the bony, freckle-faced girl behind her. Barely fifteen and in this country just over a year, Molly was Bridget's cousin. She had come in less than an hour after Justin. Her desire to make America her home and her wide-eyed wonder at the luxury all around her reminded Katrina of herself at that age.

"Me aunt says come June you're to marry the yellow-haired son and that's why you won't be working here after today."

"Yes." Katrina held out her left hand so Molly could see the simple silver band that signified her engagement. After the ceremony, she'd move the ring to her right hand and that's where it would stay until the day she died.

"I caught a glimpse of him in town this morning when me Aunt Bridget fetched me from the train. He's a dandy-lookin' one."

Yes, Richmond was an attractive man. He was the height of most men but had blonder hair and bluer eyes. Everything about him, from his dignified walk to his refined speech spoke of elegance. And then there was Justin. Of the same family yet taller, dark-haired, dark-eyed, with a determined walk, he had a way of speaking that could imply instant intimacy, with words spoken not just from his lips but from his eyes.

"Me aunt took me past the Barrison Brewery, too. Looks to be a moneymaker, that's for sure."

"Mr. Barrison provides very well for his family," Katrina said, unable to clear her mind of Justin's image.

Molly looked around. "You'll be living in all this splendor and not having to clean it?"

"That's right," Katrina said as she followed Molly's gaze, not at all surprised to realize how important it was to her that the furniture always gleam, the windows always sparkle. Even in her cozy home in Russia, with its red brick floors, white plaster walls, and blue enamel ceiling, cleanliness and order were the standards. It was only because the Barrisons recognized Katrina's class and knew she came from a once prominent family fallen on hard times that they approved of her marriage to Richmond.

"Come," Katrina said, leading the way up the long, sweeping staircase. When she reached the landing, she gestured to the left. "The bedrooms at this end of the hall are reserved for guests." She gestured to the right. "These rooms are for family." Her gaze lingered on the closed door of Justin's room. She hadn't seen him all afternoon. He was probably sleeping, tired from his trip. "The family rooms have all just been cleaned, so you're to start with the guest rooms."

"And which is the one you'll be sharing with your mister?"

"This one," Katrina said, as she opened the door and for the second time that day stared at the cherry sleigh bed in the center of the room. For the second time that day, she felt a deep-rooted desire she could neither define nor dismiss. If this desire had to do with Richmond, why hadn't she felt it before?

Hoping to clear her thoughts, Katrina led the way down the hall toward the guest rooms, but with each step she found herself trying all the harder to picture what her mother had told her years ago about the joining of husband and wife, and this was still her concern when she opened the door to the guest room at the end of the hall and walked in.

She gasped and turned beet red. "Molly, cover your eyes!"

Molly crossed herself. "Jesus, Mary, and Joseph!"

Justin, clad only in iridescent bubbles and thick white lather, dropped the cake of soap into the bowl on the stand beside him and grabbed a towel. He turned around, and, until he fastened the towel about his waist, gave both women a second view to remember.

"Hurry, Molly," Katrina said as she shooed the girl out into the hall ahead of her. Slamming the door, Katrina gripped the knob with one hand to make sure it stayed closed and with the other covered her heart, as though that would still its thunder. She had never, ever, seen a grown man naked.

From the noises she heard inside the room, she imagined he was scrambling to dry and dress as quickly as possible. But she knew she would never forget the expanse of skin covering his broad shoulders and the hard wall of his chest, smooth but for a small patch of dark hair still wet and glistening from the soap and the afternoon sun pouring through the window. She would always remember watching the water trickle down his flat stomach and disappear in the triangle of dark curls below.

Katrina felt a flush of heat that, while not altogether new, had never been this intense.

"You still out there?" he called through the door.

"Yes. I'm sorry. I was just showing Molly—you shouldn't be in there, you know. This is a guest room. You should be down at the other end of the hall."

"I like my privacy."

Molly cupped her hands around her mouth and whispered, "He's the other brother?"

Katrina nodded.

"The wild one just come home from Germany?"

Katrina gave Molly a look intended to let the girl know her comment was out of line, but it apparently had no effect.

"Me Aunt Bridget says he's a rebel and a heartbreaker and she loves him like a son. Says he left a princess waiting at the altar—a genuine *princess.*"

"Molly, you go on down to the kitchen. Tell your Aunt Bridget I sent you and that she's to keep you busy for at least a quarter hour. Then you can come back up here and clean the guest rooms, starting with this one."

Wide-eyed, Molly said, "I don't know as I ought to be leaving you alone up here with that stallion."

"Molly!"

"Well, that's what he is, sure enough. You saw good as I."

"To the kitchen. *Now!*"

Katrina watched Molly race down the stairs and disappear around the corner. She waited a moment, then cleared her throat and rapped on the door. "Are you decent?"

"Come on in."

"I wanted only to apologize. I—"

"I can't hear you. Open the door."

She squared her shoulders, lifted her chin, and very, very slowly turned the glass knob.

With his back to her, he said, "Just hanging up my towel."

Even from the back he looked handsome. But he should have finished dressing before he draped his towel on the washstand. Instead, he stood there buttoning his clean white shirt, sleeves billowing slightly around his arms. His tan trousers were already tucked into his high black boots.

He turned around and caught her staring at him. She silently cursed the blush that once again stained her cheeks. He smiled. The silence that followed unnerved her.

"As I said, I was showing Molly around. She's to clean

the guest rooms today. I didn't expect anyone to be in this room. I didn't mean to startle you."

He looked amused by her comment. "No harm done."

No?

When she didn't respond, he walked right up to her and went on. "Forgive me, Katrina. I should have done this sooner." Before she knew what was happening, except that her heart was drumming loud enough to be heard down the hall, he kissed her lightly on the lips. "Welcome to the family."

With that, he slipped past her, leaving her with one finger lingering on her lips and a faraway look in her eyes. At the top of the stairs he turned around and winked.

"And all these years I thought you were waiting for me."

Katrina was stunned. His words echoed in her mind long after he'd disappeared down the stairs. He'd never said or done anything to show he was interested in her. As far as she knew, he'd never asked about her in his letters. He'd certainly never written to her. And to walk up to her the way he just did, bold as you please, and kiss her like that . . . ?

She pressed her hand to her heart again, feeling the need to protect it. Wait for him? Heaven help her, she almost wished she had.

Later that afternoon, her ability to concentrate was shaken again as she stood at the entrance to the Barrisons' grand dining room and scrutinized the table one last time. The snow-white linens had been bleached, starched, and pressed. The white china gleamed. The crystal stemware and silver flatware sparkled. She nodded to Molly, who placed an oriental vase of deep-pink azaleas in the center of the long table between the tall white tapers. They both stood back to admire the effect.

From behind her, Katrina heard the front door open and a smooth, familiar voice.

"Were there no roses in the hothouse?"

Katrina turned to face her fiancé, who looked as perfectly polished as the silver. "Oh, Richmond! Justin is home. Have you seen him?"

"What? He's not supposed to be here yet."

The critical look on Richmond's face made her enthusiasm suddenly seem inappropriate, as did the traitorous feeling in her heart. But Justin and Richmond were brothers. They should be happy to see each other. And so she asked, with less fervor, "Isn't that wonderful?"

"For whom? Certainly not me. I had a full agenda to tend to before he showed up. Not for Mother. She's not even here." Richmond combed his fingers through the straight blond hair he kept tucked behind his ears. "How like Justin to upset everyone else's schedule in favor of his own."

From the kitchen came Justin's deep voice. "Did I hear my name?"

"Well, well," Richmond said quickly, extending his hand in the well-mannered way Katrina had seen so often. "I trust you had a good trip."

Justin shook his brother's hand, with nothing of the warmth he had shown her that morning. "Yes. I even managed an early train."

"How fortunate for us all."

Bowing slightly toward Katrina, Justin said, "I understand, little brother, that congratulations are in order."

"That's correct."

Katrina felt a strange discomfort as Richmond stepped close to her and took her arm in his.

"Come June," he said, "I will have a wife."

"A most beautiful wife," Justin said, his gaze on Katrina.

She felt the slightest tightening of Richmond's arm. She knew him well enough to recognize the hurt in his voice when he said, a little too sharply, "I suppose you've had your fill of the beauties of Europe."

"All I did in Europe was study."

"You left no trail of broken hearts? No princess at the altar, as I've heard?"

"I studied. That's all."

"Yes, of course."

"It's true. In fact, I can't wait to talk to you and Father about the breweries I saw there, the fields of hops—"

"Justin!" At the sound of the booming voice coming from the front door, Justin straightened his shoulders and Richmond squeezed Katrina's arm. Eberhard Barrison was home. "Why the hell didn't you come straight to the brewery as soon as you arrived?" he asked as he entered the room.

Eberhard was Justin's height, but heavier, hard looking. He puffed out his chest and arched the thick gray tangle of his eyebrows. "Well, I see you found your way home all right."

"Yes, Father, I did." Justin walked over and extended his hand. "It's good to be back."

Shaking his son's hand briefly, Eberhard said, "It's good to be back in the lap of luxury. That's what you mean. Your five-year holiday is over. I hope you know that."

"I didn't come home to loaf, Father. I came home to work."

"Good. Because that's what you're going to do." He looked at Richmond. "Both of you."

"I'm looking forward to it. I learned a great deal in Europe, Father. I saw massive breweries, endless fields of hops. There are many things we can do to improve—"

"We still dine at eight," Eberhard said as he scrutinized the table. "I trust you'll be dressed by then."

"Yes, Father. Of course."

"See to it." He left the room and went upstairs.

Katrina felt an overwhelming relief as Richmond released her arm. Richmond and Justin exchanged commiserating looks.

"What did you expect?" Richmond asked. "Tears and a hearty embrace?"

"I know better than that." Justin shoved his hands in his pockets and shrugged.

"So," Richmond said, "what *did* you do today?"

He kissed me. Katrina averted her eyes, unable to keep the thought from her mind or the blush from her cheeks.

Justin walked to the window and gazed at the fresh green pasture. "I saddled up and took a ride."

"You saw the two new Hanoverians?"

"Yes. They're magnificent. I saw the river, too." He looked at Katrina. "Your bakery suffered more than you admitted, didn't it?"

"We did lose the flour. All of it. But Poppa will get more."

"I don't know how," Justin said. "From what I heard today, every mill along the river has been flooded."

Richmond waved a dismissing hand. "Don't concern yourself, Katrina. I'll see to it that your family gets more flour. Just remind me."

"*Danke.* I mean, thank you. My family will be grateful. And now I must get home, for Gretchen needs my help."

Richmond took her arm in his once more. "Why don't we step out into the garden for a moment. The azaleas you've picked are pretty enough, but I think sprays of yellow forsythia would look handsome too."

"But I must get home—"

"Now, now. There's no need for you to worry, my dear. I'll have the stableboy bring the buggy around and drive you to town myself."

She hesitated, then felt the slightest increase of pressure from Richmond's hand on her arm.

"Surely you would enjoy my company?" he said. "Or am I no longer the love of your life?"

Clearing his voice, Justin said, "You two will excuse me?" He nodded to Richmond, then looked directly into Katrina's eyes. "I don't know that I ever thanked you for your warm welcome this morning."

"I did nothing."

Richmond eyed her curiously, while Justin added, "Oh, but you did. You made me glad I came home." With that, he walked away.

Katrina could see nothing in Richmond's demeanor that betrayed his thoughts, except the set of his jaw as they stepped outside. She didn't think he liked having his older brother home.

Gazing at the beauty all around them, Richmond said, "This time next month the roses will be in bloom. All women like roses, don't they?"

Katrina nodded. "*Grossvater*—my grandfather had a beautiful rose garden."

"The blooms in *this* garden are as big as doorknobs."

"I know," Katrina said, realizing that all Richmond really wanted at this moment was an audience.

"There I go again," he said, "rambling on about such nonsense when we have so many more important things to discuss." He smiled. "Like our wedding."

She fought the image of the cherry sleigh bed in the room at the top of the stairs and the image of Justin, naked, in the room down the hall. "Last night I embroidered the last stitches on a dresser scarf for our room. It's covered with honeysuckle." She reached into her basket. "Here, I'll show you."

"No, my dear, don't bother. I'm sure it's beautiful."

While she appreciated his confidence in her work, she would rather have shown him the scarf. But he was a busy man and she was eager to get home. Knowing he would see it soon enough, she tucked it back into place. "I picked a wild pansy this morning. Two of the petals had four lines. That means my wish will come true."

"I'll see to it myself."

"One petal had seven lines. That means I have a faithful sweetheart."

Richmond laughed. "The old folklore is charming, I suppose. But please, Katrina dear, don't mention such things when we're in the company of others. I wouldn't want you to be embarrassed."

"Of course." She didn't say anything about the last two petals, the one with five lines, which foretold of trouble waiting in her path, and the one with nine lines. Nine lines on a pansy was unusual. It meant she would soon go over the water to wed—a prediction that made no sense at all.

It had been five years since she crossed the ocean. And even if the Missouri River flooded again—so great a flood that she had to swim to safety—she wasn't about to be uprooted from her new home. Not now, not ever.

2

Like stiff white sheets clipped neatly on a line, the pristine half-timbered wood and stucco homes of Merriweather, Missouri, stood in orderly rows on narrow streets surrounding churches with lofty white spires and a school built of locally made salmon-colored brick. A colorful hand-painted WILLKOMMEN sign graced the bakery's front door. Katrina waited for Richmond to help her from the buggy, then quickly said good-bye. The leather strap of sleigh-bells slapped against the door as she rushed inside.

"I'm sorry I'm late," she said as she scurried past Gretchen who was scrubbing the floor, and ran up the stairs to put away her things. Back down in less than a minute, she stopped to catch her breath and explain. "I got here as soon as I could. Richmond gave me a ride in his buggy—"

"*Ja, ja, ja.*" Gretchen looked up from the arc of suds in front of her. Her bright blue eyes had lost their luster. Her silver-blond braids sagged against her ears. And her round

apple cheeks looked dull. "So this was your last day as a hired girl?"

"*Ja*, my last."

"Lucky for you. When you and Richmond are wed, you will not have to worry about a flooding river. I think I will marry a man who lives on high ground too. And I will take Momma and Poppa to live with me."

"You go sit down," Katrina said as she knotted the hem of her skirt, knelt on the floor, and picked up the frayed and sloppy cloth from where Gretchen had left it.

Gretchen stood, stretched her back, and groaned, then sat on the red bench Poppa had made. "From where you found so much energy?" she said, letting her dark dress sag between her ample thighs. She yawned. "Together we have not had enough sleep for one."

Katrina noticed the tidy shelves, with all the colorful tins of cocoa and tea and jars of jewel-toned jellies arranged just so. Gone was the brackish odor of river water, mud, and spoiled yeast. In its place was the clean smell of lemon oil. The counter sparkled, too. At one end stood scales and a set of weights, a mill to grind coffee, another for pepper and spices. At the other end, a gleaming black cash register. "You've already done a week's work," Katrina said. "No wonder you're so tired."

"Momma too," Gretchen said. "And I am worried. She washed all the baskets in hot suds, scrubbed all the crockery, then scalded the sink with lye. She took to her bed an hour ago, yet tomorrow she plans to wash and starch the curtains."

"Momma wants more than just an agreeable appearance."

With another gaping yawn, Gretchen nodded. "I hope Poppa finds a way to get more flour. I heard the millers suffered greatly from the flood too, but someone must have flour they are willing to sell."

After rinsing a section with clean water, Katrina sat

back on her heels. "Richmond said not to worry. He will find more flour for us."

"At what price?" Gretchen glanced toward the stairs and lowered her voice. "This morning, after you left, I heard Poppa say to Momma that searching for flour will be useless for he has no extra funds to spend this month—unless some of the accounts pay early, and that is not likely."

"What did Momma say?"

"She said, 'You find the flour. I will find the funds.'"

"And?"

Gretchen shrugged and looked up at the cuckoo clock. "We will know when Poppa gets home. Or when your Richmond shows up."

Half an hour later, Katrina mopped the last of the suds from the floor and the sweat from her brow. "When the wood is dry I'll rub in the beeswax and sweet oil, if you'll polish."

"*Ja,* sure. And then," Gretchen said, with the hint of the smile that usually defined her face and a flickering gleam that rarely left her eye, "as soon as Poppa gets the flour, I will bake a big batch of my delicious sticky buns."

"You have a particular customer in mind?"

With a noncommittal shrug, Gretchen said, "Maybe. For I am a young and beautiful woman who intends to plot her own future and marry for pure love. We live in America now."

"Gretchen, when will you learn? You know of the danger in picking your own husband. You could get one who hides that he is sickly. Or one who has no trade. Or one who uses his fists. Let Poppa pick for you. He will pick to ensure your future as he did mine."

"Poppa didn't seek Richmond. Richmond sought you."

"Yes, but Poppa approved."

Gretchen merely smiled. Katrina knew there was no point in trying to convince her of the danger in abandoning the old ways. Since coming to the golden land, all she and Poppa talked about was the importance of becoming Americans. For Poppa that meant picking the president. For Gretchen that meant picking her own husband.

That evening, Poppa returned carrying a fifty-pound sack of rye. A boy he had hired carried another, just as large, of wheat. Momma had found enough ingredients to make a pot of noodles and cream for dinner, so all seemed back to normal—until it was time to eat.

Neither sister said a word when they noticed the absence of the silver candlesticks their mother always used for dinner. Katrina saw a knowing look pass between her parents, both sad at the measures they'd been forced to take, both determined to do whatever else was necessary to have a life that was not rich but yet was richer than the one they'd left behind. Gretchen seemed relieved, but Katrina had to blink back tears. Those were the candlesticks Momma had always hidden from the czar's soldiers, the candlesticks that had belonged to Great-grandmother.

The next morning, as Gretchen sat at the dressing table braiding her hair, she said, "Katrina, what is ailing you? Your mouth, it droops like a rag. You are to be a wife soon. You should be the picture of joy."

Sitting on the edge of the bed, Katrina yawned. "I am in need of more sleep, that's all."

"You are not planning to change your wedding date, are you? Sophie Schulz did that. Two times, each one closer than the one before, all of which leads people to talk."

"No, the first of June is still the date."

"Good. Soon I will have all this space to myself. And already I have big plans for it."

"For this little room?"

"*Ja,* I plan to set up a writing desk and make a cooking

book of all the new recipes I will create. I will record breads—wheat and rye, and kuchens—plum and cheese—and . . ."

Katrina was only half listening, surprised to feel such hurt at knowing Gretchen's eagerness to see her go. Never again would they whisper in the dark about their fears and dreams. Never again would they tiptoe down to the bakery in the middle of the night to share a sweet or make a cup of hot soothing tea for the one whose time of the month had come. But then, Gretchen was afraid of nothing, not an unknown future, not a life of loneliness, not even the criticism of those who mocked the accent she tried so hard to erase.

"Katrina? Your brain—it still works?"

Startled from her reverie, Katrina surveyed the sparsely furnished room that, even after five years in America, held only half of what she'd left behind. "So you plan to write cookbooks after I marry Justin—" She covered her mouth with her hand. "I mean Richmond."

All teasing left Gretchen's voice. "To predict your marriage to the wrong brother is no small matter."

"It was a slip of the tongue, that's all." How could she even think of marrying another man? She was betrothed. Her nerves instantly jangled as she pictured Justin, naked but for soap bubbles, then saw him standing before Eberhard, waiting for the welcome he had a right to receive, hiding the disappointment he must have felt.

"Why did you slip?"

Why indeed? Katrina folded her hands in her lap and twined her fingers in a knot, angry that she wasn't able to control her feelings, doubting her ability to explain to Gretchen what she couldn't explain to herself.

"Well?" Gretchen pressed. "Out with it."

"It's nothing. He just confuses me, that's all."

"When did he confuse you? You told me he arrived only yesterday."

Katrina groaned as she looked up into Gretchen's eyes, but she couldn't answer.

"When?" Gretchen said. "Did he close the door without slamming? Did he greet you without shouting?"

"Justin isn't like that. Neither is Richmond. It's their father who is so harsh."

"So when did he confuse you?"

"When he kissed me!"

Startled, Gretchen paused, considering the revelation. "An innocent brother's kiss, *ja*?"

"For sure that's all it was. Just a brother's kiss."

"Not a man's kiss?"

"No. He meant nothing by it, I'm certain."

"Then why should it confuse you?"

"I don't know."

"Did he say anything when he did it?"

Instantly reliving the moment, with its warmth and excitement, with its hint of seduction, Katrina could do nothing but repeat Justin's words. "'Welcome to the family.'"

"Ah, of course. He was showing his manners."

"He said that all these years he thought I was waiting for him."

"Why would he say that?"

"How should I know?"

"Why, that pompous oaf! Just what gives him the right to be so bold? A prosperous name?"

Katrina stood and paced the floor. "I can't see into his mind!"

"You must have shown him some encouragement."

Turning sharply, Katrina said, "How could I have encouraged a man I haven't seen in five years. And even then, he never knew I was there!"

"And that angers you?"

"Of course not!"

Gretchen looked confused. "Then why you are getting

so upset? If I didn't know better, I would say not only has
Justin turned your head but you have been unfaithful in
your heart. Tell me I am wrong. Please."

Groping for a logical explanation but finding none,
Katrina blurted out, "I saw him naked."

Gretchen gasped. "When? How?"

"I was showing Molly around and we walked in on
him. For sure Molly has told Bridget." Katrina groaned.
"What am I going to do?"

"You are to put him out of your mind, that's what."

"Gretchen, I saw him naked!"

"So? Has the image spoiled your brain?"

"You know as well as I that if we were in the old country I could be forced to marry him. How would one man
feel knowing the woman he planned to marry had seen
another man in his altogether? The first man would
worry. 'Am I as pleasing to her eye as he? Whose endowments are better for giving her healthy children, his or
mine?'"

"Now you listen to me, Katrina Swann. Though I know
you always long for the old country, be glad you blun-
dered in America. In America anything can be fixed. So
cease your worries this instant. You will never be forced
to marry Justin. But you must stay clear of him."

"How can I? We'll be living under the same roof, eating
at the same table, passing each other in the hall, brushing
against—"

"Halt." Gretchen shook her head, as though disaster
had befallen both of them. Then she said, "Katrina, you
have never been one to tingle over the sight of a handsome
man. This is not the time to start. More important, keep
this in mind. When Justin was home five years past, his
name was linked with Verena Aberle. And before that
Helga Utley. His reputation is none too fragrant."

"That was idle gossip. At last year's *Oktoberfest*, I went

promenading with Bert Kleinert, but that doesn't make me a trollop."

"Why do you defend him, this man you care nothing for?"

"I'm not defending him!"

"I think your head has been in the oven too long."

Frustrated by her tangling thoughts, Katrina blurted out, "There's more." Gretchen looked at her expectantly. "When I saw him standing there . . . without his clothes . . ."

"*Ja?*"

"I liked it. I felt something . . . something . . . I felt drawn to him."

"Hmm." Gretchen tilted her head to one side.

Katrina knew that whatever Gretchen said next, it would be for Katrina's "own good."

"Katrina, I love you and I say this for your own good. Richmond is a smart man. He may believe like all the others that the prettiest flowers are picked early, yet he still picked you. Now here you are with the best catch in town right in your basket and still you are tempted to shop the market." She stood and made her way toward the bedroom door. "But you remember this. Married to Richmond, your children and your children's children will prosper. Momma and Poppa will be secure in their old age. Best of all, you will be only two miles down the road from me. Only a fool would cast such a blessing aside." She paused, then added, "Besides, I would hate like poison to be the one to tell Poppa that your heart has taken a turn. He is so proud of securing the match for you."

"Wait." Only because she trusted Gretchen with her heart did Katrina give words to the seed of the dream she feared to plant. "What if Justin felt the same about me as Richmond does? He is a Barrison too. My future would be as secure with him as with Richmond."

Shaking her head sadly, Gretchen said, "I believe you have a handsome face that would bother any man to distraction, but you must face facts. You are a good cook, yes, but you are not husky for hard work and your hips are not wide for bearing babies. You have no dowry. *And* you are all of twenty."

"What are you saying? That I should be on my knees every night thanking God that at least one man wants to marry me?"

"I am saying only that you have been lucky once. You would not be wise to count on being lucky twice."

Katrina had never been given to lofty ambitions, and though Gretchen's advice rankled, she knew her sister was right.

"Now come," Gretchen said, "help me with the kuchen. It will only be apple, but until the plum trees bear it will do. Anything to fill my bakery again. Tonight we will wax the floor."

As Katrina approached the door, she saw a spider crawl between her and Gretchen. Pointing, she said, "Look. A spider."

"So we are to quarrel." Gretchen grinned as though the idea of sparring with her sister was a source of pleasure, but a barely visible tick at the corner of her mouth betrayed her concern. "Do you wish to quarrel about who will wax and who will polish? Or about which breads to bake today, wheat or rye?"

Katrina watched the spider disappear beneath the bed. The quarrel with Gretchen wouldn't be about either cooking or cleaning. She knew it. She saw the determination in Gretchen's knuckles as she gripped the wooden doorknob, just as she herself had done to avoid the temptation of seeing Justin naked again. Gretchen was afraid of this quarrel too.

Katrina couldn't shake the feeling that Justin's sudden appearance was about to shatter both Gretchen's world and her own. Because she didn't know what else to do,

Katrina found new appeal in Gretchen's simple solution to combat the crazy thoughts that troubled her heart. Remind herself how lucky she was to be marrying Richmond. And avoid Justin, simply avoid him.

Once downstairs, the sisters scrubbed their hands in the washbasin, and Gretchen retrieved two large brown striped bowls from the shelf under the counter. Giving one to Katrina, she said, "I will make the dough. You soak the apples and raisins and grate the cinnamon. And I will tell you all about Lukas Heinz."

"Lukas Heinz. The chemist?"

"*Ja,* the chemist. Before the flood he was in every day for one week. He buys one sticky bun at a time. Just one. I hear he's worth catching, but I think he's a slow-molded man, the kind that never gets excited. Yet he praises my baking, saying it is fit for the President Cleveland."

Katrina noticed the blush that colored Gretchen's already sun-kissed cheeks. Faithfully, Gretchen read the column in the *Gazette* that instructed young women on the rights and wrongs of looking and acting like a *real* American girl: what style of dress was appropriate for what time of day, how to hold and use a handkerchief, and the art of witty conversation. Not once did she complain that she had only three dresses, two for work and one for church, or that her threadbare hankies were edged with only the tiniest bit of lace, not the elaborate flounces illustrated in the newspaper, or that her conversation always betrayed her difficulty in learning the new language. Gretchen deserved better. If picking her own husband would bring her the happiness she deserved, Katrina would support her goal.

Having made that decision, Katrina prayed there would be nothing else of such importance for them to quarrel about.

*　　　*　　　*

Justin stepped into the bakery and inhaled the aromas of fresh bread, baked apples, and cinnamon. "I brought you some flour," he said, as he lowered the sack he'd carried on his shoulder.

He couldn't help but smile and stare in admiration. Gretchen had grown into a beautiful woman. Thick braids of hair as pale as new cornsilk wound around each ear. Her pale pink cheeks rounded as she smiled in return. But her eyes . . . her big bright-blue eyes narrowed slightly. He wondered if she was suspicious of him for some reason, though he couldn't imagine what.

"There's no charge," he said, suddenly realizing what was probably troubling her. "My brother told Katrina yesterday that he'd try to find some. I understand the flood ruined all you had."

"*Ja*, it did. So this free flour, it is from Richmond?"

"It's from my family."

"Poppa has already bought flour for us."

"Oh, I'm glad he found some. But you can keep this anyway."

"For free?"

"Yes."

"*Danke.*"

He gripped the edges of the sack, ready to hoist it over his shoulders again. "Where would you like it?"

Wiping her hands on her apron, Gretchen came around the counter and directed the placement. "There. Against the wall." When he'd finished, she said, "So, you must be Justin."

"And you're Gretchen. Last time I saw you, you were twelve years old."

"*Ja*, well, much has changed around here since then."

"I see."

"It's good you could come home in time for the wedding."

"Is Katrina here?"

"*Ja*, she is here, but she is very busy. The wedding, it takes much of her time."

He didn't know exactly when all this talk about the wedding began to bother him, but it did. "I only wanted to say hello."

Going to the stairs that led to the living quarters, Gretchen called, "Katrina. Katrina, come down."

Justin endured one long and awkward moment as Gretchen eyed him from head to toe, while pretending to be interested in the loaves of pumpernickel on the shelves. He'd eyed a woman that way once or twice—well, maybe three or four times, certainly often enough to recognize the ploy when he saw it. He wondered if the women he'd looked at were ever as uncomfortable as he was right now. Unlike those earlier experiences, he had the distinct feeling that Gretchen didn't like what she saw.

He forgot all about other women as soon as Katrina came down the stairs. If ever the mere sight of a woman could make his body betray his desire, it was now. He recognized the danger.

"Justin!"

She had a beautiful smile. "I know you're busy—"

"Nonsense. I was just folding laundry."

Gretchen interrupted, pointing to the new sack leaning against the wall. "Look, the flour from Richmond."

Katrina looked first at the flour and then at Justin. With a look of sincere gratitude in her eyes, she said softly, "*You* bought the flour, didn't you?"

"It's from the family." Was he supposed to tell the truth? That he rode up and down the river until he found a miller who had some? That he knew his brother would forget? That he didn't want to see that worried look on Katrina's face . . . especially when there was something he could do about it?

"We appreciate it," Katrina said. She turned to Gretchen "Don't we? But Poppa was able to buy two sacks from a miller upriver. You should take it back. I'm sure your family can use it."

"*Ja*," Gretchen said, "there will be plenty of baking going on for the wedding."

Justin kept his gaze on Katrina. "No, I—I mean we—we want you to have it."

"All right, then. Please tell your family how grateful we are."

"I will." Standing several feet away, he could still smell the soap in her clothes, the fragrance of her skin. He'd bet anything that her hair, when unbraided, when spread invitingly about her shoulders, carried the scent of rainwater.

"I guess I'd better go now," he said, heading for the door. "Let me know if you need anything else."

"Thank you," Katrina said.

Before he could reach the door, it opened and in came Richmond. "What are you doing here?" Justin asked.

Directing two small boys behind him to carry in two large sacks, Richmond said, "I'm bringing flour. I said I would."

Katrina and Gretchen rushed over and helped the boys place the sacks next to the wall while Justin stood stunned. Not for one minute had he believed Richmond would carry out his promise.

Richmond noticed the other sack of flour. Under his breath he said, "Don't interfere with my life, big brother. And don't underestimate me. A lot has changed in five years." In a louder voice he went on. "Come now. Mother would like to see you, and I must get back to the brewery." With hasty nods, the brothers left.

"Wouldn't you know," Gretchen said when they were gone. "No sooner does Momma sell the candlesticks than we get all the flour we need."

"I told her Richmond would provide the flour, but she said Poppa will do the providing for this family."

"You wait and see. When your marriage brings an easier life to Momma and Poppa, she will not be so hard on herself or on Poppa."

"I hope you're right."

"Of course I am right. So, now that Justin is back, you think he will take up with Verena Aberle again?"

"Why would he do that?"

"Come now, Katrina. Look at him good next time. His back is straight like an obedient soldier, yet his eyes move with the quickness of an animal. His clothes show his high station, yet his hair, it needs a good cut. To my eyes he is a man in conflict. And the desires of such a man get aroused easily. He will not stay a bachelor long. Not that one."

"Verena Aberle is too serious for him."

"What about Helga Utley?"

"Too wild."

Gretchen picked up a tray of rolls and headed for the back room where the oven was. "And who are you to pick his woman?"

Turning so Gretchen couldn't see the sudden tears in her eyes, Katrina busied herself straightening items that needed no further hand. She had no right to feel possessive, no right at all. Yet to think of him with someone else tore at her heart with a feeling she couldn't understand and a desire she couldn't permit.

Not all prison bars are forged of iron.

Controlling his growing frustration, Justin Barrison carried a load of wood into the parlor, stacked it beside the hearth, and stoked the fire he knew his mother would want. Though it was warm outside, a massive oak tree kept the room shaded and the windows filled with shadows. The sky had turned cloudy and the air cool, making the dark walls and dark floors look somber despite the expensive trappings at the windows and underfoot. It was his mother's favorite room.

"Thank you," Rosamond said as she stepped into the parlor. "You don't know how pleased I am to have you home, dear. It seems like only yesterday you arrived, so full of modern ideas."

Ideas his father refused to listen to. "It's good to be back."

She gave a little nod. The high stiff collar of her dress held her head erect. The narrow black stripes on the cream satin emphasized her image of order and control. Only the silver filigree pin at her throat softened the effect. She moved closer to the fire, shivered, and rubbed her hands along her arms. "I can never seem to get warm."

"Bridget brought coffee. It's hot."

"You'll join me?"

"Of course." Pouring from the service on his father's desk, Justin filled two delicate cups while his mother sat in one of the burgundy velvet chairs. He noticed how her hands trembled when she lifted her cup. No one had been spared the tension caused by his homecoming.

"Do you expect Father home on time this afternoon?"

"Your father is always on time. You know that."

A moment of tense silence hung between them as she peered into her cup.

"Don't argue with him tonight, Justin. Please. Not tonight."

"Not tonight," he said through gritted teeth. He'd been home more than a week and he and his father had done nothing but argue, which is why he'd spent the day working the horses instead of going to the brewery. "What about tomorrow? Will he listen to me then? What about next week? Next month?"

"Please." Looking pained, Rosamond slipped a lace-edged hankie from her sleeve and delicately pressed it to her forehead.

Justin knelt on the floor beside her and took her hand. "I don't want to upset you, Mother, but I can't go on like this. I'm twenty-five years old and still living in his shadow."

"His shadow?" She shook her head. "You speak nonsense. Your father means nothing by his harsh words. He is merely preparing you for the day when he places the Barrison Brewery in your hands."

"I've spent the last five years in Munich—at his request— learning from master brewers. I come home knowing why our lager, pilsner, and bock are so much better than English ale, knowing how much hops is needed to cut the sweet taste, knowing the secrets of yeast, knowing how to make improvements in transportation—but he won't listen to me. I told him all he has to do is read the papers. The big brewers are getting bigger and the small ones are disappearing every day. Does he listen? No. I can't tolerate any more of his stubbornness. I don't even want the great Barrison Brewery! I never did!"

"Bite your tongue. There's not a man for a hundred miles who wouldn't wish such a fortunate fate—your brother included."

"Then let Richmond have it. He knows the need for progress. He can run the brewery. I want to strike out on my own."

Rosamond's fingers tightened around her cup. "You're the eldest son. The brewery should belong to you. You have a right! You also have a duty."

"I have my own life to lead."

Justin stood and looked down at the woman who had crossed the ocean as a pretty girl of sixteen to join the handsome boy she'd married a year earlier. She rarely talked about those early days, and he always wondered if it was because the man she loved had become a stranger after he came here. Justin found it hard to believe that his father had once been the dashing hero of his village, volunteering—without knowing the language or the layout of the land—to investigate America first-hand to find out if its streets were truly paved with gold, or at least if it was a land where his neighbors could prosper. But that was the story Justin always heard.

"A man's destiny always exacts a high toll from those he loves, Mother. You told me so yourself."

"So I did," she said, "so I did." She straightened her shoulders in that resolute way he'd seen so often. Staring into the fire, she said, "I imagine you have things to do now."

"Yes." His mother's bitterness had turned to apathy long ago. There would be nothing from her now but silence. Only the soft pliant curls of her hair, stripped years ago of its youthful color, betrayed her memories of happier times. He felt sorry for her.

He also felt frustrated. As he'd forced himself to do time and time again, he held his temper and walked away.

He headed for the barn. He'd ride his horse through the hills. Rid himself of this growing need that threatened to rob him of his sanity. Then he'd come back, swallow his anger, and play the dutiful son for his mother's sake. But even his love for her couldn't keep him restrained forever.

Only when he reached a point in the hills overlooking the town, where the little Swann bakery lay, did he admit his other, equally powerful, equally threatening source of frustration. Katrina was going to marry Richmond.

3

Richmond drew back on the reins, controlling the horse's exuberance with a light hand and setting the silky black canopy fringe to tremble. He turned to Katrina. "You've been awfully quiet this afternoon. Is something wrong?"

"No, nothing."

"You look so grim. I've bored you with all my talk of business. That's it, isn't it?"

"No, Richmond. I just have much on my mind."

"Don't let your family forget about coming to dinner next week. Father wants to extend a formal welcome, and I'm sure Mother wants to discuss arrangements for the wedding."

"We're looking forward to it."

He reached over and patted her hand. "Soon all your troubles will be over. And you won't have to worry about anything except which dress to wear."

He doubted there was a woman alive who didn't envy

Katrina's good fortune. His parents sympathized with her family's loss of fortune. Indeed, it was tragic: Gustav Swann, once a prosperous landowner, now nothing but a common baker, one daughter a baker's helper, the other a lowly domestic. Richmond thought of how their lives would improve, and how grateful they would be, once he wed Katrina. He didn't know what he had ever seen in that haughty bitch from St. Louis. But he had been younger then. What did he know?

Gracefully, he stepped from the surrey and helped Katrina down. Taking her hand, he led her to a high point in the meadow, overlooking the sun-drenched valley laced with the pink and green of apple orchards and grape arbors. The glittering Missouri River with its gently scalloped banks ran alongside.

"I told you I would take you to the most beautiful spot in all of Merriweather," he said. "I'll bet you've never seen anything like it."

"It reminds me of the Dniester River winding to the Black Sea. And the Danube too, though I picture it only from Grandfather's stories."

Why did she always have to best him? Why couldn't she have just said, "Yes, thanks to you, I have seen the most beautiful sight on earth"? Lately, she contradicted him at every turn. It was getting on his nerves. He reminded himself that he too was nervous about the wedding, about having enough room for the out-of-town guests, about having enough food and drink, about the music, about whether or not he'd be embarrassed by the gown Katrina's mother insisted on making for her. He had offered to send Katrina to his mother's seamstress. The woman had silks and laces from the finest shops in Europe, but Frau Swann stubbornly refused. In fact, he couldn't be sure she found the idea of having him as a son-in-law all that appealing. But then, she'd only made a halfhearted attempt to learn

English. She probably resented the fact that he was a real American—something she would never be.

Composing himself, he said, "I trust your family has recovered from the flood."

"Yes. It was only a few days until we had the bakery cleaned and whitewashed. Poppa managed to buy more flour. Gretchen and I baked day and night to refill the shelves. Poppa has had to delay work on the gazebo he is building for Momma's anniversary, but, other than that, things are back to normal."

"You were able to use the flour I gave you?"

"Oh, yes. Thank you."

"I'm glad." He paused. "I heard your mother had to sell a pair of silver candlesticks. Didn't you tell her I would provide the flour?"

Katrina's eyes widened.

"Don't look so surprised," he said. "In a small town such as ours it's impossible to keep anything private."

"They belonged to my great-grandmother on my mother's side. Whenever we heard that the soldiers were coming, we put the candlesticks in a pail and lowered them into the well. When we prepared to leave the village for good, Poppa said we could each take only one memento. Gretchen took her doll with the porcelain face. I took the carving my grandfather had made of Strudel—he was my dog. Poppa took a book of Latin. Momma took the candlesticks."

He was pleased to hear how much the candlesticks meant to her, for he'd managed to find them and buy them back. He planned to give them to her as a wedding present.

They stood silently for a moment and then he said, "I've always heard Merriweather mirrored the Rhine River valley, though I've never been to Germany myself. I was born right here." He waited for the look of appreciation in her eyes.

"Though it's the home of my ancestors, I've never been

to Germany either," Katrina said. "My grandparents were just children when Napoleon marched through their village. They had to flee or risk being killed instantly or starving over the long winter. That's why they settled in Russia—the promise of free land."

"Your father is going to take the test and become an American, isn't he?"

"He studies for it every day. He wants to vote."

"Good." He linked her arm in his and led her to where she could look down and see the Barrison Brewery dominating the valley. He took a deep breath to settle his thoughts, for the enormity of his own dreams astounded him. "Someday soon, Katrina, Barrison Brewery will all be mine. I will decide what kind of beer to brew, how much, and where to ship it. And I will set the price."

"I don't understand. I thought you and your brother—"

"No." He pressed his fingertip to her lips to quiet her. "The brewery will be mine, all mine. Just as you will be mine."

She lowered her gaze. He would have liked to have seen more enthusiasm on her face at the mention of being his wife, but no doubt the idea still overwhelmed her.

"You have discussed your ambitions with your father? With Justin?"

Richmond let his head fall back in a laugh. "Hardly." He patted her arm. "I know you can't understand all the complicated transactions necessary to advance a business, and I don't expect you to."

She eased her arm free. "My family runs a business."

He liked the way she bristled at his words, like a spirited horse yet to be broken. "A little bakery, a giant brewery—surely you see there's no comparison."

"I can see much that is the same."

"Now, now. There's no need to get cross. I don't know why you insist on contradicting me. I'm only telling you my plans because that is what husbands and wives do, isn't it? Share their dreams for the future?"

"I suppose you're right."

"Of course I am. You see, Father finds Justin even more volatile than he's ever been."

"Justin? Volatile?"

"He's a keg of dynamite. His ideas for the brewery are good ones, I'll grant him that. But unlike Justin, I know better than to try to force new ideas on Father. He may have said he sent Justin to learn, but what he really wanted was for Justin to come home from Germany and confirm that his ways of doing business are still the best ways. That's not what Justin told him. And I must admit, Justin is right."

He sighed, trying to seem resigned to the situation, and went on. "Father intends to place the running of the brewery in the hands of his son—one son. It's only a matter of time before my brother's temper flares again. And when it does, Father will be forced to cut him loose. He has already threatened as much, and as everyone in this town knows, Father is a man of his word."

"Cut him loose?"

"Disinherit him. Throw him out of town."

"For merely disagreeing? Surely your father wouldn't be so cruel."

Richmond laughed. "You've been around him for five years. You know what a tyrant he is. Would he do something so cruel? Of course he would." In fact, Richmond was counting on it.

"But your father? What will happen to him if you take over?"

"I don't intend to kick him out of his own business, if that's what you mean, but he can't work forever. His limp has worsened. He tires easily. Mother wants him to take her to see San Francisco, an idea I heartily endorse."

"What will become of Justin?"

He drew back. "Why should you be concerned with my brother's welfare?"

"It was a reasonable question, Richmond. I'm to be a member of your family. Of course I'm concerned."

"Well, I'm not heartless. You know that. I would give him a job of some sort, but I doubt if he would accept being second in command. I certainly wouldn't, in his place." He searched her eyes for some sign that she supported his strategy, but all he saw was pity for Justin—poor, handsome, educated, world-traveled Justin. "Lest you forget, Katrina, *I* am the one you're going to marry."

"Of course I am going to marry you."

"You don't have to sound so unenthusiastic. Is the idea of marrying me an unspeakable torture?"

"No, I'm sorry. That's not how I feel at all. I'm eager for our wedding. Truly. But with the flood my thoughts have been heavy of late. That's all."

She was trying to convince herself, and he knew it. Richmond felt an old and ever-present anger. As he always did when the feeling surfaced, he reminded himself of just how superior he was. He dressed with impeccable taste. He entertained his mother's dinner guests with witty conversation and masterful piano music. He shared his father's passion for fine horseflesh. He made a point of studying the soil and knew how to lay out a garden to ensure blooms across three seasons. He had organized the town's *Oktoberfest* for the last two years, singlehandedly.

Justin's absence had finally—*finally*—allowed Richmond to earn his mother's smile and his father's respect. It had also made Richmond the most sought-after bachelor in town. Remembering this usually made Richmond feel better, but not now.

As though it were yesterday and not five years ago, Richmond recalled the day he noticed Justin gaze with blatant male appreciation at the family's new maid. Ah, sweet Katrina. Barely fifteen, her slender body was indeed worthy of any healthy man's glance. With a sheen of silver cast on her dark brown hair, a whisper of pink to her flawless skin, and big brown doe eyes that widened often in awe of her new surroundings, she would bloom under the right man's careful hand. That's what Justin had said. With a wink, he had added that it would be *his* hand.

But Justin was wrong. Richmond would be the one to have her.

Now, with her standing beside him, his band of silver on her hand, it was time to take what was his. He stroked Katrina's cheek with his fingers. Running the pad of his thumb across her lower lip, he relished the look of anticipation in her eyes. She wanted him. He knew it.

Just as he'd envisioned it a hundred times, he wrapped his arms around her and pulled her close. He'd imagined that little gasp too. He pressed his lips to hers.

"No!" she said, bracing her hands on his chest and trying to get away.

She must mean only to increase his ardor. All women were like that. "Yes," he said, pushing her hands aside. He drew her close again, this time keeping one hand on the back of her head, forcing her to accept his kiss. Her struggle excited him.

She turned her head aside, and he released his hold.

"What's the matter with you? You're to be my wife! Surely I'm entitled to taste what will soon be mine?"

She stood there staring at him as though he were the one who had done something wrong. He raked his hand through his hair. "Do you find me so unappealing? Is that it?"

For no reason at all, her eyes filled with tears.

Women! he thought. "Here," he said, giving her his handkerchief.

"*Danke.*" She dabbed at the corners of her eyes.

"You mean 'thank you.'"

"Thank you." She took several deep breaths. "Richmond, I find you most attractive. Any woman would. Yet I refuse to allow such liberties without benefit of marriage." She gave him a tenuous smile, the kind that begged his forgiveness.

"I understand," he said, clasping her hands in affection as well as frustration. "You're still an innocent. It's the man whose passions become unbridled, not the woman's."

He lightly squeezed her hands, all the while delighting in the fire that flared in her eyes. He was a gentleman. He could wait until their wedding night if he had to. "Indeed," he murmured as he envisioned her lying beneath him, begging for his touch, "you do arouse a man's passions."

Katrina came home to find her mother working in the bakery. As they always did when they were alone, the women spoke in German.

"Momma, you shouldn't be on your feet. Go. Sit. I'll finish that." Katrina took the paring knife from her mother and chopped away at the rhubarb stalks on the cutting board. A huge bowl of hulled strawberries sat next to it. Gretchen had obviously planned strawberry rhubarb tarts. "Where's Poppa? And Gretchen?"

"Strolling," Truda said, as though her husband and daughter had gone to the moon. "Gretchen took your poppa strolling." With effort in every step, she walked across the room. Bracing her arm on the back of the bench, she eased herself down, her skeletal frame giving little shape to her faded dress. "Katy, dear. Have you a notion of what's cooking in Gretchen's head?"

A chunk of rhubarb flew across the room, and Katrina's heart thundered against her chest. "I think I do."

"It's the chemist, yes? The Heinz boy. From my room I can see him walking toward the bakery. Every morning at eight, just as the sticky buns come from the oven. Your sister's giggling starts five minutes before he arrives and continues five minutes after he leaves." Truda sighed with contentment. "I hear he is good husband material, the chemist."

"So I hear." Katrina wondered if Lukas Heinz would do to Gretchen what Richmond had done to her. Paw at her like an animal? Force her to accept his kiss?

"Katrina, what has you so troubled?"

Katrina wiped her hands and knelt at her mother's side. She didn't know why she felt so reluctant to tell her mother about Richmond, except that it would give her mother even more reason to worry over the welfare of her daughters.

"Come, come, out with it."

"Well," Katrina began after a lengthy pause, "this afternoon when Richmond took me riding, he . . . he . . ."

Truda looked grave. "He didn't take advantage of you, did he?"

"No, Momma. He didn't." Katrina took a deep breath and told her mother everything.

"I've been afraid of this," Truda said when Katrina finished.

"Nothing happened, Momma. When I protested, he stopped."

Truda leaned forward and gently brushed a stray wisp of hair from her daughter's face. "Of course nothing happened. I know that as long as it was up to you, you wouldn't allow it."

"Then why do you look so worried still?"

Giving careful consideration to her words, Truda hesitated and then said, "You have never spoken of Richmond in the way Gretchen does her chemist. Never talked about his eyes or his smile."

"I'm just not one for giggles. It means nothing."

"Then why is your heart so troubled?"

Why? Because she couldn't think of anything without

thinking of Justin. She couldn't close her own eyes without seeing his. She couldn't look to the bakery door without wishing to see him cross the threshold. She couldn't even embroider her wedding linens without picturing him standing beside her next to Richmond's bed, without feeling traitorous because of the intimacy it suggested. Every time she bathed, she pictured his broad chest streaked with creamy white lather. More powerful still was the memory of his tender kiss and the forbidden desire it evoked.

"Oh, Momma, I don't know. I just don't know."

Truda stroked her daughter's hair. "You are troubled because today the man you plan to marry seeks to sample what lies in store, and while you were right to stop him, your telling of the incident lacks the signs of your own anticipation. In fact, I have yet to see evidence that your heart flutters over this man you intend to live with the rest of your life."

"I'm twenty years old, Momma. I should have made you a grandmother several times over by now. I don't need to have my heart flutter in order to have a good marriage."

"And who is it you are trying to convince with all this force in your words? Me? Or you?"

"I don't need to be convinced. I know the facts. Richmond is a healthy man. Handsome, too. And American by birth. He knows his mind and is ambitious for his future. He cares for me and I for him. He plans to take over the brewery one day, which means that long and forever he will stay right here in Merriweather."

Truda sighed. "Ah, I hear the importance you place on that. He will stick fast to this valley that looks so much like home. Katy, you must never be afraid to move on. Life doesn't always deliver on its promises. You must be willing to strike out for what you want. Look at your poor poppa. He gave up so much to come to this country."

Katrina couldn't keep the bitterness from her voice. "We *all* did."

"Are things truly so bad here in America? We have our own home—not as fancy as what we left behind, but our own. We have our bakery, and business is good."

"What about the candlesticks, Momma? They were your only treasure from the past."

"Candlesticks. What are they? If we had stayed behind, the czar would have taken them. He would have taken everything. Each time the soldiers came, we had to hide the candlesticks—"

"I know the story. Poppa tells it every time he comes from the *Biergarten*."

"You know the story , but you don't remember the feelings. You can't. You were too young. Listen to me now. This is America. Your own poppa, an ordinary man, has a say in the running of this entire country. He can *vote* to pick the president. We have *freedom*."

"But we had Grandfather, and now he's gone. We had our friends and they are gone. We had land, a fine house. I had poor Strudel."

"I know. I know."

"Would you do it again, Momma? Would you leave your home and all your dreams?"

"My dream was to keep my family together."

"You could have made Poppa stay."

"No. On this matter I could not have swayed him. Even if I could, I would choose not to. It would have killed your poppa to stay under the yoke of the czar, just as it *did* kill my poppa. I know that in my heart. Your poppa did what he thought was best."

And if Poppa had not brought them to America, Katrina would not have met Richmond. *Or Justin,* a little voice inside of her added. "I know, Momma."

"That's better," Truda said. "Now, talk to me some more about your Richmond Barrison. You know he would not have been my first pick for you—I am still fond of the

Wolter boy, Wilmot—but perhaps the problem is in my hearing, and your affection for Richmond has been there all along. You've told me he is steadfast and responsible. He's not dull, I hope."

"Oh, no," Katrina answered quickly, eager to put her outburst behind her and oddly grateful for the chance to convince her mother of Richmond's fine qualities. "He tells amusing stories, and he makes me laugh."

"And your wifely duties? Tell me true now. How does it make you feel to think of your young man in that way?"

"It would not be too unpleasant."

"It would not be too unpleasant? Would it be filled with passion? Love? Katy, listen to me. Your poppa and I, we were matched by a coupler, yes, but we had seen each other many times and exchanged smiles and glances that set my heart to fluttering. So when we wed, it was not as two strangers, resigned to make the best of what we had, but as two hearts eager to express the love we already felt. My own heart would break to see you settle for less."

"But if I were being matched by a coupler, I might have to settle for less."

"A good coupler knows the young people of his own and neighboring villages and can see the wisdom in joining two strangers. So while love is not always a guest at the wedding of a match made by a coupler, the chances are good that love will grow." Truda sighed. "But you and Richmond . . . oh, Katy, I'm just not sure he is the right one for you."

"Momma, don't worry on my behalf. I'm old enough to know what it is I want. And married to Richmond Barrison, I'll have it. We'll be happy."

"You know this in your head or in your heart?"

"In my heart."

"As you wish." Slowly, Truda levered herself from the bench. "I'm going upstairs to rest a few minutes before getting dinner. Please, think on our words before you act in haste. For while a full purse does bring its own brand of security to a family, there is no greater security than love."

Katrina stood and helped her mother walk across the room. "You're saying I don't love Richmond?"

"Do you?"

"Am I so selfish to want a better life, Momma? For me and for my children? Is it so wrong?"

"No, child. I know your intent is not selfish in nature. But you are not being matched by a coupler. You are making decisions of your own. And so you must know how important it is to love the man first, not the fancies. Ah, but that was not my question. Do you love Richmond Barrison?"

Katrina answered clearly. "I will learn to."

"A ladybug with five spots!" Gretchen rushed over to Katrina, who was chopping the rest of the rhubarb. "It landed on my very own hand while I was walking with Poppa. Five spots!" She held her hand in front of her face as though recapturing the moment. "I am guaranteed a good harvest."

"And what do you plan to harvest? We have no fields of wheat or rye, no great garden of our own."

"It is not a crop I want, silly. It is Lukas Heinz."

Katrina scooped the juicy chunks of rhubarb into the bowl and wiped her hands. "You did talk to Poppa. I thought as much."

"Oh, *ja*, I talked to Poppa, all right. He was overthrown with joy. Already he knows that Lukas would make a fine husband. He is a chemist with his own apothecary. He is healthy, not big and strong like a bull, but he has superior shoulders. And I would make a good wife too. I told Poppa, though he said he already knew. Not only am I young and beautiful and healthy, I know how to bake as well as cook and sew. Poppa may bake much of the bread, but I am the one who bakes the fancy pastries and I am the one who is learning more about the American way of cooking—they like a lot of butter, no lard. Lukas could find no better match if he hired a coupler."

"And what did Poppa say?"

Gretchen grinned. "Oh, you know Poppa. Like a goose feather he can be pushed over."

Katrina remembered another side to her father, one not easily pushed. "What about a dowry?"

Only for a second did the look of doubt cross Gretchen's face, but she quickly recovered and said, "American girls don't have to have dowries."

"Does Lukas know he will get no cows, no pigs, no land, no gold, but just you?"

"Not yet, but he will. Soon. And he will be happy. I predict it. For I have been touched by a ladybug with five spots. Besides, you are being wed without a dowry."

"Only because Richmond said he knew it would be a hardship for Poppa to come up with one." What Richmond had actually said to Katrina's father was that anything Gustav could put together would surely be inconsequential to Richmond's own already substantial holdings. Katrina had overheard her parents talking about the conversation. Her mother said if Richmond had any respect for his elders, he would never say anything so keenly designed to wound a man's pride. Her father said Richmond was just telling the truth, painful though it was to hear.

"There, you see?" Gretchen said. "There are no blocks in my path to wed Lukas Heinz."

"Just one."

"What?"

"Lukas Heinz himself. Does he know you plan for him to be your husband?"

"He'll find out on May Day."

"May Day?"

"*Ja*. From now on, each morning when Lukas comes in

for his sticky bun, I will unload on him some of my many charms. Then on May Day, at the May fair lumber auction I will catch him for a year, and after a year in my sparkling company he will be eager to wed."

Smiling with confidence, Gretchen slipped a bibbed white apron over her head, tied it about her waist, and went to the back room, where she added two small logs to the fire to keep the big brick oven at the perfect temperature.

Katrina couldn't help but compare Gretchen's view of marriage to her own. Gretchen was so eager, so determined, so sure that joy, and only joy, awaited her life with Lukas. And they weren't even betrothed yet.

Katrina rushed to the back room. "Gretchen, how do you feel about your . . . your wifely duties?"

Gretchen winked. "I have a feeling I will like them even more than baking." She paused. "What is it? Why you are looking so sad?"

"I'm not sad. It's just that . . ."

"*Ja?*"

"Well, I can't say that I share your enthusiasm at the thought of . . . you know, coupling."

"Katrina, you may be older than I am, but I don't believe you are dried up like a prune. All you need to do is let Richmond sample some of your many charms. A little holding of hands. A little kiss. Maybe a little squeeze."

"Gretchen!"

"I know that's what Lukas wants. I see it in his eyes, and of course the idea of kissing and squeezing holds appeal for me too."

Well, it didn't appeal to Katrina. Not at all. Richmond had done all those things and would have done more if she'd let him. And she'd have to let him soon.

4

Friendship aside, Katrina had clashed enough times with Bridget O'Malley to know how crotchety the woman could be. It didn't matter. Not today. For though she told herself she was going to the Barrisons' to see if Molly had any questions about her new duties, Katrina knew in her heart that wasn't entirely true.

She had to see Justin. She knew it would be wise for her to avoid him and let time erase his effect on her, for she was sure that, given time, his power over her would fade away. But she didn't have time. She was to marry Richmond in less than six weeks. She had to know if what she felt for Justin meant anything, and she had to know now, before it was too late.

She also had to know if there was any chance at all that Justin felt something for her. And, if so, what did he feel? The affection of an older brother or something far more serious?

With Gretchen's advice ringing in her head like an

alarm, Katrina knocked on the frame of the open back door and stepped into the kitchen. Bathed in sunlight from large sparkling windows, the room was filled with every convenience, including a large sink complete with a drain running underground, a row of pegs overhead to hold an assortment of neatly hemmed and looped dish-cloths, separate ones for delicate stemware, dirty dishes, and greasy pots and kettles. Above all this was the large clock Bridget always cursed, for Herr Barrison had put it there to ensure the regularity of his meals.

"Come slummin', have you?" Bridget groaned as she bent over and dropped the large oval basket of wet laundry on the floor.

"Good morning, Bridget."

"If you're looking for the missus, you'll not be seeing her till noon."

"I really just came by to say hello and see if Molly had any questions." Katrina sounded insincere, and she knew it.

"Come to say hello, is it? Sure, and I suppose come June when you're prancing round here in your fancy new duds you'll be wanting to pop in at all hours to have a bit of tea with me just like old times."

"You could hardly blame me," Katrina said as she sat on one of several stools at the table. "I don't know anyone who brews a pot better than you."

"Ah, go on with you."

Katrina could tell by the way Bridget fussed with the wet laundry rather than look Katrina in the eye that the older woman felt just as uncomfortable as she did about the change in her station, for until Katrina had been given the role of companion to Mrs. Barrison, she and Bridget had worked side by side. It was Bridget who had patiently shown Katrina how to clean a stone hearth and how to use oxgall and potter's clay to clean grease from marble, for Bridget knew how much Katrina needed the job.

"How's Molly?" Katrina asked.

Bridget shook her head. "The girl tries hard, that she does, but she's as much a greener as she was the day she stepped off the boat. She needs a bit more time than most to learn the ways of a place big as this." She inclined her head toward the living quarters. "That old goat. There's some just ain't got an ounce of patience in them."

"Herr Barrison?"

"Who else?" Bridget eyed the kettle of simmering water on the stove. A few moments later she poured the golden brown brew into two cups she took from the cabinet above her. "Here," she said, handing a cup and saucer to Katrina.

"*Danke.*" Katrina sipped, but the hot tea did nothing to calm her. "I suppose Richmond has already gone to the brewery this morning?"

"Sure as mud on a rainy day. Ain't had one day of lolly-gagging in five years, that's for sure." Bridget inclined her head toward the living quarters again. "Still scratching for a grain of that man's attention, he is."

Bridget didn't have to explain. Katrina knew she was referring to Eberhard Barrison. The man would sooner choke on a word of praise than give it, even to his own sons.

"And Justin?" Katrina asked, immediately turning her attention to the cup she held in her hands so Bridget wouldn't see the interest in her eyes.

"He'd be in the library goin' over the accounts for the time he's been gone. Mark my words. The day both them boys is working each by side the other is the day I'm leaving. Me poor heart couldn't take the ruckus."

"But they might work well together if given the chance. After all, they are both gentlemen."

"Them boys has been scrappin' since they was tiny, fussin' over who gets the best pony, blamin' each other for wackin' the rooster with the slingshot. Pushin' always led

to shovin' with them two. Now they'll be fightin' over
who gets the brewery." Bridget crossed her muscled arms
in a show of defiance. "I ain't stayin' round to be caught in
the middle, no, sir."

"Surely you don't mean that, Bridget! The Barrisons are
good employers, and you've been with the family for years."

Bridget looked at Katrina oddly. "Now *that* I have, that's
for sure. I come when Justin was but a tot, apple of his
father's eye, that one, but a black-haired devil just the
same, always taking me pot lids outside to play gladiator.
And the younger one, he was no better. Bangin' on the
piano. Screamin' like a banshee. Pickin' his mother's flowers off by the heads. Begorra, the sufferin' those two have
caused me!" She set her teacup down with a clatter and
looked Katrina straight in the eye, as if about to deliver a
profound message. "I know them boys. Know them like
they was my own. Know their weaknesses. Know their
tricks."

At the sound of footsteps coming from the hall, Katrina
turned, trying to control her trembling.

And there he was. His dark gray suit had been tailored
to typical Barrison perfection, framing his broad shoulders and long legs, though he seemed restricted by the
stiff-fronted white shirt and even stiffer collar. Considering the way his brow furrowed, the dark tie about his neck
could have been a noose.

"Katrina."

She told herself not to read too much into something as
simple as the way he said her name, but he made it sound
so intimate. Was he as pleased to see her as she was to see
him?

He greeted Bridget and entered the kitchen to join
them at the table, straddling the stool across from Katrina. Somehow, it didn't surprise her to feel so content just
by being near him. She didn't flinch as his eyes drank her

in, flicking quickly over her just-washed hair and her very best blue cotton dress, the one with the sprigs of purple lilacs embroidered about the neck. Nor did he seem bothered by the appreciative look she gave him in return. In fact, he smiled, showing something far deeper than the grin she usually saw on Richmond's face, and in that instant Katrina knew without a doubt that her feelings for him were not just a passing fancy.

"*Guten Morgen*," she mumbled, then cleared her throat to say it again, this time in English and less nervously. "Good morning."

He regarded her with a tender look that said he recognized her discomfort, that just maybe he felt it too. His voice barely above a whisper, he said, "You look fetching this morning."

"*Danke*." She felt a blush warm her cheeks.

Craning her neck toward them, Bridget said, "And what do I look like? A side of beef?"

Justin broke his gaze. "Only the highest grade," he said with a teasing grin.

"Ah, go on with you!"

Bridget's customary words sounded uncommonly strained, as though it troubled her to see Justin and Katrina get along so well.

To Katrina he said, "Mother said you and your family are coming to dinner tonight."

"Yes."

"To talk about the wedding?"

She nodded.

"So you are going through with it?"

Bridget interrupted. "Now what kind of question is that? Of course she's going through with it."

He ignored Bridget. "Are you?"

"The date has been set. The long-distance guests have all been invited. Momma has nearly finished my dress—"

"I was afraid something like this would happen one day."

"What do you mean?"

He lowered his voice. "That I would finally find the perfect woman for me, only to learn that she wanted to marry someone else."

She prayed the panic she suddenly felt didn't show in her eyes. Was he teasing her? With Bridget in the room, he couldn't possibly admit to such strong feelings. Yet there was no trace of humor in his voice, no playful wink. She didn't know what to do or what to say.

After a moment or two of uncomfortable silence, Justin looked around the room, focusing on nothing. "So, what brings you here this morning?"

"I came to see how Molly was doing. That's all."

"Molly's doing fine." He glanced toward Bridget. "Isn't she?"

Like a cat stalking a mouse, waiting to catch it off guard, Bridget stepped over to the table. "She can dust and polish with the best of them, she can." She paused and looked at Justin first, then Katrina. "She's put to memory the right spot for every ladle and skillet." As though concentrating on something far more important, she slowed her words. "She's still a wee bit fuzzy on which dish towels to use for tumblers and which for dishes, but she's a good worker, that she is."

Katrina squirmed in her seat. "I'm glad to hear it," she said, though she'd barely been listening. If Justin spoke from his heart—*if* he felt something as strong for her as she felt for him—what was she to do about it? Anxiety overtook her.

Bracing her arms on the table, Bridget looked in Katrina's eyes. "You're not gettin' sick on me now, are you? You're all fevered lookin'."

"I'm fine," she said, too quickly for anyone to believe her, least of all Bridget.

Then came the warning look in Bridget's eyes, the look that said she was well aware of something of which she did not approve. She took Justin's cup from his hands and set it on the table. "You'd best be goin' now, Mr. Justin. Ain't nothing for you to do round here except get into trouble."

"Maybe Katrina wants me to stay."

Stammering, Katrina said, "No. No, you go on."

"Well, then," Justin said to Bridget, "I guess you're right."

"'Course I'm right. Now off with you."

Justin stood. "Let me give you a ride back to town."

"No!" Bridget nearly barked. "She ain't finished visitin' just yet. You go on."

Justin seemed to take his time walking toward the door. Much as Katrina's heart told her to go with him, common sense told her to stay.

"It's a long walk back," he said.

"I'll manage."

Bridget glared first at Justin, then Katrina. "I been with this family a long time, and we don't take well to upheaval. You two hear me?"

With a confident air, Justin said, "Sometimes upheaval is the only way." He smiled at Katrina. "Next time, then."

Knowing it was best, at least for now, Katrina let him walk away. She didn't take well to upheaval either. Upheaval always brought tears.

"I propose a toast."

Eberhard Barrison, his face flushed from too much wine, pushed his chair back, stood, and raised his glass. "To my second son, Richmond, the first to carry on the Barrison name."

Justin didn't miss the pride in his father's tone. Lately, it seemed that everything Richmond did was perfect and everything Justin did was worthless. Being out of his father's favor was nothing new. What bothered him far more was seeing how much both families looked forward to the marriage of his brother and Katrina.

All evening long the two mothers had talked about clothes and flowers and decorations. His mother insisted the flowers come from her own garden—they were exquisite this year. Several times she asked about Truda's progress on Katrina's wedding dress. Each time Truda assured her the gown would be lovely—periwinkle silk, lavishly beaded across the shoulders and bosom with white seed pearls. Rosamond also expressed concern about what Truda and Gretchen would wear. "Please," Rosamond had said, "no aprons, no matter how fancy the embroidery."

The two fathers talked politics. Both were Republicans. Both agreed that Richmond had a fine future ahead of him.

Gretchen asked Richmond about the food for the giant celebration, for he had insisted on making all the arrangements. He rattled off a menu that seemed to impress her.

And all the while Katrina laughed and nodded at the appropriate times. She gave her approval, needless as it was, to every arrangement both sets of parents discussed. She didn't disagree with a single detail. Worse than that, she lowered her eyes demurely when Richmond held her hand to show everyone the ring and said how much it pleased him to see his ring on her finger.

Was that what she chose? Justin could only assume that, despite his indirect way of telling her he wanted her, she still didn't realize how much he cared for her. Or she did know, and it didn't matter.

He knew that a woman valued a man who had a prosperous future. How many times had Helga Utley told Justin not to show up at her house unless he was driving the surrey? Though she had said it playfully, he knew she meant it.

The more he thought about it, the more Katrina's reluctance to go with him that morning made sense. She already knew that Richmond was intelligent, that he had good business sense. She didn't know much about Justin. He knew he was smart and could run a business. He even considered himself an innovative thinker. But Katrina had yet to see this side of him. Tonight she would find out.

As dessert was being served, Gustav Swann said to Justin, "And you, young man, with your big opportunity to study with the masters. What age-old secrets did you bring home in your trunk?"

"Indeed, I learned a lot in Germany. First of course, that all beer drinkers there are protected by the *Reinheitsgebot*—"

"There's no need to go into that," Eberhard said. "The purity ruling has been around since the Middle Ages."

"Yes, but controversies are already rising over it." Justin turned to Gustav. "Beer is to contain nothing but barley malt, hops, yeast, and water. Absolutely nothing else. But the secret of each recipe is in the yeast: how hot to have the water, how much water to use. When to extract the malt. There are so many variables. Recipes are kept under lock and key."

Eberhard interrupted. "Another time, Justin. I doubt the women are interested in business talk."

"You are a lucky man," Gustav said to Eberhard. "Two smart boys."

With a tight-lipped smile, Eberhard nodded.

"I learned a lot about the business of breweries, too," Justin said, ignoring the stern look from his father. "In this country, the way of the future is with the giant brewers in St. Louis and Chicago and Milwaukee."

"Is that so?" Gustav said.

"Oh, yes. By the turn of the century the small breweries in this country will disappear."

"Not all of them," Eberhard said.

"No, Father. Not all of them. But certainly those that don't take advantage of the great rail system—"

"Thank you, Jus—"

"Those that refuse to modernize their equipment or add their own cooperage—"

"Justin—"

"Those that turn a blind eye to new products, those that refuse to acknowledge the need to grow, the need to compete—"

"That's enough!"

Justin barely heard his father's booming voice. He paid no attention to the controlled anger creasing his mother's brow, to the discomfort on the faces of Katrina's family, or to the decided pleasure in Richmond's smile. All he saw was Katrina's wide-eyed shock.

Eberhard took a deep, deep breath, lifted his wineglass, and said, "Please forgive my son. Perhaps by the time he's thirty, he will have outgrown his childlike exuberance." He sipped and then, added, "If I can tolerate his presence that long."

"Perhaps that won't be necessary," Justin said. Then, because it was never his intent to make Katrina and her family feel uncomfortable, he swallowed his pride and said to them, "Please accept my apologies. Father is right. I shouldn't have gotten so carried away."

His words had the desired effect, for they accepted his apology and quickly resumed the kind of chitchat, awkward as it was, that meant they were just as eager as he was to put his outburst behind them. As soon as he could, he would explain to Katrina, for she still looked distressed.

Then Richmond stood. "A toast," he said, lifting his glass. If his long pause was for effect, it worked, for every eye was on him. His attention, however, was focused solely on Justin as he said, "To Katrina. My bride."

* * *

Three stories high, the brewery was an imposing building
for a small town. Built by local hands using locally quarried stone, the massive salmon-colored walls cast long
shadows. Louvered windows that hung on pivots had
been cranked open as far as they would go, begging a
whisper of an April breeze. Only in the cavernous cellar
was the air cool, for the countless kegs of amber lager,
deep brown bock, and light gold pilsner needed time and
controlled temperatures to age to perfection.

Before opening the heavy black walnut door, Justin
read the broadside nailed to its face: *By Popular Request,
the Barrison Brewery Will Sponsor a Harmonial Social
Soiree at the Biergarten After the May Day Celebration
Next Week.* Richmond's name was all over the poster.
With the industry changing so fast and competition everywhere, it would take a lot more than knowing how to
throw a party to keep this brewery profitable.

He tapped his breast pocket where he'd put the list of
items he would insist on talking to his father about. If the
old man had any hope of surviving in this modern world,
he'd have to listen.

Gripping the wrought-iron railing, Justin climbed the
stairs two at a time and walked briskly down the hall. He
passed the accounting office, where a dozen men in starched
white shirts hunched over a dozen massive desks, each man
straining his eyes over one of many hardbound ledgers
stacked in front of him. Business was good. For now.

He took the stairs to the third floor. The deafening
sounds of workingmen and machines rose from the bowels
of the building, as did the ever-present smell of yeast and
malted barley. A glass showcase of stoneware and pewter
steins announced the entrance to Eberhard Barrison's office.

With the din all around him, Justin could hear his

father yelling at Richmond. As usual, there was no sound of Richmond yelling back.

As soon as Eberhard saw Justin, he bellowed, "Get in here and talk some sense into your brother before I lose my temper!"

Poor Richmond. Despite his expensive suit and his polished shoes, he looked pitiful standing there raking his hair with his fingers. Justin was still smarting from his father's wrath of the night before. He didn't wish that on Richmond or anyone else. Nor could he blame Richmond for delivering such a pointed, possessive message in his toast to Katrina. If the situation had been reversed, Justin would have done the same thing. Now, just for a second, a look of camaraderie passed between the brothers.

"Problems, brother?" Justin asked.

"Father and I were discussing our strategy for the future."

"I'm glad to hear that. These aren't the Middle Ages."

Mouthing his words so their father wouldn't hear, Richmond begged Justin, "Tell him!"

Justin took the slip of paper from his pocket and handed it to his father, saying as he did, "Father, I apologize again for my outburst at dinner last night. But the world *is* changing. We can't continue to operate as we have been all these years and still compete in a market that grows day by day."

Justin watched his father's fists clench as he read down the list of recommendations Justin had prepared that morning and then crushed the paper in his hands.

"This is nonsense!"

"It's reality," Justin said. "The small brewers—"

"Barrison Brewery is not a small brewery!"

Richmond cleared his throat, but still his voice trembled. "Yes, Father. As far as Merriweather is concerned, Barrison Brewery is huge. But compared to the rest of the country, the rest of the world—"

"Shut up!"

Richmond closed his mouth and pressed his arms to his sides.

"Richmond is right," Justin said.

"What's the matter? Merriweather isn't good enough for you anymore?"

"Merriweather is a small town."

Eberhard studied the list again and looked back at Justin. "We don't need to have our own cooperage. That's a waste of money."

"If we want to grow, we do. The quality of the kegs is critical—"

"What do you think I am, some kind of idiot? I know the importance of a sturdy keg. There's not one in this entire brewery that's not made of thick white oak and heavy steel. The best. Only the best."

"But where do you send them when they need repair? St. Louis. We have to wait our turn while all the other small brewers are having their kegs repaired, too. We can't afford to wait, so we buy more new kegs. I saw the books, I know. With our own cooperage we could not only build our own kegs but repair them as well. If we don't grow, we'll die."

Eberhard marched across the room, waving his hand in an all-too-familiar gesture of dismissal. His leather chair groaned as he sat down and smashed the crumpled list against the uncluttered surface of his desk. "So you think I should start brewing stout and porter?" he asked with a smirk.

Justin stepped up to his desk. He took the wadded list, unfolded it, and spread it out where his father could see it. "I'm not sure, but I think we should at least consider it. The English represent another market, a lucrative one, but they like their beer brewed from the top."

Eberhard's face took on the look of controlled patience that always preceded his wrath. "Richmond, what do you think about this?"

Richmond cleared his throat again. "The railroads go

to all the big cities now. All across the country. We don't have to limit our market to towns on the river. We could tap into the New England market, the south—"

"Enough!" Eberhard glared at his sons. Focusing on Justin, he said, "I made it possible for you to study with the best. You were supposed to learn something *useful*!"

"I learned a wealth of useful information. If you would just listen—"

"You learned to defy me!" Eberhard said in a voice of steel that grew harder and colder by the minute. "We brew good German lager here. Lager, pilsner, and bock. All brewed carefully—*and expensively*—from the bottom. If either one of you pea-brained idiots thinks for one minute I'll sully my reputation by making that cheap English swill, you're even more stupid than I thought."

He raised himself, braced his palms on the desk, and leaned forward.

"Now you two listen to me. This is *my* brewery. I will not set up a cooperage. I will not brew from the top. And I absolutely will not contribute any of my hard-earned money to the Society for the Promotion of Good Morals!"

"I only thought to enhance our image in the community," Richmond said quietly.

"My image doesn't need enhancing. Do I make myself clear?"

Just as he had when he was a boy bracing himself for a slap across his cheek or a blow to the side of his head, Richmond stood still. "Yes, sir."

Justin glared back at his father. "Perfectly clear. All you want us to do is take orders."

Like the unfolding fury of a storm, Eberhard straightened till he stood upright, eye to eye with Justin. His sardonic smile showed his deep pleasure as he ripped Justin's list in half. "If you don't like taking orders from me, you can always leave. I don't need you."

"Leaving sounds better all the time."

Justin turned and walked away. Anger weighted his steps as he descended the stairs. He had to get out of here. Do something. Go somewhere. He couldn't be his father's slave any longer.

Back on the street, he loosened his tie in an effort to calm down. That wasn't enough. He stuck his finger between his neck and collar and tried to stretch the stiff fabric. That wasn't enough either. The brewery itself wasn't the issue. He didn't give a damn about it, except that it provided security for his mother and employment for half the town. All those years in Germany he'd tried to picture himself at the head of his father's empire, but the image always frustrated him. He wanted to build his own empire.

Richmond, on the other hand, found his identity in the brewery. And, as always, he would buckle under rather than fight for what he believed. In fact, the only thing Justin had ever seen his brother exert any real effort to get, and keep, was Katrina.

Justin climbed into his buggy and flicked the reins with more force than necessary. There was a whole world out there waiting for him. Didn't his father have enough confidence in him to think he could make it on his own? Didn't the old man know how much he wanted to try?

Sometimes upheaval was the only way. That's what he'd told Katrina. Maybe it was time for some upheaval of his own making.

"Is this a weed or a flower?"

Kneeling in the dirt, Katrina sat back on her heels and wiped her brow on her sleeve. "Look at the leaves, Gretchen. That's one of Momma's Sweet Williams. Don't pull it up."

"In my herb garden I know every leaf. Here I'm still a

greener." On her knees too, Gretchen hunched forward and scrutinized the variety of plants. "But I will learn."

With Momma tending the customers and Poppa down at the river helping to strengthen the levee, Katrina had reminded Gretchen that the garden needed tending. Weeks of sunshine had left a jungle of sprouting plants.

Gretchen removed her garden gloves. From her apron pocket she took two chunks of shortbread. "Here," she said, handing one to Katrina. "We need our strength."

Katrina removed her gloves too. "*Danke.*"

"I still cannot believe what happened at the Barrisons' last night. For Justin to openly defy his father—"

"Justin was merely trying to give his views on business."

"*Ja, ja, ja.* Don't tell me it was his views on business that had you so shaken. I know you too well."

"What are you saying?"

"Only that there you were with Richmond's ring on your finger, and there was Justin buzzing around you like a bee to honey."

"He wasn't buzzing around me. He *lives* there."

"*Ja*, and there you were with your eyes full of pity for him when his father scolded."

Katrina jabbed her garden trowel into the dirt. "You saw no such thing."

"I saw enough to agree with Momma. She says Eberhard's coffers may be full, but that doesn't make the man all wool. Also that Rosamond Barrison must have been desperate to the point of needing even bread and butter to take his name. I know from how he sticks his nose in the air when he steps into my bakery that he is a man with a small brain. In fact, I fear he has Prussian blood in his veins. Prussians have to have their name on everything."

"You're right about that."

"And Justin is just like him."

"How can you say that?"

"You heard him with your own ears. Shouting at his father with defiance and disrespect. Saying that only he knows the best ways for business."

With a pain far deeper than mere disappointment, Katrina looked away. Everything Gretchen said was true. Last night they had all seen for themselves how explosive Justin was. His anger was just like Poppa's the day he argued with the czar's soldier. Katrina remembered how he had shouted that no one was going to make him change his name to a Russian name. Then he had stormed out to the stables. He rode away and was gone for hours. When he came home, he told each of them to pack their things, for they would leave the next day. And leave they did. Momma always said Poppa was brave to defy the czar, but Katrina didn't agree. Poppa lost everything because he had to have his own way.

Katrina would never let that happen to her. She would never lose her home. Her children would never be uprooted. She could not accept a man with a nature as wild as Justin's. One of the qualities she admired in Richmond was his ability to remain calm under all circumstances, to pursue his future with a plan of logic, not emotion.

Thinking of Richmond now, she set aside several small plants she'd just dug up and turned over another patch of soil. "Here," she said, passing the tender shoots and their fragile root balls to Gretchen. "These are pink phlox. Plant them right there behind the Sweet William. That's where Momma placed them in the old country. When the red and purple flowers come, the garden will look pretty."

Gretchen pointed to a space beside a patch of white and purple pansies. "I think they would look better over there."

"No. The phlox grow too tall. They have to be behind the Sweet William. That's the way it's always been."

"So maybe it's time for something different, *ja?*"

"Why must you be so eager to change things?"

"Change things?"

"Yes. Look at you. For years you have worn your hair in braids about your ears, and today you cross them over your head. What are you going to do tomorrow, cut them off?"

"Katrina?"

"You know what I'm saying. You are supposed to make pumpernickel on Mondays and instead you make cardamom. You are supposed to use lard in the turnovers and instead you use butter."

"Americans like their butter."

A familiar anxiety strained Katrina's words. "You fiddle with your schedule. You fiddle with your recipes. You fiddle with your hair. What will you do next?"

"Maybe I will demand my right to vote!"

Katrina couldn't take it anymore. She stood and removed her gloves. She liked being able to recognize a plant by just a few small leaves. She liked knowing that she could control the look of the garden. She liked staying in one place where her roots could sink deep and anchor her to the soil. She liked knowing who she was and what was expected of her. Why couldn't Gretchen understand that?

"Where are you going?" Gretchen asked.

"Inside. To help Momma."

No sooner were the words out of her mouth than the worried sound of her mother's voice drew the attention of both sisters to the back door of the bakery.

"Quickly, Katrina. There's a gentleman here to see you."

Katrina dropped her gloves into the basket she left on the ground and headed for the door. "Who is it?"

"Justin Barrison."

5

Lust. Maybe that was all he felt. Still, it could make a man do dangerous things. Justin slipped his hands into his pockets as he watched Katrina walk toward him. What the hell was he doing here? She was a pretty woman. That much was obvious. But there were other pretty women in town. Why did he feel such a strong desire to see her, to be with her?

With Katrina's mother standing right behind him and her sister right on Katrina's heels, he knew he wouldn't get as much as a minute alone with her. Not that it mattered. With that frown on her face, she didn't look at all pleased to see him. After last night, he wasn't surprised.

When she got closer, he removed his hands from his pockets, straightened his posture, and gave a slight bow. "Afternoon, Fräulein Swann—Katrina."

She nodded. "Good afternoon."

He hadn't given any thought to what he wanted to say, an error that was now obvious.

"Did you want to see me about something?" Katrina asked.

"Come, Gretchen," Truda said, waving her hand. "Let's go inside and see to our customers."

"But what if Katrina needs my help?"

Nudging Gretchen's shoulder, Truda said, "Your sister doesn't need your help. Now, come along."

As Gretchen passed him and followed Truda inside, Justin heard her say, "But Momma, people will talk."

Justin ignored her comment. People had talked about him for years. When he was a boy, they said he was uncontrollable. When he was a lad in school, they said he was wild. When he was a young man about town, they said he was a rebel. True or not, what people said about him or might say about him didn't matter. All he cared about right now, this minute, was Katrina.

She looked everywhere but in his eyes, increasing the awkwardness of a silence filled with words unspoken.

He cleared his throat, instantly hating himself for adopting the nervous gesture Richmond always used. "I see you have a garden."

"A small one."

"Vegetables as well as flowers?"

"Just flowers. This is Momma's garden. The vegetables are behind that pile of lumber. Poppa is building a gazebo for her. All the way back, at the edge of the woods."

He surveyed the long narrow plot of land and the heavy canopy of trees at the far edge, not because he was interested in the gazebo or the trees or the flowers but because he had to have something to talk to her about. "He picked a good spot."

"Momma needs the shade."

"Katrina?"

She looked straight into his eyes. "Yes?"

He laughed nervously. Lower passions, that was what

he felt. He felt them every time he saw her, every time he heard her voice, especially now. Just being in the same room with her made him want to scale a mountain or break a wild horse, something requiring skill, a strong body, and a keen mind, something dangerous, something that would impress her. But he'd tried to impress her last night and look where it got him.

"Katrina, I'm sorry about last night."

"You already apologized to everyone."

"Not to you."

"That's not necessary."

"Yes, it is. I didn't want to ruin your evening."

"You didn't."

"And I don't want you to think I'm some hotheaded fool."

He waited for her to assure him that she didn't see him that way at all, that she found him intelligent in his thinking and brave in asserting his views.

"He is your father. Why do you insist on antagonizing him the way you do?"

"For God's sake, Katrina, he's a tyrant."

"Maybe so, but—"

"You think I should submit to him as if he were some kind of king? Suffer his wrath like a helpless child?"

"Why does my opinion matter so much?"

"It just does." Along with everything else that he felt was slipping away, the charm he'd always counted on vanished, leaving him feeling unsure of anything except that no woman had ever affected him this way before.

Katrina smoothed her hair in a nervous gesture and began walking. "Do you . . . do you want to see the garden? It's not very big."

"The garden. Yes. The garden."

He followed her to the area where she'd obviously been working, wondering for the second time that day how to set things right with her. He looked at the tidy, symmetrical rows of freshly turned earth and at the young plants packed so carefully in little mounds. "You've been busy," he said.

"I still have much to learn about what will grow in this soil, but Richmond is teaching me."

"Richmond?" Justin suddenly felt an inch shorter and shrinking by the minute.

"Yes. He also offered to arrange for someone to help Poppa finish the gazebo—Poppa has so little time to work on it—but Poppa insists on finishing it himself, though he is new to the tools of a carpenter."

"I can understand your father's feelings. I'm not sure I understand my brother's."

"What's to understand? Richmond is a generous man."

"Everything has its price."

He had to have said the wrong thing, for she turned around, slowly folded her arms across her chest, and in a calm and steady voice said, "Justin, why are you here? Tell me the true reason."

"I wanted to see you. I wanted to apologize."

"I'm engaged to your brother."

"Engaged. Not married. Not yet."

Where was that soft expression on her face, the twinkle in her eyes that said she was pleased to see him, the tender smile that acknowledged whatever this feeling was that had passed between them?

"I will marry your brother on the first of June," was all she said.

Her words came too quickly, as though she'd rehearsed them; if that was the case, maybe she was trying to convince herself. Justin took heart. "Are you sure that's what you want?"

She looked down at her garden, and Justin had the feeling she had already asked herself the same question. Her face was resolute when she looked up. "I want roots for my children."

"But what about you? What do you want for you?"

"I want a stable life. A calm life."

He reached for her hand.

"Don't," she said, pulling away. "This isn't right."

Had he imagined it? Had she, just for one small and fleeting second, grasped his hand?

"Go, Justin. Please. Now."

Her lower lip quivered, betraying the turmoil inside. He should never have come here. He knew that now. Not wanting to upset her any more than he already had, he mumbled a simple good-bye and left.

Justin had only been gone a few minutes when Gretchen came marching out the back door and down to the steps of the gazebo where Katrina sat, her head hung low, her fingers entwined in a tight knot.

"What did he want?" Gretchen asked as she sat next to Katrina.

"Nothing."

"He wanted to play with your heart, didn't he? I saw the hungry look in his eyes last night and again today. Tongues have been wagging the whole town over since he came home. Five and twenty years old and still with no wife? Something is defective about that man." Gretchen paused. "Do you hear me?"

"You don't know anything, Gretchen. Just go away and leave me alone."

With an indignant grunt Gretchen bunched her skirts, rose, and stomped back to the bakery.

Katrina leaned against the railing of the gazebo. In the space of five minutes she'd driven away two people she cared for.

May Day. Every man, woman, and child in Merriweather had gathered around the flower displays in the center of town to celebrate the arrival of summer. Many were exhausted, having spent a night of firing guns and cracking whips, all in an effort to protect the village from the magic of witches who run wild on the last day of winter, for in the old country there were only two seasons, the growing and the dying. Now, the older citizens stood quietly admiring the greens and flowers that crowned the colorful *Maibaum,* while the younger folk clapped as gaily dressed children danced around the pole to loud and lively oompah music, holding aloft one end of the many rainbow ribbons that radiated from the wreath at the top of the pole.

Earlier that morning, Katrina had found a small birch tree under her bedroom window. She knew the tree was from Richmond. The significance of the traditional May Day gesture only added to her nervousness, and Gretchen teased her unmercifully as the two of them dressed for the day's festivities.

"You flounder like some fish. For months you keep his company in public. From his pew in church he makes dog eyes at you instead of giving his attention to the sermon. You primp your hair and pinch your cheeks before you go out. So why pucker your face now because he gives you a birch?" She wove a length of pink ribbon through each pale silver braid and smiled at her reflection in the mirror. "If it is a shriveled shrub beneath your window, then sure, fall to pieces, for Richmond's affections have died. But he knows you still cling to the old ways, so even though he is an American he gives you a birch, the sign of love." Gretchen grinned and added, "Maybe over his bed he hangs a green fertility wreath, waiting to test its powers on you."

"Maybe you should mind your own business!"

Katrina hadn't meant to sound so sharp. She waited for Gretchen to laugh or reply in kind, but Gretchen said nothing. She merely grabbed her shawl from the edge of the bed and hurried from the room, leaving Katrina to regret her hasty words and to acknowledge the growing fear inside her.

An hour later, her nerves still on edge, Katrina joined her mother at the annual celebration.

"Here you are," Truda said, slipping her arms around Katrina's waist. "Richmond has been looking for you. I told him to be patient. You'd be along."

"He planted a birch tree under my window last night."

"Gretchen told me all about it—with more enthusiasm, I might add."

Katrina understood that tone. Her mother wanted to talk about Katrina's despondence these past weeks; Katrina didn't feel like talking. Along with everyone else in town, she'd heard about the escalating arguments between Eberhard Barrison and his older son. Every time she allowed herself to think about Justin, she pictured him saying something defiant, doing something rash. Justin Barrison certainly wasn't the kind of man Katrina wanted for a husband or a father to her children, but he fueled a fire deep inside her that, despite her misgivings, both excited and disturbed her.

"Momma, where is Gretchen? I need to talk to her."

Truda gestured toward the grandstand, where a group of girls Gretchen's age stood together on stage, covering their mouths to muffle their giggles.

"Right up there," Truda said, "in the front. She has decided to enter herself in the lumber auction. I heard her instruct the auctioneer that when it is her turn, he is to describe her as a flowering plum tree, not a sturdy old oak, and definitely not a gnarled knotty wood. Apparently, her chemist likes plums as well as sticky buns."

Katrina panicked at the thought of her sister taking such a risk. "But what if someone else bids for her?"

"Don't worry so about your sister. She wouldn't risk a year of keeping company with an eligible young man unless she was certain she'd be spending it with her chemist."

Truda held her daughter's arm as they watched the festivities, laughing as the auctioneer encouraged interest in the matchmaking game.

"Katy, dear, stay here and keep me company. Poppa has been gone for over an hour, talking to Herr Barrison and Richmond. Oh, look, here comes Poppa now."

Katrina's stomach knotted the moment she saw her father.

Gustav Swann, his barrel chest lifted with pride, strutted toward them. In one hand he carried a stein of beer, in the other a clarinet. Spotting his wife and daughter, he grinned, fanning the bristly salt and pepper mustache that bordered his upper lip.

"You will all be glad to know that the Barrison boy is ready to quit the state of single blessedness and go to double cussedness." He tilted his head to the side, making his goofy smile even more pronounced.

Truda arched her brow. "Have you been looking too deeply into your stein?"

Tucking his clarinet under his arm, Gustav said, "Nonsense." His eyes watered as he took his wife's hand. "I've been sealing the fate of our lovely daughter."

Katrina's stomach knotted.

"It is still so hard for me to think of your getting married and moving away," Truda said. "Are you sure about this? About Richmond? There will be other young men, you know."

"Your mother is right, of course. But come, Katy, there aren't many like the Barrison boy around. You're a lucky young woman. Now it doesn't matter in the least that long-distance invitations have all been sent. But there is the matter of that ride you took with him in his surrey. Alone. *Ja?*"

"Gustav, don't pressure the child like that."

Katrina drew her mother's attention. "I'm not a child,

Momma. And it's true. Richmond took me for a ride to show me the land his father will give us for a wedding gift. Don't worry about me so. It's all right. Richmond and I are both eager to begin our life together. The first of June can't come too soon."

Gustav glimpsed someone out of the corner of his eye. "Aha! Here is my future son-in-law now." He passed his clarinet to his wife and with his free hand waved to Richmond. "Come, come!" he shouted.

Wearing his best suit and a politician's smile, Richmond joined their circle. He bowed to Katrina's parents. "Frau Swann. Herr Swann."

He took his place next to Katrina. "Fräulein," he said, with a kind of respect that made Gustav nod his head and jut his lower lip in a show of satisfaction.

"Herr Swann, I want to thank you and your wife for your willingness to accept me into your family. I want to assure you that my family is equally as eager to embrace your Katrina." To Truda, he added, "I will treasure your daughter as the jewel I believe her to be."

Truda nodded as though he'd said exactly what she'd expected. All the while, she kept her hands fisted and her arms braided tightly across her waist.

Katrina remembered the last time her mother acted so annoyed. It was the day Richmond came to the bakery saying he assumed Truda had no silk from France or lace from Belgium with which to make Katrina's wedding gown. Politely, he suggested that the task be given to his mother's seamstress, reminding Katrina and her mother that it was important Katrina not embarrass him. She remembered the fire in her mother's eyes as she assured Richmond that she would manage on her own. She had. The gown was nearly finished, and it was beautiful.

Her thoughts were interrupted by the sound of her father's voice.

"Come, come, my son. This calls for a celebration."

"Indeed it does, sir. A glass of my family's finest schnapps?"

"An excellent idea." Gustav winked at his wife.

Bowing to the women, Richmond and Gustav headed for the *Biergarten.*

"Herr Swann, you must come out to my family's stables more often and study our fine Hanoverians. I also have Belgians, trotters, and a champion thoroughbred. Katrina praises you as a fine judge of horseflesh."

Katrina heard their voices fade as they walked away, arms across each other's shoulders. For the first time in a long time her father carried himself with the same importance he always had in Russia.

Suddenly overwhelmed by the thought of marriage in just a few short weeks, Katrina looked all around her—at the *Maibaum,* the costumed children, the bandstand— anywhere but into her mother's eyes.

Truda finally broke the silence. "Well, then?"

Katrina knew that tone too. Momma had sized up the situation and was about to pass judgment. Wishing she could avoid the conversation, Katrina slipped her hands into the pockets of the white-on-white embroidered apron she wore on special occasions and stared into the crowds.

"Come, Katrina, I need to sit. My legs are weary."

Katrina helped her mother to one of several benches in the shade of a giant tree. When Truda had settled herself comfortably next to Katrina, she patted her daughter's leg.

"What does it take to marry a man? Tell me."

"Certainly not love."

"It would be nice if all marriages began with love, but such is not the case. For many, love takes time to bloom. Of that we have talked already. So what does it take for a woman to marry a man?"

"I don't know, Momma. Respect for the man?"

"For sure, respect is good. A woman wants to hold her head high when she says to another, 'See that man there? He is my husband.' *Ja*, to have respect is good. What else?"

"Momma, please. No lecture. Not now."

Katrina flinched as her mother's bony fingers squeezed her wrist. In the older woman's eyes burned an ageless fire that had been tested and tempered generations before her, a fire not dimmed by her weakened body.

"It takes courage. Raw like the winter wind." Truda tightened her grip. "With boldness in the eye you must look at life and know that together with your husband you can face whatever hardships come to your door. You must trust him to be honest and to work hard and to have the welfare of his family as his chief concern. A woman must have great courage to marry and risk so much on one man. Do you have such courage, Katrina?"

Katrina couldn't answer.

Early the following week, a booming baritone drew Gretchen to the bakery door. Halfway down the street a sturdy-looking man in a long dark coat and high hat tapped his ribboned cane against the door of each home and business. Gretchen cocked her ear and listened.

"Greetings!" the man shouted. "Greetings from Richmond Barrison, who is well known to you, and from his bride-to-be, the beautiful Katrina Swann."

Before stepping outdoors, Gretchen turned back to Katrina, who was arranging fresh poppyseed rolls on the shelf. "You stay inside," she ordered. "It's the *Hochzeitslader*."

Knowing that the hired wedding inviter was just outside the door made Katrina's heart begin to pound. Before the day was over, everyone in town would be making plans to attend her wedding to Richmond.

She hadn't spoken to Justin since the day he came to her

in the garden. She told herself to be grateful, for his nearness tested her will and challenged every vision she'd ever
had of her future. Yet, try as she might, she couldn't keep
him from either her thoughts or her dreams. And now
here she was, her wedding plans in faster motion, her
future spinning out of control.

With a sickening curiosity, Katrina stepped closer to the
open door. The *Hochzeitslader* had prepared an elaborate
invitation.

"You will find roast mutton and baked ham, generous
portions all. Pitchers of beer, as many as you like. Prepare
for dancing until the light of dawn. . . . And now, let me hear
your answer! Will you be there to honor the happy couple?"

Katrina covered her ears to the thunderous applause of
the crowd in the street.

Stepping back into the bakery, Gretchen leaned against
the door and pressed her hand to her heart. "Before another
year has passed, the *Hochzeitslader* will invite the town to
my wedding." Imitating the man outside, she strutted across
the room. "The handsome and prosperous Lukas Heinz
and the beautiful, talented, and *young* Gretchen Swann."

Katrina smiled but couldn't bring herself to banter.
Instead, she thought of how much Gretchen, too, had suffered coming to this country, how hard she had to work,
how some of the town's more critical citizens—Germans
who had been in this country longer and English who considered themselves the only true Americans—poked fun at
Gretchen's constant struggle with the language. But
Gretchen didn't seem to mind. She took things in stride,
blooming wherever she was planted.

"I'm sure you're right," Katrina said, working to lift her
own heavy thoughts. "Soon Momma will be stitching your
wedding dress too. Your strategy at the lumber auction
paid off handsomely."

Gretchen perched one hand on her hip and the other

on the coil of silver-blond hair around her ear. "Lukas Heinz paid handsomely."

"As well he should."

The two sisters went to the side window and stood close to each other as they watched the *Hochzeitslader* make his way around the corner.

"Gretchen, I didn't mean to snap at you before. On May Day—when you teased me about the birch tree. I'm sorry."

Gretchen squeezed Katrina's hand. "Forgotten."

Within three weeks, Gretchen was offering advice freely and frequently. Katrina stood on a bench in the kitchen while Truda slipped the nearly finished wedding gown over Katrina's small shoulders, down her slender torso, and around her narrow waist. Gretchen looked at the periwinkle satin, white lace, and seed pearls. She stepped closer to the bench. "Tell me, Katrina, where went all the meat on your bones?"

Katrina grinned, for she loved to tease with her sister. "There's nothing wrong with my bones."

"Katy, hold still and keep your chin up," Truda said. "I must mark the hem. We have only two days."

Two days! Katrina bit her lower lip. Surely, the worry that filled her heart was common to all brides.

Gretchen lifted Katrina's wrist as though it were that of a rag doll. "Look at you, with the arms and legs of a chicken. And your endowments. You can't call that chest a bust."

"Girls," Truda said, through lips pressed to hold an assortment of pins, "don't try my patience."

From her lofty position on the bench, Katrina looked down at her sister and forced herself to return the banter. "I have a silhouette for fashion, not farming."

Truda leaned back on her heels and took the pins from her mouth. "Enough! Must you two always be at each other's throats?"

Katrina said, "We didn't mean to upset you, Momma."

Truda waved her hand to dismiss the subject. "I'm feeling my age, that's all." She braced one arm on the edge of the bench and raised herself up. "Take the dress off. Leave it on the table. I'll work on it tomorrow." She sighed, a faraway look having snuffed the fire in her eyes. "Watch out for the pins."

The sisters looked at each other as their mother walked down the small hall and firmly closed her bedroom door. Without asking, Katrina knew that Gretchen shared her thoughts. Momma wasn't happy about this wedding.

In an uncomfortable silence, Gretchen helped Katrina remove the gown and then said she had a few things to tend to in the bakery. Back in the room she shared with her sister, Katrina began assembling the items she'd be taking with her to her new home on the day after tomorrow: her best pale blue dress and black embroidered shawl for church, two second-best dresses and bodices, a plain black shawl for every day, a nightgown, a white shawl for bed, undergarments, a few hair ribbons and toiletries.

With all her possessions folded and stacked neatly in a corner of her room, Katrina sat on the bed and turned the carving of Strudel over and over in her hand. Her grandfather had died the year after they came to America. The news came in a letter from a neighbor, who mentioned that the dog had died too.

Katrina recognized the sound of Gretchen's footsteps. Gently stroking the carving, Katrina said, "Richmond doesn't have a dog of his own. I don't even know if he likes dogs."

Gretchen glanced at the meager pile of belongings in the corner. "He has fine sleek horses and fat, meaty chickens."

"I know," Katrina said, reminding herself of the importance of a well-stocked pantry. She glanced at the pile of her belongings. "You'll have more room for your own things now."

Gretchen shrugged. "I never felt cramped."

"I'm not going far. Only two miles."

"*Ja*, not an ocean. I know."

Until they climbed into bed that night, Gretchen didn't say much of anything else, except how beautiful the wedding gown had turned out and what a lovely bride Katrina would make.

Just as Katrina was about to fall asleep, Gretchen whispered, her voice quivering, "You remember how on the ship I could sleep only by holding onto your nightdress?"

"You were just a child."

"I feared I would be lost at sea unless I held fast to your shift. Only then I would be safe."

"I know," Katrina whispered, understanding this admission of fear was not easy. "I was afraid sometimes too."

"But sometimes you rolled to the very edge of the cot, seeking to be free of me."

Katrina didn't need the light to know that her sister was fighting back tears. "I was stupid," she said.

"And so I would wait till your breathing grew deep. And then I would inch my fingers toward your back. I would hold my breath and pinch your shift—just a tiny pinch, one so small you wouldn't notice and wake up. Then I felt safe. And then I could sleep."

Katrina fought back her own tears. "We're both safe now. We should sleep."

"*Ja*." Gretchen yawned, shifted in the feather bed, and clutched her pillow. "Morning will come. Like it or not."

The sisters closed their eyes, each knowing that after tomorrow neither of their lives would ever be the same again.

Katrina couldn't sleep. She listened to Gretchen's soft breathing, reminding herself that they would be no more than two miles apart. She told herself that again and again, but still sleep eluded her. Only when she felt Gretchen's hand brush against her back and pinch her nightdress did Katrina, too, find peace.

6

At one end of the beer hall a firecracker popped, and someone threw another piece of crockery to the floor. The noise was guaranteed to banish evil spirits that could ruin the happiness of married life. A man's last night as a bachelor demanded the revelry of a good *Polter-abend*.

The aroma of spicy sausage and tangy sauerkraut mixed with the smell of beer in the air. The long, heavy oak tables groaned under the weight of platters of salami, roast beef, and hard-boiled eggs. The band summoned those who could still carry a tune to join in another drinking song. Those who could no longer hold themselves upright leaned their heads on their arms and dozed off.

Richmond, the guest of honor, staggered from table to table, through the haze of pungent pipe tobacco, thanking his guests for coming. Waving his hand over the table laden with gifts, he thanked everyone again for their generosity. Much earlier in the evening Katrina and her family had been present to join with the Barrisons in introducing the out-of-town guests. Now only the men remained.

At three in the morning, Gustav finally left the beer hall and stumbled home, for he wanted to make a special bridal bread for Katrina. He would give it to her at the banquet, along with the customary salt, the insurance for a happy marriage. Now, in the back room of his bakery, he mixed the ingredients. Humming a drinking tune, he stepped out the back door and returned with a generous armload of seasoned wood for the oven.

In her bedroom above the bakery, Katrina tossed and turned, her mind on events earlier in the day. Justin hadn't even come to the party. She heard he'd gone to St. Louis on business. Richmond had danced with her; then, in front of an appreciative crowd, he had presented her with a pair of elegant slippers to be worn only in their home, the traditional symbol of her subjugation to him as his wife. "Tomorrow," he had whispered in her ear, "you will be Katrina Barrison. And you will be mine."

The slippers sat on the floor by the chair, propped beside the wedding gown Truda had finished only that afternoon. This time tomorrow, Katrina Swann would be no more.

This time tomorrow, thoughts of Justin—or any man other than her husband—would be forbidden.

Before going to bed, Gretchen had held the gown to Katrina's face, fussed with the skirt, fiddled with the cluster of pearls at the shoulder and the row of never-ending pea-sized buttons down the back. She told Katrina there had never been a more beautiful wedding gown or a more beautiful bride.

In the morning Gretchen would weave a wreath of white rosebuds for Katrina's hair. The scent of the roses would be so sweet. . . .

Katrina turned her head into her pillow to avoid the odor.

Smoke!

She bolted upright and shook Gretchen's shoulder. "Get up!"

Gretchen didn't need to be told why Katrina had roused her. Barefoot, they ran past the kitchen to their parents' room.

Empty.

Smoke came from the bakery downstairs. Covering her nose and mouth with her hands, Katrina flew down the narrow stairs, squinting at the smoke.

"Momma?" She listened and called again. "Momma!"

A small voice coughed and answered. "Help."

Smoke belched from the room that held the great oven. Following the sound of her mother's voice, Katrina plunged into the black fog. Orange flames licked the wall behind the oven, lapping at the heavy wooden shelves filled with supplies. Odors of scorched flour mixed with the smell of blistered paint.

Her eyes burning from the smoke, Katrina found her mother on the floor and rushed to her side.

"Help your poppa," Truda cried, as she crouched over her unconscious husband, frantically beating the fire from his clothes with her bare hands.

Katrina grabbed the braided rug by the door and threw it over her father, effectively smothering the flames.

"Outside, Momma. Get outside. Try!"

Truda wouldn't budge.

"Gretchen!" Katrina cried. "Where are you?"

With no time to summon outside help, Katrina stood behind her father's head and slipped her arms under one of his shoulders. Gretchen appeared, clutching Katrina's wedding dress.

"Help me get Poppa out." She saw the dress. "Leave it."

Gretchen dropped the gown and slipped her arms under her father's other shoulder. Coughing and fighting for their own breath, they dragged him along the floor. Truda crawled behind.

Despite all the noise still coming from the *Polter-abend* at the beer hall down the way, someone must have heard or smelled or seen the fire at the bakery, for Katrina and Gretchen had moved their father only a few yards when the front door flew open and an army of neighbors rushed in.

Two strong men carried Gustav to the street. Katrina and Gretchen supported their mother by the arms and hurried her outside. The fire brigade, with their wagons and hoses, took over. The rest was a blur.

The local surgeon, Dr. Bitner, ordered Gustav and Truda taken to his office and summoned Lukas Heinz.

Following the doctor's orders, Katrina and Gretchen stood no closer than the door to the surgery. With blankets wrapped around their shoulders, the sisters held hands and cringed as they watched the doctor lean over the examining table and cut away what remained of their father's clothing.

"Carron oil," Lukas said as he handed the doctor the amber bottle he'd brought from his apothecary.

With Lukas's assistance, Doctor Bitner soaked strips of gauze in the gray-white lotion and spread the dripping patches over the patient's blistered body. Katrina searched their faces for signs of optimism. She found none.

While the doctor continued with Gustav, Lukas turned to Truda. Her injuries weren't as severe as those of her husband. Still, her hair was singed, her lungs were contaminated with smoke, and patches of skin on her hands and arms were red and blistered. As she lay slumped in a chair, her feet propped by a hassock, she moaned softly and called her husband's name. Tears trickled down her parchment cheeks. Lukas treated her burns, then administered a needle to her spindly arm. She closed her eyes.

"I'm keeping them both here tonight," Dr. Bitner said to Katrina. "We'll set up a cot here for your mother."

Katrina struggled to steady her voice. "They *will* survive, won't they?"

"That's not for me to say," Dr. Bitner answered, ushering both girls from the surgery and into the outer hall.

"No." Katrina balked. "We want to stay nearby."

"Out of the question. I have no room. You will be in my way."

"But we can't leave them."

"Do you want what is best for them or don't you?"

"Of course I do."

"Then go. Get some rest. I don't have the energy tonight to tend to four patients."

"But they *will* survive, won't they?"

"I don't make predictions. I don't make promises."

Katrina tried to remain calm for her own sake as well as for Gretchen's, but the fear inside her gathered momentum like a locomotive whose engines have been stoked to capacity. "They *will* live, do you understand?"

Gretchen pulled on Katrina's arm. "Come with me, Katy. We can't do anything here."

Katrina let her sister lead her toward the front door. "I'll be back here in the morning, doctor," Katrina said, as though it were a threat. "You *are* going to stay with my parents?"

"Of course I am. All night." Turning to Lukas, Dr. Bitner added, "You go with them. Get them to the Barrisons'. Then come back. I'll need you here tonight."

Lukas nodded and went to the door. He tightened the blanket around Gretchen's shoulders before leading the way.

The night was still busy with the helpful and the curious. Easily guided by dozens of kerosene lamps, the sisters retraced their steps to the bakery. In her bare feet, Katrina winced at every pebble. Runoff from the hoses had cut watery veins in the dirt street, draining what looked like the lifeblood of the bakery. The fire had been extinguished, but steam rose from the rubble. The charred wooden frame hissed and the stone foundation sizzled. Even the air smelled burnt.

One of the firefighters approached them. Soot clung to the sweat on his face. "Your parents. How looks it for them?"

"They will be better in a few days," Katrina said.

"Goot," he said with a smile. "Very goot. We pulled a few things from the topside before the roof caved in. Over there." He pointed to the two traveling trunks sitting on the doorstep of someone else's home. "I'm sorry we could not save more."

Momma's linens, a few odds and ends, Poppa's books and tools. "*Danke*," she said to the fireman before he returned to the task of clearing the debris.

Feeling an urgent need to ensure that the trunks had survived, she walked over and bent down. The wide leather straps on Poppa's trunk were singed. The brass fittings on Momma's were black with soot. Otherwise, they were all right. There was still something left of the life they once knew.

Grateful for small miracles, Katrina stood up. That's when she saw her wedding gown, lying atop a pile of debris in front of the neighboring cottage.

Her hands trembled as she reached for it. So wet. She held it by the shoulders. So heavy. Water slipped from the pearls and chilled her fingers. Doused by the firemen's hoses, the bruised satin dripped an endless stream of purple tears and bled to death in Katrina's hands.

She carried it with her, draped across her outstretched arms.

Then she looked for Gretchen and saw her leaning against a huge oak tree, her head lowered, her shoulders sagging, her hands cradled between those of Lukas Heinz. Katrina watched, the weight of her own burden wearing her down. How tenderly young Lukas kissed Gretchen's hand, stroked her cheek. How gently he slipped his arms around her and held her against his chest while she cried.

Where was Richmond? He should have been here by now. He should have been with her at the doctor's office.

Rosamond Barrison rushed over. "You poor thing, look at you," she said, as she draped a cloak around Katrina's shoulders. "Your parents?"

Katrina huddled under the warm woolen cloak and gave Rosamond the details.

"I see," Rosamond said. She looked around, sizing up the situation. "It's not hopeless, but it's not good."

"We'll be fine," Katrina said. "We'll have everything back to normal in no time."

"Yes, of course you will. In the meantime, you and Gretchen will stay at our house."

Katrina nodded. "*Danke*. I'll tell Gretchen." Katrina took a step away, then turned back sharply. "The wedding—I can't go on with the wedding. Not now. You understand."

"There will be plenty of time to talk about that later. For now, let's get the two of you out of this night air."

Katrina walked over to where the two trunks sat like orphans on the neighbor's stoop. "These go with us," she said. "And my dress."

"Of course." Rosamond's eyes filled with compassion as she took the dress from Katrina's arms. "I'll drape it over the side here. Your mother did a beautiful job." She directed a man to load the trunks in the back of the less-than-elegant wagon she'd brought. "I'm sorry the conveyance is not more fitting," she said, "but the wagon was already hitched for the day's work and I didn't want to waste time getting a buggy."

It occurred to Katrina that she would have never pictured Rosamond Barrison as having either the initiative or the compassion the woman now displayed. Perhaps some people showed their true selves only under stress.

Lukas held Gretchen's arm and administered little pats as he walked her over to the wagon. It must be his handkerchief Gretchen was using to dab her eyes.

Katrina couldn't explain the discomfort she felt as she told her sister they'd be staying with the Barrisons. Gretchen nodded and thanked Rosamond.

"Look, girls," Rosamond said. "It's nearly morning."

Bands of pale peach and yellow stretched across the sky, chasing the last of the night, lifting the sun, lighting the way.

While Rosamond took the seat next to the driver, Lukas helped both Gretchen and Katrina into the wagon. He waved as the wagon rumbled down the road and around the bend.

How odd, Katrina thought, to be reliving the scene again—Gretchen huddled beside her, their parents' trunks at their backs, their home fading in the distance. Just as it had been in the old country, the day they left.

How terrifying to feel it all again.

"Richmond is still asleep," Rosamond explained as they entered the foyer. "I tried to wake him before I left, but I'm afraid he sought too much celebration in the stein. He will know of your tragedy soon enough."

Rosamond motioned for the sisters to follow her up the wide staircase. Stopping in front of one of the many doors along the hallway, she explained, "I would prefer to give each of you your own room, but the house is filled with guests for the wedding. I hope you don't mind sharing accommodations." She opened the door to the bedroom

Katrina knew was second in size only to the one occupied by Eberhard and Rosamond.

"I admit to feeling awkward about this, dear," Rosamond said, patting Katrina's arm. "However, this is the only room available."

Katrina felt awkward as well, more so, she was certain, than Rosamond. "We are grateful for your hospitality," she said. She stepped inside and motioned for Gretchen to join her.

Rosamond clasped her palms together and held her hands at her waist in her usual formal pose. "I'll leave you now," she said. "The trunks will be aired and brought up later. Katrina, you know where everything is kept. Please help yourself. Tell Bridget if you need anything." She paused, then added, "There are several new nightgowns in the dresser. You might as well wear them now. By the time you wake, I'll have apparel for you both. The cobbler will be here by noon. Now, try to get some sleep."

Once Rosamond had gone, Gretchen gaped at their surroundings. She had been to the house before, when Katrina worked there, but had never seen the elegant upstairs chambers. Heavy forest-green silk draped the tall windows. A white lace spread covered the cherry sleigh bed. The wide floor boards had been freshly scrubbed, showcasing the intricate pattern of two deep blue oriental carpets. There were also two green velvet chairs, a desk, and, on the dressing table, a crystal vase of white roses.

She walked to the window and slumped against the frame. Her posture betrayed her exhaustion, her voice her sadness. "Morning has broken. Your wedding day has come."

Katrina slipped her arm around her sister's shoulder. "Not today. Not until Momma and Poppa have recovered. I told Mrs. Barrison. She will explain to everyone."

"You don't sound disappointed."

"I just can't think about my wedding when Momma and Poppa are hurting."

"But they will be good as new?"

"For sure," Katrina said as she gently squeezed her sister's shoulder.

"And your beautiful wedding gown. All Momma's hard work. I ache for your loss."

"Maybe with Momma's help we can salvage the pearls and buttons."

"*Ja*, maybe."

They took comfort from each other a moment longer before Gretchen spoke again. This time anger sharpened her voice. "There was no need for Poppa to be baking at that hour. I had readied everything before I went to bed. He should not have been fooling with the oven at all. And he should not have quenched his thirst so much at the *Polter-abend*. That's what I believe is the cause of the fire."

Katrina sat on one of the tapestry chairs and ran her fingers through her tangled hair. She was so tired. "Poppa was making a special bread for the wedding. Momma told me. Maybe it was the oven. I did notice it was running too hot, but I never told him. I forgot." The realization brought a lump to her throat, but tears wouldn't come.

"It was the beer." Gretchen yawned and unbuttoned her dress. "Now we must rebuild the bakery. How many days do you think before Momma and Poppa are well?"

Katrina shrugged her shoulders. "Soon," she said with more hope than conviction.

Gretchen accepted the answer. Turning toward the door, she sniffed. "I know the smells of breakfast and the sounds of early risers, but I, for one, am going to bed. Where can I wash?"

Katrina inclined her head. "The door to the left."

Once Katrina was asleep, hours passed like minutes. She pulled the sheet over her head to muffle the rapping, but the sound persisted. She lifted the fine linen sheet and opened her eyes, squinting at the noonday sun that poured in through the windows. "Who is it?" she called.

"Katrina, my love. Only now did I hear of your ordeal."

Richmond. She was surprised at how annoyed she felt. She saw the glass doorknob turn.

"May I come in?"

"No! Please. I'm not prepared."

An inch at a time, he opened the door, just wide enough to poke his head through and squint his bloodshot eyes. He wrinkled his nose. "This room smells like a furnace." He paused and smiled. "But you look enchanting."

She didn't feel enchanting. "I'll join you downstairs in a few moments, but, please, allow me privacy now."

He looked offended, but he quickly recovered. "Of course, my dear." He stepped back and pulled the door closed another inch. "Mother says you have decided to postpone the wedding. For how long?"

Katrina cleared her throat. It hurt to talk. "Until Momma and Poppa have recovered."

He sighed. "Ah, then it will be only a few days. The house guests had planned to stay several weeks anyway, so I see no problem. I'll have everything rescheduled for—"

"No! Richmond, please. Until I know Momma and Poppa are well, I can't put my mind to any thoughts other than their recovery. Can't you understand?"

"What do you take me for, an unfeeling lout? Of course I understand. But, Katrina, love, I want you to think how wonderful your life will be when we are wed—trips to St. Louis, your own servants." He opened the door a few inches more. "We have received so many gifts. I can't wait to show you."

Katrina felt like screaming.

Gretchen stirred. Katrina pressed her finger to her closed lips, begging for quiet.

Richmond nodded, then backed into the hall, pulling the door behind him.

For most of the next four days Katrina and Gretchen took turns keeping vigil at Dr. Bitner's, either upstairs at their mother's bedside or downstairs in the hall just outside the surgery where their father lay. The doctor thought it best they not get too close to him. The odor was near unbearable.

On the fifth day, Katrina's hopes shattered as she stood outside the surgery and listened to Dr. Bitner.

"Poppa's dying? No, you must be wrong. The night of the fire you said—"

"I said I don't make predictions." The doctor patted Katrina on the shoulder, as though he wished he could do more. "The burns are bad enough, but the infection is worse." He shook his head slowly. "I give him laudanum and keep the dressings wet, but there's nothing else we can do. Your poppa won't make it through the night."

"I thought you didn't make predictions."

"Some things are certain."

Instinctively, Katrina steeled her heart. The anticipation of such unbearable pain deadened all feeling. "And Momma?"

"Still very weak. She's sleeping."

"I can see Poppa now?"

The doctor nodded and led the way into the surgery. "The smell," he cautioned her.

Katrina had smelled it before, back in Russia, the stench of rotting flesh. A forest fire had killed a boy. She remembered seeing his stiff little body, all black and charred like a piece of wood, his hands fisted and curled as though he had tried to punch the flames away. She remembered hearing the boy's mother cry that he should have known not to go into the woods. He should have known.

Katrina noticed the open windows. *To permit the exit of the soul.* The padded examining table had been turned so Poppa's feet faced the door. *To hurry the soul's departure.* She felt the rush of tears but bit her lip to keep from crying. *Weeping disturbs the spirit.*

"Poppa," she whispered as she rested the tips of her fingers next to his face, "Poppa, I love you. We need you. Please get better."

She kept her vigil until she felt Dr. Bitner's gentle hand on her shoulder. "Your mother won't be awake for a few hours. There's nothing you can do here. Go now."

Katrina didn't want to leave, but she knew she'd only be in the doctor's way if she insisted on staying. She'd go back to the Barrisons', get Gretchen, and together they'd return in a few hours on the chance her mother would be awake by then.

Katrina found Gretchen seated in the parlor with Rosamond, Richmond, and a number of out-of-town guests. Quickly, they bombarded Katrina with questions about the fire, her parents, and the wedding plans.

Gretchen made no effort to hide her nervousness. "You've been to see Momma and Poppa? They are better? Why you didn't get me?"

"You were asleep," Katrina said, as though Gretchen's rest, too, was important. "Dr. Bitner said we could come back in a few hours." Turning to her hostess, Katrina added, "If you don't mind, I must speak to my sister alone for a few moments."

Katrina hated to see the look of hope slip from Gretchen's face. She hated to see the fear behind Gretchen's eyes, knowing it mirrored her own.

"Katrina, love, what about the wedding? We've been waiting four days."

"I'm sorry, Richmond, but my mind can't think of that right now." She beckoned Gretchen. "Please excuse us."

Once outside, Katrina told Gretchen everything Dr. Bitner had said. Neither wanted to wait at the Barrisons', so they walked back to town.

Lukas Heinz was in the surgery when they arrived. He took Gretchen's hand as she stood next to her father. Again Katrina noticed how attentive the young man was to Gretchen, and she to him. When the time came for them to wed, for surely they would, they would be happy together.

Katrina went upstairs to see her mother. Looking even thinner and more fragile than usual, Truda lay in the narrow bed. So still, almost weightless, she barely dented the crisp white pillowcase under her head. Her bandaged hands rested above the sheet. She smiled as Katrina came into the room.

Katrina had never lied to her mother, so when Truda asked about her husband, Katrina told the truth. He was dying.

Truda didn't gasp, or sigh, or cry. She just stopped listening and sank into the pillow behind her. Feeling totally helpless, Katrina stood with her arms at her sides and watched her mother fall back to sleep.

Against the doctor's wishes, Katrina and Gretchen stayed in the surgery all night. They were there when their poppa died.

7

Katrina was not surprised to find a generously sized *Totenhemd* in her mother's steamer trunk. She fingered the soft white "dead man's shirt." Poppa would wear it when he crossed the ferry into heaven. Katrina found a smaller *Totenhemd* beneath it. It, too, was sewn without knots that might impede the final journey.

The thought that Momma, too, might die was once inconceivable, but Dr. Bitner had cautioned that for Truda the loss of her husband could have devastating effects on her recovery. She had inhaled a great deal of smoke, and she either couldn't or wouldn't do the painful deep-breathing exercises Dr. Bitner ordered to keep her lungs expanded and empty of fluids. He was right. Momma's condition had worsened in the last few hours. It was only at the doctor's insistence that the sisters went back to the Barrisons' to get some needed sleep.

Despite the comfort of the featherbed, the cool linen sheets, the softness of the down-filled pillows, Katrina and Gretchen found sleep impossible.

Now, kneeling on the floor beside the trunk, they both started at the knock on the door. Rosamond's voice faltered as she opened the door. "Dr. Bitner sent a message. He wants you at his office immediately. It's your mother. I have a carriage waiting." The woman had tears in her eyes.

Along the road to town, they saw the old *Leichenbitter*, moving from house to house, tapping each door with his black stick, announcing that the baker Gustav Swann had been called to eternity. Katrina thought of her mother and swallowed hard. "Pray he has no need to retrace his steps."

Gretchen couldn't speak, fear had so gripped her throat.

Katrina continued. "I should have known this would happen. Momma always said her heart beat as one with Poppa's. I should have insisted Dr. Bitner let us stay in the surgery. I should never have left her side. And now she's alone."

"Stop it!" Gretchen cried through trembling lips. "You frighten me."

"I'm sorry. I don't mean to." She reached for Gretchen's hand. "Maybe Momma has taken a turn for the better, after all."

Gretchen looked suspicious. "You think?"

"All things are possible."

"*Ja?* Then why do you carry her *Totenhemd* with Poppa's in your lap?"

Katrina couldn't answer.

Suddenly, the air around her changed. She smelled the faint, sweet fragrance of her mother's skin, felt her warm tender touch; then, just as suddenly, the sensations were gone.

The carriage pulled up in front of the doctor's office. He stood in the doorway, his arms hanging limp at his sides. The sisters were barely out of the carriage before he gave them the news.

"She is gone. Peace be to her ashes."

*   *   *

Richmond insisted on taking care of the burial details.

"Here," he said as he handed Katrina two gold coins. "To pay for their ferry ride across to the distant shore." He stood back while she approached the two wooden coffins in the Barrison parlor and placed a coin in each of her parents' hands.

At the cemetery, he stood back while she threw a clump of earth on each coffin.

He made the arrangements for the banquet following the funeral, making sure there were generous quantities of both food and *Leichenbier*, the beer of the dead.

"Drink up," he said to the hundreds of guests gathered later in his parents' house. "Drink up."

Katrina looked at the bounty around her and felt empty. She'd cleaned this magnificent house enough times to know exactly where everything was, and still she felt lost. She might not have remembered to brush her teeth or comb her hair if it hadn't been for Gretchen, though, unlike Katrina, Gretchen had spent the night weeping. For Katrina, tears wouldn't come.

Katrina wandered through the rooms. She didn't know what to say when people offered their sympathies and assured her that time would heal the wound. Liars! Fools! She hadn't cut her hand or broken her foot. She'd lost her parents!

Inside, she was shaking.

Richmond stood across the room. She watched him. He moved so easily through the crowd, addressing each guest, looking appropriately sorrowful, nodding at all the right times. Katrina needed his strength to get through this day.

"Richmond," she said, barely above a whisper. When he did not answer, she repeated his name a little louder.

He looked in her direction, and his image began to spin. "Just a minute, darling. I'll be right there."

"Richmond!"

Suddenly weightless, Katrina slumped to the floor.

The pain-free euphoria didn't last long. Her bones felt like brick; her eyelids like lead. Someone was calling her name.

"You just fainted," he said. "Relax now. You'll be fine in a moment." The familiar voice sounded reassuring.

"Justin?" She opened her eyes and focused.

No, not Justin. She saw Gretchen, her face pale, her hands folded in prayer. Lukas Heinz, gentle, dedicated, comforting, eased his arm under Katrina's head and passed a bottle of ammonia under her nose. The odor was unpleasant but effective.

Richmond appeared and helped her up. "Katrina, darling, are you all right?"

Looking for an anchor, she flattened her palms against his shirt. She could feel her lip tremble, but she was helpless to stop it. "They're gone. Dead." She rounded her shoulders and made herself small as she leaned into his chest.

Quickly, he cuffed her wrists with his hands and gently drew them back. "Tell me what you need, Katrina. A glass of wine? Water?" He turned to Lukas. "What does she need? Just tell me."

"Time," Lukas said. "But for now, a little rest. Something to eat."

Richmond guided her to a chair. "Here. Sit. I'll have Bridget get something."

"I want to go upstairs and close my eyes." Katrina braced her hands on the arms of the chair to get up.

Richmond knelt on one knee in front of her, blocking her path. He glanced quickly toward the center of the room where Eberhard stood, then whispered, "Darling, how would it look for you to leave our guests now? People wish to pay their respects. You understand how these things are, don't you? I'll stay right here beside you. You will have nothing to worry about."

Katrina sat back and locked her hands in her lap, as surely as she locked her feelings in her heart. "As you wish," she mumbled.

"Look, Father Lipp just arrived. I must greet him. Wait right here. I'll only be a moment."

Katrina looked around for her sister. Gretchen had been shuffled by the crowd into the other room. She stood next to Lukas, his arm draped protectively across her shoulders. Her eyes were red and swollen, but Lukas was there to soothe Gretchen's pain, to let her know she wasn't alone. Katrina took comfort in seeing her sister so cared for.

She dismissed the idea that she might also be jealous. After all, she reminded herself, she was the one who was engaged to marry the most eligible bachelor in town, an attractive man who had wealth and position. What more did she want?

What more indeed?

She needed to think. With everyone eating and drinking, it wasn't as hard as she feared to get away. She slipped out the back door and blended with the twilight.

The fresh air felt good. Following her instincts, she headed for town.

Vines of fragrant honeysuckle crawled over the stone fences along the way. Pan-sized leaves canopied the grape arbors. There was no breeze this evening, just perfumed hothouse air. She inhaled the honeysuckle, Justin's favorite flower, then quickly chastised herself for thinking about him now, for thinking about him at all. She pinched a sprig of the small creamy trumpets and, lifting her veil, tucked the flowers in her hair.

The moon had been growing for days. Tonight it would

fill the sky. Knowing she'd have the light of the heavens to guide her, she kept walking.

She continued along the narrow road and down the empty streets of town, not surprised to find herself in front of the bakery. How painful it looked, wounded and scarred. In the distance behind the crusty black remains, safely tucked on the edge of the woods, sat the gazebo. It was to be Poppa's anniversary gift to Momma. It had survived.

As she drew closer, she imagined hearing the forest weep, lonely sounds to lament the end of life.

Trampled to the ground, flowers still lined the walkway, soot dulling the once-colorful petals. The fine black film had settled in the curves of the valentines cut in the gazebo's wooden trim. She slid her hand along the smooth sanded finish of the railing as she climbed the steps.

The structure closed around her like a pair of comforting arms. She slid to the floor, wishing she could cry, but the tears stayed locked inside, as they had for days.

Lost in her sorrow, she didn't hear his footsteps until he reached the gazebo. The cut of his business clothes may have been proper, but the hair that defied the boundaries of his collar and the purposeful step to his walk reminded her that he was a man of his own thinking, a man of strength. Just the sight of him brought consolation to her abandoned heart.

"Justin!" Her joy at seeing him filled her voice. "You're back." Even in the dim light, she could see the worry lines creasing his high forehead, the mournful look filling his dark eyes, and the compassionate smile on his generous lips. How clearly she had memorized his features.

"I just got in. I stopped at the livery to water my horse. Old Otto told me about your parents." He paused. "Oh, Katrina, I'm so very sorry." He held out his hands and helped her to her feet. "Are you all right?"

"No . . . but I will survive."

"I came by to see the damage, get an idea of how much help you'd need. Looks like a lot."

She looked at her poppa's unfinished labor of love. "This is all that's left," she said, unable to still the tremor in her voice.

For a second she thought he might say that everything would be all right, words she knew to ring false. He didn't.

"I'm glad to hear you and Gretchen are staying at the house."

"Your mother has shown us every kindness."

"You're practically family."

"Actually, the wedding is off for now. I know some guests have traveled great distances, but when I get married, I want it to be a happy day." She thought of the pansy with five lines and of the hard road ahead it predicted. She didn't see any happy days in her future.

"Your wedding day *will* be a happy day, Katrina. Somehow I just know it." He glanced toward the street. "My horse is out front. I'll take you back to the house whenever you're ready."

"No, no, I don't want to go back there. Not yet. I just can't." The trembling rocked her shoulders.

"It's all right. I understand." He wrapped his arms around her and gently drew her close. "Take all the time you need."

Nothing felt more natural than being cradled in his embrace. Nestled against him, she finally began to cry. The harder she cried, the tighter he held her. When she felt her legs give way, he braced her against his chest and helped her to the floor, where they knelt facing each other. Murmuring her name, he held her until her breathing eased and the flow of tears subsided.

Tenderly, he pressed his lips to the heavy black veil that covered her forehead. His simple nearness brought comfort. She tilted her head to look into his eyes, grateful for his presence.

As though tortured by his own need, he slowly lifted

her veil, then lightly touched his lips to hers, stirring the air as the few inches between them disappeared, inviting the ritual of the kiss to begin.

As powerful as death had been to numb her feelings, so too was the power of his kiss to rekindle them. Just when she thought she'd never savor the excitement of life again, she was feasting on it. Desperate to keep the feeling from slipping away, she ran her fingers through his hair, boldly pulling him closer, deepening his kiss. She gloried at hearing him moan. With the tip of his tongue he spread her lips and dipped into the softness of her mouth. She arched against him, aching for more.

With his heartbeat thundering against her breast, she mirrored what he'd just taught her and plundered his mouth with her tongue. He held her tighter, confirming her belief that somewhere in this private oasis where their shadows mingled she could find life again.

His hands spread heat that both soothed and excited as they ran up and down her spine. Still, the emptiness inside her cried to be filled. When his hands cupped her breasts, she gasped, not in fear or shame but in a wanting so intense it hurt.

He stopped only to unbutton her bodice, to push it off her shoulders, to drag it down her arms. The same with her chemise, until the light of the silver moon played on her bare flesh.

As though he ached for her loss, as though he wanted nothing more than to ease her pain, he lowered his head and kissed first one breast, then the other.

He eased back, his breath as ragged as her own. Caution in his eyes, he waited for what she knew was a sign of her willingness. She knew that shame might come in the morning, but still she unfastened the waistband of her skirt and let the fabric fall. She wanted everything this man could give her.

He fumbled with the buttons on his shirt, yanking the

last one loose, sending it skipping across the wooden floor. He removed his pants. Nothing prepared her for the sight of his arousal or for the primitive longings it evoked.

"Are you sure?" he asked.

Never more sure of anything, she reached for him, the brother of the man she was to marry.

Richmond looked frantic as Justin rode up to the house, Katrina sitting sidesaddle in front of him. She didn't miss the look of contempt that Richmond gave his brother.

Taking a pistol from his waist, Richmond shot twice in the air. "Everyone's been out looking for you," he said to Katrina. "Where have you been? I was worried. Do you know how late it is?"

"I didn't mean to worry you," she said. "I just needed to get away. I started walking and found myself in front of the bakery. I lost track of the time. And then Justin came."

Like dozens of fireflies, lanterns appeared from every direction.

"I've got her!" Richmond shouted. "She's safe."

Gretchen ran down the front steps, her arms outstretched, fresh tears streaming from her swollen eyes. "I thought somehow you too had . . . oh, Katrina, why you leave me like that?"

Katrina slid from the horse and felt her sister's agony as they embraced. "I didn't mean to worry you. I'm sorry."

"And everything about you is fine?"

Katrina nodded. Fine indeed.

She started as she felt Richmond's hand on her shoulder.

"I think I should get you inside," he said, leading her to the door.

At the top of the stairs she turned around. Justin had dismounted and was surrounded by townspeople slapping him on the back, thanking him for finding her, she supposed.

He looked up at her. The distance between them couldn't disguise or diminish the pain she saw in his eyes. She knew he saw the same in hers. The weight of Richmond's arm felt heavy on her shoulder as he urged her toward the door. Dear God, what had she done?

"Katrina, as soon as you have rested, we must talk about the wedding," Richmond said.

"No. Not now."

"But, Katrina—"

"Please. We must wait a year. Out of respect. I've lost both my parents."

"Forgive me," he said, shaking his head. "I'm afraid I haven't been much comfort to you. I'm sorry. I mean no disrespect to your parents. I am just eager to begin our future, to restore joy to your life." He kissed her hand. "Go inside now. Get some rest."

Something wasn't right. Richmond couldn't put his finger on what it was, but ever since the night Justin found Katrina at the bakery and brought her home, he sensed a change in his bride-to-be. More often than not, he found her standing by herself at the parlor window staring at the road back to town. He assumed it was her grief making her so contemplative, but whenever he tried to comfort her, she flinched and pulled away. Whenever he asked her a simple question, she fumbled over her words as though she didn't know what to say. For a woman who usually spoke her mind freely, this was a new development.

He played several new tunes for her on the piano, but he could tell she wasn't listening by the way she gazed into space. He offered to take her for a ride up to his favorite spot high on the hill, but she declined. She said she wanted to see what was left of the bakery, but as soon as he made plans to take her there, she changed her mind. One minute she looked soft and, while not content, at least accepting; the next minute tortured. She didn't make sense.

He would have been even more concerned had she not also distanced herself from Gretchen. She even, he noticed, refused to talk to Justin.

"Enough!"

Eberhard Barrison pounded his fist on the dining room table, causing the stemware to tremble. His cold eyes turned colder still as his face darkened with rage.

Gretchen reached for Katrina's hand beneath the table and clutched it tightly. Katrina wanted to assure Gretchen that everything would be all right, but she couldn't, for the tension in the Barrison household had been building for days, particularly since this morning, when the last of the wedding guests departed.

Eberhard glared at Justin. "I will not be challenged. Do I make myself clear?"

"Then you will not survive. Do I make *myself* clear?"

Eberhard rose, his hands fisted at his sides. "Why you insubordinate lout. Get out of my sight. Now! Go!"

Justin's chair clattered to the floor as he shoved it back. He stood, balled his napkin, and tossed it on his plate. "Half the men in town depend on the wages we pay to feed their families. Will you have them go hungry?"

"*We* don't pay their wages. *I* pay their wages. *I* am Barrison Brewery."

"When I am running the brewery—"

Katrina tensed as Eberhard picked up his glass of wine and threw it against the wall.

"I will rot in hell before you run my brewery."

Katrina and Gretchen gasped. Rosamond stared at the wall as she reached for her water. Richmond sat still and silent.

Justin said, "You owe the women an apology."

"I don't owe anyone anything." Eberhard looked with disgust at his wife and younger son, then at Justin. "Least of all you." He stormed away from the table.

Immediately following the slam of the library door, Richmond reached for the carafe of wine on the sideboard. "It's the business," he said by way of explanation, as he quickly topped off everyone's glass. "Father has so much on his mind. He didn't mean to be rude."

"Well now," Justin said with a bitter smile. "I never thought I'd hear *you* defend him, but then it'll all be yours now, won't it?"

"Can I help it if you antagonize him?"

Desperate to outrace her fears, Katrina blurted out, "You can't go, Justin! You can't! Apologize to your father. Tell him you're sorry. He'll forgive you. But you must do it now. Hurry!"

His eyes narrowed, and when he spoke to her she knew exactly what he meant. "Unlike you, Katrina, I'm *not* sorry. I'm not sorry at all."

"But you'll lose everything!"

He looked at her. "I've already lost everything that matters." With that, he left the room.

"You can't go!" she called after him. "You can't!"

Only then did she realize how Gretchen, Rosamond, and especially Richmond were staring at her.

8

One of the qualities Richmond admired most in Katrina was her ability to keep her temper in check. Marriage would curb her outspokenness, to be sure, for that's what marriage did for all women; it made them docile, appropriately submissive. After all, to honor and obey was an essential part of a woman's obligation in marriage. But temper? That was another issue altogether. For Katrina to become so easily and so emotionally provoked by Justin's violent outburst earlier that night deeply concerned Richmond. He had no intention of living his life on the fret of his wife's sharp tongue. Not Richmond Barrison, heir to Barrison Brewery. No indeed.

He smoothed the front of the black dress coat he'd worn at dinner and checked his reflection in the full-length mirror in his bedroom. He had always enjoyed making little demonstrations of his affection. He liked giving Katrina boxes of chocolates, flowers and such, though he couldn't say he ever found her as appreciative as he expected.

When her parents were still alive, he made a point not

to visit too frequently. He didn't want to ever be accused of being too aggressive. No, other than that one day he had tried to kiss Katrina, he had been careful not to ever exhibit any obtrusive familiarity toward her. True love was delicate and timid. He would bide his time.

He was, however, equally careful to pay her mother both marked attention and respectful homage, always assuring her of the many advantages he would provide for her daughter: a well-appointed home, a position of honor in the community. He couldn't say that Truda Swann had been appropriately impressed. But Katrina was. He was sure of that. And Katrina's affections were all that mattered.

From his admittedly few conversations with Gustav Swann, Richmond knew that Katrina would be agreeable to the match. He would never have asked for her otherwise, for no gentleman likes the humiliation of being refused the hand of a lady, even if only for a quadrille. He remembered that haughty bitch in St. Louis. How could he have ever thought her equal to him?

To Gustav's credit, he had been frank about his daughter's outspokenness. The man actually admitted encouraging both his daughters to speak their minds. Richmond raised an eyebrow and thought to himself that if Herr Swann expected his younger daughter to make as good a match as Katrina, he had better teach her the virtues of humility and a low and gentle voice, for both sisters had far too much liberty of expression and there weren't many eligible men in this world willing to exert the effort to reform them.

Richmond opened his wardrobe and rifled through the frock coats, double-breasted waistcoats, and trousers of both dark and light colors. He always wore a dress coat to dinner. Someday, when he had sons of his own, he would see to it that they did the same, for it was the observance of these seemingly minor matters of etiquette that marked a true gentleman.

He would wear the light gray flannel tomorrow, a soft blue shirt, a small-patterned tie. Having decided that, he closed the door. Though he certainly sympathized with Katrina's loss of her parents, the loss of her clothing provided the opportunity for him to dress her in a manner befitting her new station. He was so tired of seeing her in those drab rags and admittedly relieved that with her mother gone—peace be to her ashes—there was no chance of Katrina's wearing one of those Old World birdcages on her head when they finally got married.

His head pounded. He'd come up to his room on the pretext of getting a clean handkerchief, for he'd given his to his mother when his father's wine splattered all over her dress. Closer to the truth, he needed a minute to himself, to try to make sense of what had transpired between his brother and his bride-to-be.

What could have made her show such extraordinary concern for Justin's welfare? Why was she so anxious to have him make amends with his father when she knew full well that after his vulgar display, he would never be given control of the brewery? It would all go to Richmond, just as he had planned. What was the matter with her?

If he didn't know better, he'd say Katrina felt some sort of affection for Justin. The pounding in his head grew stronger, and he pressed his fingers to his temples. He knew full well how Justin felt about Katrina. He'd known it for years. Justin thought she was beautiful. Richmond remembered that once, when he was only fifteen, Justin had said she reminded him of a prize colt. Then he had laughed in his boastful way and said he was going to be the man to break her in.

Richmond didn't think she was all that beautiful. Attractive, yes, but he'd seen more comely women in New York, Philadelphia, St. Louis. He wasn't marrying her because of her looks but because, in spite of her sharp tongue and her lack of proper respect, she bolstered his confidence. Unlike a certain ignorant woman in St. Louis, Katrina recognized his worth.

He lifted his chin a bit higher. He wanted her for one other reason too: Justin wanted her.

Richmond smoothed his black dress coat one more time before opening the door. He and Justin had fought over toys and cookies, over who got to place the angel on top of the Christmas tree, over puppies, over horses. Now they were fighting over Barrison Brewery and, if Richmond's suspicions were correct, over Katrina Swann. But Richmond wasn't a boy anymore. He was a man. He knew how to win. Hadn't he already won the brewery?

With what little pride he had left, Justin threw several pairs of Levi's and a handful of shirts, socks, and undergarments into his battered leather valise. He was the one who had said upheaval was necessary. He was the one who had said he wanted to build his own empire, seek his own destiny. Well, now he'd have the chance. He laughed at himself, knowing the joke was on him. He'd lost. He'd barely begun to fight, and he'd lost. Worst of all, he'd finally found someone worth fighting for.

He buckled the valise and headed for the door. He had to give Richmond credit. The man was a strategist.

He stepped out into the hallway. The door to Katrina's room was open. Her light was on. He was tempted to go to her, at least to say good-bye. But would she speak to him?

These last two weeks had been hell. When she wouldn't join him for even a simple walk in the garden, he told himself to be patient. She'd lost her parents. Her home. This couldn't be an easy time for her either. But she wouldn't let him help. She wouldn't accept so much as a drink of water from him. Every time he looked at her, she turned away, making it clear she didn't even want to be in the same room with him.

What the hell had happened? Was it so easy for her to forget how powerful their loving had been? He couldn't.

Now he heard Richmond's voice coming from her room and he heard her gush with appreciation. It hit him like a blow to the chest.

"But it would take me a lifetime to repay you, and even then—"

"Now, now," Richmond said, "I'd planned to give them to you on our wedding day, but I understand and can accept your delay—as long as it's not forever."

"Oh, Richmond, *danke*. I mean, thank you."

"You need time to grieve. After all, you wouldn't want to come to me on our wedding night with a broken heart, now, would you? Poor Katrina, you've suffered so much already. That's why I wanted you to have these now. To ease your sorrow."

Justin stood in the doorway, his presence startling both Richmond and Katrina.

"Leaving, brother?" Richmond said.

"Looks that way."

The smug expression on Richmond's face didn't affect him. He'd seen it for years. It was the sudden and powerful longing in Katrina's dark eyes the moment she saw him that made Justin question his decision. She hadn't said a word to him in days except for her outburst tonight, and that was to urge him to stay. Maybe he'd been mistaken. Maybe he hadn't lost her yet. The possibility empowered him. Richmond might be able to strengthen her link to the past, but Justin could show her the future. All he had to do was convince her that a future with him was worth having.

Clutching a pair of candlesticks, Katrina asked, "Where will you go?"

"I'll take a room in town."

Richmond stiffened. "You mean to say you aren't really leaving?"

"I'm leaving this house."

"Well, you aren't welcome at the brewery. Surely, you know that. You'll draw no money, not a cent."

"I'll get a job." He didn't bother to say that he had a little money of his own from years of scrimping. What he had in his pocket wasn't any of Richmond's business.

Katrina's voice sounded hopeful. "And then what will you do?"

He shrugged, not with indecision but with the power of a man who suddenly has options. "Haven't made up my mind." He picked up his valise and smiled, knowing how much his show of confidence would irritate Richmond, hoping it would tell Katrina that he had no intention of going anywhere. Not yet, anyway. "So I'll see you both around town. Goodnight, Katrina."

"Gave her the candlesticks already, did he?" Bridget washed another potato in the bowl of cold water.

"That he did, Aunt Bridget. Said he didn't want her coming to him on their wedding night with a broken heart."

Addressing her comment more to Gretchen than to Molly, Bridget said, "He's a good boy, that Richmond. He'll be giving her every fancy she can think of. That sister of yours is in for a fine life, a fine life indeed. You mark my words."

Gretchen nodded. She knew Richmond had given Katrina the candlesticks. Katrina had shown them to her last night. They'd both shed a tear or two and taken comfort in shared memories. It would take a long, long time for wounds so deep to heal. Fortunately, both she and Katrina had plenty of time.

She sat on the stool and tapped her foot while Bridget

peeled another potato and Molly carried the skins to the slop bucket.

"Hand me down the biggest of the fry pans there, Molly girl. And fetch me the crock of butter from the ice chest."

Gretchen groaned. Fried potatoes. Again. Katrina had told her not to invade Bridget's kitchen, and for more than three weeks she'd complied. But Gretchen's hands itched to knead bread and roll dough, and her stomach wanted to taste a potato in a creamy soup, or a tangy salad, or a golden onion-flecked pancake.

"Let me help," Gretchen said, as she hopped off the stool and headed straight for the sack of potatoes.

Bridget raised her paring knife. "You'll be doing no such thing!"

"Please."

"No. You sit yourself back down and have another cup of tea. You're a guest in this house. Besides, I don't want no foreign hands in my kitchen."

Foreign? Gretchen stood her ground. Using every ounce of control she could muster, for she didn't want Bridget to know how deeply her words had hurt, she said, "I am an American. Same as you."

"Well, of course you are! For crying out loud, I didn't mean you was still a greener. I just meant that other than Molly, here, and your sister when she was working, I ain't let another pair of hands—German, French, Eye-talian, English, even Irish, or what have you—mess up my kitchen." She put the knife down. "Now, don't go crying on me! Jesus, Mary, and Joseph. What am I going to do with you?"

"I am not crying." Gretchen sniffed and drew an old frayed hankie from her sleeve. Dabbing her eyes, she said, "You could let me make a batch of potato salad. I know you have vinegar, and I saw the dill in the garden."

"Wait just a minute here."

"Or potato soup. Or potato pancakes. I could show you how. But please, no more fried potatoes."

Gretchen felt Bridget's scrutiny as she tucked her handkerchief away. If it weren't for the look of kindness in the older woman's eyes, Gretchen would have been worried.

"Suppose I let you play with the potatoes this one time. What'll you be wanting your hands on next? The chicken? The beef?"

"The bread."

Molly piped up. "Aunt Bridget, ain't you always saying anybody's bread tastes better'n yours?"

"Hush with you!"

More eager than ever to help, Gretchen blurted out, "You don't let it rise long enough. That's why your bread, it's so tough."

"Hmm. Tough, is it?"

"Oh, *ja*, and you got to keep the heat in your oven just right. If it gets too hot—" Gretchen stopped, suddenly overwhelmed by memories she'd been so sure she could control.

Surely Bridget knew, as did everyone else in Merriweather, that the bakery had burned and Gustav Swann had died because the oven ran too hot. To her credit, Bridget didn't mention it. Instead, she marched to the pantry and took a clean apron from the tidy stack in the corner. "Here," she said, handing it to Gretchen. "Nobody works in my kitchen 'less they wear an apron."

Gretchen held the apron to her chest. "So I can help?"

Bridget pointed to various stations about the room. "I knead the bread on that end of the table. I roll dough in the middle. Prepare my pans on the other end. If I'm shelling peas or snapping beans, I sit in that chair by the window. Over here in this corner I churn the butter—unless the air is too warm, and then I haul it out to the springhouse."

Gretchen looked around, wanting so much to be useful again, to create with her hands as well as her heart. "You have pudding cloths? Jelly bags of white flannel?"

"Never used 'em, but I have 'em."

"A waffle iron? A griddle?"

"Them too."

Molly looked at Gretchen with something close to worship. "You know everything about baking, don't you?"

"*Ja*, I do."

"Will you teach me?"

"Sure. Soon as we fix the potato salad, I'm gonna show you how to make the sweetest kuchen dough. We gonna fill it with juicy cherries. Then we gonna whip up the freshest cream and make a Bavarian peach torte. And then, the best of all, I'm gonna show you how to make the biggest sticky buns, filled with plump raisins, swirled with cinnamon, and crowned with crunchy pecans."

She grinned from ear to ear and blinked back tears all at the same time. Tying the apron around her waist, Gretchen felt happy for the first time in a long time. This was a grand house, with a kitchen equipped for a czar. She would have to remind Katrina of what a rich life she would have when she finally did marry Richmond. She would remind Katrina soon, for not once in showing Gretchen the candlesticks last night did Katrina show the tiniest flutter of her heart for Richmond.

"Gretchen," Katrina said one morning a couple of weeks later, "Richmond has offered to take me into town. I want to see how bad the damage is to the bakery. Will you come with us?"

"I do want to see the bakery, but—" Gretchen looked over her shoulder at the empty bread basket on the dining room table and shook her head. "I can't leave now, not with so much bread and so many rolls to be baked—not to mention doughnuts and tarts. Is a mystery to me how the Barrisons have survived."

"Richmond recommends we raze the lot and sell it, then invest the money. What do you think?"

"If we invest in a new bakery, sure, for I have no coin in my pocket and I won't go to Lukas as a pauper."

Richmond joined them, holding the cup of coffee he'd taken from the sideboard. "I assume you've no more candlesticks to sell. Your poor parents didn't even have assets enough for a dowry—not that a dowry matters to me."

Annoyed by Richmond's comment, Katrina said, "There are many customers who owe to the bakery. Once they pay—"

"I'm afraid not," Richmond said. "You see, I have already encouraged them to settle their accounts—which they did, of course."

Gretchen cocked her head to one side as though she couldn't believe what she was hearing. "The money my customers owed to me and Katrina they paid to you?"

"That's correct. They didn't want to deal with women in matters of commerce, which is understandable, nor did they want to bother the two of you in the midst of your grief. Knowing that if not for the tragedy Katrina and I would be wed by now, they felt it appropriate for me to handle your financial transactions, since, as Katrina's husband, I would be doing so anyway."

"Then where are our funds?" Katrina asked, not at all comfortable with the idea of Richmond getting involved with the bakery.

"*Ja*, where is the twenty-two dollars and eighteen cents, for that is what we are owed on the books?"

Richmond sighed. "I had so hoped to avoid this discussion. If you girls would only let me take care of everything for you—"

"Where is our money?" Katrina asked again.

He gestured to the voluminous folds of Katrina's rich black silk. "The seamstress. The cobbler. Mother wanted to pay for everything, but I told her you two still felt the need to be independent and would be offended to have her absorb your debt. Of course, if I was wrong I would want you to tell me."

Katrina tried to squelch the anger that was making her voice rise. "I would never want your mother—or anyone—to incur debt on our behalf," she said. "But cotton would have sufficed. We don't need silks and jet beads."

"Oh, Katrina, there you go again, getting upset over something as trivial as a few gowns. I didn't mention any of this before because I assumed we would soon be wed and from then on I would take care of such things—both for you and your sister. It's unseemly for either of you to be working, not when I can provide for both of you. So you see there's no need to rebuild the bakery, no need at all."

"Oh, but there is!" Gretchen said at once. "I aim to have personal liberty. I can have it through my bakery."

"Now, now," Richmond said, "there's no need for either of you to be upset. I'm told grief can induce irrational behavior."

Gretchen dug her fists to her hips. "I am not irrational."

"I only meant that once you have had enough time to grieve, you will see that the bakery is not your security. I am your security. "

"No," Katrina said. "We owe it to Momma and Poppa to rebuild. They did not cross an ocean to see their dream die so easily. While Gretchen and I are both grateful for your generosity, bringing the bakery back to life will be good for us."

He paused. "Well, then, if you insist on pursuing a course of commerce, you needn't worry about the bakery. Not for a minute. I will obtain the funds. I will arrange for construction to begin immediately. After that lavish feast you prepared for us last night, Gretchen, that is the least I can do."

Sounding suspicious, Gretchen said, "So, how much money for this dress?" She lifted just enough black fabric to show the tip of her toe. "And for the shoes?"

"Now, now, now," Richmond said, "it's not important. Let's forget it, shall we? I never should have brought the subject up."

"More than twenty-two dollars and eighteen cents?" Gretchen asked.

"The amount is insignificant."

Katrina pressed. "How much?"

"One hundred sixty? One hundred seventy? I'm not sure."

"Whole dollars?" Gretchen's eyes widened with both surprise and alarm.

Staggered by the figures, Katrina glared at him. "You collected our money so we would not be in debt for the funerals. Then you put us in debt just the same, and for something we didn't need."

"Calm down," he said. "For one thing, you *did* need those dresses, both of you. Proper mourning gowns should be of silk. I've ordered others, too. Gray. Lavender. The mourning period must be observed properly. Beautiful women should not go about in rags. Katrina, you in particular need a whole new wardrobe, but that's another issue. More important, how can you possibly consider yourself in debt to me when you are soon to become my wife, when I am so eager to share all I have with you? A few dollars. What can a person buy these days with a few dollars?"

"Pride!" She grabbed a fistful of fabric from her skirt. "For twenty-two dollars and eighteen cents you bought my pride."

"Katrina, don't say such a thing. Please. I never meant to anger you. Only help you."

Gretchen looked at Katrina. "I hate like poison to say this, but Richmond is right. We could not have paid for dresses, even plain cotton dresses, and shoes and a roof over our heads—especially a roof such as this—with twenty-two dollars and eighteen cents. We should be grateful."

Katrina felt sick to her stomach. Gretchen was speaking in that matter-of-fact tone Poppa often used, the one she suspected spoke the truth while it hid the anger building inside.

"Look at us," Gretchen continued. "We have no funds and nothing to sell. This is our reality."

"Not forever. We'll rebuild the bakery—"

Richmond interrupted. "You don't need the bakery."

"Yes, we do. At least for now. And we need to live there as well. For now."

After a long pause, Richmond said, "Then I suppose you will simply have to rebuild."

"*Ja*, sure, but with what?"

"With a loan from Barrison Brewery, of course."

"A loan?" Katrina asked.

"It appears that's the only way. I can see how much this little bakery means to the two of you, and though I find your insistence on living there a foolish notion indeed, I suppose I will have to accept this last stand of independence. So I will arrange for a loan, with interest and penalties, the same as a loan from a bank. I have such authority now."

Katrina chided herself for being suspicious. "To arrange a loan would be generous of you. But I think we should go to a bank."

"Katrina, dear, there isn't a bank in this entire United States of America that would lend a sizable amount of money to two unmarried immigrant women with no collateral."

"You don't have to remind me of how this country thinks of greeners."

Gretchen opened her mouth to add something, then thought better of it.

"Well?" Richmond asked. "Shall I draw up the papers?"

"Gretchen? What do you think?"

Gretchen shrugged. "What choice we have?"

"If we want the bakery, none."

"Then it's settled," Richmond said. "I'll arrange for a loan, all proper and legal. That way you won't feel as though you are accepting my charity, though I must say it hurts me that you see it that way." Offering his arm to Katrina, he said, "Now let's go have a look at that pile of rubble, shall we? And see just how deeply in debt you will be to me." He turned to Gretchen. "Will you change your mind and come with us?"

Gretchen shook her head and walked into the kitchen. Katrina knew her sister well enough to know that tears were close at hand and that Gretchen, like Katrina, would only weep in private.

Katrina felt a wave of uneasiness sweep over her as she took Richmond's arm. She had wanted to make some kind of decision, some kind of move forward, and now she had. But at what price? The implication of Richmond's words was clear. As long as she still planned to marry him, she and Gretchen would have the funds to rebuild their lives. Without him, they would be destitute.

Feeling weak, she held his arm tighter, a gesture he seemed to like.

Halfway into town, on a stretch of deserted road, Richmond stopped the carriage. For a second or two he just sat there, as though gathering his thoughts. Katrina straightened her back against the seat and clutched the strings of her reticule. She prayed he wasn't going to remind her again of how poor she was, how needy.

"Katrina," he said, as though he'd been pondering some great mystery, "Katrina, we are engaged to be married and yet we have never spoken of love."

Caught by surprise, she didn't know what to say.

He continued. "Does that bother you? I hear that romantic love is important to American girls. You, of course, come from the old country. Still, I would think it might concern you—that you might at least wonder about my feelings."

"Momma always said that while love might not be a guest at the wedding, it could easily come to live with a couple over the years."

"Your mother was a wise woman."

"Yes," Katrina said with conviction. "She was."

"In any event, I want you to know that I love you." He nodded, and Katrina could picture him standing in front of a mirror trying the words on for fit and finding them to his liking. "I love you," he repeated.

He had that expectant look about him. Was he waiting for her to say the words? She prayed not, for she didn't love him. She assumed she would at some point, but she didn't now. So she said, *"Danke."*

His blue eyes widened in surprise. "Thank you? Thank you?"

"Richmond, I'm sorry. I care for you, but—"

He tossed his head back and laughed. "There's no need to apologize. I'm the one at fault here. You aren't really an American girl now, are you? I keep forgetting."

"Now just a minute."

"Tsk, tsk, there's no need to look so peeved. You're certainly not just another immigrant. You know that. I meant only that you have a more old-fashioned, more traditional view of marriage, one that does not necessarily include love, one that sees marriage more as an arrangement. I suppose I should be grateful. Yes, in fact, I am. After all, I wouldn't want a woman who was so eager for a man's admiration that she would toy with his fragile heart and break it like a matchstick."

"Do you think that's what I'm doing? Toying with your heart?"

He sighed. "I think perhaps you are the only one who can answer that question." When she didn't answer right away, he asked, "So are you? Are you toying with my heart?"

Until now, Katrina had thought the dilemma of her feelings affected only her own life and that of her sister. She had never thought of a man as being vulnerable to his own heart's desires, but hearing Richmond admit to the pain a man suffers from a broken heart made her feel terrible, for she never meant to hurt him. No doubt she had caused such pain for Justin too.

"That has never been my intention," she said.

Richmond looked crestfallen, but what was she to do? Until she could firmly and without reservation give her heart to Richmond, everyone she cared for would suffer. And she couldn't do that until she resolved her feelings for Justin once and for all.

She had tried to avoid Justin, hoping to put him out of her mind, if not her heart. Yet she couldn't deny the desperate ache she had felt when she saw him standing in the doorway to her room the night he left his home. Afraid she would never see him again, she had clutched the silver candlesticks to her heart, praying her mother's wisdom would somehow come through to her and tell her what to do. She'd felt so relieved when he said he planned to stay in town.

Her stomach lurched at the memory of making love with Justin, and the thought of the chaos that the act might someday cause.

She looked over at Richmond, sitting perfectly straight, as though by the sheer power of his will he could control his world. He forced a smile, but it didn't reach his eyes, and Katrina felt he'd once again managed to quiet some festering turmoil of his own. To her relief, he said nothing, simply flicked the reins and headed down the road and into town.

Muffled by the creaking wagon wheels, barking dogs, and laughing children, the sound was faint at first: a single hammer pounding away in the summer heat. Katrina gripped the edge of her seat as Richmond passed between rows of sturdy white stucco buildings with their dark exposed beams and steep red tile roofs, their window boxes heavy with ivy and red geraniums, up to what was left of the bakery.

There, in the midst of the charred ruins of her parents' dream, the remnants of a nightmare, a scrap of the life she'd once known, stood Justin, with his shirt unbuttoned, his sleeves rolled past his elbows, and a red bandanna around his head. He was rebuilding her bakery.

Overwhelmed with gratitude and other feelings she wasn't ready to admit, Katrina burst into tears.

9

"There, there now," Richmond said, handing her his handkerchief. "I should have realized how traumatic it would be for you to see all this again. Perhaps I should take you home."

Katrina wiped her eyes and fought for composure. "No. I want to stay."

Richmond glared at Justin, who was now heading their way. "As you wish."

Justin buttoned his shirt as he walked toward her, but not before Katrina got a glimpse of his chest and, with it, the flash of a memory. He grinned at the sight of her. She bit her lower lip to control her smile, but couldn't deny how happy she was to see him.

"Katrina, I didn't expect to see you down here so soon." He nodded to Richmond.

"I had to face the bakery at some point," she said. "It's been over a month."

"A month can seem like forever."

"Yes," she said, feeling more confused than she had ever imagined possible.

"Here," Justin said as he offered her his hand. "Let me show you what I've done."

She turned to Richmond, a questioning look in her eye.

"Yes," Richmond said with the slightest crack in his confident air. "Let's do have a look."

She took Justin's hand and stepped down.

She'd always thought the foundation that formed the cellar and the lower half of the first floor would withstand anything, but the weight of falling timbers had cracked the masonry, freeing more than a few stones and loosening others. Strewn about, they looked like fallen tombstones in an abandoned cemetery. There wasn't a blade of green grass in sight. The damage was worse than she'd thought. Soot clung to the brick walls of the bank on the left and the singed beams of the general mercantile on the right.

"The neighbors got together and hauled away most of the debris," Justin said by way of explanation. "But, as you can see for yourself, there's still a lot left."

"Obviously," Richmond said. He kicked a piece of rubble at his foot, releasing the stench of burning air.

Katrina reached down and picked up the object. "Our teakettle," she said as she brushed away the dirt and grime.

"You don't need that filthy thing," Richmond said, taking it from her and tossing it onto the pile at the edge of the property.

"But—"

"Bridget makes the tea." He put his hand on her shoulder but pulled it away when she flinched.

Justin drew her attention to the small pile of lumber he'd been working on when they arrived. An odd assortment of sizes, each board was neatly stacked, each board singed by the fire. "I think I can salvage some of the wood," he said, "though I've had to saw off both ends of some pieces. I know I can salvage the nails." He reached into the pocket of the narrow canvas apron he wore about his waist and rifled his hand through the nails he'd already collected.

"You've worked so hard," she said, not wanting to hurt him by adding that the task he'd set for himself was clearly too daunting for one man, that his efforts to collect nails looked foolish, and the lumber he'd managed to salvage looked useful for firewood but nothing more.

He seemed to bask in pride. "There's a lot to be done."

"But why are you doing all this?" she asked.

Richmond joined in. "Yes, tell us, dear brother. Why have you devoted all your time and what little funds you might have to rebuilding the bakery? Could it be you have nothing else with which to occupy your time? Would no one in town risk father's wrath and hire you?"

"That's nonsense," Katrina said quickly, then turned to Justin. "You have found employment, haven't you? Tell him."

He looked in Katrina's eyes but said nothing.

Richmond smirked. "I'm right, aren't I?"

"Yes, dear brother, you are. I don't have a job. No one will take me on."

"And so you squandered what money you had on bed and board in a town where you aren't welcome and a few tools for a project that's clearly beyond your capabilities." Richmond shook his head. "Reckless as always."

"Go to your father," Katrina said. "Apologize. He would take you back. I'm sure he already regrets his words. Please, Justin, for your future."

"My future isn't in Merriweather. I can't wait to get out of this stifling town."

"Then go," Richmond said. "What's keeping you?"

Katrina felt an urge to say something, to admit aloud that she cared for Justin. But reality came crashing down all around her and fear trapped her words inside. Though his heart might be in the right place, Justin's actions proved him reckless and irresponsible. He always would be. Dreams of a future with him would have to remain only dreams.

Her heart ached for both of them as she looked at his crumbled efforts to succeed. "You'll never know how much I appreciate what you've tried to do here, but—"

"I'm taking care of rebuilding the bakery," Richmond said. "I plan to hire a crew this very day. So you see, your meager efforts aren't needed. Appreciated, of course, but not needed."

"I'll stay as long as I feel like it," Justin said, his shoulders squared. "And when I feel like moving on, I will." He looked at Katrina.

"But where will you go? How will you live?" she asked. He didn't answer.

Thanks to the loan Richmond arranged through Barrison Brewery, work on the bakery began immediately. Every morning a crew of experts labored to restore the home and the livelihood of the Swann sisters. To everyone's surprise, Justin showed up every day to help, though Richmond made it clear he wasn't to be paid. Richmond added his own labor in the form of supervision for a quarter hour or so every afternoon, but with his days spent increasingly in managing the brewery, he had little time to spare. He told Katrina that while he didn't welcome Justin's presence, if the fool was willing to work for free, Richmond certainly wasn't going to stop him.

Katrina and Gretchen worked alongside the men, fetching tools, hauling water to drink, laying out food provided by the neighbors. Progress was remarkable by anyone's standards. By the end of the second week, it was obvious the bakery would be back in operation soon and the sisters could move into the new two-room living quarters above the business.

To anyone who cared to notice, something else was obvious too. Katrina Swann wasn't speaking to Justin Barrison.

Late one afternoon, after most of the men had returned to their own homes and other obligations, Gretchen poured two cups of the cold cider Frau Epple had brought from her cellar. "Katrina, come sit. I need the truth from you."

Kneeling in what would soon be a flower garden, Katrina returned the tools she was using to the basket beside her and stood up. "What is it?"

"Why are you not sharing words with Justin Barrison? Don't think I don't see. He works hard like an ox and you pour water for everyone but him. He tries to talk to you and you turn your head. I thought the two of you shared a friendship."

"In case the obvious has passed you by, Gretchen, Richmond and Justin don't get along. I don't think Richmond would be pleased to find me cavorting with his brother."

"Cavorting? You exasperate me. I worry that you turn rude without reason to a man destined to be your family. You huff and puff like the day I told you Poppa was considering Wilmot Wolter as a match for you. I say only that you should talk to Justin, not kiss him. And don't say 'Gretchen' like I don't know my own name."

"As far is Justin is concerned, he is no longer part of the Barrison family. He doesn't want them and they don't want him."

"And why is it you don't open your heart to me anymore? Am I no longer part of your family too?"

"Stop talking nonsense. I don't have the patience for it."

Katrina turned on her heel and walked away, behind the bakery, toward the gazebo, all the while wishing for the old days when she could share her worries with

Gretchen. For her worries were mounting as she marked each passing day.

The gazebo beckoned. With its gentle curves and halo of cut-out hearts and flowers, it called to mind all that was beautiful the night she'd taken the comfort Justin offered and given him her heart. How fitting that the gazebo should sit unfinished, its once clean wood dirtied with soot.

It would be dangerous to surround herself with memories of Justin's arms and Justin's kiss and her own sweet surrender to Justin's love. She had to forget him and let the healing start.

Still, she walked up the stairs and into the gazebo. She'd been there only a few minutes when she heard his voice, and the strength she'd tried so hard to find disappeared.

"Katrina."

She turned to see him standing on the ground at the bottom of the stairs. "This mean anything to you?" he asked.

She looked at the object in his hand. With recognition came a flood of childhood memories that brought a lump to her throat.

He handed her the charred piece of wood, then watched as she gently brushed away the soot and debris.

"My grandfather carved this for me. It's my dog, Strudel. I had him since he was a puppy."

"He was a talented man."

"Yes, he was." Knowing there was no way to stop her heart from aching, she focused on the pain of a past long behind her and sighed. "Poor Strudel. He was born an idiot dog. His head was huge and his eyes wandered. When he walked he would trip over his own feet. They were so big and flat. Poppa said he was useless and we had to drown him. I begged him not to. I promised to take care of the pup. I promised to feed him, and brush him, and train him not to bark at birds. But I was only five years old and

Poppa said I was too young for so much responsibility. When he came with the bucket, I grabbed Strudel and ran away." She swallowed to steady her voice. "I came back, of course. And Poppa let me keep him. Every night for ten whole years he slept at the foot of my bed."

Her heart cried at the memory of having to leave Strudel—and everything else—behind. "But Strudel is dead now. So is Grandfather." She cradled the carving in her hands and let the silence settle between them.

Finally, Justin spoke. "I'm leaving Merriweather soon."

He had a hesitant look in his eyes and Katrina wondered just how eager he was to go. But just glancing at him weakened her, so she kept her eyes on the carving in her hands and said, "I thought you might."

"I've worked a bit down by the docks. Keep hearing about free land up in the Dakota Territory. A lot of Germans have already settled there. All along the river. Inland, too."

"That's good. You'll not forget your roots."

"And I won't have to worry that I'll never taste another Wiener schnitzel. But that's assuming I'll find a good German cook for a wife."

"Damn you, Justin Barrison!" Their eyes met in a clash of dreams. "Why do you have to make this so hard on both of us?"

"I'm sorry."

"Sorry? For what? Sorry that I lost my momma and poppa? That you gave up your birthright? That I lost my innocence?"

"Look, if I took advantage of your grief, I regret it more than you can ever imagine. But I thought—I know—you wanted me as much as I wanted you. You didn't lose your innocence. You *gave* it."

"I was consumed with grief and my thoughts weren't clear. I had little choice."

"You *always* have a choice. You have one now. Leave here. Come away with me."

"Don't do this to me."

"But we'll be happy. I'll find a job somewhere. We'll have a fine house. Beautiful babies. Come on, Katrina, please. Say you'll do it." He grabbed her hands, forcing the carving to fall to the ground.

Katrina looked down with panic. When had the freedom to choose her own destiny become so frightening?

Drawing on every ounce of determination, she pulled her hands away. "I can't," she said, her voice catching, "I can't live knowing every day will be a challenge."

"What do you mean?"

"I want a man I can depend on. A man who won't let his pride destroy his life and the lives of his family. A man who has a solid plan for his future, a man who won't throw everything away in a moment of anger or run with his tail between his legs when trouble comes."

"That's not fair—"

"Listen to me! I want a man who isn't too proud to work in another man's shadow." She stood there trembling, tears streaming down her cheeks.

"Then you don't want me, do you?"

She sniffed and straightened her shoulders. "No."

He held his head high, but his eyes showed defeat. "Did you ever? Did you ever think you could love me?"

She considered his question and all its ramifications. "I don't have the courage to love you."

She let him walk away, praying she'd done the right thing.

That night, and for several thereafter, Katrina fell into bed sedated by exhaustion, though she could never truly rest. She clutched the hem of the sheet between her fingers and pulled it close to her chin, telling herself that, truly, all was right in her world.

*   *   *

Gretchen grinned as she shelved the new shipment of sugar from New Orleans. A row of fifty-pound sacks of freshly milled flour stood against the wall, waiting to be mixed into muffins, kneaded into bread. She turned the tins of lard so each colorful label faced front.

"Who would ever believe," she said to Katrina, "that only two months after the fire we could open for business? If not for the generous purse of the Barrisons— Katrina! Pay attention!"

Katrina looked at the sack of sugar she was about to empty into the flour bin. "A simple mistake," Katrina said, irritated more with herself than by Gretchen's criticism.

Katrina was just as distracted the following day. She used only four eggs instead of eight in the cheesecake. She burned her hand on the stove. That night Gretchen scolded her for posting the day's totals in the wrong column of the journal.

The day after was worse. With a customer standing at the counter waiting for her special order, Katrina dropped the item in question on the floor, creating a mess of chocolate cake, dark cherries, and whipped cream.

Katrina burst into tears and scurried from the room, leaving Gretchen to clean up the mess and to convince the customer that a blueberry-filled torte would make an equally fine birthday treat. Once the customer left, Gretchen followed Katrina's path upstairs to the bedroom they shared. Katrina was lying on the bed, staring at the ceiling. Gretchen marched into the room and stood at the foot of the bed, her arms akimbo.

"Katrina, you give fresh proof to the world that a woman past twenty can still be as addle-brained as a girl of twelve. My patience is spent. I want the full story of what troubles you to distraction. No more of this 'I'm so tired' and 'I'm so hot.' It's not your time of the month, so don't tell me you are unwell."

Katrina pulled herself up and sat on the edge of the bed. She sighed. The facts were so clinical. With a delicate touch of her fingers, she smoothed her dress over her midriff. She could tell from the unsuspecting look in Gretchen's eyes that the news would shock her more than it had Katrina. She gathered up the black fabric and exaggerated a bulge in her abdomen. "I'm in the usual condition . . . for a married woman."

Her own composure fractured as she saw the disbelief in Gretchen's eyes. Katrina had not believed it either, at first, but after missing two menses, she could not deny the shameful truth. "From my calculations, I'm expecting early next spring, mid-March to be exact."

Though Katrina's concerns were many, the immediate one was that Gretchen would take offense and feel ashamed to be her sister. Already, Katrina could see the disappointment on Gretchen's face, eroding her easy smile.

Katrina felt she died a little as she watched the mental calculations flash by Gretchen's eyes, as if only the issue of *when* she'd conceived mattered.

"Just after Momma and Poppa died?"

"I know how bad it sounds, but let me explain—"

"He forced himself on you. He couldn't accept the mourning period that delayed the wedding, so he forced himself on you."

"No. I was willing." Katrina's voice grew softer, to a silent prayer that Gretchen's righteous anger wouldn't be directed at her, though where else could it go? She stared at her lap and flattened the fabric, wishing that her condition would disappear.

Katrina knew Gretchen's common sense didn't come from the ceiling, or the walls, or the floor, but that's where she was looking.

"These things have been known to happen." Gretchen said. "You must tell Richmond at once. Dispense with the rules of mourning and wed him immediately. He will be only too pleased."

Katrina took a deep breath. "I can't marry Richmond."

"Why not?"

"He isn't the father. Justin is."

Gretchen gasped. "*Justin*! How could you do such a thing? You are betrothed to his brother!"

Katrina's heart raced. "It was but one night. Just one time. I am so sorry."

"Does Richmond know?"

Katrina shook her head. Just the thought of saying the words constricted her throat.

Gretchen glared at her. "You will tell him before the proof shows? Or had you thought to deceive him until after the wedding?"

"Of course I will tell him. In the morning. I plan to tell him in the morning. What do you take me for?"

Gretchen put her fists on her hips. "A selfish fool. You got us out of the Barrison house with all its comforts because for you it was upsetting—and the reason doesn't escape me now. So quick to spread your legs and destroy our livelihood. For unless Richmond marries you, you have thrown away the future for both of us. No decent citizen will patronize a bakery run by a . . ." Gretchen bit her lip, unable to say the word.

"I have already confessed to God and have begged his forgiveness. Richmond is a compassionate man. My hope is that he can find it in his heart to forgive me as well. He loves me. He told me so."

"You think his love for you is bigger than his pride?"

"I think he is an understanding man. I thought you—"

"What world do you live in? Richmond will never have you now."

The jingle of sleigh bells on the bakery floor drew Gretchen's attention.

"I must hurry. *Someone* must watch the bakery, and you haven't even the brain to watch your virtue. You have ruined everything for us. All for a selfish night of passion. Richmond may forgive you in an instant, but I won't. Not now, maybe not ever."

Katrina didn't think anything could make her feel worse, but Gretchen found a way. Before marching out of the bedroom, she added with unmistakable malice, "I never thought I would be glad to see that Momma and Poppa are dead, but at least they are spared having to live with your shame."

Katrina stood there trembling. On the tip of her tongue was a plea for Gretchen to wait, to listen, to try to understand. But tears kept the words inside. Besides, Gretchen was already gone.

A *whore.* Even to think the word drew her breath up short, pressed down on her chest with the weight of a hundred stones. No one would patronize a bakery run by a whore, or by the sister of a whore. Lukas Heinz was a decent man with a reputation to uphold. He wouldn't marry the sister of a whore.

Richmond, who had to have only the best, Richmond would never marry her once he knew the truth.

She thought about Justin. To go to him now would only make matters worse, for though his pride had been hurt, he had a sense of honor. If he knew she carried his baby, he'd do the right thing and marry her. But then what?

She sat on the edge of the bed and waited for the sudden dizziness to pass.

The feeling of dread was all too familiar: hearing her father shout at the czar's soldier, hearing Justin shout at his father. Just like Poppa, Justin valued his wild ways, his precious freedom, more than the well-being of his family.

She reached for her pillow and held it against her chest, praying it would muffle the pounding of her heart, for to hear its loud frantic beat terrified her.

Would Justin spend a scant moment worrying about their future? No, of course not. There was nothing too rash or too reckless for him to pursue. Together, he would stand tall while she would tremble with the knowledge of the disaster that was sure to come. Once again, she would be the one to pick up the pieces of her life. Only this time, an innocent child would suffer too.

She held the pillow tighter and rocked softly back and forth even as she fought to steady her breathing. There had to be another way. There had to be. For if she married Justin, the uncertainty, the fear, and the panic that right this minute made her want to scream would become her constant companions.

A soft summer breeze heavy with the scent of rain fluttered the curtains. Sneaking in its wake came an idea, one so horrid that if she weren't desperate she would never even consider it.

But she was desperate. Not only for herself but for Gretchen and for her unborn child.

What if Richmond never knew the truth? What if he thought the child was his?

Along with a fragile hope and the glimmer of a plan came a sinking feeling in the pit of her stomach. She sat still, very still, praying the feeling would pass but knowing it would only get worse.

Beads of sweat broke on her brow as she thought of the deception. If she succeeded, she would be a whore not once but twice. If she failed, she would be branded a whore for the rest of her life.

She couldn't do it. Yet she knew she had to.

*   *   *

Richmond removed his hat and set it on the counter next to the small ribbon-wrapped box he'd brought with him. He looked around. "No customers?"

Katrina walked toward the still-open door. Half of her prayed that someone, anyone, would come through the twilight shadows and she would be forced to abandon her scheme. The other half willed her hand to hold steady as she took down the *Willkommen* sign and slowly, carefully, closed the door and lowered the latch. "No," she said, keenly aware of Richmond's smile. "No customers. Not at this hour."

"Your sister. Where is she?"

"Gretchen is keeping company with the chemist, Lukas Heinz. They are meeting friends at the *Biergarten*. She . . . she won't be back till late."

"I see." He nodded as though he understood the unspoken communication between them. Again he smiled. He wore a white shirt and a dark suit with a deep blue cornflower poking from his breast pocket. Katrina didn't miss the implication of the test he'd set for her. If the flower retained its color by morning, his sweetheart would marry him. If the flower faded, she would marry someone else.

She didn't think it was possible to feel dirtier than she already did, but she shuddered at the way Richmond gazed appreciatively, not at the little purple lilacs embroidered about the neck of her dress but at her full breasts. Could he tell?

"We baked hermits today. Would you like one?"

He laughed and opened his arms. "Katrina, come, come, you didn't ask me here to sample your cookies, now, did you?"

She couldn't move. If only she could smile in return and share his suggestive banter. . . . If only she could set her fears aside and do what she had to do. . . . If only she could stop thinking about Justin. . . .

Seeing her hesitation, Richmond picked up the small box and said, "You said you wanted to talk about the wedding and that pleases me. As foolish as it sounds, there was a moment when I thought you might reject me. But you wouldn't do that, would you?"

Despite his confident air, she could see a look in his eyes that begged reassurance. "I've always seen the wisdom in being married to you," she said.

"And well you should. But you asked me here for another reason, didn't you?"

Katrina nodded and gathered the inner strength for what she had to do.

"You asked me here because you're grateful for the loan I arranged and you want to show me that gratitude. Am I right?"

"Yes, Richmond, I am grateful."

"Of course you are. Here," he said, handing the package to her. "I want you to have even more reason to be grateful."

She untied the ribbon and opened the small black jeweler's box. She caught her breath at the dazzle of the earbobs.

Richmond looked pleased with her reaction. "Those are genuine diamonds and emeralds. They clip on and will cover those unsightly holes."

Piercing ears was meant to protect against evil spirits, to trick them into thinking they were passing through the entire body.

"Try them on," he said.

Her hands shook as she fastened the payment to her ears. She should be glad Richmond was looking at her with such admiration. It would make what she had to do now a little easier, for Gretchen would be home in a few hours, and even if the opportunity to be alone with Richmond came again, Katrina didn't have the luxury of time to wait.

"I have a looking glass in my bedroom," she said, heading slowly toward the stairs, knowing she had to make sure he would follow her. She fingered one of the earbobs. "I want to see how they look. Would you . . . would you like to—"

"Why, Katrina," he said with mock reproach, "you surprise me. And here I thought you planned to torture me until our wedding night."

He followed her up the stairs and into the bedroom. Knowing what she was about to do, she couldn't explain the sudden feeling that somehow she was the one being tricked.

10

Richmond knew exactly what she was doing: making sure he knew she'd broken free of Justin's spell. And it was about time.

Justin had such an easy way with women. He always did. How many times over the years had Richmond thought a girl was interested in him, only to find out she was using him to meet his devil-eyed older brother. For nearly two months now Justin had toyed with Katrina's affections, taking advantage of her grief, pretending to console her, all in a futile effort to make Richmond feel inadequate.

Well, well, well. Wouldn't Justin love to see his younger brother now? Right here in Katrina's pitifully sparse bedroom. Invited, no less, by the woman Justin had thought under his spell. Just thinking about the victory that would soon be his made him hard.

He was glad to see she was nervous. He wouldn't want anything to do with a woman who made it a practice to invite men to her room. She didn't have to shudder, however, when she looked into the mirror. There was no reason for her not to like what she saw. The earbobs cost a pretty penny, and he knew good and well she didn't own anything that even remotely compared with their value.

He removed his jacket and draped it across the chair, adjusting the cornflower to keep it visible. He had a handsome face and a good physique. The women at Ivy's in New York City always told him so. They fought among themselves for the chance to be his companion. Why? Because he knew how to satisfy a woman. They told him so, and they would know.

He removed his cuff links and tucked them in the pocket with the cornflower. He unbuttoned his shirt, took it off, and draped it beside the jacket. Then he removed the rest of his clothes—delighting in the look of awe on her face—and lay down on the bed.

Poor pitiful Katrina, standing there like a statue, overcome by the sight of a naked man. Without appearing conceited, there was no way to let her know just how fortunate she was to be marrying a man of his talents. But she'd know soon enough. That is, if she ever came to bed. She obviously didn't know what to do next.

"Take your clothes off," he said. "That's why we're here, isn't it?"

All she could do was nod.

When she reached for the earbobs, he sat up. "No. Not those."

"But—"

"I said no." He took a deep breath and continued in a hypnotic voice. "I want you stripped of everything *but* those. Next time I'll add a necklace. Then a bracelet. Then a navel jewel with a long fringe of seed pearls to slip and slide over your belly. I'll make you beautiful."

"A navel jewel?"

"Relax. It's just an ornament, not an instrument of torture."

Her fingers fumbled as she reached for the top button of her dress, and just for that second, when her eyes filled with nervous tears, he thought she'd changed her mind.

He laughed to hide his own nervousness, for he did want her to like him, to be impressed. "Don't look so scared," he said. "We're going to be married."

That seemed to comfort her, for she unfastened the rest of the buttons, slipped her dress off one shoulder and then the other, and let it fall to the floor.

"Now the chemise."

Though she had to look at the ceiling while she did it, she loosened the frayed satin cord that gathered the garment over the swell of her bosom, slipped it off her shoulders, and let it fall.

"Your breasts," he said with admiration. "I never imagined them so large."

She blushed, a sign of innocence he found exciting.

"Now take your hair down."

With trembling fingers, she removed several combs. A waterfall of silken brown locks fell past her shoulders.

"Aren't you going to say anything?" he asked.

"I . . . I don't know what to say."

"How could I forget. This is all new to you, isn't it? This mating." He sighed with growing anticipation. "Now your drawers. I want them off as well."

"Oh, Richmond," she said, quaking. "I can't—"

He jumped from the bed. He wrapped his arms around her, pressing her breasts against his chest, grinding his sex against her pelvis so she'd know how much he wanted her. But she trembled all the more. "Yes, you can," he said. "You want to. You know you do."

She struggled, and he thought he would explode from the exquisite torment. He grabbed her hair and held it tight. Pulled her head back. Kissed her hard. Plunged his tongue into her mouth. Then he thrust against her, giving her a taste of the pleasure that awaited her on the bed.

"No!" she cried and with surprising strength pushed him away. "I can't do this. It isn't fair. Not to you. Not to me. Not to Justin."

He stared at her. "Justin? What does he have to do with this?" He didn't like the sudden look of determination in her eyes. Though she was breathing hard, she looked somehow powerful. Again, this time with a feeling of dread, he asked, "What does Justin have to do with this?"

"Richmond, I'm sorry. I never intended to hurt you."

"Hurt me? How?"

She lowered her hands to rest on her stomach. "Your brother's child grows within me."

In that moment, everything seemed to freeze. Richmond's face turned ugly, his green eyes narrowed to slits. "I've been denied." The words spewed like venom as he said them again, louder. "I've been denied."

"I'm sorry," she said, her lips trembling, her hands shaking. "It happened but once. I'm so ashamed."

His eyes darted back and forth as he tried to think clearly. "You'll get rid of it. I'll make the arrangements myself."

"No! Don't ask me to do that. I can't."

He grabbed her wrist and squeezed it tight, wanting to burn his anger into her skin. "You'll abort the bastard or you'll leave town."

"I know how hurt you must feel—"

"Do you?" He squeezed again and spit on the floor. "You know how stupid I'll feel when everyone finds out I nearly married a whore?" He cupped one of her breasts as though assessing a fair price. "You have a birthmark here, Katrina," he said, staring at a small raspberry-colored mark just below the nipple. "A flaw."

Her tears only made him angrier. He jerked away and

yanked his clothes from the chair. He shoved his arms into the sleeves of his shirt, pulled on his trousers, yanked on his boots. "You know how humiliated I'll feel when their eyes mock me? When they say you could resist me for a whole year of mourning, but you couldn't resist my brother for one night!"

How could he have been such a fool? Well, he wasn't going to be made a fool of twice. He marched toward her and snatched the earbobs from her ears, delighting in her startled pain. "You're nothing but a whore, except that you're smart. At least you think you are. But we'll see about that."

He grabbed his jacket and paused at the door, suddenly knowing exactly what he would do.

"Leave town, Katrina. Leave or I'll ruin you, your sister, your bakery—everything."

"This is my home!"

"Leave. I can't bear to look at you."

Her eyes brightened with tears and she shook her head with just the kind of panic he wanted her to feel.

"You can't do that to me," she said. "You can't."

"Oh, but I most certainly can. Just as my father made sure no one in town would give my brother a job, he can also make sure no one in town will patronize your little bakery. He'll do it for me, you know. And he'll do it gladly. And then where will you and your sister be? On the streets."

"No. I'll say the child is yours and you turned your back on me."

He snickered at her desperation, then scoffed. "Who do you think the town will believe? You, the unwed shop-keeper? Or me, heir to the town's largest employer? You surprise me, Katrina. I didn't think you capable of stooping so low. Then again, you've obviously stooped much lower."

She tugged the engagement band from her finger. "Here. Take it," she said, holding it out to him.

He gave it and her a look of dismissal. "Throw it away." He took the cornflower, already starting to fade, from his pocket and tossed it on the floor. "Throw that away too."

Then he turned and left. Empowered by his new resolve, he marched down the stairs and slammed the bakery door after him.

Sitting on the edge of the bed at the boardinghouse he called home, Justin squinted at the morning sun as he pulled on his boots and made a mental list of the tools he'd need to finish the gazebo. He was surprised Richmond hadn't told his crew to do it. Surprised, but glad. Knowing the sentiment Katrina attached to the structure, she'd probably welcome the chance to help. She could sand the flat surfaces and paint the trim. He wanted a reason to talk to her again, because, despite all she had said to him, he wasn't about to just give up and walk away. Not from her.

She said she didn't have the courage to love him. Well, fear could cripple a person. That was her problem plain and simple: she was afraid. But he planned to help her. All he needed was a chance.

He straightened the faded quilt as he thought of how he'd approach her. If she really wanted to marry Richmond, she wouldn't have postponed the wedding for a whole year. A few months, yes, out of respect. But with her parents dead, she and her sister were left alone with no means of support other than the bakery, and even in these modern times, people usually frowned on the idea of a woman in business. They would have understood the need for Katrina to shorten the mourning period.

She had to be brave to keep the bakery running. That was the first thing he planned to tell her. The second was that he loved her.

A knock on the door interrupted his thoughts. He went to open it.

"Richmond? What are you doing here?"

With a sheepish grin, Richmond smoothed the uncharacteristic wrinkles on his starched white shirtfront and straightened the deep V of his waistcoat in what Justin knew to be a nervous gesture. Most surprising of all was that Richmond's hair was uncombed, as though he'd just risen from bed and hastily dressed.

"I've come to make peace."

"So early in the morning?" Justin arched a suspicious brow as he stepped back and gestured for Richmond to come in.

Glancing around the clean but sparsely furnished room, Richmond said, "I always wondered what one of these places looked like."

"Now you know."

"Yes," he said, looking more nervous by the minute. "You don't have to live like some indigent, however. Katrina was right. All you have to do is apologize to Father. Not that I think it would be easy, mind you. If he'd screamed at me the way he did to you, well, I wouldn't blame you if you just took off. It would serve the old man right. I'm just pointing out your options."

Justin grabbed the spindly wooden chair from the corner and straddled it. "What do you really want?"

"I told you. Peace."

"Why?"

Richmond looked at the sagging wing chair in the corner. "May I?"

"Help yourself."

He sat down and fussed with his clothes again, leaving Justin to wonder why his brother hadn't taken the time to groom himself before he left the house.

"I won't lie to you, Justin. You're my brother. Mother

sent me—not that I wouldn't have come on my own, but she doesn't want bad blood between us. Not now." Leaning forward, he added with emphasis, "Especially not now."

"Because the Barrison dynasty is about to change hands?"

"No, but something equally important." Richmond smiled.

"What are you talking about?" Justin had a discomforting feeling but couldn't explain why, except that if his mother had sent Richmond over, and if her reason had nothing to do with the brewery, the matter must be serious.

Rapidly twirling a gold stud, Richmond continued. "You see, Katrina has decided that it is in her best interests to waive the mourning period. She feels we should wed as soon as possible."

No! Justin curled his hands around the back of the chair, desperate for an anchor, for between Richmond's words and the confident, joyous look in his eyes, Justin sensed real and imminent danger to his beautiful future. "I don't believe you."

"Oh, but it's true. That's why she asked me to the bakery last night. To tell me of her decision." Richmond tried to suppress a grin, as though debating on whether or not to give more details, then blurted out, "Well, with her sister away for the evening, that wasn't the only reason—if you capture my meaning."

"What are you saying?"

"Only that with Katrina in my marriage bed, I'll have no reason ever to go back to Ivy's." He stood, walked to the window, gazed outside, then turned back to Justin. "Everything I've ever thought of as feminine is exaggerated in her. She's beautiful! I simply can't wait to dress her in silk and satin. A little too educated, but I can't hold that against her. Above all, she aims to please and—well, look at me." He gestured to his disheveled hair and unkempt clothing. "I had but a few hours' sleep last night."

"You slept with her?"

Richmond smiled as though sharing a secret. "Oh, you've had so many women, you know how it goes. First a glimpse of petticoat, then stocking, then thigh, a finger welcomed into the honey pot, a—"

Justin jumped up, sending the chair clattering to the floor. "You're a liar!"

Richmond stepped back against the wall, his eyes wide with shock. "What's the matter with you? You know how it is between a man and a woman. Especially when they are to be wed." Then, as though he suddenly saw the situation for the first time, Richmond took an apologetic air. "Oh, Justin, I'm so sorry. You fancy her, too, don't you?"

Justin hated knowing that his pain showed on his face, but it cut too deep, hurt too much, simply to will it away. What was he supposed to say? *Yes, I've fallen in love with a woman who has told me all along she wants nothing to do with me.* Until this morning, Justin would never have believed Katrina loved Richmond, but if Richmond spoke the truth, she must love him, for she would never share such an intimacy unless she did. Grasping for a shred of dignity, Justin said, "I'm just surprised, that's all."

With a sigh, Richmond said, "Oh, I'm so relieved to hear you say that. I assured Mother that the tension between us had everything to do with the brewery and nothing to do with Katrina."

"Mother thought I cared for Katrina?"

"Apparently, though she pointed out that you're much too noble a man to interfere if your feelings weren't returned in kind."

Noble? Justin swallowed hard to hold back feelings of anger, hurt, betrayal—all far from noble. Suddenly, he needed to get out of this room, away from Richmond's star-struck eyes, away from the possibility of running into Katrina.

Then, one scrap of hope dangled before him, one explanation that could banish this nightmare brought so innocently with his brother and the dawn. Richmond could be lying.

Richmond resumed an air of wonderment, and went on, as though he couldn't contain himself. "Her breasts. Oh, Justin, except for a deep pink blemish on the left one—I think of it as a patch of pink lace—her breasts are beautiful. And surprisingly full for such a slender woman."

Only snatches of Richmond's deadly words found their mark. To let them all in would be to die. Powerless to banish the memory, Justin closed his eyes and saw Katrina's white breasts, bathed in silver moonlight, filling his hands, the nipples hardening under his lips. On her left breast he remembered seeing a pink birthmark. Richmond wasn't lying.

He opened his eyes to see his brother smoothing the front of his coat.

"Well, I suppose I'd best be on my way," Richmond said. "I've so much to do. A week from now I won't have to worry about whether or not that sister of hers is about. I'll be bedding my wife whenever I've the whim."

"Do you love her?"

"What a question to ask. Of course I love her. She's everything I ever dreamed of in a woman. Mother and Father approve of her. It goes without saying she loves me. So we'll marry, throw lavish parties, make frequent trips to New York—Katrina said she couldn't wait to see the shops. I told her I'd show her Philadelphia too, though I've no intention of showing her the place where we grew up. All in all, we're going to have a fine life, a fine life indeed."

Justin shoved his hands in his pockets and stared at the cracked glass covering the picture on the wall, feeling the threat of tears. He flinched when Richmond patted him on the shoulder.

"I do hope you spoke the truth when you said you didn't fancy Katrina. For if you do, my coming here must have caused you pain and that was never my intention."

"I'm fine," Justin said. "I wish the two of you happiness."

"Thank you, brother." Richmond walked toward the door. "Now *if*, just *if* you did, at any time, fancy her, isn't it better that you know the truth about her now, while you can still salvage your pride?"

Justin nodded.

Richmond walked toward the door. "If there hadn't been so much bad blood between us lately over the brewery, I know I wouldn't have to ask this," he said, as he twisted the glass doorknob, "but I'd like you to stand up for me at my wedding."

Justin was a brave man, but not that brave. "Sorry," he said, hoping his voice didn't crack. "I'd planned to leave town pretty soon." He turned around to face Richmond. "Today, in fact."

"Today? I see. Then I'm glad I came over this morning. Now I can tell Mother we've made peace, so even though you won't be here for the wedding, her heart will not be troubled."

"Yes. That's good."

"Where are you going?"

He had to think fast. "There's a settlement up the Missouri in Dakota Territory. Free land."

"Oh, yes. Mother said you'd spoken of the Dakota. And a little town called—what was it?"

"Prosperity."

"Oh, yes, Prosperity."

Even as he wrestled with the knowledge that he'd been a fool, a complete fool, Justin grasped for a new sense of purpose to his life. "So, I . . . I wish you a good life, brother, and I wish you and Katrina much happiness."

"Thank you. Your goodwill means a lot to me."

"You'll say good-bye to Mother for me?" He feared he could not be able to keep his composure in the face of either her anger or her tears. "Tell her I'll write as soon as I'm settled."

"Of course I'll tell her. There's no need for you to delay your plans. I believe there's a northbound boat leaving this morning."

"How convenient."

"Yes. Well, I suppose this is good-bye." Richmond reached for Justin's hand.

"Good-bye, brother." Justin shook Richmond's hand. "Good luck."

"Same to you."

Richmond stepped out into the hall. As Justin closed the door to the room, he closed the door to his heart and accepted the simple truth he'd denied all along. Katrina didn't want him. She wanted Richmond.

He turned around and busied himself by gathering his things. She'd never be satisfied without trunk loads of clothes. He went downstairs and settled his bill. She had to have a big fussy house, with servants, stables, gardens. She wanted to go to New York, not the Dakota Territory. He had to think of this morning as a turning point in his life, the day he decided finally to get out of this town and take a chance on himself. She'd always be an albatross around his neck.

He walked down to the docks, the morning sun at his back. He wasn't about to stop at the bakery to say good-bye. She had her life, he had his. Richmond would tell her he was gone, but after today she'd never give him a second thought. He squinted his eyes and looked back one last time. He'd never think of her again either.

*   *   *

Katrina dressed hurriedly. She'd spent the night barely sleeping, hating herself for what she'd done, worried over what Richmond might do. Gretchen's avoidance gave her a taste of what they could both expect from the good citizens of Merriweather if Richmond, the man she'd always thought of as generous and mild-mannered, carried out his ugly threat.

If he did, she'd be forced to leave.

She went downstairs, where she could tell from the scent of soap and lemon that Gretchen was scrubbing, a task she performed for the good of the store as well as her spirit. First she would tell Gretchen what had happened last night, for she deserved the truth. Then she would relieve Gretchen's worries with the news that she planned to go to Justin, tell him the truth, and thwart disaster, for he was an honorable man and surely he would agree to marry her. Knowing he had family obligations now, he would settle things with his father and they would stay in Merriweather. Gretchen would forgive her. The bakery would flourish. All would be right again.

The sound of sleigh bells slapping against the door told Katrina that someone had just left. "A customer so early?" she asked. "All we have is day old."

With a grim expression on her face, Gretchen looked up from wiping the counter. "No. Richmond Barrison."

"Richmond?" A gathering of fears weakened her.

As though forcing her anger down to her hands, Gretchen wrung water from the rag into the bucket at her feet. "*Ja*. He said to tell the whore who is my sister that Justin has left town and is gone for good."

"Justin's gone?" Katrina murmured. She could hardly believe it.

"*Ja*. You heard me. And Richmond, he said he would

be back for your answer. What does he want from you now? Surely not your vow to be faithful and true."

He wants me to leave.

The windows were open, the door unlocked, the cash box unguarded on the counter, loaves of bread unprotected from any thief who might decide to enter. How was Katrina to protect herself? Her baby? Gretchen?

"Katrina?"

In a few hours the shelves would be full, but one word from Richmond and the town would scorn Katrina for her sin. One word from the Barrisons, and the contempt of the good citizens of Merriweather would extend to the bakery as well. People might not buy as readily. God forbid, they might not buy at all.

"Katrina?"

Filled with emptiness and the sudden realization that she had no future, Katrina opened her mouth, but words wouldn't come. What a fool she'd been to think life would ever turn in her favor. What a fool.

With Gretchen's voice receding in the background, Katrina turned around and somehow managed to walk back upstairs.

How could Justin have gone away without even saying good-bye?

Except for Gretchen's shunning, everything appeared normal the next day. Still, Katrina found no way to escape anxiety. It ignored the lock on the door, the curtains at the window, and visited her again that night when she was too tired to think, too sad to cry. The day after, despite the oppressive August sun, she felt dark days gathering. A thunderstorm ushered them in.

Unbeknown to Katrina, the eager wind stirred round like a gossip, tempting the curious townspeople to lift their faces to its breeze, to wonder aloud why the young Mr. Barrison had called off his wedding, to heed his suggestion that perhaps they should shop at another bakery.

True to his predictions, in less than a week the sleigh bells on the bakery door ceased to jingle as once-loyal customers of the little shop ceased to buy. The following Monday, he called the loan.

There was no mistaking the look of triumph on his face as he stepped into the bakery and up to the counter.

His father, grim-faced and resolute, followed and stood to his right. On his left, stood portly Herr Krause, the banker, a man who'd been her neighbor for years. There he stood, slapping an envelope against the palm of his hand. The two older men looked around as though passing judgment. The bread baskets were empty, the shelves bare of cookies and cakes.

"Good morning," Katrina said, though she sensed it would be anything but.

Richmond smirked. "Where is Gretchen? This concerns you both."

"Right here," Gretchen answered as she marched down the stairs. For the first time in over a week, she didn't make a point of establishing distance between herself and Katrina, but stood next to her. Close. She even put her arm around Katrina's shoulder and gave a little squeeze before turning to face the men.

Both grateful and confused, Katrina hazarded a smile, hoping Gretchen would know how much she appreciated the show of support, even if it was only for the moment.

Taking the envelope from Herr Krause, Richmond removed the contents and laid the papers on the counter. "I believe you'll find the documents self-explanatory. The two of you owe me and my family four thousand dollars. The note was made with the understanding that I would marry Katrina, which we all know is out of the question"—he stared openly at her abdomen—"now that I've discovered her true character. That being the case, I'm here to collect. Father is here to verify the position I've taken. Herr Krause is here to padlock the door."

Disgraced anew, Katrina's voice quivered. "Richmond, please. Have you no compassion? Gretchen should not be made to pay for my sin." She turned to Herr Barrison. "My sister is a good baker and a good businesswoman, worthy of your family's trust."

She saw nothing but ice in his gray eyes as he answered, "The decision is Richmond's."

Richmond wiped his index finger along the counter as though looking for something else to criticize, but the counter was spotless, as were the floor, the walls, everything. With knowing vengeance, he spoke to Katrina. "There is one thing you can do, of course. Leave. Leave and I will honor the agreement with your sister."

She felt the walls closing in. "I need time. Please. A few weeks."

Gretchen turned to Katrina. "Leave?" With the astonishment that comes from realizing the extent of disaster, she covered her heart with both hands and said, "Is that what he wants from you?"

Katrina turned to her sister. "Yes."

Gretchen shook her head. "We can sell Poppa's books and Momma's linens. Momma's wedding ring."

Poor Gretchen, Katrina thought. It was one thing to pay for her own mistakes, but to make Gretchen suffer too was unbearable. Selling everything they had would bring only a few hundred dollars, if that, and it would mean the loss of the only mementos they had of their parents. Knowing Gretchen was willing to take such a step in order for the two of them to survive only made Katrina feel worse.

Richmond looked at this watch. "You have one minute."

"One minute!" Katrina cried.

Addressing Herr Krause, Richmond said, "You brought the lock?"

Katrina pressed her hand to her chest to assure herself that her heart was still beating while Herr Krause retrieved the metal toolbox he'd left at the door. He opened it and took out a sturdy padlock.

Gretchen marched to the door and flung it open, anger flashing in her eyes. To Richmond she shouted, "You don't need a lock to keep our patrons away. Your sour grapevine has done the job for you."

Katrina knew she was right. Even if they could somehow manage to pay the loan, it wouldn't guarantee future business.

"Thirty seconds," Richmond said.

Filled with foolish courage, Katrina grabbed the papers from the counter and held them in the air. "You win. I'll leave."

She hated to see that satisfied smile on Richmond's lips. Even more she hated to see the tears fill Gretchen's eyes.

"But you must promise, before these witnesses, that you will not utter one word to discourage the community's patronage. Furthermore, you must promise to use your influence to see that the townspeople support the bakery until Gretchen can pay off the loan. Agreed?"

"And you will leave within the week?"

"No. I need a month."

"That's too long."

"I need to search for a place. I need to amass funds to travel."

Richmond seemed to consider the ramifications of her staying that long in town. "Two days," he said. "And Gretchen, you will tell people that Katrina has gone to New York to meet relatives arriving at the docks. Yes, that's it. Two days. Under the circumstances, I think I'm being generous. Agreed?"

Her heart said no, but knowing that to argue could make matters worse for Gretchen, she said, "Yes. Two days."

Katrina surrendered the papers into Richmond's waiting hand. He tore them in small pieces, smiling as he littered the floor with his triumph.

Gretchen maintained her hardened stance as the men filed by her and out into the street. It was still there when she closed the door and leaned her forehead against the wood. As though she couldn't bear to look at Katrina, she said, "You have ruined it for us. You have ruined it for both of us. Forever."

Unable to speak, Katrina stood silently while tears wet her cheeks. When Gretchen finally turned around, Katrina saw nothing but sadness in her eyes. Sadness and more tears.

11

Sunlight warmed the wood of the gazebo, lulling Katrina into believing that it held the solution to her problem. She leaned against one of the pillars at the entrance and closed her eyes. Though she missed Momma and Poppa, Gretchen was right. They'd been spared the shame Katrina had brought on her family, and for that she was grateful.

She thought about going to a big city like New York or Philadelphia, but they were rumored to be dangerous places for a woman alone, or a woman with a child.

How could she possibly leave Merriweather? In a new world, with a new way of life and a new language, her family had sacrificed everything they had to establish their bakery. She and Gretchen knew how to run it. They could make it a success. She knew they could. It was all they had.

Until then, Katrina didn't realize how tightly she was gripping the railing. She'd find a way to get back to Merriweather. She might not have any choice in the matter right now, but someday she would. No one, not even

Richmond Barrison, could keep her away forever.

But until then, where could she go? She'd asked the question again and again, until her head spun from the frustration of having no answer. Now, here in the gazebo, the memory of loving arms closed around her, giving her not only a precious moment of peace but an answer.

She could go to Justin. He was, after all, the baby's father. He had cared for her once. If he refused her, she could hire out with one of the other families in the community. She'd have to lie and say she'd been widowed, but she would do that to protect her child from being branded a bastard. If Justin wouldn't take her in, surely someone would.

Even as her heart warmed to the idea of going to Justin, her head reminded her of why she hadn't done so before. If he had gone to the Dakota as he said he might, then theirs would be a hard life, for she'd heard the prairie was a frightening place and no place to raise a child. She would have to try something else before becoming so desperate.

The next morning, after she knew Eberhard and Richmond would have gone to the brewery, Katrina went to see Rosamond Barrison.

Standing in the parlor, declining to take the seat Rosamond offered, Katrina said, "I am pregnant. With Justin's baby."

Rosamond held a glass of brandy in her hand. "Please, Katrina, sit down."

"Did you hear me?"

Rosamond glanced at Katrina's belly, and a fleeting smile crossed her lips. "Yes, I heard you. I know all about the baby. And about the loan. Richmond told me last night."

"Then you know why I've come to you."

"No," Rosamond said as she sat down. "What can I possibly do?"

Katrina sat down in the small chair she'd come to think of as hers, another reminder of how big a fool she'd been to expect a place in that house. "You can convince your husband and son to let me stay without foreclosing on the bakery." She leaned forward, knowing her eyes betrayed her desperation, hoping her plea would not fall on deaf ears. "Not only for me but for your grandchild."

Rosamond's tight, thin lips arched at the corners, and Katrina dared to hope. "There's nothing I would like more than to be close to my first grandchild. I've dreamed of the day. But I cannot go against my husband. And I will not come between my sons."

"But I've worked for you all these years!" Katrina blurted out.

"I know, dear." She glanced at the glass she'd placed on the table beside her. "And for that I am forever grateful. But I cannot do as you ask. Try to understand."

"No." Katrina folded her hands in supplication. "Please. What will it take? What do I have to do? I don't want to leave. Why would it be so terrible for me to stay? I don't understand."

Rosamond looked away as though the sight of a desperate woman begging for help was painful to her. "Listen to me. If you stay and claim that Richmond is the father, people will wonder what is wrong with Richmond that he doesn't give you his name. If you admit someone else is the father, people will say there must be something lacking in Richmond that you preferred another man. So, you see, my dear, you must leave."

Tears Katrina had sworn not to shed filled her eyes as fear took the foremost place in her heart. "No. I don't see. I don't see why such weight is given to what people say, to what people think of Richmond. *I* am the one whose life is being ruined! *I* am the one who is losing everything! I think Richmond is hateful!" Gasping with emotion, Katri-

na took her handkerchief from her pocket and wiped her
eyes. She wasn't about to apologize for what she said. She
meant every word of it.

Calmly, Rosamond reached for her brandy and took a sip.
When Katrina had composed herself, Rosamond continued.
"At some point in our fragile lives, each of us must search for
our own substance. When a man begins his search and
comes to fear that, in the end, he *has* no substance, then, for
that man, appearance becomes the most important thing."

"If you are saying that Richmond has no substance, no
soul, no heart, you are absolutely right. But, still, why
should it be *his* wishes that are granted and not mine?"

As though the answer was obvious, Rosamond replied,
"Because he is the one with the power."

Katrina saw a look in Rosamond's eyes that said she'd
either accepted or found it too tiring to question this conclusion. "So that's how it is to be," Katrina said. She
vowed silently that one day *she* would be the one with the
power, and when that day came it would be *her* dreams
that would come true.

"Try not to judge him too harshly," Rosamond said.
"His life has not been without its sorrows."

"But he is not the one shedding tears today, is he?"

"We are all brought to tears at one time or another."

The woman was not going to help. That was clear. Katrina did her best to gather her composure before she
stood. "Then I won't waste any more of your time."

"One more moment. Please. Where will you go?"

To the only place she could go. Why was it so hard to
say? "To Justin, if he'll have me. I'm praying you know
where he is."

"The Dakota Territory. I believe he is headed for a town
called Prosperity. On the river."

"Prosperity," Katrina said, committing it to memory.

"Dear Katrina, take heart. Going to Justin is not a

death sentence. Surely you feel something for my son. If not, how could you have—"

"Of course I feel something for Justin." Rosamond had asked the question Katrina had asked herself a hundred times. But what was it she felt for him?

"Then why such reluctance to go to him?"

"Because with him I have no idea where I'm going. First he says he wants to roam the world, and then he says he wants to homestead—in a place that is an ocean of land away. And all I want is to stay right here." Again it hit her that she had to leave, and fresh tears came to her eyes. "I just want to stay here. Near Gretchen and the graves of my parents."

Rosamond walked to the small secretary, unlocked an inner compartment, and withdrew an envelope. "Two hundred dollars," she said, as she came back and faced Katrina. "Enough to pay your passage and help you get settled. If Justin is not in Prosperity, this is enough to get you settled somewhere else."

There was a time when Katrina would have been too proud to accept charity, but that time had passed long ago. She had a child to think of now, a child who would never know the comfort and security of a well-appointed house and a well-stocked pantry, or the luxury of an education, or the prestige of a settled place in the community. With a trembling hand, she took the envelope.

She said good-bye to Rosamond and headed for the door, finally accepting that all her hopes were gone. Pausing at the door, she turned around and said, "You knew it would come to this all along, didn't you?"

"I know my sons. Give Justin a chance."

"What choice do I have?"

Katrina went home and posted a letter to Justin.

*   *   *

"You can take Momma's trunk," Gretchen said. "And half the linens and housewares, though only a few items survived. And Poppa's hammer."

"Thank you." Katrina prayed for Gretchen to say something more, to extend forgiveness, but Gretchen's concern was only for items, not hearts. The frost between them had melted a little in the twenty-four hours since the Barrisons had come to foreclose, but the closeness they once shared had yet to be rekindled and Katrina feared there wouldn't be time to set things right. She was leaving in the morning.

Into the trunk she layered softened dish towels, carefully mended sheets, and the dresser scarf and pillowcases she had embroidered. "You keep the candlesticks," she said. "I think Momma would want it that way."

Gretchen didn't argue.

Katrina sighed as she caught a whiff of the smoke that had invaded the trunk only two months past. So many losses. So much more to lose. For a moment she considered it fortunate that neither she nor Gretchen had managed to break the reserve that was between them. After tomorrow, they might never see each other again. Even a simple good-bye was going to be difficult.

The crowded dock hummed with the hurried to and fro of those leaving and those staying behind. Over and over again, Katrina coiled and released her fingers around the handle of the tin of raisin cookies Gretchen had packed for her the night before. The bakery shelves were once again filled with the evidence of her sister's talent. Richmond had kept his word. If anything, the bakery had more customers than ever before. This knowledge afforded Katrina the assurance that she was doing the right thing by leaving.

Lukas nudged Gretchen as though prompting her to say something, but she remained as silent as she had been all morning. To Katrina he said, "Don't fret that this will be like the ocean voyage. Never will you lose sight of land. Small towns line the route. In fact, some people make this trip for pleasure."

Katrina nodded, trying to calm herself with Lukas's assurance. She knew that thoughts of shipwrecks and starvation were illogical, but they were far less painful to contemplate than to contemplate the gulf that stretched between her and Gretchen.

"I know I won't starve," Katrina said. "I have my delicious raisin cookies." She hoped Gretchen would acknowledge the compliment, but Gretchen remained silent, her stare fixed straight ahead.

Katrina remembered how her hopes had so foolishly gathered last night when Gretchen gave her the tin of cookies, how those fleeting hopes vanished when Gretchen stiffened to her embrace. Now, afraid her own tenuous composure would shatter if she looked into Gretchen's eyes, Katrina stared ahead as well.

Muscled stevedores unloaded crates and sacks and bales for the good citizens of Merriweather and took on the barrels and boxes and trunks of those eager to be under way. Katrina envied those passengers who laughed and waved as though beginning a great adventure. She watched those who tenderly grasped the hand of a loved one as they stepped aboard the gangplank. She longed to share the pain of leaving with someone who loved her enough to hate seeing her go.

Dear God, how she regretted ever having met Justin Barrison.

Off to her right she heard a baby cry, a reminder of the changes to come. She carried a new life. She'd always assumed she'd have children someday—someday in her future, when she was married, when she had a nice home, a nursery, tiny cotton gowns with crocheted lace on the edges. But once again, her plans clashed with reality, this time through no one's fault but her own.

Lukas heard the baby, too, and patted Katrina on the shoulder. "You are strong and healthy. Your child will be strong and healthy too."

Sadness gripped Katrina like a vise. Pleading for acknowledgment, she looked at Gretchen and whispered, "I know you are disappointed in me. I know my sin has ruined the future for both of us. But Gretchen, please, don't make me leave without your forgiveness."

Gretchen said nothing.

"You may never feel my little one nestle in the crook of your neck. Never hear him cry. Never see him smile." Katrina could see the tears as they brightened Gretchen's eyes and feel them as they spilled silently down her round apple cheeks, for tears spilled down Katrina's cheeks too. "And my baby will never know his *Tante* Gretchen."

Gretchen's eyes remained averted. She lifted her chin and, though her lower lip trembled, she said, "Two miles. You were to go no more than two miles."

"I'm sorry!" Katrina stretched out her arms, aching to give her sister comfort and obtain her forgiveness.

But Gretchen stiffened as she had the night before. "Happy is he who can forget what can't be changed."

So that's how it would be between them. Katrina added the weight of Gretchen's anger to her already heavy heart and turned away. On shaking legs, she stepped toward the gangplank. With one sweeping look, she tried to commit her surroundings to memory, for she knew she would never see them again.

Her eyes focused on Gretchen, cocooned in her own arms. Trembling inside, Katrina couldn't stop her voice from quaking as she called, "*Auf wiedersehen.*"

Gretchen didn't answer.

Katrina turned and boarded the steamer, not once looking back.

Fall 1887–Summer 1888

Prosperity, Dakota Territory

12

The white painted paddle wheel lapped up the dappled gray river as the steam-driven engine purred, headed on its northbound course, away from the community she'd come to call home, past the familiar rolling green landscape that reminded her of her childhood. With the passing of each watery mile, Katrina cried inside as, one by one, her symbols of security slipped out of sight.

At each port of call, some passengers left; others came aboard. New faces. New dress. Sometimes new languages. She avoided them all, walking the decks in the evening when most were in the dining room. She didn't have much appetite for either food or company, but she forced herself to eat for the baby's sake.

When the boat docked for long hours or days, to load up on fuel and supplies, Katrina walked into town. The same wide streets, houses, and shops huddled side by side, clinging shoulder to shoulder. A white church and steeple sat in the center of town or at the end of the street. People were the same everywhere, she thought. So eager to come to America, the land of opportunity, only to re-create what they left behind, especially when they discovered that America's streets were not made of gold.

Her wanderings, however, had a purpose. If she could find employment, she wouldn't have to go to Justin. At least half a dozen times she got off the boat and spent her precious money on lodging for several days, all to give her time to find a job. She was skilled at taking care of old women, but she found out quickly that without someone to stand for her character, she wouldn't be given a chance. She could bake, and from the loaves of burnt bread and watery custards, there were several shops in need of a woman who knew her way around an oven. But no one would hire her. Husband and wife would each arch a suspicious brow at her woeful tale of being recently widowed, a babe on the way.

With her funds shrunk to near nothing, she would board the next steamer north, heading toward her destiny.

Day by day, the view from the boat reminded her of just how far she'd gone. Eventually the landscape flattened, dwindling under an ever increasing expanse of sky. Trees became noticeable by their decreasing numbers. Not all of America was like the docks of New York or the village of Merriweather, Missouri.

Katrina felt as much a foreigner as she had when she first came to this country, but this time was worse. Except for the little one she cradled inside, Katrina was alone.

Day after day, night after night, Katrina heard someone somewhere tell frightening stories to anyone who would listen of prairie blizzards so fierce they would freeze a man's eyelashes, of whirling, twisting winds that picked up barns and tossed them about like toys, of wild animals that prowled the prairie at night. And now, whenever Katrina strolled the deck, her efforts to calm her fears were made hopeless with each belch of black smoke from the bubbling chimney as it scraped the clear blue sky. So desperate for a word of encouragement was she, Katrina said yes when the wizened old woman in the corner of the passengers' lounge offered to tell her future.

A faded gray kerchief covered the woman's head. A heavy black shawl with long tangled fringe draped her sloping shoulders. Poor woman. Despite the heat of the sun, Katrina imagined Madam Agata, as she called herself, hadn't known warmth in years. But her pale gray eyes saw everything.

With her gnarled finger she beckoned Katrina to the wooden table and the frayed red velvet bench facing her. "Sit, my dear, for the worries that burden you are many and grow heavier with the passing of each new moon."

Hesitantly, Katrina sat down. For one moment Madam Agata's nearly toothless smile looked kind and reminded Katrina of her long-departed grandmother. Then quickly, the smile turned cunning, almost like that of a witch.

The old woman chuckled. "Ah, yes, the imagination both comforts and scares. No need to be frightened of me, for I am but an old woman."

From an intricately carved wooden box in front of her she removed several small colored stones, a piece of branched red coral, and a crucifix, positioning each in an arc on the table. Reverently, she unwrapped the piece of deep blue silk that remained in the box and from its folds took a deck of well-worn cards.

She placed her hands on the crucifix and closed her eyes. "A moment, please, to prepare myself." She paused. "And now," she said, opening eyes so silver they were almost white, "to the reason for our encounter."

She shuffled the cards and turned one face up.

"While you struggle to hold on to what little you have,

you risk losing all." She seemed to stare not at Katrina but through her. "This hardship and downfall, you have brought it on yourself. While not a comforting thought, still, a lesson in knowing your own shortcomings. You will find a different solution the next time."

Oh, yes! Katrina said to herself, remembering the pansy petal with five lines. Next time she would be the one in power and it would be her dreams she would make come true, for two of the velvet petals had four lines. She watched as Madam Agata turned the next card.

"Ah, an engagement. Harmony of the masculine and feminine. You have such harmony?"

"Had."

"I sense a reconciliation."

Katrina felt a glimmer of hope, until Madam Agata turned over several other cards, shaking her head.

"The pain is necessary, for you can no longer cling to your blindness. The way of life you knew is no more. You must accept it. But understand this, child, the cleansing flames of tragedy bring enlightenment in their wake."

A sweat broke on Katrina's brow as images flashed of her father's burned body, her mother's scorched hands. "I'm going to be in another fire?"

"The flames have already touched you, but not for the last time. The final fire will not be one of destruction but one of purpose. You will feel the flames on the inside. You must be strong."

Light-headed now, Katrina wanted only to leave the old woman and her disturbing prophesy.

She stood, but before she could leave, Madam Agata turned over one last card and said, "Do you not want to know the outcome?"

Katrina stared at the crudely drawn pictures on the cards, particularly the last. "What does it mean, all those cups?"

"Could be great joy. Could be great sorrow. When falsehood is brought to a marriage, the marriage is doomed to die, for only when the shadows of both partners are brought to the light can love flourish."

"At least in the end I will find happiness?"

"What you seek is what you will find. The cards merely show you the paths being offered. Where you choose to tread is your decision and yours alone."

Though Katrina didn't exactly understand what Madam Agata meant, she did know that only an empty home and a life of strife lay ahead.

Most of the riverboat passengers got off in Yankton, where a thriving German population had carved a respectable community. Katrina reasoned that if Prosperity, nearly two hundred miles north, was as well established, she stood a chance of finding employment, though she'd have to learn to lie without turning red. Of course, she'd be looked down on, as all hired girls were, but at least she'd have a roof over her head. She prayed she wouldn't be made to work outside, under a sun that would turn her white arms to shameful brown. She adjusted her kerchief with the grim knowledge that if sun-darkened skin proved to be the greatest of her misfortunes, she would fare well indeed.

Finally, four weeks after leaving Merriweather, rays of painfully bright morning sun drew the boat close to the shore of her destination. A few wooden buildings sat in some semblance of order on either side of a wide dirt path leading straight from the single dock, where a small stand of scrawny cottonwoods struggled to get a hold. There were no neat white houses, no church with towering steeple, no village green, no trees. The place looked ugly, desolate, beyond the end of nowhere. This was supposed to be a community of farmers. Where were they?

A young Norwegian couple who'd boarded in Yankton

were the only passengers other than Katrina getting off in Prosperity. The wife, younger than Gretchen, spoke only Norwegian and clung to her husband's side the entire trip. The husband spoke a few words of English. Katrina gathered they had family in the area, which would explain the relief and excitement on the girl's face.

The husband, after arranging for a wagon and loading his own things, took Katrina and her trunk to the door of the Rhinedollar General Store, where a sign advertised rooms for rent, riverboat tickets, service by a competent representative of the United States Post Office, and merchandise extraordinaire, all at reasonable prices.

She'd had endless days of lonely hours to decide how she would approach Justin. She didn't expect him to be pleased at the idea of taking her in. He'd left Merriweather without so much as a wave. If he'd truly cared for her the way he said he did, he would have said good-bye. But then she really didn't want him to care for her. Not really, for that would only complicate matters. All she wanted was a place to stay until the baby was born and old enough to travel. If he'd give her that, she'd set up housekeeping for him. She'd bake, cook, clean, mend, make curtains, plant flowers. And then she'd leave. She didn't know where she'd go, but it would only be for a short time, just long enough to make the story of marriage and widowhood believable. Then she would march right back to Merriweather, Richmond be damned. It was with such resolve that she stepped out of the hot dusty air and through the open door of the Rhinedollar General Store.

Overwhelmed by the rich smell of leather saddlebags, baskets of golden brown bread, barrels of pungent kraut and pickles, and by the sight of sparkling bottles of tonics and colorful tins of salves, jars of peppermint sticks, and licorice whips, Katrina started when a cheery woman's voice greeted her from behind the counter.

"Get yourself in out of that heat, honey. My, my, but you will definitely need more protection from this sun than that old kerchief. You're new here, aren't you? Just off the boat? Speak English, do you? *Sprechen sie Deutsch?*"

"English," Katrina said, determined to make her abilities as marketable as possible should the need arise.

The woman was shorter than Katrina but just as slender. As she scurried over, she held her hands out while she rubbed her thumbs and fingers together, reminding Katrina of a cricket. Merchandise piled against every window blocked most of the light, so it wasn't until they were face-to-face that Katrina could see the lines in the woman's face and guess she was thirty-five, maybe even forty.

"Nadine Rhinedollar here. Proprietor—along with my husband, Godfrey. Postmistress—I handle that on my own. Ticket agent—that's my sphere too. Fashion consultant—now that's definitely my area of expertise. And you'd be . . . ?"

More than a little overwhelmed, Katrina said, "I'm looking for Justin Barrison's place."

Nadine gave a look of surprise, but recovered instantly. "And you'd be his . . . ?"

"I'm . . . " Katrina didn't know how to answer. "I just need to find him. Can you direct me?" A little too desperately, she added, "He *is* here, isn't he?"

"He's here, all right."

Katrina exhaled, feeling the tautness in her muscles relax, as she dismissed the visions of being stranded, alone, with just a small amount of money left, no place to go, and a baby on the way. Only then did she realize how anxious she'd been.

"Please. Can you direct me?"

Arching her brow, Nadine stepped back behind the counter. She turned to a wall of at least fifty dark wooden cubbyholes, most of them empty, and pointed her finger left to right, then right to left, again and again. When she stopped, she retrieved an envelope, studied it, and said, "You from Missouri?"

Her letter. Justin had never gotten her letter. He didn't even know she was coming. Instantly light-headed, Katrina grabbed the edge of the counter.

"Hold on now!" Nadine cried as she hurried back around the counter again. "Here, sit on this pickle barrel. It's that dadblamed sun. Until you get used of it, not that a body ever does, why, it'll just boil the blood right out of you. Scorch your hair, burn your skin. What you need is a good bonnet and a big bottle of Miss Laurieann's Lotion. It's from Paris, France. I carry it standard. Here, you sit. I'll fetch you a drink of water."

A moment later, Katrina gulped the cool water, knowing it was impossible to steady her trembling hands.

"How about a slice of bread and jam?" Nadine asked. "Or a pickle?"

Katrina turned pale as she felt a twinge of nausea.

Nadine shook her head. "Oh, dear me. Are you bringing Mr. Barrison a surprise of some sort?"

"I . . . I just need to see him."

"Well, he's not in town, of course, or he'd have picked up his mail. He filed on a place about eight miles southeast."

"But where is his house?"

"Eight miles southeast."

Katrina didn't understand. In the old country, everyone lived in town, where there was strength in numbers and comfort in knowing a friend was but a few steps away. The land they farmed might stretch for miles from town and that was where the farmer would go each day to work, but everyone lived close together.

Katrina feared this isolated way of living was but the first of many surprises. "Thank you for the water," she said, handing the glass back to Nadine. "And for the chance to rest a moment. I'd best be on my way now." She stood, grateful for the return of her balance and, far more important, for the confirmation that Justin was here. Eight miles southeast. "Can you tell me where I might rent a buggy?"

"Not much call for buggies in these parts, but you can rent yourself a horse and a wagon over at the livery. Out the door and to your left. Can't miss it. As for the Barrison place, now that's a two-hour ride, three if you ain't used to a wagon, four or five if you ain't familiar with section markers."

"Two hours?"

"Honey, out here that's nothing. Here," she said, reaching for the letter she'd left on the counter. "You can deliver this yourself if you're of a mind."

"Of course."

Katrina took the letter and hurried out the door, before Nadine could pry any further and before Katrina turned red at having to lie.

She'd driven a buggy before, but never a wagon, which was much longer and heavier. An hour later, however, thanks to the help of the man at the livery, Katrina set out, directions memorized, for the Barrison place, eight miles southeast. "Follow the ruts for the first five miles, then keep your eyes keen for the markers," he'd told her.

The hills on the other side of the river made Katrina think of the backs of hard-worked men, bare and muscled, desperate for relief. On this side there was nothing but a never-ending stretch of the most monotonous, hopelessly ugly country she'd ever seen, scorched by air as hot as a blast furnace.

Dust, dust, and more dust. Was there ever an end to it? Katrina sought her handkerchief again, though it repulsed her to even think of pressing the soiled cloth to her face.

After two hours, the powdery dirt stuck to her skin, coated her hair, gathered under her nails. Jarred and jostled with every turn of the wagon wheel, she had all she could do to maintain her balance on the hard wooden seat. Her back ached. Her feet were swollen. Her hair felt like wet plaster. If she didn't get out of this corset soon and get these hot stockings off, she'd scream.

But it was much easier to focus on physical pain than to think about what she'd say when she saw Justin.

After another hour, with a throbbing red sun pounding on the horizon, the land just waiting to be swallowed up by darkness, Katrina heard what sounded like the piercing howl of a wild dog, forcing her to acknowledge another and more immediate worry.

She was lost.

13

"*Put up a house.* Doesn't have to be anything fancy. A dugout is good enough. A soddy is better. Whatever you choose, give it a window. Plow at least ten acres into crops. Live on it for five years, then pay your proof fee of four dollars, and she's all yours. Any questions?"

"No, sir," Justin had said.

Justin remembered counting out his fourteen-dollar filing fee and handing it over to the land officer in Aberdeen as though it were yesterday, the middle of August, not a full month later. He remembered beaming with pride as he took the paper and shook the man's hand. Justin Barrison, newest landowner in the central Dakota Territory.

Now his homestead application with its official seal and signature sat safe and secure in a coffee tin underneath the bed. The Homestead Act gave him six months to start proving up on the place, and he hadn't wasted a single day. The enormity of the challenge excited him. It also gave him plenty of room to bury his sorrows.

With a bundle of stakes and ripped red bandannas in his saddlebags, he'd ridden a day and a half from Aberdeen to Leola, another two days to the growing town of Eureka, two and a half more days to Prosperity, then finally two hours across rock-strewn land that he just knew would reward his hard work.

Just as the officer in Aberdeen had described, the land was punctuated every square mile with a metal section marker. The pipe, an inch and a quarter in diameter, poked up a foot and a half from the flat ground, high enough for a man to see. Screwed to the top of each pipe was a brass disk etched with the appropriate section and township numbers.

Justin found one of nature's landmarks, in his case a triple-peaked butte the officer had described, then slowed his horse, his eyes keen for the next section marker. When he found it, he got down and compared the numbers on the disk with those on his certificate. Then he let out a yell, and with the heel of his boot he dug up a chunk of soil. He scooped the rich black earth in his hands, felt it, smelled it, rubbed it between his palms, and imagined a bright new future as he let it sift between his fingers and fall back to the ground.

He stood there for a spell, dizzy on the edge of the vast emptiness that was now his. He compared the numbers again, just to be sure he hadn't made a mistake, then took three stakes, three nails, and three red bandannas from his saddlebags. As every homesteader before him had done, he stretched his legs to measure an estimated yard and stepped off a half mile north. Using one of a thousand nearby rocks, he drove the first stake into the ground and nailed a bandanna to the top so it would flutter in the ever-present breeze. He turned east and stepped off another half mile, drove the second stake into the ground, turned south, stepped off another half mile, drove in the third stake, then turned west and stepped off the final half mile back to the metal section marker where he'd tied his horse. This quarter of Dakota Territory belonged to him. Nothing but prairie and sky. And it was all his.

Now, though the sun was setting quickly, washing the sky with peach and blue, it felt just as warm, just as welcoming as it had nearly a month ago. As he had done then, Justin shaded his eyes and looked in every direction at his own piece of heaven. He could see future acres of rich black soil tilled to face the sun, a sea of golden wheat, another of rustling corn, a big red barn, a green fenced-in pasture, beef cows, milk cows, pigs and chickens, and a bountiful vegetable garden.

He had traded in one dream for another. This one lacked the sweetness and fire of the woman he had loved—the woman who had betrayed him—but it was a good dream just the same.

The horse was an old farm animal. That's what the man at the livery said. He also said that if Katrina got lost she was to give the horse its head and let it lead the way. It would know where to find food and water.

Katrina didn't like the idea of letting the reins go slack and giving control to the animal. What if the man at the livery was wrong and the horse just wandered deeper into nowhere?

The howling startled her. This time the call was answered by another. She pictured a pack of wild dogs, large, hungry, keen-eyed animals, surrounding her even now, watching, waiting.

One by one, her choices slipped away. She couldn't find her way in the dark, and she didn't want to stop and sit until morning. What if she fell asleep? What if the horse took off in the middle of the night and she lost her bearings? What if the wolves attacked?

Straining her eyes at the unseen danger all around her, she slackened the reins as she'd been instructed. The horse stopped for a moment. "Go on," Katrina said, her heart beating faster by the second. "Go on. You know the way."

The howling came again.

"Hurry, boy. Hurry!"

As though the horse understood her, it set out again, but it kept the same slow pace, following an invisible trail in the coarse, shriveled grass, past a triple-peaked butte jutting up from the land. Katrina forgot about her aching back, her swollen feet, her restraining corset. She wanted to see civilization. She wanted to see Justin.

With twilight at her heels, she sighed with relief when she saw the tip of a spinning windmill, churning up the deep purple sky. "Oh, what a good boy you are," she said to the horse. "*What* a good boy."

Suddenly, the land dipped slightly and there, sheltered against the wind, sat Justin's homestead. Her new home.

As the horse plodded along, Katrina's mind denied what her eyes clearly saw. She hadn't seen one good solid tree since she'd gotten off the boat. Those she did see were too thin and spindly for good lumber. All this time she'd assumed dwellings out here were built with some kind of local brick, or quarried stone, or at least the whitewashed bricks of mud and straw used by some in the old country. She didn't expect a big house, or a barn or corral. But this? Surely the shadows fooled her, for all she saw was one low square building. It appeared to be made of grass.

Justin heard the noise, closed his ledger, and put it on the shelf. He stepped outside. He'd finished his chores for the day and was recording both his progress and his plans. Big plans. Now that the railroad had come as far as Eureka, rumor had it that a big terminal station would be built there. Carloads of new settlers would be coming every week, maybe several times a week. He liked knowing he was one of the first. He liked knowing he was part of history.

He strained his eyes. He didn't recognize the wagon, but whoever was headed this way was coming to see him. There wasn't any other reason a person would travel this far out, unless he was lost. Well, he'd invite whoever it was in for a cup of coffee and a chance to rest. With any luck, whoever it was had news from Prosperity. He'd been so busy he hadn't had time to get into town. He'd sweated more in the last month than he had in the last year. Not that he was complaining. He wasn't. In fact, if he hadn't been so busy, he'd have had time to think about being lonely, and he really didn't want to do that. It hurt too much.

The wagon drew closer. The driver was a woman. He could tell that from the clothes. What the hell was a woman doing out here? Something about the way she moved . . . no, he was imagining things. Memories could trick a man so easily. Still, the way she covered her heart with her hand, as though the sight of him took her by surprise, that was so like Katrina.

Katrina. He'd always liked the sound of her name on his lips, but he hadn't said it aloud since the day he left. He'd tried, but just the way an old song could dredge up a memory best left in the past, so could the sound of her name.

It still angered him to think of her with Richmond. Not that she wasn't entitled to make her own choice. She was. But damn it, after that night in the gazebo, he thought he'd be the only one ever to share that kind of intimacy with her. What a fool he'd been.

The woman slowed the wagon. The stiffness in her shoulders and the lift of her chin said she regarded him with a kind of wariness. She didn't have to worry. He wasn't the kind of man to take advantage of a woman. Or to stand in the way of her happiness.

He bandaged his broken heart as he walked out to meet the stranger.

Katrina caught her breath. Everything about him bespoke strength, from the square set of his shoulders to the long determination of his stride. He walked with an air of authority, like a man who has staked his claim and has no intention of giving an inch. His dark hair had grown longer, slightly unkempt, surprisingly attractive. His shirt, faded blue, sleeves rolled to the elbow, fit snugly across his chest. He wiped his hands against his thighs as though readying himself to greet a stranger who'd come to his place.

In the time it took him to take one stride, Katrina questioned every excuse she'd given herself, every argument she'd rehearsed to give Justin, all to explain why she'd come. If just the sight of him could send her blood racing, how could she ever look him in the eye and be calm when she asked him to let her stay?

Whether she was ready or not, the old horse took her down to him. She forgot all about the howling dogs.

Justin started as though he'd seen a vision.

Katrina? Could it be? He walked faster, explaining an eagerness he knew he shouldn't feel by saying he was simply trying to satisfy his curiosity.

It was Katrina, all right. There was no mistaking the way she held her head so high. What the hell was she doing out here? If someone was ill or had died, he'd have gotten a telegram, or at least a letter. He knew she wouldn't come all this way to gloat over the lavish way of life she now had with Richmond. As it always did, the thought of them together opened a wound he feared would never heal. Well, he had another dream now and she wasn't part of it.

But here she was. Alone.

She wanted to jump from the wagon and run toward him, to fall into the safety of his arms, to take the comfort of his embrace, but she couldn't. She'd hurt him enough already. She risked hurting him even more just by being here, but she had no choice. To encourage him falsely would be unfair, for though there was no denying the hold he had on her heart, she could never share his life, a fact she reminded herself as he came closer. Besides, he didn't look all that happy to see her. She couldn't blame him.

She stopped the wagon and willed her voice to hold steady as she greeted him.

"Hello, Justin."

"Katrina. Is it Barrison yet?"

"No," she said firmly, not ready to admit that the decision of whether or not to marry Richmond had not been hers to make.

Justin looked startled, then quickly shrugged. "Well, I thought it might be you, and then I told myself I was crazy. But here you are, sharp tongue and all. What are you doing? How did you get here?" He looked at the horizon behind her as though expecting to see another wagon. "You didn't drive all the way from Prosperity by yourself, did you?"

"Indeed I did." His reference to her sharp tongue recalled Madam Agata's words about the hardship and downfall she'd brought on herself.

Justin looked far from impressed. "And you said I was foolhardy." He shook his head. "Everything all right back in Merriweather?"

"Yes."

"Good."

"Your parents are fine as well."

He said nothing.

Silence fell between them, affording each a moment just to look at the other. Katrina saw bitterness in his eyes. It was hardly justifiable. He was the one who had run away from her without so much as a wave. She hadn't come this far, however, to argue with him. She was the one at the mercy of his hospitality, the one with the empty hand held out. Still, if there was to be more hardship and downfall in her life, she knew he would be its cause.

Without any sign of enthusiasm, Justin stepped up into the wagon, sat beside Katrina, and took the reins. "We might as well get inside," he said, as though it was his obligation, not his desire, to give her shelter. "The temperature drops fast as darkness falls." He glanced in the back of the wagon and saw her trunk. Flicking the reins, he said, in a tone that was civil at best, "I take it you're here for at least the night."

"A bit longer, if that's all right."

"What the hell."

"It won't be for too long," she said quickly, causing Justin to look confused and, if she didn't know better, hurt, causing her to regret all over again why she was here. "A few months . . . well, actually, several months." She entwined her fingers as though doing so helped her focus on what she had to do. Though she wished she didn't have to sound so impersonal, she said, "That's something I need to talk with you about."

She tucked her skirt to keep the fabric from brushing against his legs. A knowing look on his face said he knew she couldn't stand the thought of touching him and he didn't relish the idea of being close to her either. Though distance was exactly what Katrina wanted, somehow it hurt.

*　　　*　　　*

Justin berated himself for the power she still held over him. He had to keep a clear head. A person—especially a woman—didn't come all this way for nothing. She had to want something important and want it bad. He liked to think she'd come just to see him, but that was as impossible as thinking he could build a soddy, dig a well, build a corral, plow, plant, and harvest, all in his first year. He had built a house and dug a well, bought an old stove too—more than what most settlers had accomplished in a year—but he couldn't have done it all so fast without his neighbors. No, indeed. Justin wasn't a man of heroic means. He was an ordinary man with a big dream and an even bigger broken heart. It wasn't going to heal by letting her back in.

Not that he thought she wanted a place in his heart. Hell, there was a moment back there when he thought she might turn and head back to town any minute. Even now, as he drove the wagon down toward the soddy, he noticed how careful she was to keep her distance from him, as though the few inches that separated them wasn't nearly enough.

Then why was she here?

From the corner of his eye he caught her wince as she got a better look at the house, with its poor excuse for light flickering through the window.

"It's called a soddy," he said.

"Grass and dirt?"

The disdain in her voice wounded him. "That's how most people live out here, at least for a while. In case you haven't noticed, you can count the trees out here on one hand. It could take years to gather enough wood for a frame house."

She turned around to the stand of cottonwoods she'd passed on her way in. He knew what she was thinking. "That's my landmark," he said. "I won't cut those."

When they reached the door, he jumped from the wagon

and helped her down, then lifted her trunk from the back of the wagon and set it by the door. "I'll be the first to admit this kind of house is unique by Missouri standards. But it's not as bad as you might think."

"Oh, no, I think it's . . . it's fine." She hesitated. "I didn't mean for my words to injure. Your soddy, it has a sturdy look."

Her lack of sarcasm surprised him. "It is. The walls are thirty inches thick. It's only got one room, but it's a big one. Pius Pettibone—he's my nearest neighbor—and his boys helped me build it. We even used a plumb line to keep the walls straight inside and out. I reinforced the four corners and the roof myself. Should last a good six or seven years." He appraised his handiwork and nodded in satisfaction, then reminded himself not to care what she thought of his home. Still, when he noticed her looking at the window, he couldn't help but brag. "That's real glass. Most folks out here have to make do with oiled cloth."

"You've done well for yourself."

He'd never expected to hear her say that. He quickly snuffed the flicker of pride that could so easily allow him to make a fool of himself and reminded himself to be careful. "It's the law. That's all. To homestead you have to have a dwelling of some sort with at least one window. Glass or cloth didn't matter much to me, but I could afford to go with the best, so I did. Dug my own well, too. Out here you've got to dig ten times deeper than you do back home to hit water—if you hit it at all." Despite the past, or maybe because of it, he wanted her to know that his decision to purchase had been based on sound reasoning, not some sudden whim. "I'm going to put a corral over there." He gestured to his left. "I'll be getting some cattle pretty soon. Pigs, too. Chickens. Everything."

Katrina looked suitably impressed with his accomplishments. She studied the door with its leather hinges and the rag-stuffed space between the top of the door and the roof.

"That's to allow for settling," he said, "though I'll admit it does allow for a good amount of dirt to get in."

"Just like the *semljanka* in the villages at home. Cool in summer. Warm in winter."

"You've seen a soddy before?"

"My own village was in the Black Valley with dense forests. But in the outer villages, all the buildings, from church to horse barn, were made of clay and straw."

His suspicions mounted. Why the hell was she making such an effort to show her approval of his place? She planned to stay for a few months, not a lifetime. And she still hadn't told him why. Above all, why—God help him—why did he still care about her?

Fortunately, the prairie was big enough to give him the space he would need while she was here, because the thought of being close to her for even a few hours, much less a few months, was already tearing him apart. As though she'd set the tone of being civil and he'd agreed to follow, he kept his voice calm as he said, "Come on inside. I'll get you settled."

Katrina lifted the wooden latch, opened the door, and saw the dirt walls, as black as the dirt floor. And to think, she'd always been worried about keeping dirt *out*.

Justin turned up the wick on the kerosene lamp he'd left on the table, sending a curl of black smoke to the ceiling. Refusing to wallow in self-pity, Katrina forced herself to remember how fortunate she was to have a roof over her head. She looked up.

"I just put that ceiling up a few days ago," Justin told her.

"Oh," she said, wondering how he could speak with such pride, hoping her revulsion didn't show. He'd covered the grassy sides of a dozen strips of sod with bleached-out flour sacks and coated the new ceiling with a thin wash of white plaster. The faded red letters of Swenson's Fine Flour still bled through. Here and there clumps of dirt, loosened no doubt by some burrowing rodent, bulged down in a most unattractive manner.

She noticed the bed.

He did too.

"Look," he said. "I'm going to go feed and water the horse. I suppose you rented it and the wagon in town."

"Will you help me return them?"

"We'll take care of that later. Have a seat. There's coffee on the stove and an extra mug on the shelf over there. I'll be back in a while. And then . . . and then we can talk."

She nodded, but before she had a chance to say anything, he was gone.

The headboard was nothing more than a rainbow-shaped loop of pitted brass. Two pillows, in nothing but blue ticking, were jammed against each other as though separately they'd been found lacking in their ability to provide a good night's sleep. A quilt, a staircase of pastel squares, lay rumpled across a wrinkled white sheet, all atop an old-fashioned frame of wood and rope.

Would he expect the rights of a married man if he gave her the shelter of his home? She hoped not. For, as she'd learned the hard way, a woman dare not welcome a man between her legs unless she can also welcome him into her heart. To do otherwise brings nothing but pain.

She looked around the room that, if Justin agreed to her proposition, would be her home for the next ten to twelve months. He'd fastened pegs on the four corner posts of the room. A frying pan, a big black pot, and a red checkered dish towel hung from one peg. His winter coat, a pair of overalls, and a gray flannel shirt hung from another.

He'd fashioned two thigh-high shelves, though each consisted of nothing more than a plank stretched between two barrels. One shelf already held several tins of food, an odd assortment of dishes, and a neatly folded white shirt. She wondered how many of these things he'd bought himself and how many had been loaned to him by the neighbor he'd spoken of. Had he bought the crudely framed and faded advertisement for a De Laval cream separator that hung over the kitchen table? Or the scrap of sagging lace nailed above the window? Probably not.

What did he cook on the old black cast-iron stove in the corner? From the looks of the items on the shelf, he existed on beans and coffee. She examined the items more closely.

"Not much of a larder, is it?" he said as he entered.

Caught with a can of figs in her hand, she stammered, "I didn't mean to pry. I just—"

"No, go ahead. Have a look around. It's not much. Not yet anyway. But one of these days—" He stopped himself.

She returned the can to the shelf. "You've done a lot in a short time."

"I've had a lot of help."

"Your neighbors?"

"Pettibones. Pius, his wife Dulcie, nine boys. Scogginses, Hemmelers, Roundtrees. A few others. Couldn't have done all this without them, not this fast anyway."

"Oh."

"And the Morehouse family. They used to live in these parts but went back east. I bought the stove from them. A few other odds and ends, too: the picture on the wall, the dishes, the bed."

"I see."

She didn't know how much longer they could just stand there, looking at each other, talking about people Justin would never see again or neighbors Katrina had yet to meet, talking as though today was no different from yesterday for either of them.

Justin, too, seemed impatient to get to the heart of Katrina's sudden visit. He went over to the table. "Here," he said, pulling out one of two heavily scratched ladderback chairs. "Come sit down. I know you've got something to say. And I'd just as soon hear it now, if you don't mind."

"You're right." Each step felt like a mile. When she reached the table she placed a steadying hand on the back of the chair and looked into his eyes. "There's no pretty way to say it. I'm here to unburden my soul and ask for your hospitality."

He looked puzzled as well as guarded. She expected that. She didn't, however, expect an oddly hopeful look to soften his eyes. Seeing it, her own eyes suddenly brimmed with tears, for all the people she'd hurt and for the dream of his she could never fulfill.

"Don't cry," he murmured, drinking in her image as though it quenched a powerful thirst. "Whatever it is, I'll take care of it for you." He faltered. "I mean, it can't be that bad."

"Oh, but it can."

He reached down and took her hand. There was no wedding ring. "You didn't marry Richmond, did you?"

"No."

He ran his thumb along her bare finger. "I hated seeing his ring on your hand. Hated it."

She slipped her hand away. "Please, Justin, don't read more into this than there is. I don't want to hurt you now. I never did."

Though he didn't move as much as an inch from her, his heart moved miles and miles. She could tell.

Knowing it was just as well, Katrina continued, "The only reason I'm standing here with you now is because your brother wouldn't marry me. *Wouldn't.*"

That he could look so suddenly confused meant he still carried hope, and once more Katrina felt the pain of hurting someone she cared for.

"I don't get it," he said. "Richmond told me you wanted

to shorten the mourning period so the two of you could get married immediately."

"He what? Oh, no, that's not the way it happened. Not at all." Relieved to be telling him the truth, she focused on Justin's questioning eyes. "He wouldn't marry me. He drove me out of town—not that he can keep me out, because I'm going back. I *will* find a way."

A touch of his former wariness returned. "Why? Why did he make you leave?"

"Oh, Justin." She sighed with despair, knowing the moment of truth had come. "Because I carry your child."

While his eyes widened with emotions she couldn't begin to discern, she went on.

"So you see, I've come to you because I need a place to stay; but just until the baby is born and is old enough to travel. I wrote you a letter; it was still at the post office in town when I arrived. The woman gave it to me. I told her I'd deliver it. But none of that matters now anyway, does it?"

When he said nothing, she braced herself for the worst, "May I? May I stay?"

"You're pregnant? With my baby?"

She nodded.

He looked straight at her belly just the way Richmond had that day in the bakery, but the expression on Justin's face was tender, as though he'd just been humbled in a way he could never have imagined. His expression was also more guarded than ever.

"March?" he asked.

"Yes." She knew they'd have to talk about the baby eventually, but this wasn't the right time. She couldn't imagine a right time. Just the fact that he'd correctly calculated the timing of the event meant he'd thought about the night of conception. Her cheeks flushed at the memory. She braced her hand on the edge of the table to steady the dizziness that followed.

"What is it? Are you ill?"

"It's nothing. Just the strain of the trip." She smiled with a weary recognition of the sad turn her life had taken. "Justin, I don't mean to press, but I can't go another day without knowing your decision. Will you let me stay?"

"For God's sake, of course you can stay. Now sit down."

Even though he kept his focus on the edge of the table she gripped so solidly as she sat down, she knew he hadn't missed her sigh of relief.

"Are you all right?" he asked. "I mean is everything going . . . well, you know, the way it should?"

"Mornings are far from pleasant, but other than that I feel fine."

"Are you taking any kind of pills or tonic, or whatever it is women do when they're—"

"Lukas Heinz supplied me."

"You have enough to carry you through? I can get some for you in town."

"I have plenty." She looked around the room. "I'll clean the house tomorrow, then wash the clothes. I'll bake the next day. If you have any mending, I can do that in the evenings. If you'll give me free rein at the stove, I'll take over the cooking." When he didn't comment one way or the other, she added, "I won't take charity."

"I can't say I like my own cooking."

She smiled, the first time in weeks. "Good."

"You take the bed," he said. "I'll sleep in the sleeping bag."

"*Danke*, Justin. Thank you."

"It's the only decent thing to do. Let me go get your trunk. I'll help you unpack tonight if you want."

"I just need a few things."

The night air rushed in as he brought her trunk inside and set it by the bed. Gesturing toward the shelves, he said, "Take whatever space you need."

"I won't need much. I won't be staying long."

He frowned, then said, "Whatever you want." He grabbed the water bucket from where it stood on the floor. "Be right back," he said and stepped outside.

His throat hurt from all the words he'd swallowed, words like "mockery," "manipulate," "second best." The night chill hit him in the face as he walked to the windmill. Sure, she could stay. Why not? He liked to think of himself as an honorable man, and with a woman carrying his child, what else was he supposed to do? Tell her no? Kick her out?

Of course, it might not be his child. It probably wasn't. Still, his concern at the moment wasn't so much the baby as it was Katrina.

She looked more wrinkled and rumpled than an unmade bed. Her shoulders drooped as though they carried the weight of the world, and, considering her position, that was probably how she felt. Countless strands of hair had escaped the braid she coiled at her neck and now fell around her dust-streaked face. She needed something to eat, a good night's sleep—hospitality he'd extend to any stranger. Trouble was, he wanted to give her more. A shoulder to cry on. A comforting arm. A tender kiss. But all she wanted was a place to stay. She hadn't said anything about wanting him to marry her, certainly nothing about love. Richmond, that boot-licking peacock, still owned her heart.

He reached the windmill, grabbed the pump handle, and pumped till fresh cold water gushed from the pipe and filled his bucket. The sloshing weight pulled on his arm as he headed back to the soddy.

The stars had just come out. Like huge jewels strewn across the sky, they crowned the prairie night with a radiance unmatched in the heavens. They hung low, close enough to tempt a man to reach. Close, but not close enough.

* * *

Katrina had grown up on stories of fair damsels imprisoned in dark dungeons. Here she was, too old and too pregnant to be anyone's fair damsel, but imprisoned in a dark dungeon just the same. Not by some evil king or even a wicked czar. No. She was imprisoned by her own lack of power. Someday, however, that would change.

Exhausted from a day she thought would never end, she knelt beside her open trunk and rubbed her temples. Pain stretched across her shoulders and up the back of her neck and into her head. She longed for a hot bath and clean clothes. She closed her eyes and sighed. What was done was done, at least for now. As soon as she got her few items of clothing, her toilette, and her medicine unpacked, she would feel better. Then starting tomorrow morning she would do everything she could to earn her keep for the time she was here.

Only now did she admit the unspoken dream, the broken hope, she'd nurtured all the way from Merriweather. What on earth made her think that, on hearing about the baby, Justin would not only agree but want to go back to Merriweather. He would apologize to his father and take his place at the head of the brewery. And, of course, marry Katrina and give the baby his name. What a fool she'd been. He hadn't once mentioned going back. He certainly hadn't mentioned marriage. Perhaps it was just as well. If he wouldn't go back, she didn't want to marry him. She would still, however, find another way to get back home.

Katrina looked around, hoping she could find some reason to be optimistic about the upcoming year, but the place was all too dirty, too impoverished, too desolate. The *semljanka* were made of clay and straw, yes, but inside they were stuccoed with plaster and white-washed, the ceilings painted with bright blue enamel. They had more than one window, more than one room. Frustration made her head throb all the harder. Didn't it bother Justin to live like this, especially when his life could easily be better?

She went to the door and stared into the darkness. She hadn't seen stars this big or this bright since the old country. She could barely make out Justin's tall, lean silhouette at the well. Clearly, however, she could hear the heavy, wheezing draw of the pump handle, the even heavier sound of resisting weight, the gush of water splashing into the bucket, and finally the loose, clanging rattle of the pipes as they relaxed. Accompanying it all was the soft, fluttering click of the windmill in the breeze. With the infinite night sky overhead and an infinite prairie underfoot, she felt trapped in her new home.

If she'd married Richmond and this was her wedding night, the wedding guests would be doing the *Kehraus* now, merrily sweeping into her new home, dancing on her polished wooden floors, beating time with spoons and pans, rolling pins and mixing bowls. The reflection of twinkling chandeliers would twirl in the tall windows. The entire town would be celebrating her fortunate union.

She returned to her trunk and knelt down. Wedged tightly along the sides were two baking tins, one for muffins, one for bread. She tugged to get them free.

"Wait," Justin said as he came through the door and saw her struggling. He set the bucket down and went to help her. Effortlessly, he freed the tins and placed them on the shelf, next to the dishes.

"Thank you," she said. The baking tins reminded Katrina of Gretchen and pulled at her heart. She swallowed hard. This was no time for sentimentality. But then she lifted the threadbare towel she'd brought with her and saw not only a pair of pillowcases her mother had embroidered but the lace collar she had worn on her wedding dress, over a quarter of a century ago. There were several dresser scarves, too, including the one Katrina had embroidered with honeysuckles. Gretchen must have put them all in the trunk.

She saw her father's hammer, hardly the only tool of a professional carpenter, but it made her remember how he'd tried to learn a new trade in his blessed America, simply because he had the freedom to do so, and how sore his thumbs had been until he learned to hammer properly. His American flag was there, too, folded in a tight triangle. He got it in New York from a soldier who'd fought in the great war between brothers. It was the very first thing he'd bought in this country, with money that should have gone for food.

And there was the carving of Strudel. Her eyes watered so quickly she had to blink repeatedly to gain control.

"I'll get those things for you," Justin said. He reached into the trunk.

"No! I mean, no, thank you. I've no need for them now. They can stay in the trunk. That way they won't get dirty or lost."

"Fine. Keep them there." He walked away.

He probably wasn't too happy about having someone just drop in on him and take over his home, especially with the news she brought. And even though she planned to earn her keep, he probably wanted a better idea of how long she planned to stay. After all, he couldn't sleep on the floor forever.

"If I'm delivered in March," she said, "and if everything goes well, I should be able to leave in August or September, one year from now." She couldn't read the shadow that crossed his eyes. "Is that too long?"

"No. I can manage that."

"*Danke.*" She hesitated. "There is one other thing."

"What's that?"

She leaned back and rested on her heels. "What do you

think we should tell people about me? How will we explain my presence?"

He shrugged. "I imagine you've already given that some thought. What do you want me to say?"

"That I am your sister, recently widowed."

"I could. But why not say you're my wife?"

She grabbed the edge of the trunk. "Heaven forbid, Justin. Don't say that."

"A fate worse than death?"

"Please, it's not that. It's just . . . well, what will you say when the time comes for me to go?"

"Maybe you won't. Who knows? Maybe you'll learn to like it here and decide to stay."

She stood and glanced around the room. "No, that will never happen. I'm sorry."

"No, I'm sorry. It was a joke, Katrina. A bad one. You're not cut out for the rigors of the prairie. I can see that."

"What do you mean?"

"Well, look at you. You're too thin, too frail. You're going to have a hard time just pumping water. Your skin still looks like buttermilk. Believe me when I tell you, it won't stay that way."

She pressed her palms to her cheeks, remembering the warning the woman in the general store had given her about the harsh sun turning her skin to leather.

Nonchalantly, he turned away from her, added a chunk of some kind of coal to the embers in the stove, and filled the kettle with water. He took a lantern from a peg on the wall and fitted it with a candle from a box on the shelf. "Are you hungry?"

"No. Just exhausted."

"There's some biscuits in that pan over there if you change your mind. They're hard, but they won't kill you."

She nodded her appreciation.

He continued. "I've got some things to do outside before

it's time to turn in. I imagine you'll want to wash up." Pulling a large washtub and a bar of soap from the shelf, he added, "This is all I've got."

"It will do nicely."

He lifted the latch on the door, then hesitated. "You said it was my child?"

"Of course it's your child. Do you really think I would come all this way if it weren't?"

"I think you'd do just about anything."

14

A Peeping Tom, that's what he was. Justin didn't like thinking of himself that way, but the label fit. Standing outside in the dark, he couldn't look away from the window.

She'd dimmed the light of the kerosene lamp down so low she might as well be bathing in darkness. She knelt in the washtub and sponged the soapy water over her narrow shoulders and down her slender arms. He remembered how that strong soap had made him itch the first few times he'd used it. He hated the thought of what it would do to Katrina's tender skin.

She turned toward him and he saw her breasts. She was only three months along, but already they looked fuller. Maybe it was the way she cupped them with that scrap of soapy cloth, the way the frayed, sopping edges splayed along her curves.

Her movements, however, were far from gentle, her demeanor far from calm. He'd upset her by asking about the child. Well, he couldn't pretend to be her brother, or her husband, or anyone else for a whole year and not know the truth. As outspoken as she was, he was surprised she didn't just come right out and say, Yes, the child is Richmond's and what difference does it make? But if that was the case, she'd still be in Merriweather. Richmond would have married her immediately.

Justin watched her, and as he did he remembered how his hands had stroked her warm flesh. He didn't need a memory to recall how his body responded.

Hard with desire, he went to the door, pressed his palm against it, and stepped inside.

Katrina crossed her breasts with her arms. "What are you doing!"

"I didn't mean to startle you," he said, surprised at how thick his voice sounded. "I'll go back outside."

But he couldn't move.

She was standing in the tub, ribbons of iridescent bubbles running down her body. A crimson flush spread across her chest, up her neck and into her cheeks—not that he could see it in the dim light—he could feel it, for she radiated heat. A patch of foam settled on the tawny curls between her legs. With both desire and wonder, he looked at her belly, at the little pouch that had barely begun to take shape.

She met his stare, then shivered and turned her back to him.

Cautiously he stepped closer, feeling a tremor rattle his body with every step. He reached for the towel she'd placed on the stool and held it out to her. "Here," he said, ashamed to admit how much he wanted her to step into it and into his arms.

Katrina looked over her shoulder and reached for the towel. "Are you leaving now?" she asked. Her fingers moved quickly to wrap and tuck the towel over her breasts. She stepped from the tub and, keeping her back to him, walked toward the bed on which she'd readied her night-gown and white shawl.

In a strained and empty voice, far too empty to be natural, far too strained to be harmless, she said, "Why did you ask if the child was yours? What made you think it could be otherwise?"

Before he could answer, she added, "Whose did you think it was? Richmond's?"

Frustration sharpened his words. "From all he told me, yes."

"What did he say?"

"That he'd been sharing your bed for some time."

She stiffened. "And you believed him! Why?"

"Because I felt he spoke the truth."

"Because he's your brother?" She shook her head. "No. The friction between the two of you was obvious. You had to have strong reason to believe such a lie." With boldness in every step, she came toward him. "What did he tell you, Justin? What was it that so easily convinced you?"

"Look, I want to talk to you about this, not argue."

"Was it simply because I gave myself to you without benefit of marriage, and, if you, why not someone else as well? Was that it?"

"No!"

"Then what?"

He yanked her towel away. She didn't flinch. She didn't cover herself. She didn't turn away.

Despising his inability to control his trembling hand, he reached out and cupped her left breast. With his jaw clenched like a vise, he stroked with his thumb the pink birthmark just below her hardened nipple. "Because he knew about this."

Katrina's expression changed. As though caught in a lie, she looked startled, resigned, humbled. She reached for the towel and, when Justin released it reluctantly, wrapped it around her body. As she tucked one corner securely over another, she took a deep breath and let it out slowly, as though uncovering the truth was painful but liberating at the same time.

Justin continued, but the anger was gone from his voice. "He said everything a man thinks of as feminine is exaggerated in you." Moving closer, his voice just above a whisper, he added, "He's right."

She brooked the distance between them with an out-stretched arm. "But he lied."

"It doesn't matter."

"Oh, but it does."

She lifted her chin. If she thought the gesture made her look defiant, she was wrong. It let Justin see how easily her pulse throbbed in the little hollow of her throat. It emphasized how vulnerable she was.

"I'm thinking it best to lay all this in the open," she said, "for I lack the energy to be wary of either your words or your silence."

"Meaning?"

"Your brother knows of my blemish because I disrobed in front of him."

"You did what?"

"I tried to seduce him."

He stepped back, pulled out a chair, and straddled it. Now it was his turn to look shocked, for all along he'd imagined Richmond the aggressor. "Why? He was eager to marry you. Everyone knew that."

"Oh, Justin, how can you be such a fool? Because I was pregnant and it was not his child. Without marriage, I would ruin not only my own chances for happiness, but also those of my child and those of Gretchen. I . . . I schemed to trick your brother into thinking the child was his, with the idea that we would marry soon. But in the end I couldn't go through with it."

Warring inside him were the revulsion at what she'd tried to do and the relief that she hadn't been able to do it. "So what happened?"

"I confessed I was pregnant with your child."

"And that's when Richmond made you leave town."

Her eyes brightened with tears. "I didn't want to, but he called the loan on the bakery and said if I didn't go, he would destroy everything for both Gretchen and me. The bakery was all we had. What else could I do?"

"Damn it, Katrina. You could have come to me."

"I tried, but you were gone! Without so much as a good-bye!"

Justin gripped the back of the chair to steady the longing rising inside him. "Why didn't you come to me right away, when you found you were pregnant? Why didn't you come to me then?"

Standing there shivering, she said, "And what would you have done, marry me?"

"Of course!"

"And you would expect me to give up my roots, to wander the world because your anger makes it impossible for you to settle down? No. The wildness in you frightens me."

"Woman, are you blind? Look around! I've settled down. Can't you see that? I'm not selling out. I'm already making plans to buy more land, plant wheat—"

"Big dreams!"

"Yes, big dreams! That's how success starts."

"Ah, but now you are the blind one, for your dreams are not my dreams. That's why I couldn't come to you when I realized I was pregnant. We don't want the same things from life. We didn't then. We don't now." She looked down at her trunk, as though gauging how long it would take her to repack her belongings. "I should never have come here."

"I pity you, Katrina."

She stiffened and held her head high. "I don't need your pity."

"Yes, you do. You see, I may dream big, but you don't dream at all."

"What's that supposed to mean?"

He couldn't just sit there and see her tears, hear her pain. Purposefully, he stood up and slowly walked toward her. "Don't pretend there's nothing between us. You feel what I feel. I know you do."

She stood her ground, tears spilling down her cheeks. Choking on her words, she said, "I can't."

In less than a heartbeat, Justin closed the distance between them and drew her to him. "Yes, you can," he whispered. "Just have faith in me." Her body, slender, wet, and just as soft as he remembered, responded willingly to the firm pressure of his hands as they stroked a path down her back. He sculpted her waist, fanned his fingers over her hips, and cupped her buttocks, just as he had done that night. The memory begged to live again.

His clothes felt damp now, moistened by the water still clinging to her skin. His need for her was painful. "Katrina," he whispered as he moved closer.

Her lips parted easily, assuring Justin that she too felt the need. He relished the scant weight of her arms as they circled his neck. He tightened their embrace, wanting always to keep her this close. He wanted to kiss her, feel her, love her, all before she had another thought of Richmond and the life he could have given her.

He deepened his kiss, claiming Katrina's mouth with his own. He would erase Richmond altogether if he could. Katrina was here with him now. He would do whatever he had to do to make her stay.

She kept her fingers entwined with his as he released her from his embrace and led her to the bed.

*   *   *

Katrina willed her conscience to a place remote and silent. Was it so wrong to want a moment of happiness? To take the pleasure Justin offered? To feel close to someone again? There had been another time when she desperately needed comfort, needed to know that life could go on. Justin had given her that comfort. It shamed her to remember how bold she'd been that night. Then it thrilled her to remember how satisfied.

She made her decision and slipped beneath the quilt.

What little light there was danced in Justin's eyes, telling her how much he wanted her. He knelt on the floor beside the bed. Katrina held her breath as he skimmed his hand along the quilt, right up to the hem she clutched in her fingers. One fold at a time, he eased the fabric from her hand until he controlled the patchwork curtain. As he drew it back, he whispered, "So beautiful."

She had not covered herself because she needed modesty but because she lacked trust. Even now, as she lowered her head to the pillow and watched Justin's hands cover her breasts, as she shuddered with pleasure as his fingers spread to gather the fullness, even now she knew he was incapable of giving her the guarantees she wanted for her future. But he was trying. And for that she would always be grateful. Besides, she would only be here for a year.

Her head sank deeper into the softness as he massaged her in a firm and rhythmic way that would have been tranquilizing had she not been so aroused.

His lips closed over the nipple he'd teased. She closed her eyes to enhance the sensation. Another caress, another kiss. Then nothing. With her own hands she covered her breasts, suddenly bereft of his touch.

Opening her eyes, she saw him standing by the bed, unbuttoning his shirt. Once bare-chested, he pulled off his boots. His black eyes hinted of pleasure to come. His lips formed a confident smile. With increasing impatience, his fingers unbuttoned his pants. He dropped them on the ground. He reached for her hand and drew it to him.

Hesitantly, she closed her fingers around him. Justin closed his eyes and groaned.

With his hand over hers, guiding her, Katrina stroked his length, feeling its heat. Her own body found pleasure as well, starting the spiral she knew would grow unbearably tight before it would give her release.

"You don't know what you do to me, do you?" He eased her hand away and climbed in bed beside her.

She remembered and smiled.

As he took her in his arms, his kisses, first tender and unsure, then hard and demanding, wound the invisible coil inside her. Thinking of nothing but the moment, and the moment to come, she raked her fingers through his hair and squirmed to place more of her body in contact with his, crushing her breasts against his chest. With every movement, she smelled the freshness of the hay in the mattress beneath her, mixed with the remembered scent of Justin's body.

The anticipation mounted. Just when she thought she could stand no more, she felt his hand glide down her body and slip between her legs. As though patiently waiting for a flower to bloom, he stroked her petal-soft skin.

Eager now for the ultimate euphoria this man had given her once before, Katrina welcomed him once again.

Her mind played such a cruel trick. Sometime in the night, in the drowsy, floating moments just before dawn, while she lay curled beneath the tent of quilt created by Justin's broad back, Katrina dreamed of her childhood home nestled in the hills. With Strudel barking at her heels, she ran barefoot through the lush countryside beside a forest so thick it cloaked the hills in black, beckoning Gretchen and their friends to help empty the overflowing picnic basket the cook had prepared that morning.

Still asleep, Katrina hugged her pillow and snuggled into the warm spot next to her, willing a faintly intrusive noise to be still. It didn't work. A cacophony of animal sounds jarred her, and she woke to see a cow's face at the window. Abruptly, she sat up.

First she heard Justin's voice, then the crackling laugh of another man.

"Son, you ain't planning to let that bride of yours lolly-gag like this every morning, are you?"

Bride. So Justin had told the man they were married. After a night of loving and sweet caresses, it only seemed natural. She couldn't hear Justin's reply.

More important, they had a visitor and she wasn't dressed. She jumped from the bed, grabbed her dress, and slipped it over her head. She raced to braid her hair and splash some cold water from the wash basin on her face, then tied an apron around her waist and a black shawl about her shoulders. Through the window she could see Justin and the man herding three cows and a calf to a small feed trough. She couldn't believe they'd have company at this hour. It couldn't be much past dawn.

A thin band of dust-filled sunlight poked through the rag-stuffed crack above the door, shedding light on the black walls, the tousled bed, and the brown mouse that suddenly scurried across the floor. Katrina screamed.

Blindly, she rushed outside, only to sink her bare foot in a pile of fresh manure.

She bit her lip to keep from crying, for screaming at a mouse and shedding tears over something so trivial as soiling her foot was nothing but foolish. She scooped up her skirt and hobbled as far as she could from the yellow-brown mush, scraping her foot on every clump of prairie grass she could find. Just as she reached the water trough at the windmill, the morning retching that had plagued her for months gripped her again, this time with a vengeance. It occurred to her to just lie down and die. Instead, she crossed her arms, clutched her belly, and heaved.

"Katrina!"

She heard the concern in Justin's voice as he rushed toward her, felt his strength as he grabbed her from behind, slipped his arms under hers, and braced her so she wouldn't collapse. Willingly, she let him absorb the weight of her body as she leaned back against his chest.

When the retching was over, Justin snatched his bandanna from around his neck and dunked the cloth into the cold water. After wringing the bandanna as best he could, he wiped Katrina's brow. "It's all right," he murmured. "It's all right. You're going to be just fine. I promise. You'll see."

Katrina never doubted anything more in her life, least of all his ability to make promises about her future. Even as Justin smoothed her cheek and brought to mind the tenderness they'd shared the night before, she was aware that his hands were rough and calloused and hers would soon be too. His dirt-caked coveralls showed his desperate attempts to sink roots in this stubborn rock-strewn soil. And smack in the middle of it all, she remembered every horrible story she'd ever heard about birthing children. No. Everything was not going to be all right, and she knew it.

The spasms finally stopped, but now her mouth and nose burned with an acid taste. Her stomach felt as twisted as a wet rag that had been wrung tight.

The man with the gravelly voice strolled over to them and said, "Doused yourself in prairie perfume, did you?"

Justin didn't move. "Katrina, this is our neighbor, Pius Pettibone. Pettibone, this is my wife, Katrina."

"How do, ma'am."

Katrina nodded.

"Stand still now," Justin said. "This is no time for modesty." He lifted the edge of Katrina's skirt, revealing her foot. Mr. Pettibone's chuckle sounded patronizing and did little to ease her embarrassment.

"Lean on me," Justin said, "and stick your foot out here."

Katrina did as she was told and in a moment Justin had rinsed away all traces of her initiation to the prairie. When he was finished, Katrina scooped up the soiled hem of her skirt to keep it from contaminating her skin. "I must go change," she said as she hurried toward the house.

She wasn't three feet away when she heard Pettibone saying to Justin. "Your wife's got *two* dresses? You can't be spending your money on fancies like that if you're planning to build a wheat farm."

"Katrina's worth a dozen dresses. Besides, don't you play the skinflint with me. Honestly, I don't know how Dulcie puts up with you."

Katrina hadn't yet met poor Dulcie Pettibone, but already she pitied the woman.

Back outside, Justin rinsed his bandanna in the water and debated on what to tell Pius about Katrina.

"You know, son, I figured you for the big husky type. The Jaegers got a girl about fifteen. I seen her in town a week or so ago. Looks ready enough. I was fixing to do the intros, if you was of a mind, and low and behold, all along you had yourself a wife. How come you never mentioned her?"

"We were married back in Missouri, before I came out here."

"Hmm. Well, she sure is a looker, I'll give you that."

"That she is."

"You know, them fine-boned kind are like china. Get all chipped and cracked in no time."

"I'll take care of her."

"Sure you will, son. But you know my first wife was

like that. Ooh-wee," he said with a shiver, "I can still picture them slim ankles of hers. Good God almighty."

"So Dulcie's your second wife?"

"My third. I'm telling you, the little ones don't last out here."

"Practice what you preach, Pius. Dulcie's not much bigger than a sparrow."

Pius grinned. "But I already got my nine boys. I can afford to have me a little wife now."

"Well, Katrina will be fine."

"And the babe? This the first, I take it."

Justin started. "How'd you know about the baby?"

"Come on, boy. All that morning retchin'? Don't forget I been through it nine times. Been through it ten times actually, but things just don't always work out. You know what I'm saying?"

"I do," Justin said. He knew about Dulcie's recent loss.

Pius scratched his whiskers, then sucked on his teeth. "Ain't none of my business, but you want to make a go of this place, you're gonna need a lot of kids. You know what I'm sayin'? You don't survive on this prairie by yourself."

"I know."

"No, I don't know as you do. Just give that wife of yours a good study one of these days. She's barely got the strength to hold up her head, much less whelp you a dozen kids. Like I said, she's pretty enough, but she sure ain't the healthiest woman I've seen. Fact is, I've seen a half-drowned cat look livelier."

"Katrina will be fine," Justin repeated.

"Well, maybe you're right. Loves farming, does she?"

"She will, in time."

"I hope so. 'Cause when your woman don't think much of your work, well, let's just say it makes for a mighty long day in field."

A short time later, Justin inhaled the aroma of fresh coffee and invited Pettibone in for a cup. Pius accepted eagerly and sat down as though he owned the place. Between sipping and slurping, he offered to have Dulcie show Katrina how to fry up some cornmeal and molasses till it made a fine burnt powder.

"You boil that," he said bracing his elbows on the table, "and you got yourself a good cup of coffee."

Unlike the swill he was drinking now? "*Danke*," she said stiffly as she wiped an invisible spot of grease on the top of the stove. "I'll try that."

"You one of them Deutschmen?"

"*Ja*," she said, more defensively than she realized until the word was out of her mouth. "I am German."

"So what do you think of our big American prairie? Pretty grand, ain't it?"

She paused in her scrubbing and looked at him. "The Russian steppes are much like this, vast and flat with no trees. If what I heard on the boat is true, that many from the steppes are coming here, they will be happy, for the land looks much the same. But I am from the Gluckstal region, the village of Neudorf in the Black Valley. My homeland is green with dense forests, gentle hills. My home in Missouri is much the same. Your prairie is flat and brown."

"Hmm. So tell me now, back in that old country of yours, could a man get a hundred and sixty acres of land from the government, free?"

"No. Not anymore."

"And a plain man such as myself, could I ride in the same rail car as your high-mucky-mucks?"

"Absolutely not." She thought of the argument she'd heard as a child—it comforts a poor person to know his place, it ensures he will never be disappointed by aspiring to something beyond his station—but she didn't mention it. She had never liked the idea.

Pius leaned toward her. "Bet you couldn't thumb your nose in the middle of the street at your king either. Or your czar. Or whoever it was had a hold on you."

"No, but—"

"Could you send him packin' if he didn't do you right?"

"No, but—"

"Well, we can here. In the U. S. of A., no man is more equal than another. That's freedom, little girl, and freedom gives a man true power." He sat back and scratched his shoulders against the chair. "My pappy's generation sent a skinny country lawyer from a log house not much better than this to Washington, D.C., to be our president. I've sent a few up there myself."

Katrina lifted her chin. "We had a fine big house, made of stucco and wood, three stories. Brick floors. Glass in every window. We had cows and horses, pigs and chickens. Trees that gave plums, apples, cherries, and nuts. Arbors heavy with grapes and rivers filled with fish."

Pius slapped his thigh and looked toward Justin. "Talk about your high winds! You got your work cut out for you, son. You don't watch it, you'll be going the way of old Art Morehouse. Had to sell out and get himself back to the East Coast, to an ocean he could swim, not plow."

"That'll never happen," Justin said. Then, seeing the crestfallen look on Katrina's face, he added, "But I'm going to plant wheat as far as the eye can see. Raise a few cattle. And turn this place into a palace."

"What do you make of that, little girl? Can you see this old soddy of yours as a palace?"

How he infuriated her! "You can put your mittens in the oven but that doesn't make them biscuits. And free land or not, this prairie is hopelessly ugly."

Pius smiled. "I reckon there's all kinds of pretty. Who knows? One of these days you may find the prairie so pretty it'll hurt your eyes just to look at it."

If you
have a passion
for great
historical
romance,
here's an offer
you'll love...

4 FREE NOVELS

SEE INSIDE.

Introducing
The Timeless Romance

Passion rising from the ashes of the Civil War...

Love blossoming against the harsh landscape of the primitive Australian outback...

Romance melting the cold walls of an 18th-century English castle —— and the heart of the handsome Earl who lives there...

Since the beginning of time, great love has held the power to change the course of history. And in Harper Monogram historical novels, you can experience that power again and again.

Free introductory offer. To introduce you to this exclusive new service, we'd like to send you the four newest Harper Monogram titles absolutely free. They're yours to keep without obligation, no matter what you decide.

Free 10-day previews. Enjoy automatic free delivery of four new titles each month — up to four weeks before they appear in bookstores. You're never obligated to keep a book you don't want, and you can return any book, for a full credit.

Save up to 32% off the publisher's price on any shipment you choose to keep.

Don't pass up this opportunity to enjoy great romance as you have never experienced before.

Reader Service.

Yes! I want to join the Timeless Romance Reader Service. Please send me my 4 FREE HarperMonogram historical romances. Then each month send me 4 new historical romances to preview without obligation for 10 days. I'll pay the low subscription price of $4.00 for every book I choose to keep--a total savings of at least $2.00 each month--and home delivery is free! I understand that I may return any title within 10 days and receive a full credit. I may cancel this subscription at any time without obligation by simply writing "Canceled" on any invoice and mailing it to Timeless Romance. There is no minimum number of books to purchase.

NAME

ADDRESS

CITY   STATE   ZIP

TELEPHONE

SIGNATURE

"I think not."

"I hope you're wrong, little girl, seeing as how your man is diggin' in deep." He took on an innocent look. "Unless you're thinking of dragging him back to Missouri. Are you thinking that?"

Katrina said nothing.

Pius looked over at Justin as if passing some unspoken message. Katrina wondered if Pius had known there'd been trouble between them all along and thought it was about time Justin faced up to it. Then he stood, scratched his whiskers, and said, "Well, I'll let you two get back to your business. I got to be getting back to work too. Fun is fun, but it takes money to buy whiskey."

He shook Justin's hand, nodded to Katrina, then said, "If you want, I'll hitch the horse and wagon to the back of my wagon and trail them back to town for you. I'm headed that way."

"I'd appreciate it," Justin said.

The two men stepped outside. A short while later, Pius drove away, towing the rented horse and wagon. Katrina wasn't the least bit disappointed to see him go.

Justin came back inside. "I know he's a little rough around the edges," he said, as he poured himself another cup of coffee, "but that man is my best friend, and he's been a great help to me. What do you think of him?"

"I think he is loud and insensitive."

"He thinks you're pretty."

"He thinks I'm weak and lacking in respect for America."

"No, he just thinks you're too frail for prairie life. But I told him I planned to take good care of you." He put his mug down and walked toward her. Everything from his slow and deliberate steps to his seductive smile let her know that his thoughts had turned amorous.

She turned away and busied herself with the dirty mugs, hoping he'd see that her mind was simply not on thoughts of loving. Besides, they had something to discuss and there was no time like the present.

She could feel his presence close behind her. Squeezing the wet rag she'd used to wash the mugs, she asked, "Why did you tell Mr. Pettibone that we were married?"

"I don't know. It just seemed the logical thing to say."

"But we discussed it. I wanted you to say I was your sister, recently widowed."

"I like my version better." Standing behind her, he slipped his arms around her waist. "Come on, Katrina, what's the harm?" He pressed his lips to the back of her neck, nuzzling the wisps of hair that had managed to free themselves from the long braid that hung down her back. "Especially after last night."

He could weaken her resolve so easily and she had so much at stake. Knowing that, she turned to face him. "The harm?" She looked at his shoulders, grown even broader than she'd remembered. At his arms, tanned and muscled by the prairie sun and the weight of the task he'd set for himself. She looked at his hair, wild and unruly, waiting for her fingers to entwine, to pull his lips toward hers. She looked into his eyes, darkened with lust.

"The harm," she managed to say, "is that people will expect certain . . . certain behavior of us."

He smiled in a teasing way. "You mean they'll expect us to be civil toward each other? Or bicker from dawn to dusk?"

Exasperated, she said, "Don't pretend you don't know my meaning."

He nodded slowly, taking her image in as though it was his right. "You mean they'll think we should act like newlyweds."

"Exactly!"

"Gazing into each other's eyes. Sharing secret smiles. Looking for excuses to touch each other." He pressed his finger to her lips. "Each of us knowing the other's needs. Each of us craving to be satisfied. Is that what they'll expect to see?"

Fighting a longing so intense it frightened her, Katrina dropped the rag she had gripped so tightly and wrapped her arms around Justin's neck and blurted out, "Let's go back to Merriweather, Justin. Let's get married for real and go back where we belong."

He looked startled, unsure of himself, and yet he spoke as though he knew her idea to be a joke. "Are you admitting your affection for me at last?"

"No, I'm—" She stopped short as a curious look hardened his features and he stepped back. "Of course I have affection for you, Justin. But affection isn't—well, it isn't love."

Folding his arms across his chest, he asked, "Then why did you just suggest we get married?"

Flustered by the change in him, she stammered, "I—I don't know exactly. I suppose because Momma told me that love is not always a guest at the wedding, but that it becomes one of the family in time."

He walked across the room and took his hat from the nail on the door. "Oh, I get it. You don't love me. You might in time. But at least you like me enough to . . . to what? Take you back to Merriweather? Give you all the benefits that come with the illustrious Barrison name? Move you into the big house where there are floor-to-ceiling windows, real glass. Where someone else does the cooking, the cleaning, the sewing?"

"What is the matter with you? Why are you talking this way to me?"

"What way? I'm just bringing everything out in the open, the same way you do."

She couldn't see a spider, but there had to be one around here somewhere, a big one. Because she and Justin were about to have a big fight. She knew it.

"Don't you dare talk to me as though I am above hard work. For five years I worked in your household. I'm the one who washed the windows, waxed the floors, and polished the marble."

"But you didn't like it, did you?"

"I did what I had to do for the welfare of my family. I had no choice."

"A person always has a choice."

"My family needed the wages I earned."

"Ah, but once you became my mother's companion, you didn't have to clean and scrub, did you? All you had to do was sit with her, read to her, pen her correspondence. You liked that a whole lot better than scrubbing, didn't you?"

"What are you saying?"

"Only that you found a way to better your circumstances. You used a Barrison."

She gasped at his mean words while inside her heart something fragile died.

Justin didn't stop. "You're willing to do it again, too, aren't you? One way or another, you need to marry a Barrison to lead the rich life you want back in Merriweather. And you don't care if it's me or Richmond."

"You can't possibly believe that."

He opened the door. The strain in his voice spoke of his own torture. "I have to believe it. It's the only explanation that makes sense."

15

Standing on the section line, a sheet of canvas stretched over his and Pius Pettibone's head to protect them from the rain, Justin looked out at the quarter next to his, a prime piece of bottomland.

"Son, you look like you didn't know it was fixin' to rain. Didn't you check the sky last night? I told you, a moon with a circle always brings water at her back."

"I'll know next time."

"Sure you will. You're doing fine. Go on and take yourself a deep breath. Lift your head to that sweet rain and smell that dirt. That's *your* dirt. All yours." Pius let his half of the canvas go and rubbed his knees as though they'd stiffened on him. Lifting his head to the rain, he said, "Most times I'm a believer in getting out of the rain so that every single solitary drop makes it to the ground, but not today."

The rain wasn't much more than a sprinkle now, too little to do the ground much good. Justin dropped the cloth and stared straight ahead. A blanket of soft green prairie grass stretched across a hundred and sixty acres of fine flat farmland. With a creek that would give water for cattle and a thick stand of cottonwoods for shade, this was a prime quarter of land.

Pius continued, "Eyeing that piece of bottomland, ain't you?"

"I asked around town before I scouted out a quarter. The Rhinedollar woman told me this one was taken. I didn't even ask when I got to Aberdeen. If I had—"

"That's an old trick. Likely, she and her man are saving to buy it themselves. That or she's protecting it for somebody else. Now that's a known game."

"I know I've got to have a lot more than one quarter if I want to make it out here. And this is the quarter I want next."

"You're a hard worker, boy, I can tell, but you oughta concentrate on what you've got first. You'll have all this land plowed and seeded and that place of yours proved up in no time. And then she's all yours. Why, look at how much you already plowed these last few days with that single-bottom of yours."

Justin looked at the wide expanse of turned earth. "It took me all day to plow two acres. It's your big double-bottom that's making the difference: five acres a day versus two. If I can impose on you for another two weeks, I could turn over enough sod to do some serious planting come spring. I can't stand the thought of waiting another year. I can't afford to."

"You ain't imposing, son. I'm happy to help."

Justin thought of how most homesteaders could do nothing the first year but erect a house and plant a truck garden. But they didn't have neighbors like Pius Pettibone, who had nine hardworking sons and nearly every piece of modern farming equipment money could buy.

Justin shook his head. "How's a man supposed to make it out here by himself?"

Pius scratched his whiskers. "Well, I got only three things to say about that. Number one, if the truth be known, sod-bustin' ain't work to me. I get out there on that breaking plow, driving these six draft horses of mine, and damn if I ain't the king of the prairie. Number two, ain't nobody does it alone out here, son, and don't you ever forget it." He sucked on his teeth. "And number three, you got a wife. You ain't supposed to feel alone."

Justin shoved his hands in the pockets of his overalls and turned his face to what was just a few scattered drops now. It had been several days since he and Katrina had spoken their minds so freely and wounded each other so deeply. Since then they'd been civil to each other but nothing more. There was no question in either of their minds now that she would leave as soon as the baby was old enough to travel. He might have a chance of patching things up with her if he agreed to go back to Merriweather, but one look at a boundless sea of prairie grass swaying in the breeze, one look at a sky broad enough to roof a man's biggest dreams, and Justin knew he could never leave. Not if he were still to be a man.

He thought about what Pius had just said. "You ever think that any of your wives married you because you've got such a big spread?"

Pius pondered the question while he munched on a carrot he pulled from his back pocket. "Hard to say what's in a woman's mind when she takes up with a man, but Desiree LaFleur—she was my first wife, the one with them slim ankles—Desiree was a wild woman. And I'm sure it comes as no surprise to you that I'm a wild man myself. I met her in a bar in Wichita. Prettiest woman I ever laid eyes on. Tiny, like a doll, but, like I said, she was wild. We was both young, both looking for adventure. So we come up here to homestead. She got herself a quarter in her own name right next to mine. Built us a house, sod of course, half set on her land and half on mine. So together we had us two quarters right off. She give me my first five boys in five years."

"And then?"

"Died breaking a horse. It threw her. Trampled her." He sighed. "Then there was Dinah. Got her to homestead the quarter on my rear flank before we was hitched. Built a house half on her land and half on mine, same as I did with Desiree.

"Now Dinah, she was a castoff from a trapper headed up to Canada. They was laid up in Prosperity a few weeks storing up supplies. I seen her with him a few times. I always tipped my hat, 'cause as you well know, I am a gentleman. She turned beet red the first time, which surprised me no end. She weren't the most beautiful woman in the world, but she sure had a pretty smile.

"Now she was a woman of substantial size, which is why I could never figure how she saw fit to let that trapper beat on her the way he did. Anyway, the day they was to head north, she just up and walked off. Those that saw what happened say he come after her with a whip. She took one lash across her back and then she grabbed that strap in her bare hand, yanked him close and stomped on his foot so hard he screamed like he was dying, and then she let him go. Broke his foot, she did. Broke it all to hell. Then she walked all the way out to my place, come up to the door, and asked if I was looking for a wife. I was. So I took her. She give me the twins and two more boys on top of that."

"And then she died too?"

Pius didn't answer. "You know, one night she told me that trapper of hers, with all the money he got from his furs, he only bought her one pair of shoes in the eight years she was with him. Shoot, she was only ten when her folks traded her to him for a set of traps. That's when he bought her the first pair. Her feet did a lot of growing over the years, but not her shoes. She always said a man don't know agony till his feet hurt. So I bought her two new pair every year, one for work and one for fancy."

"That must have made her happy."

"I'd like to think so, but if she was really happy, she wouldn't have walked off the way she did . . . just walked off one morning saying she was hunting berries. Never come back. Left all her shoes, too. Lined up by the bed, nice and neat, her red mules first. They was her favorites."

"And there you were with nine kids."

He nodded. "Messed me up bad, that it did. But you know she just wasn't right in the head. There was signs all along. Still, I like to think I give her a few years of luxury. She deserved it."

"You ever hear from her?"

"Not directly. A woman matching her description was found floating in the river a hundred or so miles downstream, but I didn't even hear about that till long after. You know, son, sometimes a person—man or woman—has a hole that just nobody can fill. And Dinah, well, she had a hole in her heart big as Texas."

"What about Dulcie? How'd you wind up with her?"

The mention of Dulcie's name brought a big smile to Pius's face. "It's this modern age brought Dulcie to me. I tell you, when I think of the backwoods way my grandpappy, and my pappy too, had to live, and then I look at all the conveniences we got now, well . . ." He shook his head in wonder. "I went down to the telegraph office in Prosperity, sent a wire to the big newspapers in Boston, Massachusetts, saying I had a big spread, nine sons, and I needed a wife. I liked the idea of having a Back East wife. They all got class. And I'm a classy man myself. I just don't go for all them la-de-das. Anyways, a few months later I got a letter from her saying she was interested in my proposal. I sent her the fare and met her at the train. 'Course you know the rest."

"So Dulcie was the only one interested in your spread."

"Oh, no, son. She didn't want me for my land. Poor thing, she don't have a head for ciphers at all. To this day she don't know how much land I got—not that I ain't tried to tell her. I'm a modern man. I don't hold with keeping my wives ignorant. She wanted me for my boys. See, she grew up in an orphanage, no brothers, no sisters. She saw a ready-made family, and that's exactly what she wanted."

"So you gave one wife adventure, one luxury, and one a family. You're a regular humanitarian, you know that?"

"I just give 'em what they wanted, that's all. Makes them happy. Makes me happy."

"But what if you didn't have whatever it was each of them wanted? What would you have done then?"

Pius gazed at the horizon, shaking his head. "A woman always knows what she wants. Maybe not so she can speak it out loud even to herself, but somewhere inside, she knows. Now that doesn't mean I know what it is. No, sir, not by a long shot. But I do know this. If I didn't have whatever it was she wanted, she wouldn't have come to me in the first place. That goes for all three of my wives."

Not all that certain he wanted to hear the answer, Justin asked, "What if a man has what his woman wants, but he can't bring himself to give it to her?"

Pius chomped down on the last bit of carrot. "God almighty, son, I ain't as wise as Solomon."

"I still want to know what you think."

"Well, I guess it all depends on why the man is holding out. If he's got a good reason and he thinks what he's doing is best for his family, the man deserves a medal, 'cause doin' what's right can break a man's heart."

"What if he doesn't have a good reason?"

"Son, if you can't come up with a good reason for doing what you're being asked to do, you damn sight well better come up with a good reason for not doing it."

"You didn't answer my question."

Pius looked him square in the face. "Then he's a selfish son-of-a-bitch bastard who don't deserve a good woman by his side. There. That answer your question?"

Justin nodded.

Pius walked over to the six horses that stood hitched to the big plow he'd already raised for the drive home. One by one, he patted their damp hides. "There's just one other thing," he said to Justin as he climbed in the seat.

"What's that?"

"Sometimes no matter how hard you try, you just can't give a woman what she wants. She's got to find it for herself. You know what I'm saying?"

"You mean like Dinah?"

Pius held the reins in both hands. "Don't mean you can't have a good life in the meantime, though. Just means you got to be ready to let go when the time comes."

Justin nodded, thinking of Pius's words as the old man drove away.

The rain had stopped altogether, leaving the air heavy with the fragrance of rich black earth. Justin loved the way the sod, broken by the disk, curled over on itself, eager to soak up the sun. Now, thanks to Pius, his horses, and his plow, Justin had all of forty acres ready to receive his seed come spring. It wasn't much, but it was a start.

He couldn't give up and go back to Missouri.

Katrina wanted a home until the baby was born and old enough to travel. He could give her that, gladly. But if she was looking for that elusive something, and he suspected she was, then getting married and going back to Missouri with her wasn't going to make her happy. Not really. It sure wouldn't make him happy. Hell, she said right out she didn't love him. Maybe he really was a dreamer, but he wanted a wife who believed in him, a wife whose eyes would light up at the sight of him, just the way Dulcie's did at the sight of old Pius Pettibone.

So he'd do just as Pius suggested. He'd make the best of the time they had together. After the way he'd talked to her the other day, he'd have to apologize. He meant what he said about her using his family to better her circumstances. But he had no call to criticize her for trying to find a way to survive. Hadn't he done the same thing himself?

So when it came time for her to go, well, he wouldn't be able to stop her. In time, he would forget how sweet she looked, asleep in the bed beside him, how she instinctively sought the warmth of his body. He would forget. She was right when she said they wanted different things. He accepted that now.

He got back in his wagon and looked toward the soddy, like a child's wooden block on a blanket of grass. Damn it. He just wasn't ready to give up.

Katrina had dishes to wash, a stove to clean, and a pile of mending. Justin wanted her to come and look at his new cows. She told him she didn't want to, though she'd done exactly that while he'd been gone that afternoon.

He'd said he was sorry he'd yelled at her the other day. Sometimes he sounded just like his father, she realized. She didn't tell him that, but she suspected he knew.

He'd said the beans and cornbread she'd made for dinner was the best meal he'd ever had. He didn't have to lie. She knew she was a fine cook. She also knew that until they made a trip to town, she wasn't in a position to fix a decent meal. Still, he was trying to make amends and she would do well to remember why she was here. So she dutifully followed him to see his new purchases.

"These two reddish ones with the white faces are the beef cattle. Then there's the momma; she's a milk cow. And that's her calf. Pettibone got them for me from a man up in Bismarck. They aren't purebreds, but they're solid stock."

Katrina swatted the ever-present flies. "I thought you wanted to raise wheat?"

"I do. I will."

"So you will both farm and ranch? On the boat I heard men talk on the subject. They said a man must choose."

"I'm a wheat farmer first. But I plan to raise a few head of beef as well. My land is rich enough."

"Every man thinks of his own copper as gold."

Either ignoring her words or refusing to be riled by them, Justin walked over to the calf as it foraged in the stubbled grass. "The little one here needs a name. You have the honor."

Katrina shook her head. "No, thank you."

"Come on. I can't believe you haven't been running baby names through your head. Women in your condition do that." He took her hand and forced her to pet the calf's trusting face, not knowing that she'd done exactly that a dozen times that afternoon while he was in the fields.

She jerked her hand back. "My baby is not a cow."

"That's not what I meant and you know it."

He was trying to heal the wound. She was making sure to keep it open. Why?

"I have work to do," she said as she turned and headed for the soddy. "Cleanliness is the jewelry of a house. Even a house made of dirt."

That night in bed, despite the ecstasy that could be hers for the taking, Katrina turned on her side, away from Justin, and drew the sheet up to her neck. She'd been here less than a week, but it had been time enough to confirm what she already knew: she could never stay.

She could tell by the way Justin fidgeted this way and that, pulling the sheet with him, that he found being in the same bed just as disconcerting as she did. She hadn't asked him to sleep on the floor and he hadn't offered again. This was his house. It wouldn't be fair. But she didn't want to sleep on the floor either, not with the bugs and rodents. She decided to simply accept his presence and do her best to put it out of her mind. She'd slept next to Gretchen all her life. Having Justin next to her would be no different.

In the stillness she could hear him breathe. It wasn't familiar to her yet, not that it ever would be.

He turned on his side facing her and lowered the sheet away from her back. "The sheet is rough, I know," he whispered. "That's because it's new. I bought it when I came out here. It'll get softer with time. You'll see."

"And turn threadbare and fade." She could tell he had been bewitched by the prairie. It wouldn't happen to her.

He seemed to consider her comment, then lifted the long braid of her hair and stroked the paintbrush end along her neck and shoulders. "I know you don't plan to stay. But in the meantime, I thought we could—well, make the best of the situation."

"Best? Best for whom?" Unless a woman loved a man, letting him get close enough to make love was too close, much too close. She knew that now. She inched away to put distance between them. "I'm sorry, Justin."

He said nothing. In the dark she couldn't tell if he was angry, except that he didn't yank her hair or force her on her back. Instead, he gently released her braid and, after a moment or two, turned on his side away from her.

*　　*　　*

The next afternoon, after Justin worked in the fields and Katrina did what she could to get the soddy in order, Justin insisted on taking her for a ride in the wagon. She was suspicious of his enthusiasm, but she went willingly. After traveling for what seemed like forever beneath a scorching sun and a cloudless sky, he slowed the wagon to a stop.

"There," he said, stretching his arm in an arc over the vast emptiness. The horizon was so wide and low it distorted her perception and made her dizzy. "Have you ever seen anything like it? Nothing but prairie and sky."

He jumped from the wagon and helped Katrina down.

"Look at your feet," he said with awe in his voice. "You're standing on the floor of the sky."

The wild native grass, sparse and uninviting, swallowed her ankles, seeking to devour her. The hot dry wind that never stopped slapped her in the face. Standing next to Justin didn't help. Even together on this prairie, they were less than nothing.

"Look over there," he said. "Forty acres of straight black furrows just waiting to be planted. This time next year, this whole prairie will be covered in wheat—an ocean of gold. And one hundred and sixty acres of it is all mine." He pointed to the adjacent parcel. "And that's the next quarter I plan to buy."

With its wide creek and full stand of cottonwoods, it was a prettier piece of land than the one he had. But what did she care? Why did he persist in trying to share with her a dream she wanted no part of?

"One hundred and sixty acres," he said. "I know that sounds like a lot. It did to me when I first got here. But it really isn't. Out here, a man needs that much just to graze eight cows. That doesn't leave anything for growing wheat. That's why I'm going to buy that quarter as soon as I can. And another quarter after that."

Katrina was familiar with the lure of free land. Her

grandfather had left Germany for the promise of free land in Russia, for Russia had wanted her barren steppes settled. Russia had wanted her peasants taught the industrious ways of the Germans. The czar had promised the Germans free land, no taxes, no military service. But promises are easily broken.

She could understand a woman being forced to come here with her family. She could understand a woman being willing to stay for a short time. But she couldn't imagine a woman wanting to make this desolate place her home. She wanted to shout at Justin, to tell him he was being fooled, just as her father and grandfather had been, but she restrained herself. She didn't want to disturb the fragile peace they'd somehow managed to find.

He continued. "Right this minute, the United States of America would give me another quarter free just for planting a bunch of trees."

"Trees?" she snapped, no longer able to hold her tongue. "Out here?" Katrina waved her arms. "Even God hasn't seen fit to put trees out here."

"I didn't say I had filed a tree claim. I just said I could. I know how hard it is to grow trees on the prairie. I'm not ready to tackle that yet."

A thousand frustrations loosened her tongue. "Why this monotonous prairie, Justin? Why did you pick this place? It has nothing of beauty, nothing."

He seemed to choose his words carefully. "I want something more than to be free of my father's tyranny. I want to settle this land. To help build a new community—one with schools and churches. To have my own home unencumbered by debt and mortgage. That's what I want."

"A home in the ground?"

"For now, yes. But not forever."

"Oh, Justin, how many times did I tell myself that if only you would settle down, we . . . we . . ." Too confused by her feelings for him to complete her thought, she snapped at him. "And here you are. Settled down, like a rodent. When you could have had a fine home, with wood and marble throughout, and library windows from floor to ceiling."

"You mean *you* could have had such a fine home."

She met his stare. His words stung, but they were true. A week of living in a sod house had made her see she was every bit as materialistic as Justin had said. What was it her mother used to say? Love is not a necessary ingredient at the wedding of two people matched by a coupler, for it is the coupler's business to know the bride and groom. But if a girl insists on making her own match, she must follow one simple rule. She must love the man first, not his fancy house. Katrina knew her mother had meant well, but this was one time when her advice did not apply.

The unspoken implication that she could have—would have—married Richmond snuffed out Justin's enthusiasm and clouded Katrina's thoughts even further.

Justin walked out onto the prairie, leaving Katrina by the wagon. She saw only his back, but she knew he was searching for answers, looking at another dream. And she could tell by the way he shoved his hands in his pockets, by the way he gazed up at the sky, that the prairie had spoken to him, just as her dense forests had always spoken to her.

He came back with a sad but peaceful look on his face.

"Katrina, you came here asking for shelter. I thought if I gave you that and more, you'd take it. I see now I was wrong. I should never have tried to force you to accept what you don't want. I won't do it again." He offered her his hand and helped her into the wagon. When he'd climbed up beside her, he added, "Stay as long as you want. Go when you want. I don't care anymore."

In silence, they rode back to the soddy.

*   *   *

That night, as Katrina sat on the edge of the bed braiding her hair, Justin went out to his wagon and brought in a bedroll. He unbuckled the straps and spread the canvas tarp on the floor by the door.

"Justin?"

"It's best this way," he said, with a decisive edge to his voice. "We both need a good night's sleep, and neither one of us is getting it. At least I'm not."

She stood. "Then I should sleep on the floor. This is your house."

"If you were going to stay here, I might suggest we take turns, but you aren't staying. You are my guest. You will sleep in the bed."

Admittedly relieved to be spared sleeping on the floor, Katrina slipped beneath the sheet and quilt. She'd also been spared sleeping with Justin. Though the bed felt unusually cold, as it would from now on, she knew it was for the best. Perhaps now at least Justin would get a decent night's sleep. She doubted she would. Not as long as she was on this prairie.

"I must have one thing however," Justin said as he walked toward the bed. "A pillow."

"Of course," she said, eager to show her appreciation. "Here, take both."

"I just need one." He reached for the pillow he usually used, then paused and took Katrina's instead. "Good night," he said.

He turned down the lamp. In the darkness, Katrina could hear him groan slightly as he settled himself on the bedroll. For a moment she thought he might punch the pillow, taking out his frustration at her on the object that carried the scent of her hair, her skin.

Instead, she heard him inhale, as she had just drawn his essence from the pillow she now clutched close to her heart.

She listened as his breathing deepened and he fell asleep.

Hard and monotonous, those were Katrina's days, but she didn't complain. She'd get up every morning at four to fire up the stove and brew a pot of coffee. While Justin tended the stock, she'd fry a few slabs of bacon Justin had bought from Pius and make a pan of cornbread. She longed for a few nuts and some fresh fruit, not just for herself but for Justin.

He worked hard too. With a jug of water in hand, he'd leave right after breakfast to plow. Katrina would set out for the open prairie, where she filled her apron with the cow chips she used along with dried corn cobs for fuel. There was a vein of shingle coal in a washout about two days away. Pius's boys went there at regular intervals. Justin said he'd buy more coal from them before winter set in. In the meantime, thanks to the Pettibone herd that had roamed the area for years, the dried manure was free and plentiful and burned just as well as wood, or so Justin said. She'd worn gloves the first week but not anymore.

Washday took half the week, pumping, hauling, heating the water, then soaking, scrubbing, rinsing, and drying the clothes that always needed mending. When she wasn't washing clothes or cooking or baking or tending cows, she was cleaning.

Every morning she methodically dragged the kitchen table outside. It was the only thing on which she could air the straw ticking, and with bedbugs dropping from the ceiling every night, she insisted the ticking be aired every single day. She found nests of bugs in the walls. One by one, they would have to be worked out with a stick and stomped to death before she would feel comfortable.

Then she'd sweep the dirt floor. Justin had fashioned a

broom of sorts from a cottonwood branch and a bunch of local grasses. Hardly the best broom she'd ever used, but for sweeping a lumpy black dirt floor, it worked fine. Still, no matter how carefully she swept, chunks of dried mud always gathered in the corners.

True to his word, Justin didn't pressure her about staying. He didn't try to make her see the prairie as something other than the desolation it was. The only thing that made her work bearable was knowing she was earning her keep, knowing she was slowly but surely turning Justin's soddy into a home, and knowing next summer her stay would come to an end. She would go back to Merriweather with her story of being widowed. She would help Gretchen with the bakery. She would tend her parents' graves. She couldn't even consider the thought of her child being forced to grow up on this lonely prairie, not knowing his background. Thinking of her family filled her eyes with tears. Fortunately, the hot wind dried them.

Two long weeks had passed. One day she was rolling up her sleeves; the next she was wearing her shawl. If September fought so hard to hold on, surely winter on the prairie was something to be feared. According to Pius Pettibone, a thunderstorm before noon any day in September guaranteed a winter of heavy snow. Katrina didn't know about that, but she did know that a rolling thunder in the fall meant a hard winter. She'd heard far-off thunder twice this month.

Today, however, was beautiful, the sun warm, the wind little more than a gentle zephyr. Katrina had pulled her chair next to the window to take advantage of the light and sat mending the limp flour sack in her lap. Her fingers moved in a slow, rhythmic, mindless fashion, over and under, over and under, as she darned a hole to extend the old sack's life. As she found herself doing more often than not, she let her thoughts drift back to a time and place more pleasant, a life and future more secure. Absorbed in thought, she didn't look up when Justin came in from milking.

But she smelled the perpetual odor of sour milk that clung to his clothes. She heard the water as he poured it into the basin and heard the sloshing as he scrubbed his face and hands. She pictured the dirt he'd leave behind on the clean towel.

He dipped the long-handled ladle into the barrel of drinking water and drank it down in one long draw. "God, but it's still hot out there."

Katrina raised her head. The look in her eyes must have betrayed her, because he said, "You look an ocean away. What is it?"

She lifted the flour sack as though it would explain everything. "The feathers." Realizing her answer made no sense, she shook her head and added, "I was thinking of my last winter in Neudorf."

He slipped his hand under the dish towel that covered the cornbread left from breakfast and grabbed a square. "What about it?"

"I was thinking of the long winter afternoons in Momma's warm kitchen. They were wonderful days. All the young wives in the village would gather there to make feather pillows. And to gossip." She paused, suspecting that evidence of the bittersweet memory had reached her eyes. "You should have seen it. Everyone laughing. Every table and every bench covered with goose feathers."

"Why your mother's house?"

"I suppose because she always gave good advice." She glanced toward the window while the memory came to life. "Momma said at fourteen I was old enough. So that last winter I sat and stripped the fine feathers from their brittle stems and stuffed them into a pillowcase, just as the young wives did. Now and then someone would say something that made the others giggle. I didn't understand, but that was all right. I felt so grown up just being there." She sighed, reliving the feeling of comfort. "In just a few hours a haze of white down filled the air. It swirled with every movement and floated on our laughter. And then it settled, covering every surface with white."

Justin wiped the cornbread crumbs from his lips and rested his arms on the table. "I've got some writing paper. I think you ought to send a letter to your sister."

"Gretchen? Why?"

"Because you're homesick. A man would have to be blind not to see that."

Katrina clamped her fists around the flour sack. "No. I may be homesick, but writing to Gretchen is not the cure." She looked away, ashamed she hadn't told him before, ashamed to have to tell him now. "Gretchen wants nothing to do with me."

Justin rolled his eyes. "And my brother is my best friend. Come on, Katrina, everyone in that town knows how devoted you and your sister are to each other."

"Were," she said. "Though I hope to one day gain Gretchen's forgiveness."

As though he'd been a fool not to have seen it before, Justin said, "She blames you for nearly losing the bakery, doesn't she?"

Katrina said, "And for leaving her. If not for my selfish—"

"Don't say it." Justin got up from the table and walked to the far side of the room. He glanced at the bed. "If I hadn't made love to you, if I hadn't made you pregnant, you could have—would have—married my brother. You'd have a big fancy house. And you'd still have Gretchen."

She saw the torment in his eyes, but she couldn't lighten his burden any more than he could lighten hers. She straightened in her chair. "Do I want to be close to my sister? Yes. She's the only family I have. Do I want a big fancy house? I know you won't believe this, Justin, but I don't want a fancy house. Those are your words. I want a sturdy house. A safe house. One with wooden floors and a roof that doesn't leak."

Despite the skeptical look on his face, she continued.

"Back in my village, a house stayed with the family, so that even a hundred years later a stranger could ask for the Swann house and everyone would know where to send him. Sometimes the house passed to a brother and his family, or a cousin or a nephew, but always it would be owned by a Swann. Such was the custom. Is it that way on your prairie? No. People here care not for roots and heritage. They stay long enough to claim the land, then sell it and leave. I heard the stories on the boat."

"That's what some do, yes, but not all. Not even most. The prairie is a frontier. It's not settled yet, but it will be. I'll admit not everyone is cut out for this kind of life, but there are trainloads of Germans, Norwegians, Swedes, and God knows who else coming to this prairie every day."

"They, too, are chasing a dream. When they see it for what it is, they will leave."

"No. These people are digging in, not selling out. A hundred years from now they might not have a house to pass down but they will have land, lots of it. I can assure you of that."

"Is that what you plan to leave for your child? Land that no one wants?"

"I will leave him land a king would want."

Shaking her head, she returned to her sewing. Bone-weary, she didn't have the energy to argue with him. Besides, there was no point. He had his wild dreams. She had her practical plans.

*　　*　　*

The very next day, Justin made an announcement.

"It's time we took a trip to Prosperity. We're running low on staples. I've got some business to tend to. And I imagine you'll want to pick up a few personal things at the general store. I know you want to buy something other than beans and cornmeal."

Katrina's excitement caught him off guard, as did the light in her eyes. "Yes! I want to get some nuts and some fruit. Fresh vegetables, too. Coffee and sugar, of course. And I need some cotton thread, some yarn, knitting needles, sewing needles, fabric."

"There's paper in the cigar box on the shelf. Make a list. We'll head out first thing tomorrow morning, soon as I tend the animals."

"I'll pack a big lunch and a nice supper."

Justin was glad to see her smile for the first time in so long, but disappointed at how eager she was to get away from his homestead.

16

As excited as she was to be going into town, Katrina couldn't stop agonizing over the words she'd poured on paper the night before. Now, with Justin down the street on business, she brushed the dust from her sleeves and looked around the Rhinedollar General Store, in which she'd met the proprietor just two long weeks ago. Crude wood plank shelves groaned under the weight of assorted supplies, tins of coffee and tea, hat boxes, boots, and farm implements. She inhaled the aromas of ripe cheese and salted meats and feasted her eyes on a rope of fine fatted sausages. Here, and only here, did the name Prosperity seem to apply.

Her entrance did not go unnoticed by the two women studying a bolt of calico.

Nadine Rhinedollar squealed with delight and came rushing over, her fingers poised in midair and rubbing together. "Well, if it isn't Mrs. Barrison! Good morning to you. Come right on in. Why didn't you tell me you was

Mr. Barrison's bride that day you come in here? Why, if I'd known . . . well, no sense chewing on that now. Come on in here."

"Good morning," Katrina said and stepped closer. She handed Nadine the long list of groceries she and Justin had prepared and a shorter list of personal items. *Mr. Barrison's bride.* Katrina hated having to go along with this sham. She had already been run out of one town because of a scandal. She didn't know if the same social standards applied in the wilds, but if they did, and if people here knew the truth, she would have to pray they weren't as strict.

"Godfrey!" Nadine called to the back room. "We have a grocery list. A long one."

A portly, pudding-faced man appeared from a room behind a curtain and took the paper. Katrina almost missed the wide smiles he and Nadine shared, for her attention was drawn to the small, slender, sweet-faced woman standing by the calico.

"How do," the small woman said. "I'm Mrs. Pius Pettibone. Dulcie. I was hoping we'd get to meet before winter set in."

Katrina smiled. "Me too. I've wanted to thank you for all you and your husband have done for us."

"My pleasure," she said.

Nadine drew both women's attention to the fabric on the counter. "I just know you ladies have an eye for quality. This is the costliest bolt of calico on the shelf. Twelve cents a yard. Here, let me tempt you with a closer look." She flipped the bolt several times to produce a generous length for the women to observe. "Now, Mrs. Pettibone, I just know those boys of yours would love to see you in this pretty blue. How 'bout you, Mrs. Barrison?"

Katrina was distracted. So this was Dulcie Pettibone, wife of that irritating old skinflint who thought it shameful for a woman to have two dresses. Katrina couldn't imagine the woman scrubbing and cleaning in either the bright yellow gingham she was wearing or the rich cornflower calico on the table.

Dulcie slipped one hand under the fabric and fanned it out. "It's mighty exquisite, but way too costly. I don't know as I should."

Nadine grinned as though they were playing a game of some sort and the next move was hers. "I'd be happy to put it on your account."

Dulcie considered the offer for scarcely a second. "Well, all right. Eight yards then. I don't need any more dresses, but that's enough for two or three shirts for my two youngest. They do like pretty colors."

While Nadine cut the cloth, Dulcie turned to Katrina. "My mister's spoke of you a hundred times. We and the boys sure think the world of your man. We'll have to have you over to dinner some Sunday. You're not but four miles from us. Nothing but buggy distance."

"We'd be pleased," Katrina said. She felt like a married woman, making social plans with the neighbors. No doubt it was the idea of having such a nice woman as a neighbor that instantly lifted her spirits. It couldn't be the idea of being Justin's wife.

Katrina found herself staring, unable to get over how poorly her expectations matched the reality of Dulcie Pettibone. From what Pius had said, Katrina expected some hulk of a workhorse, not this slightly built woman who stood barely five feet tall. At one time her heart-shaped face must have been very pretty, without the rough patches on her cheeks, without the web of fine lines around her lips. Her bright blue eyes held a natural twinkle; the corners fanned with laughter. Katrina guessed her age to be somewhere around thirty, but it was hard to tell.

Realizing how starved she'd been for the company of

other women, Katrina listened intently to Dulcie's every word.

"More than this world, I wanted to come right over and meet you when you arrived, but with nine younguns to tend to . . . well, now that you're married, you'll find out soon enough." She smiled broadly.

Katrina was surprised. She didn't think she showed much yet, so Justin must have said something to Pius and Pius must have told Dulcie.

A wistful look filled Dulcie's eyes. She whispered, "I lost the little one I was carrying. That's the true reason I couldn't come over the day my husband brought the cattle. It was my first."

Katrina felt the woman's sorrow and wished she could do something to soothe the pain. At the same time, she was reminded of how dangerous it was for a woman to bear a child and how hazardous it was to be delivered on the prairie. She shuddered to shake her fear, but it held fast.

Just then, Nadine appeared from the back room carrying a small but bulky book. "Excuse me," Katrina said. "Is there any mail from Missouri? For me, I mean."

"No, no mail from Missouri, but I've got the new Sears, Roebuck catalogue. You'll be wanting your own, I know, but until then you can order from mine. So make out your wish lists, ladies."

Setting the book on the counter next to the calico, Nadine looked directly into Katrina's eyes. "Mrs. Barrison, I know I can get the true story from you. Word has it your husband just made a sizable addition to his livestock. Two Herefords and one Guernsey with a calf. Did I hear right?" Before Katrina could answer, she added, "I see in the Vermont farm journals that purebreds are the only way to go these days. All anybody out here has are mongrels."

"Ours are not purebreds," Katrina said.

"Oh," Nadine said, clearly disappointed. She pressed.

"Someone told me he's down at the livestock pen right now with Gilbert Bodine, fixin' to buy half a dozen hens. Maybe more. He's a right smart man, that husband of yours. Until you get your fields planted, and I don't expect that will be for a while, you'll still have butter and eggs to sell. And that's a woman's pin money: butter and eggs. You got a good churn, don't you?"

"An old one, but it will do," Katrina said, amazed at Nadine's knowledge of Justin's activities. Amazed and slightly annoyed.

"Well, I want you ladies to know I just got me a new shipment of Miss Laurieann's Lotion. It's from Paris, France, and it has a secret ingredient. A bottle on account for each of you?"

Looking at her weathered hands, Dulcie said, "I suppose I shouldn't, but—oh, well, yes. The boys do love the way it smells. And I need three blue flannel shirts. Give me a fourteen, a fifteen, and a sixteen neck; one of those baseball mittens, something for dyspepsia—Mr. Pettibone and three of the boys are plagued—and I think I'll order one of those ice cream freezers from the Sears catalogue." She studied the tall candy jars. "And ten red peppermint sticks. My boys just love peppermint."

"On your account, right?"

"Yes, that'd be fine."

"And how 'bout you, Mrs. Barrison? A bottle of Miss Laurieann's?"

"No, not today."

"Well," Dulcie said with a sigh, "I hate to see this visit come to an end, but I've got to head on over to the wheelwright and see if he's got that wagon wheel fixed. This time of year, the men are all out in the fields, so that leaves me in charge of such things. Now that I think on it, except for the dead of winter, they're always out in the fields." She gave Katrina a bright smile. "Tell your mister to bring you by real soon." With that, Dulcie left the store.

As Katrina straightened her black shawl and adjusted her kerchief, she felt Nadine's discerning eye.

"I don't know what the sun's like in Missouri, Mrs. Barrison, but out here you need a bonnet. Something with a brim. That kerchief won't do a thing for blocking the sun. You'll be squinting those big brown eyes of yours, cutting lines in that pretty face. Tsk, tsk, tsk. If I was you, I'd protect my assets. You sure you don't want some of Miss Laurieann's Lotion? It's from Paris, France. Only fifty cents."

Katrina looked down at her own hands. Always dry and sometimes red, they looked far worse than they ever had. She imagined what the prairie sun could do to a baby's skin. Thank goodness she would be leaving this place next summer.

"No, just the items on my list."

Nadine read quickly. "White cotton thread—soft. Knitting needles—small. Hmm," she said with a knowing smile. "Oh, I'll bet your mind is full of more important things than a bottle of lotion. Let's take another look at this calico, shall we?" She waved her hand across the waves of bright blue still on the counter. "I know exactly how to handle that 'inconvenient' dress problem you'll be facing shortly. If you can't work a needle yourself, there's a seamstress downriver in Yankton who can whip up a dress that's as wide and comfortable as you could want. We can send her your measurements and the cloth. I know you'll be wanting the best."

Katrina stood dumbstruck.

"And," Nadine continued, "you simply must view the newest in baby carriages in the Sears book. They're showing upholstery in peacock blue, Nile green, and pomegranate. You'll need a new wardrobe and a layette and all—and you don't have the luxury of time. Looks like you've got a March, maybe an April, mountain growing there."

"Please!" Horrified to find her condition discussed so freely, Katrina pressed her fingers to her temples, pinpointing the headache that had suddenly affected her. She studied the floor as she mumbled, "How did you know?"

Nadine whispered, though there was no one else in the store. "Let's just say word gets around."

"Oh."

Nadine opened the catalogue to the baby carriages. "Come on, now, Katrina. Can I call you Katrina? Lift that chin of yours and thank the good Lord you've passed the danger months. Cleophee Yucker's the local midwife and she's every bit a jewel—a German woman like yourself. Birthed the last three of mine." She moistened her finger and flipped quickly through the pages. "Here. Have you ever seen finer cook stoves in your life? And each one is guaranteed in good faith."

Katrina couldn't believe how relieved she was to see Justin come through the door.

Nadine began to scold him. "Now, Mr. Barrison, why can't you be like some other husbands round here and linger a spell down at the Silver Spur Café? I was just showing your missus the latest in cook stoves."

"We have a stove." Justin offered his arm to Katrina, then asked Nadine, "Is my order ready? I've got my wagon outside."

Nadine called down the basement to her husband, then spoke to Justin. "Godfrey is bringing it up right now." She smiled. "I suppose you newlyweds are eager to get back to your little love nest. Setting up housekeeping can be such a joy for young folks in love."

Katrina remembered her warning to Justin that if he told people they were married, people would expect the actions of a couple in love. She was sure he remembered, too, when Nadine looked furtively left and right.

"I can't tell you how many times I've had to explain to

folks that the two of you were married back in Missouri. Those men down at the livery—you know what gossips they can be. A pretty woman comes into town, don't give her right name, and asks directions to the home of the most eligible bachelor in these parts and—well, you can just imagine the stories they concocted. You probably don't even remember, but you used another name when you took the wagon. Swann, I think it was. Your maiden name?"

"Yes."

"I thought so. Takes a woman awhile to get used to the change."

"It does."

Nadine make a point of looking at Katrina's hand. "Nice you could afford a wedding ring right off. A lot of folks can't."

Katrina felt Justin's instant reserve. Before leaving the soddy, she'd slipped on the ring Richmond had refused to take back. Now that she and Justin were in agreement on her leaving, she didn't think he'd mind her wearing the ring. After all, a wedding ring did make their lie of a marriage look more convincing.

"But I set them straight," Nadine said. "Right off." She looked as though she expected Justin to say thank-you.

"Some people should mind their own business," he said.

Nadine eyed him suspiciously. "Don't tell me you two have already had a spat." Before he could answer, she added, "I hope you're making allowances for her delicate condition. You want her well rested when the time comes."

Justin sighed. "We'd like to get back before sundown, if you don't mind."

"Well, of course you do," Nadine said. "And here I am jawing away your time." She yelled over her shoulder. "Godfrey, you hurry up down there!"

Running her finger down the list of items by the register, Nadine said, "That was a mighty big order. I hope that doesn't mean we won't be seeing you two next month. I was just telling your missus I'd be happy to open an account for you."

"I'll pay cash."

"Cash it is."

Drumming his fingers on the counter, Justin seemed eager to leave. Katrina didn't blame him. All this talk about their being married had to remind him of two things: that Katrina never wanted to be part of such a ruse, and that come next summer she would leave. She wasn't about to change her mind, of course, but looking around the store, she thought of several things she could do to make Justin's home more comfortable. Then maybe he wouldn't regret letting her stay.

Nadine eagerly accepted Justin's bills and coins, and Katrina hid her surprise at the stack of bills Justin put back into his pocket. She had no reason to know how much money Justin had, but apparently he wasn't as poor as she thought. Good. She could make curtains for him, and a matching tablecloth. She'd make a ruffled skirt to go around the washstand. Hang a picture or two—pictures with trees. A rug would be nice too. A wood floor would be best to control the fleas, but, lacking wood, a rug would make all the difference. She'd talk to him about it and order a few things next month.

"You ready?" Justin asked.

"Yes, just as soon as I mail this letter." She pulled the envelope from her pocket and gave it to Justin, who smiled for the first time since he'd entered the store. He handed the letter, along with coins for postage, to Nadine Rhinedollar.

"Missouri?" Nadine asked as she scanned the envelope. "Gretchen Swann. Must be kin of yours."

"Let's go," Justin said.

"My sister," Katrina called over her shoulder as she followed Justin outside.

The wagon crawled along. Justin ran his thumbs along the smooth leather reins as he composed his thoughts. He didn't like seeing Richmond's ring on Katrina's finger. No. Not one bit. He knew, however, that he wasn't in a position to complain. It was his idea, not hers, to say she was his wife. He'd be the one to live with the wagging tongues when she left.

"Richmond's ring came in handy," he said.

She answered quickly. "He wouldn't take it back, I thought it wasteful to discard it, and I didn't feel right about selling it."

"Right."

They rode awhile longer in silence. He noticed how often she gripped the edge of the seat, no matter how slowly he took the horse. Her belly was growing every day. She had to be uncomfortable. All of which forced Justin to think of what he'd been avoiding, for uppermost on his mind was Nadine's comment about Katrina's delicate condition. He hadn't discussed the whole idea of being pregnant and delivering a baby with Katrina yet because he didn't know what to say. Women were supposed to talk to other women about such things.

The night his mother delivered Richmond, Justin had been sent to the empty carriage house with a jug of milk and a few cold bannocks. As usual, his father had been away on business. Several hours later, one of the women who was tending his mother had brought him a blanket and told him to find a pile of hay and go to sleep. If he wanted his mother to live through the ordeal brought upon her by the appetites of a selfish man, the woman had said, he'd better pray as if the devil himself was at his heels.

Justin had prayed. He had brushed away the hay so there'd be no cushioning for his bony knees, hoping God would recognize his willingness to suffer so his mother might be spared. But it had been a warm summer night, and the windows had been open to capture a breeze. He had heard his mother's screams.

He resolved now to do whatever he could to make Katrina's time an easy one. He'd see to it that she didn't do any heavy work. He'd make sure she ate plenty of food. With all the supplies they'd bought today, that shouldn't be a problem. And he'd see to it that she got a lot of rest. He'd also see to it that she got better acquainted with Dulcie Pettibone. But first, he'd make sure she knew he could provide for her needs and for those of his child.

"Did you get everything you wanted?" he asked.

"Oh, yes. I can't wait to make you a pot of sausage soup. Some nice chewy pumpernickel bread. A jar of pickled eggs. A crock of sauerkraut. I'll earn my keep, you'll see."

"You don't have to *earn* your keep."

"I know, but I can accept your kindness easier if I can also give."

He knew what she meant. Out here, one man might hoe another's corn in exchange for plowing. Or plant potatoes in exchange for having his laundry done. Katrina wanted no strings, no debt, nothing that might pressure her to change her mind and stay.

"You've already done a lot," he said. "And I'm grateful. But I think you should ease up on your chores. I'll take the table out from now on. You let me know when you want water for clothes, and I'll haul that too."

"Justin, there's no need to coddle me. I feel fine."

"Maybe so, but I don't want you straining yourself the way you've been doing. I just don't think it's healthy. Not in your condition." As though she might misinterpret his intent, he quickly added, "Not that I don't appreciate all your work. I do. The house is always clean. My clothes are always washed and mended." He was stammering like a fool and couldn't stop. "I can't wait to see what you can whip up at the stove. Despite what Pius says, you already make a fine cup of coffee."

"*Danke*," she said, but the word sounded hollow. She looked away, as though she expected him to say something else, but he'd be damned if he knew what it was.

"With any luck," he continued, "this time next year I'll be killing dozens of roosters and filling up the larder with canned chickens. My root cellar will be full of potatoes and carrots and onions. Pius is sending one of his boys over tomorrow to help me enlarge the chicken coop."

Katrina looked behind her at the wooden crates loaded with flapping, squawking chickens, their white feathers flying. "I think you should have enlarged the coop before you bought the chickens."

"I never expected to buy this many, but Gilbert Bodine is selling out. He offered his pullets for a better-than-fair price. But cash on the barrel only."

"Selling out?"

He knew what she was thinking. Another homesteader who couldn't make it on the prairie.

"What happened?" she asked.

"His wife said she'd go back alone if she had to, but she refused to live so far from Pennsylvania, where all her folks are. So Bodine made a choice."

"A wise choice."

"Time will tell. He's walking away from three years of hard work. He's giving up his investment just when he's close to turning a profit—at least a modest one."

"Maybe he wants to give his wife what she wants for a change."

"I wonder what she'll think of him when he has to

accept charity from her relations till he gets his family settled in a place of their own and finds a job in a factory or a coal mine. That's about all he can do." Justin shook his head. "And neither a factory nor a coal mine is going to give Bodine the freedom he had on the prairie."

"Maybe having to live with relations won't matter all that much to Mrs. Bodine. Lots of folks do it. Maybe she'll even like it. She'll have womenfolk around for company and for help with the chores. Maybe she loves her husband enough to give up a bit of freedom for the sake of security— his as well as hers."

"Maybe she doesn't understand the importance of freedom."

"Maybe he doesn't understand the value of security."

Justin glared at her. "If she loved her husband, she'd stand by him while he builds his dream."

"Maybe it's a foolish dream he's chasing."

Justin squeezed the reins in frustration. "I suppose she should never have married him."

Katrina gripped the edge of the wooden seat as the wagon bumped along. "On that we agree." She paused. "I imagine poor Mrs. Bodine just didn't know how to recognize the signs."

Justin kept his gaze on the horizon. Only a few inches separated him from the woman he was trying so hard not to love. Only a few inches—nothing compared to the difference between what they were and what they could be.

Late the next afternoon, after Clifford Pettibone rode home, Justin called Katrina to come take a look at the new chicken coop. She'd spent the day boiling, scrubbing, and starching clothes with potato water she'd collected all week. Now she was retrieving them from the scrub bushes on which she'd draped them to dry.

A dry, brittle branch scratched the back of one of her reddened hands. She winced and pressed it to her mouth. Her lips felt parched and scaly, her hand cold and water-logged. It looked as wrinkled as a prune. Her ring finger, choked by the thin band of silver, looked desperate for relief. She'd had every intention of taking it off when they got home from town last night, for she didn't like wearing it any more than Justin liked seeing it. But her hands and ankles had swollen badly and the ring wouldn't budge.

"Just a minute," she called to Justin.

"Leave it," Justin called when he saw her starting to lift the flour sack she used in place of a basket. "I'll get it for you."

He'd hauled the table outside that morning, though she told him she was perfectly capable. He'd carried the mattress out, too, and just after dinner hauled it all back in, telling her he didn't want her lifting anything heavy. He'd said he planned to help her with the laundry, too, and he was proving true to his word. Katrina smiled in spite of herself. Her poppa had always been that way with Momma.

Unfortunately, no amount of help from Justin or any-one else could give Katrina more energy, lessen her trips to the outhouse, or let her sleep better. More than once it occurred to her that if Justin slept next to her in bed, she would have his warm body to curl against. Surely then she would find peace.

Weary from the day's work and worried about the days to come, she trudged down the path that led to the out-house and the new chicken coop.

Fatigue had drained Justin too, though his eyes were still bright and his smile showed he was a long way from defeat. With a grand gesture, he waved his hand to pre-sent what he obviously considered an achievement. "Well? What do you think?"

Katrina looked at the wood and wire box, four times larger, and much sturdier, than the simple woven-wire cage he'd put up himself. Clifford must have been a big help. "It's looks to be a fine coop."

Justin beamed. "It is, isn't it?"

He reminded her of her poppa and how when they came to America he had announced that he would learn the skills of a carpenter. Instead, he had had to become a baker, forced to put his dream into the gazebo with its lopsided hearts and flowers.

Following Katrina back to the soddy, Justin hoisted the flour sack filled with clean clothes and brought it inside. "I'll put this on the bed for you," he said. "This is too heavy for you to carry." He tossed the sack on the mattress.

"Justin, I need three or four yards of cotton flannel to make some clothes for the baby. And some wool for crib blankets." Her loosened stays dug into her sides, reminding her of what else she needed. "And I'll need some fabric to make a new dress, or at least enough to make pieces to insert in this dress."

"Why didn't you buy those things when we were in town yesterday?"

"I didn't know how much money I could spend."

"You just write down what you need, I'll see that you get it." He took the long-handled dipper from the hook on the door and filled the cup with water from the rain barrel. He offered it to her. She took a sip, then he emptied it with one long swallow.

"Nadine said we can open up an account."

"I think we can manage some fabric without getting ourselves into debt with the Rhinedollars. You make a list. I'll give the money to Pius. That man goes into town more often than a thirsty drunk. With nine sons to work the ranch, he can take the time."

"I'd rather go myself, if you don't mind. There are some things I need to see in order to know how much I want."

"And you don't want Pius to take you, is that it?"

"I can make the trip myself. I would prefer it that way."

"No, that's just not safe. Maybe I can change works with Clifford and he can take you in. Not even Pius can afford to lose a solid hand this time of year, but I don't have a crop yet, so I'll fill in. I know the boy likes going into town. How would that be?"

"Don't you want to turn more land?"

"Missing one day won't make any difference. Not this year anyway."

"I don't think I would mind riding with Clifford."

"Good." Justin put two plates, two bowls, two mugs on the table. "Soup smells good."

"It's an old recipe. From my *Grossmutter*." Katrina removed the dish towel from the bowl of fresh carrots Clifford had brought over, folded it, and hung it on the board of hooks and nails Justin had built for her. He'd tacked up a calendar on the board as well, a makeshift calendar he'd figured on the back of an envelope. It was September 30. Less than six months from now she'd be cooing at little Kurt, or Hans, or Anna, or Flora. A few months after that and she'd be able to leave.

She felt an odd sense of regret. Justin wouldn't leave the prairie and she wouldn't stay, but at least they no longer argued about it. In the arguing, though, she had felt there was a chance to make a change. It struck her now just how completely Justin had accepted her decision. If she were to stay on the prairie, it would be of her own choosing.

Later, after she'd washed and wiped the dishes from the meal, and while Justin puttered just outside with his new hoe, Katrina grabbed the ends of the flour sack full of clean clothes and shook the contents on the bed.

She heard a vibrating buzz—like the tines of a pitch-fork hit with a hammer.

When she saw the spike of silver rattles in the middle of a gray-brown coil, she screamed.

The scaly head reared. Its forked tongue flicked in the deadly still air. Its unblinking eyes held her gaze.

Awash in a sudden sweat, she didn't hear Justin come in. Didn't see him grip the hoe and raise it. Didn't see him strike with lightning speed.

She saw the shattered clumps of garden dirt from his hoe soil her clean white sheets. Saw the splattered blood on her freshly laundered chemise, on Justin's clean shirt. Saw the severed body twitch. And twitch. And finally lie still.

She shuddered as he pulled her into his arms. With her head buried against his chest and her body held fast in his strong embrace, she could faintly hear him murmur her name, barely feel his lips kiss the top of her head. But nothing he did could still her trembling.

That night, lying fully clothed on the bare straw ticking, tucked in Justin's arms, Katrina stared into the blackness. With a morbid obsession, she relived the incident again and again.

What if Justin hadn't been there?

What if her baby had been on that bed?

17

Justin loved the wheat fields, the place where the wind met nature's abundance and a sea of heavy headed, once supple, green stalks undulated in waves of gold. Now it was time to harvest what seed, soil, rain, sun, and sweat had grown. By mid-October, the job still wasn't done. For two weeks, he and his neighbors had taken turns going farm to farm, helping each other cut, bind, and stack the wheat before it seeded and went back into the ground. Pius had the biggest reaper. Scoggins had the strongest team of horses, all nice and well-fed, not a sore-shouldered one in the bunch. Hemmeler provided the tools to fix anything. With countless acres of wheat ripening at the same time, changing works was the only way to harvest everyone's crop. Like all the other farmers, Justin kept a tally of the work he had done for each of them and the work each had promised him in return. He didn't have a crop of his own this year, but come next year he would, and it would be a bumper.

There was no uncertainty when he thought about next year. He still planned to stay. Even the incident with the rattlesnake didn't sway him, though it was clear from the way he held Katrina all night, stroking her hair, gently rubbing her shoulder, that he knew she was still afraid. She told him she could never forget what happened. He told her she shouldn't. He told her snakes were a part of the prairie. He told her to carry a stick and always walk with her head down. She said she couldn't wait to get away from here. The next night, because he said it was best for both of them, he returned to his bedroll on the floor. She didn't protest.

This particular morning, however, things looked a lot brighter. While the others were finishing up their coffee, Justin stood at the edge of Karl Hemmeler's wheat field and anxiously watched the sky. It was a good thing they were cutting today. A storm now could shatter the entire field, ruin a year's work. Next year, Justin would be just like every other farmer in the Dakota territory, worrying until his stand was cut, sheaved, and safely stacked.

He didn't know the migrant crew working for Hemmeler this season, but he knew his neighbors. They all had sons, healthy, strapping boys eager to be part of the harvest. Justin picked a few dry, bearded heads of wheat here and there. He rubbed the heads in his palms and blew off the chaff, then slowly chewed the grain, savoring the milky, nutty taste.

Justin wanted to share all this with his own son. He wanted to be there when his son picked up his first clump of soil and held it in his tiny hands. He wanted to see the light in his child's eyes when he smelled the dirt and grinned, to stand next to the boy when he plowed his first furrow and planted his first field. He longed for the day when he could say, "This is yours, son. All yours." But unless Katrina stayed out here with him, that day would never come, because he didn't want to share all this with just any woman. He wanted to share it with Katrina and *their* children.

Pius Pettibone caught up with Justin and slapped him on the back. Gazing at the clear morning sky, he said, "Paintbox blue. That's how my missus names that color." He gave Justin a look of mild reproach. "Son, I told Hemmeler same as I'm telling you. If you'd listened to me, you could have saved yourself a full night of worrying. You want to know if we're in for a storm, you study the birds. If they're eating more than usual, expect some turbulence. Pay attention to the flies too. They bite extry hard before a storm. I'm telling you, boy, this land's so flat you can see the weather coming two days away. You just got to learn to look."

A short while later, Karl Hemmeler gave the nod. "Stock your jugs, men, and let's roll out."

The scorching sun was halfway up the sky when Dulcie's wagon appeared in front of the soddy.

"You ready?" Dulcie called as she hopped down.

When Katrina appeared at the door, Dulcie inclined her head to the back of her wagon. "I brought three jugs of cool milk just hauled up from the well, fresh carrots, a crock of pickled watermelon rind, some cheese, and a big basket of fried cakes."

"I've got chicken stew, baked beans, pickled eggs, and pumpernickel rolls."

"My boys are going to love to hear that! They sure can eat. Here, let me help you. With food like that, those men are going to stand in line to change works with your man next year just for the chance to eat at your table."

Dulcie followed Katrina inside. "Well, I never!" Dulcie said with honest appreciation. "Will you look at what you've done."

Katrina had straightened things just so, draped one of the dresser scarves that had been her mother's on the top shelf. She'd washed and starched the limp remnant of lace

Justin had hanging above the window. Now it looked white as snow. She'd picked a bouquet of wild sage and filled a coffee can she'd set in the middle of the table. The lacy green-gray leaves and clean fragrance made the whole room look better than it ever had.

"I plan to make curtains too," Katrina said. "A matching tablecloth. A skirt for the washstand. And maybe a rug."

"You can come on over and use my machine—it's a Singer—any time you've a mind to. Makes sewing go a lot faster."

"If you're sure you wouldn't mind."

"I'd welcome the company."

Katrina told herself she fixed up the room for Justin's sake, but she had to admit it, creating such a transformation gave her a feeling of satisfaction.

She packed the dutch oven filled with chicken stew into a wooden crate and wedged it tight with flour sacks. She did the same with the jar of pickled eggs. Dulcie held a pillowcase open while Katrina filled it with rolls. "There," she said, indicating completion.

Dulcie looked hesitant. "I clean forgot dessert. What am I going to do? The men have got to have a sweet."

"I didn't forget," Katrina said with a hint of triumph. The most enjoyable part of preparing for this event was making Gretchen's famous sticky buns. Katrina had dozens of them, all swirled with cinnamon and drizzled with glaze. She took a large bowl from the shelf and lifted the red and white checkered cloth that covered it. "Think these will satisfy them?"

"They'll plant themselves on your doorstep and never leave."

"Care to try one?"

Dulcie took a bun and bit into the soft sweet dough. "Umm. If the recipe ain't a secret, would you pass it on to me?"

"Sure. It's my sister's creation. They're even better with pecans."

At the door, Katrina stopped, checked the ground for snakes, then stepped out. As she and Dulcie loaded the wagon, Katrina decided she'd write to Gretchen as soon as she had a chance and let her know her sticky buns were just as popular on the prairie as they were in Merriweather. Gretchen hadn't answered Katrina's first letter yet, but Katrina would not stand on ceremony, not when there was so much to lose.

Katrina noticed the lack of concern on Dulcie's face as she walked about. "Have you ever come across a rattlesnake?" Katrina asked.

"That I have. Mr. Pettibone told me about your encounter. You must have been scared something mighty."

"I'm scared every time I set foot outside. You are too, aren't you?"

"I sure am. Those devils can kill."

"Doesn't that ever make you think about leaving? About moving somewhere where there aren't any rattlesnakes?"

Dulcie gestured to the soddy, the wide flat prairie, the even wider open sky. "And leave all this?" She paused, then added, "'Course, I carry a stick when I'm about and I always walk with my head down. Come next August when they shed their skin you be extra careful. They're slow, then, but blind as bats. Strike out at anything that moves."

Katrina said no more. Was she the only one who saw the wisdom in being cautious?

A sharp pain gripped Katrina as she tried to step up into the wagon. She gasped and instinctively flattened her hands across her belly.

"You all right?"

Katrina nodded. "I tried to climb up too fast, that's all."

"I ain't so sure. You got a sudden washed-out look about you."

Katrina knew her washed-out look came from an ever-present fear even worse than rattlesnakes, a fear that she would miscarry, or be delivered too soon, or that her baby would be marked with infirmity or worse. Or that she herself might not come back from the black pain that overtakes women when they're put to the bed, a pain that for some is so bad it takes them from this world forever.

The pain passed. Knowing she was doing the right thing, Katrina said, "I think I'd better stay here and rest today. Please tell Justin—"

"I'll stay here with you."

"You can't. Everyone is counting on the food. Besides, I feel much better now."

"But I . . . I just don't know what I should do."

Having made the decision to stay brought its own sense of relief. "You go on," Katrina said with confidence. "I'll be fine. I know."

"Well, if you insist."

With all the plowing to do in late October, turning under the wheat stubble and readying the fields for next spring, this was hardly the time to spend the better part of a whole day visiting. But Katrina said yes eagerly when Justin offered to take her to the Pettibones. Over four months along now, she was showing good, though her work-dress and big apron still disguised her condition, at least she hoped it did. But at night, in her soft cotton gown, her belly's roundness was clearly evident.

Justin would sit her at the kitchen table while he stood behind her and rubbed her shoulders. Just as he did when she first met him, he spoke his dreams aloud. He couldn't wait to show her the town of Eureka. The first train arrived in July, and already people were clamoring for building sites to build grain elevators for all the wheat that was pouring in. He painted such an exciting picture. For a fleeting second she entertained the thought that she might want to stay.

That very morning, while she talked about the things she needed to buy at Rhinedollar's, Justin talked about the going price of wheat in Eureka.

"I don't know if you realize it," he said, as he helped her with her coat, "but with more and more factories and more and more people moving to the cities, farming isn't just a matter of subsistence anymore. It's business, big business."

With daily temperatures barely reaching forty now, Katrina already felt the cold. She bundled her knitting in a clean apron and kept her head down as she headed for the wagon. Baked by the sun, whipped by the wind, the once tender grass crackled under her feet. "I need things for the baby, Justin. Flannel for gowns. Cotton lawn for diapers—"

"I know," he said. "Don't worry. I've got ten dollars set aside for you to get all those things. Did I tell you they've already got a hotel in Eureka?"

"Two times already."

"Well, when I get that piece of bottomland, I'm going to put it all into wheat. Pretty soon I'll be hauling wagons full of it into Eureka. You'll see."

She listened to more of this talk as they rode along. She said nothing but nodded her head, for Justin was always one for grand visions.

The four-mile ride that Dulcie had called buggy distance took forever. Every few miles Justin had to stop the wagon while Katrina relieved herself behind a clump of prickly bushes as dry as tinder. She'd loosened her stays as far as possible and cut up one of the dresser scarves to add gussets to the side of her dress. If she didn't get more fabric soon, she'd have to cut up the sheet.

They continued for another hour, talking easily about

the new chickens, the calf Katrina had named Blossom, the turn in the weather, and always about the rising price of wheat. They sounded like a married couple, going over the day's events, planning out the week, looking to the future. Together.

Finally, Justin slowed the wagon. Katrina gasped at the sight ahead.

"That's the Pettibone place," he said. In one direction, countless stacks of dull golden wheat hyphenated acres and acres of dry, stubbled ground. In the other, hundreds of bright orange pumpkins lay scattered like a broken strand of beads.

As Justin took the wagon down, Katrina eyed the house. Flagged by a graceful poplar, its silver leaves shaking in the breeze, the Pettibone ranch looked fit for a king. There was a two-story lumber barn and a house made of logs. Buckets of purple-blue asters and coffee cans full of red geraniums graced the walkway. Katrina was ashamed of the envy she felt as she stepped on the porch.

Ushered inside by an eager Dulcie and the two youngest boys, Katrina gaped at the interior. "Justin, look at this!" There were four rooms, all small, but each had wooden floors and sparkling windows with starched blue curtains. The kitchen had two framed pictures of mountain scenes hung on walls of clean white plaster. The long table was covered in a flower print that matched Dulcie's apron. It was not the luxury of the Barrisons' grand house in Merriweather, but it was everything Katrina wanted.

"It's a handsome house, that's for sure," he said.

Justin didn't sound defensive, but still Katrina wondered if her praise for the Pettibones' home made him feel inadequate. On the chance that it did, she decided to keep her thoughts to herself or share them with Dulcie when the men were outside.

Dulcie took two matching cups and saucers from

shelves next to a stove that Gretchen would envy—a huge oven with a six-burner top and an overhead shelf, nickel-plated, all with more swirls and curlicues than anything Katrina had ever seen. It still radiated the heat and aroma of recent baking.

"I'm going to fix us some tea," Dulcie said. "You just sit yourself down and rest. How are you feeling these days?"

"As good as can be expected." Following Dulcie's instructions, Katrina settled herself on the delicate rose print cushion of a handsome rocker.

"Mr. Barrison, will you be joining us for tea?"

"No," Justin said. "I'm going outside to find Pius. I'll leave you two ladies to visit."

Before he left, he squatted down next to the rocking chair and placed his hand on Katrina's arm. "You sure you're feeling all right?"

"I'm fine," she answered, "just tired." His demonstration of affection was just for show. She knew that. But his concern was genuine. She knew that too. She found herself watching him when he walked out the door. He was a good man. He had learned a lot, grown a lot, living out here. As far as she could tell, he hadn't made any impulsive moves or rash decisions, just grand talk. Maybe he was changing.

"You two make a handsome couple," Dulcie said as she set a plate of gingerbread cookies on the table.

Because she suddenly realized how much she enjoyed the role she pretended, Katrina felt a sadness she'd never expected. Leaving wasn't going to be as easy as she'd once thought.

Later, after a second cup of tea, Katrina pulled her knitting from the sack she'd carried with her.

Wistfully, Dulcie eyed the six-inch white stockings. "So teeny tiny."

Katrina smiled. Thinking of her baby was the one thing that never failed to make her happy. Or afraid. "I'm hoping for a girl so I can embroider all sorts of birds and flowers and hearts and such on every piece."

"I thought all you German girls stitched the tree of life on all your fancies."

"Not on everything."

"I want to have me a girl one of these days too. I never had any brothers or sisters. Never had any children of my own either, for that matter. Clem, the youngest here—well, he was nearly three when I married his paw. I don't know as I'd know how to take care of a baby boy, what with all the—you know, differences."

Both women fell into an awkward silence, Katrina concentrating on her knitting, Dulcie on her teacup.

"I bet Mr. Barrison wants a boy," Dulcie said. "Men always do."

"I suppose," Katrina said. The question caught Katrina by surprise. She and Justin had never discussed the baby, not the way Dulcie seemed to think. Katrina had deliberately avoided the subject. It was for the best that Justin had no interest in the baby. If he did, he might try to stop her from leaving. Then again, if Justin could feel as tied to the child as Katrina already did, maybe he'd go back to Merriweather with her.

"You mean he hasn't gone around spoutin' about how he's gonna show his son how to rope and ride? How to plow a furrow straight as an arrow? How to tell when a storm's brewing?"

"I'm sure that's what he's thinking."

"Well, that's all Mr. Pettibone talked about when I was carrying."

"I'm sorry for your loss, Dulcie. It must have been hard on you."

"It was. Still is. But Mr. Pettibone—well, he was just an angel."

Katrina arched her brow at Dulcie's description.

"There he was, taking over my chores, waiting on me in bed. He tried to cook but all he could do was rustle up some eggs and flapjacks. The boys just loved it, though. Said their paw could do anything. Shoot. You know how it is when you get a good man. Well, of course you do. You got one of the finest men in these parts."

Justin *was* a good man. He'd given her exactly what she'd asked for: temporary shelter.

"So you'll be getting your visitor in March, did you say?"

"Yes, March." Nervously, Katrina fingered the tiny stockings in her lap, thoughts of being delivered never far from mind.

"You given any thought to moving into town as the time grows near?"

"No. I didn't think there was a doctor in Prosperity. Was I wrong?"

"No, not hardly. We only get a preacher once every four or five months. It's just—well, we could still be shoulder-high in snow, that's all. Travel ain't impossible, mind you. But it ain't easy either."

And what would she do if there was no one but Justin to deliver her? What if he went for the midwife and didn't get back in time?

"Ain't it queer," Dulcie said, "to be talking so free about babies and all?" She placed her palms on her nonexistent hips. "I just don't think the good Lord built me for having babies. They say you don't remember the pain, but—"

Squeezing the yarn till her knuckles turned white, Katrina blurted out, "I'm scared. I'm scared of having this baby out here." Her shoulders trembled as she bit her bottom lip, hoping the pain would somehow dispel her fears and restore her fragile equilibrium. "What if my baby dies? What if I die?"

Dulcie rushed over and knelt beside the rocking chair.

Covering Katrina's hands with her own, she said, "Oh, this is all my fault, going on like that. I'm sorry." Gently, she squeezed Katrina's hands. "You stop frettin' this minute. Cleophee Yucker don't live but six miles from here, and like I told you she's one fine midwife. She hardly ever loses either a baby or a momma. She'll take good care of you. And when your time comes, I'll be there with you if you want."

As though doomed to her fate, Katrina took a deep breath. "I'd like that," she managed to say. The fear inside, however, was not diminished.

"Good. Now you iron the wrinkles in that brow. I know there's places in the world where life's a heap easier, but, tell the truth now, can you imagine a place more satisfying? Why, you and your family are destined to be part of this country's growing up. Look at you. You and your husband already own your own home and your own land."

Eyes instantly bright, Dulcie continued.

"And just wait till next July. Nobody celebrates the Fourth like Prosperity. Every storekeep in town decks out his place in red, white, and blue bunting. The womenfolk cook like you won't believe. The men put on a rodeo. Some even do tricks. The Rhinedollars stock enough firecrackers to light up the whole sky, and of course every parent buys sparklin' sticks for their kids to wave about. Folks who can make music play for the big dance that night. We usually have at least three fiddles. For most of us that's the only time all year we make a new dress. Men who was in the war set out their uniforms, blue next to gray. And I'd be lying if I didn't admit sometimes there's a few hard words and usually a few tears shed for those who didn't come back."

"It sounds like a grand event."

"It *is*! But best of all, every store and every home flies Old Glory. Just a small flag, mind you, the kind on a stick.

Courtesy of the Rhinedollars. Only time they ever part with something for free."

Dulcie patted Katrina's hands again before she stood.

"You just wait till the Fourth. You won't be sorry you come out here. And by then, nothing and nobody could make you leave."

Dulcie's words brought back memories. She wasn't the only one who thought America's birthday was worth a giant celebration. Though Merriweather didn't have rodeos and barn dances, it did have firecrackers and a parade. Poppa always used to march. He'd hold his head high and puff out his chest and entice passersby to lay a wager that he couldn't name all the presidents, which, of course, he could. Katrina used to think his admiration for this country was to cover up his regret at having left the old, but maybe she was wrong.

Dulcie spread a clean dish towel on the table and carried over a good-sized bowl brimming with potatoes. She kept talking while she peeled. "The Rhinedollars dearly love to see Mr. Pettibone step over their threshold. They're letting him make time payments on anything he buys, everything from saddles and plows to windows and dishes. Even the inside privy."

"Time payments?"

"I hadn't heard of it before either. It's where you buy something that costs a lot but you only have to give a few dollars in the beginning and then pay a little every month until you pay it off. And you don't have to wait till you pay it off to get your purchase. You can get it that very first day if it's in the store, or the Rhinedollars will order it right away. 'Course you have to pay a little extra over time, for what they call interest, but Godfrey Rhinedollar says that's the way all the businessmen are doing things back east. He says it's the only way you can make your money work for you."

Katrina understood. "So instead of paying twelve dollars for a stove, you pay twelve dollars and get a stove and a privy."

"And store-made ruffled curtains, a rocking chair, whatever your heart desires."

More than ever, Katrina wanted to turn Justin's soddy into a home, a cozy haven just like the Pettibones' home.

She and Justin stayed there for the noon meal, an undertaking of grand proportions. Thirteen people crowded around the long kitchen table piled high with fried chicken and gravy, biscuits, potatoes, and carrots. There wasn't a left-over slice of pumpkin pie to be found. When the men and boys had all gone back outside to resume their chores, Katrina helped Dulcie clean up.

She looked out the window where the two youngest boys were raking out the barn, the long wooden handles nearly overpowering their small frames.

"Each boy seems so different." Katrina thought of Gretchen and wondered what it would have been like to have had seven more sisters. Seeing all the Pettibone boys at the table, their faces washed, their hands joined in prayer, the littlest one wanting to kiss Dulcie's cheek before he went back outside, Katrina came to a conclusion. Though she doubted life on the prairie would ever be good for her, it was a life that made some folks happy. She could see why some folks would want to stay.

Dulcie set the bucket of potato peels and table scraps by the door. "I'll have Elmer give that to the pigs. He's the fidgety one, always willing to do an extra chore. Merton wants to be a trick rider in a rodeo. 'Course at one time or another all boys want to be trick riders. Now Pitt, he won't admit it, but he likes to cook. Helped his father out a lot when I was laid up. You know, I don't know what I'd do without my boys."

"I know Clifford has been a big help to us. He's a fine young man."

Dulcie gave a sly grin. "Now let me query you on something. What do you suppose would suddenly make a dedicated young rancher look for excuses to go to town when he could be riding his horse on the prairie?"

"Clifford's in love?"

"With Amadee Ducheneaux. She's French. So was Clifford's mother, Desiree LaFleur. 'Course I never knew Mr. Pettibone's first wife, but I have met Miss Amadee. Prettiest little thing you ever saw. She ain't but sixteen and just barely. Jet black hair so smooth a bug would roll right off and pale blue eyes big as saucers. She's from back east. Her folks died and she come out here a few months ago to live with her aunt and uncle. And I'm telling you, Clifford don't want to talk about nothing, 'less it has to do with Amadee Ducheneaux."

"You sound worried."

Dulcie hesitated. "It's just I tell all my boys to keep the 'Thou shalt nots,' but sometimes I wonder if they're listening."

From the window Katrina could see Justin and Pius coming toward the house. She knew it was time to head for home. She said to Dulcie, "Justin said he would ask Mr. Pettibone if it was all right for Clifford to drive me into town one day soon. I need to buy some fabric."

"He'd love to. Give him a chance to show off to Miss Ducheneaux. I'd go with you, but this time of year I'm loading up that root cellar. That's my province. Potatoes, onions, carrots, squash, turnips—you saw the pumpkins, I'm sure."

"You had quite a harvest."

"My, yes, it has been a good year."

During the small talk of leaving, Katrina set a date for Clifford to take her to town and a date for her to come over with her new calico and use Dulcie's Singer sewing machine. Of course, Katrina didn't have any calico yet, but now she knew how to get it. The same way she'd get curtains for the window, a matching tablecloth, a skirt for the washstand, a picture or two of trees and mountains, maybe even a rug.

She mused at how strange men were at times. Justin prided himself on his skill with money, yet he never told her of time payments. She planned to do a lot with his ten dollars. Wouldn't he be surprised.

18

"I think a child needs a father."

There. The words were out. Justin had rehearsed them in his mind several times as he hoisted the bushel baskets filled with vegetables from the wagon and carried them down the steep steps to the root cellar. But practicing the words silently and saying them out loud were two different things.

Down in the root cellar, Katrina fastened the last rope of onions to the railroad spikes Justin had driven in the wall for hooks, then turned toward him. The instant her brow furrowed, he feared he'd made a mistake in speaking his mind so suddenly, but it was too late. Though he'd told himself a hundred times he had to accept Katrina's decision to leave when the time came, he couldn't make the resolve sink from his head down into his heart.

"I mean it, Katrina. I think a child needs both a mother and a father. I know we haven't talked about that, but I think we should."

He set the basket down on the hard-packed dirt floor. Skeletal trunks of cottonwood trees braced the earthen walls. Between them stretched the shelves he'd made to hold the endless bounty he envisioned as his future.

As his eyes adjusted to the dimness of the cellar, his heart sank at the expression on Katrina's face. "You aren't crying, are you?" he asked.

"Oh, no," she said, so sweetly it made Justin want to take her in his arms. Instead, he shoved his hands into his pockets. This was no time to push his affection on her. "I think you're right," she added softly. "A child does need both a momma and a poppa."

He was relieved, but when she didn't go on, he tortured himself with thoughts of how little his own family knew about showing love. No doubt Katrina was thinking that too and wondering if he could ever be capable of loving their child the way she already did. Nervously, he cleared his throat. "As you well know, my father didn't show affection to either me or Richmond, but I would not be that way. I would be different. I feel it important that you know that."

"You would be different—how?"

Having no answer ready, he turned his attention to the basket at his feet. He took several large potatoes from the basket and tossed them into the wood and wire box he'd made. "We've got enough vegetables here to last through the winter, thanks to Pius."

"Justin, how?"

He thought a moment. "I would take good care of him. I would walk with him when he had a bellyache or a new tooth."

"He would have to be sick to earn your affection?"

"No, that's not what I meant." He was about to say that he'd help to feed and change and bathe the baby, but then he looked at his big calloused hands and thought of how rough they'd be against a baby's tender skin. Instead, he said, "I don't know if I could sing him a lullaby, but I could tell him stories, and I could teach him about animals, show him how to ride, how to take care of himself."

Katrina's voice sounded even softer, farther away when she said, "I think you would make a good poppa."

"Yes." His voice choked. "I would make a good poppa." *I will make a good poppa, if you'll let me.*

He'd make a good husband too. He was glad he'd taken her to the Pettibones'. Not only had she enjoyed the company of another woman, but she'd seen the rewards of hard work and witnessed firsthand a family who loved the prairie. Now, with supplies for winter stored all around them, she had to know he'd take care of her, take care of their baby. She had to know.

Arms outstretched, he welcomed her to his embrace. Silently, she slipped her arms around his shoulders and rested her head against his chest. He drew her closer, careful to keep the power of his feelings harnessed, for realizing what he might give up for her frightened him. Pliant and trusting, she relaxed as he stroked her back, as he brushed aside the strands of hair and kissed her forehead. Next summer seemed a lifetime away, yet he already knew that when the time came, he couldn't just let her walk away.

She stepped back and drew his hand to her belly. Her hand over his, she applied gentle pressure. The sudden flutter beneath his palm made him grin. It was either that or cry.

Dulcie Pettibone was right. All Clifford wanted to do was talk about Amadee Ducheneaux. At first Katrina didn't mind. After all, Clifford had taken her into town. Justin had told Clifford to drive slowly. Into town and back, Clifford had been the perfect gentleman, except for his nonstop praise of Amadee Ducheneaux.

"Don't you think Miss Amadee has shiny hair? And did you ever see such white teeth?"

"I'm sorry, Clifford. What did you say?"

"About Miss Amadee. Don't she have the best laugh? She laughs like she knows what's really funny and what ain't, don't you think so?"

"Oh, yes. I know she enjoyed that tale you told her about the jackrabbit." Katrina didn't want to be rude, but it was hard to listen to Clifford tout the praises of the lovely Miss Amadee when there was news from Merriweather in Katrina's handbag.

"Don't you think she's pretty?"

"What? Oh, yes, even prettier than you said."

Clifford drew back on the reins and the wagon came to a stop just outside the soddy.

"Here you are, ma'am. Back by four o'clock, just like you wanted. I hope you don't mind my jawing on and on about Miss Amadee, but I had the need for an older woman's opinion."

"Of course," Katrina said, too eager for privacy to be bothered by his comment.

With characteristic exuberance, Clifford helped Katrina down from the wagon. From the back he retrieved a bushel basket of apples and five good-sized packages wrapped in brown paper and tied with string. "I'll put these inside for you. Pa says we're gonna get some rain tonight."

While Clifford helped himself to a dipper of cool well water, Katrina put a dozen apples in an empty flour sack. "Here," she said as he climbed back into the wagon. "You take these home and have your mother fix up something special."

"Hey, thanks!" Clifford took the sack of apples and set it on the seat beside him. With a nod and a flick of the reins, he was off.

Katrina stepped back inside and gazed for just a moment at the abundance she'd bought. However, as eager as she was to unwrap her packages, she had something even more pressing to do.

Moving slowly so she could summon her courage, she took her apron from the hook by the washstand, tied it about her waist, sat down on the chair, and reached for her handbag. Inside was a letter from Gretchen.

Dear Katrina, my sister,

Like a tub of butter left in the sun, my heart has softened. I am missing you every day, more and more.

Tears rushed to Katrina's eyes as quickly as the fear left her heart. The carefully creased paper trembled in her hand as she read on.

Don't worry about our bakery. Business is good. My Lukas made the tables and chairs Poppa always wanted to put in the bakery, so now the customers linger for a cup of coffee or tea in the morning when they buy my sticky buns and in the afternoon for the *Kaffee kuchen* when I have the fresh plum breads and cream buns too. Next I will try making American round pies. All the new American recipes I am trying, but I don't like so much sugar and so much butter.

What are the foods on your prairie? Lukas says you have buffalo sausage. Is this true? How are the women on the prairie? Do all of them speak good English?

I ask all these questions because your letter it was too short and so I worry. You say you have a little house made of sod. Is it like the dirt brick houses of villages in the old country? You say you have a horse, some cows, and chickens, but you say nothing about Justin and little about your babe to come. Are you yet a different shape?

Do you stick out in the back and in the front? Lukas
asks how is the tonic and do you need more?

My Katrina, between the lines of your letter I read
that much is not good. I am wanting you to be happy
and that is why I am telling you that soon the cold
heart of Richmond Barrison will warm and once again
you will be welcome in our village. His father has had a
small seizure of the heart but is better now. Tell Justin.
I think Richmond looks at life with new eyes. One day
a week he comes to my bakery. He pretends to want
bread or cakes, but his true reason is to ask about you,
which he always does. Sometimes his face gets hard
when he remembers he is mad with you still, but soon
he will soften. I am sure.

Gretchen's letter continued with admiration for
Lukas Heinz, with genuine sympathy for their neighbor,
poor Frau Epple, who had fallen and broken her hip, and
with interest in all the other Merriweather gossip.

Katrina cried when she read about poor Frau Epple,
not because of any particular fondness for the woman
but because all sorts of things made her cry these days—
the chicken whose egg somehow rolled out of the nest
and broke, the red geranium Dulcie had given her,
whose delicate blossoms had shriveled in the heat. And
that dust, that never-ending brown talc that crept into
every crevice and dirtied her clean clothes, her dishes,
her one window—all such foolish things over which to
shed tears.

Katrina composed herself and reread Gretchen's letter. She would share the letter with Justin when he came
in for supper, which would be soon. He would enjoy
catching up on the news from home. He would be troubled to hear of his father's illness, of course, but relieved
to know that all was well now. Puzzled, Katrina read that

portion of the letter again. Surely, his mother would write to tell Justin herself what had happened.

There was another matter in Gretchen's letter that Justin might find troubling: Richmond's change of heart. For if what Gretchen said was true, Katrina would not have to fight to take her place in the community. She would be welcomed. But could she go back without Justin?

Justin had said he believed her explanation of what had happened with Richmond, that she had tried to seduce him but couldn't go through with it. But both Justin and Richmond were men of pride. Both held fast to what they felt was theirs. Most of all, the rivalry that had festered for years between the brothers was not likely to go away easily, if ever. Katrina knew how miserable she had been when anger separated her from Gretchen. How much greater the misery would be for Justin to have to work beside his brother. Katrina and Gretchen were moved by love to work things out; not so Justin and Richmond. What if her wish was granted and Justin agreed to go back to Merriweather? Did she have the right to ask him to make such a sacrifice for her?

Clear answers did not come easily. Katrina folded the letter and slipped it into her pocket. Tomorrow she'd write to Gretchen and tell her all about the Pettibones and the Rhinedollars. She'd enclose a snip of the cornflower blue calico, too. Maybe she'd press a clipping of the greengray sage that made everything smell so nice and clean.

Half an hour later she'd unwrapped her purchases, arranged them on the bed, and stored the brown paper and twine for future use. In addition to the apples that had come all the way from the train station up in Fargo, she'd bought twenty yards of that beautiful blue calico, enough for a dress, a window curtain, a skirt around the washstand, and a tablecloth. She bought a white wool crib blanket, three yards of white flannel for baby sacks, four yards of cotton lawn for diapers, six skeins of colorful embroidery thread, two skeins of plain yarn, one bar of creamy sandalwood soap that had come all the way from the Orient, a new shirt, and a pair of leather work gloves for Justin.

Katrina straightened the hem of the red-and-white checked dish towel and laid it on the table, centering a brown mixing bowl on the cloth and, one by one, polished a dozen apples against her chest and piled them in the bowl. She ground enough beans for a fresh pot of coffee. With the inviting aroma drifting through the door, she scrubbed the carrots, beets, and potatoes they'd have for dinner. With tender biscuits to sop the bacon-grease gravy, and baked apples and cream for dessert, it made for a tasty meal.

She looked at the bowl of apples again, signs of luck and love. Eager as a schoolgirl to see her future, she took one apple, studied its shape, and smoothed her thumb over the taut red skin. She picked up a knife.

Holding the apple over the table so it would catch the peel, she placed the edge of the knife near the stem and carefully eased the blade down and around, relishing the sweet scent and the juice that wet her palm. With one final snip, she severed a corkscrew peel from the apple.

Then, as she and Gretchen had done so many times as girls, Katrina picked up the peel and tossed it over her left shoulder, knowing it would form the initial of the man she would marry.

It broke when it landed.

There was no sign to tell her future. No B for Barrison. No J for Justin. An ominous feeling settled over her. Hoping to chase it away, Katrina picked up the peel and tossed it into the bucket of scraps. Was she wrong to have begun listening to her heart?

It wasn't long before she heard Justin at the door. She wiped her hands on her apron and smoothed back her hair. She shouldn't worry about an apple peel, not when she had brought so many treasures from town.

He stood in the doorway and stared at the bed. "God in heaven, Katrina, what have you done?"

Both surprised and hurt, she folded her arms across her chest. "I've gone shopping."

"Did you leave anything in the store?"

"You don't have to shout."

His lips moved silently as he looked at each item, as though he was adding up the total cost. "This had to come to more than ten dollars. And that's all I gave you."

"*Ja*, it did."

"But how?" As soon as he asked the question, a knowing look crossed his face. "Damn it, Katrina. You made arrangements with Nadine Rhinedollar, didn't you?"

"It's called time payments, and it's not as awful as you might think. All I had to do was give her the ten dollars and promise that you'd pay her one dollar and seventy-five cents every month—"

"For the rest of my life. I know how time payments work."

"I didn't sell you into servitude, for heaven's sake, I merely purchased necessities. And the payments will only be for six months."

He didn't looked comforted.

"Look at the calico, Justin. There wasn't another blue like it. I'm going to make curtains and a tablecloth. And a skirt for the washstand." She looked down at her belly, visibly round now, growing. "And a dress. I would have liked to have a variety of colors for clothing and decorations, but I decided using one would be more economical. Dulcie says they buy everything with time payments. She says that's the modern way of making your money work for you."

"Katrina, listen to me. If we have a season with no rain, or too much rain, or a hailstorm or a plague of hoppers—any number of things—the crops could be destroyed and then I couldn't afford to pay a nickel a month for one month. That's what I'll be worrying about as soon as I have a crop. Right now, I've got to worry about getting enough land plowed up just to plant a crop. Do you understand?"

"But I saw all the money you had when we were in Rhinedollar's last time."

He balled his fists. "That money has to last all year! Until I get a crop, I don't have anything of substance to sell."

"Oh, Justin, I'm truly sorry. I would never have bought so much if I thought it would present a hardship for you. Maybe I can take some of the items back."

He paced the floor, shaking his head. "No, you don't have to take anything back."

"But you just said—"

"I know what I said." He sat on the edge of the bed and leaned forward, bracing his elbows on his thighs and his chin on his hands. "But I do have enough money. Don't worry. It's just that I have to make a go of this place. I have to prove—" He closed his eyes tight, then opened them as though clearing his thoughts. "I just have to do it."

She nodded, understanding a little more what kind of demon drove him.

She walked over to the bed and handed him the work gloves she'd bought for him. "Try them on. Nadine said they were the best."

He slipped his hands into the thick leather and examined the stitching. "They look well made. They feel sturdy."

"She said they would keep your hands from getting blistered."

He took off the gloves and laid them on the bed next to the soap. "Thanks." He picked up the soap and inhaled its fragrance. "I'm glad to see you bought some decent soap. That cake I've got makes me itch as soon as I pick it up. I'm sure you've noticed."

"Indeed I have. I asked Nadine if she had honeysuckle

because I know that's your favorite. She said the sandalwood was better, but she'd order the honeysuckle if I wanted."

"The sandalwood is fine. Besides, much as I like honeysuckle blossoms, I don't want to smell like them." He reached over and fingered the calico, then looked around the room. "I ought to pay it off and save the interest, but I want to hold on to the cash in case there's an emergency. I guess six months of payments won't kill me."

"The time will go by quickly."

He nodded. Katrina wondered if his thoughts were the same as hers. In light of their growing affection for each other, in light of their concern for the baby, what would she do now if he asked her to stay? And what would he do if she asked him to go?

Not one to prolong the inevitable, Katrina tapped her apron pocket where the letter waited. "Supper will be ready soon," she said. "Why don't you wash up and I'll pour you a cup of coffee. I have news from home."

He headed for the washstand. "You've heard from Gretchen?"

"Yes. And her heart has softened. All is good again between us."

"I'm glad to hear it. And Richmond?"

Katrina heard the disdain in his voice. "Richmond's heart has softened too. At least that's what Gretchen thinks."

"Hmm," Justin said as though he doubted Gretchen's conclusion.

"Business is good," Katrina said. "Though I still think Gretchen is too eager to embrace new recipes. Cooking is not just to fill empty stomachs. Cooking is to preserve the heritage."

Justin poured water from the pitcher into the bowl, leaned forward, and splashed water on his face.

"Wait." Katrina retrieved the new bar of soap and gave it to him. "Use this."

It took only a few seconds to smell the aromatic scent of sandalwood released in the soapy lather covering Justin's hands and face. Katrina inhaled.

She froze. Something was wrong.

Justin cocked his ear toward the door, grabbed a towel, and rushed outside. The sudden memory of disaster weighing her steps, Katrina followed.

Thunder rumbled in the distance. Low gray clouds with an eerie blue shadow tumbled overhead. Brittle tumbleweeds raced helter-skelter across the field. Distance prevented them from hearing the Pettibone bell, but there was something . . . a thread of sound on the wind . . . something desperate. They couldn't hear it. They could feel it.

Justin ran toward the corral. "Hurry!" he called over his shoulder. "I'll get the wagon. You get the gunny sacks. And pray those clouds are bringing rain."

In the distance she could see the smoke.

The wheat stacks were on fire. Gold and orange and red, the ordered rows blazed into the smoky purple-blue sky. Bundled sheaves of pale delicate oats trembled against the hot rushing wind until they, too, caught and flared like so many candles on a cake.

With silver-white streaks of lightning crackling behind him, Justin made the wagon fly past acres of corn drying on the stalk and straight through fields of knee-high stubble left by the harvester, past a whole year's profit in unthreshed stacks of wheat, straight to where the fire threatened the Pettibone house and barn.

He could see Pius and the older boys out in the field at the edge of the fire, slapping the flames with wet gunnysacks. Dwarfed by the six noisy, nervous horses hitched to the plow in front of him, ten-year-old Pitt was driving a furrow between the field and the buildings.

"What is that poor boy trying to do?" Katrina asked, alarm in her voice.

"He's making a firebreak."

Justin stopped the wagon by the house. Clutching his arm, Katrina looked at Pitt's efforts and cried, "What can we do? A row of plowed ground won't keep that inferno at bay."

"Pray that it will!" Justin jumped from the wagon and helped her down. "You be careful, you hear me? Stay by the water trough. Get right in it if the fire gets close."

"Here," she said. "Take these." She handed him his new gloves.

He looked all around him. For one tortured second, as though he had something to say and was afraid he might not get another chance, he placed his hand on her belly. "Your poppa loves you, little one." Then he added, "He loves your momma too." He brushed her cheek with his lips.

Before she could respond he was running toward the fire, taking her heart with him.

This was no time for sentiment. Katrina grabbed the empty feed and flour sacks from the back of the wagon and hurried to the windmill, where Dulcie and the younger boys had formed a bucket brigade. Next to the house, little Clem stood on an upturned barrel yanking the rope with all his might, ringing the bell to signal neighbors from the other direction.

Drenched from her efforts, Dulcie hoisted another bucket of water from the trough and passed it down the line. With a quiver in her voice and fear in her eyes, she looked at Katrina and cried, "Thank the Lord you're here!"

Terrified by the chaos all around her and the devastation she knew would come in its wake, Katrina clutched the sacks close to her chest. She wanted to reassure her friend, to tell her that everything would be all right, the wind would die down, more help would arrive, but even if nature and neighbor cooperated, the loss was already great.

Should the fire take a turn, it could reach Justin's place. It was coming closer. They should all leave now. That's what they should do. Get away while they still could. Run!

But Dulcie continued to fill buckets. Clem continued to ring the bell. Pius, his sons, and Justin continued to fight, all in the hope of saving the Pettibones' future. Where there was hope, there was courage.

Swept up in the struggle, Katrina plunged the sacks she'd brought into the cold water. With half a dozen of them weighing down her shivering arms, wetting her to the skin, she ran toward the field, as fast as her swollen feet and swollen belly would allow. She got as close as she could to the fire to bring the sacks to Justin. She was not foolish enough to try to fight the fire herself.

But suddenly the fire snapped and popped, shooting sparks high into the air. Acrid black smoke darkened the late afternoon sky. Thick swirls of dust made it hard for her to see anything but the flames. She dropped all the sacks but one on the ground, then hoisted the one remaining sack over her right shoulder, ready to do battle.

"Katrina, no!"

She felt the pull as Justin yanked the cloth from her hands.

"Get back!" he cried. His face was smudged in black, his hair and eyelashes singed. He gripped her shoulders and drew her several yards away. "God almighty! I told you to stay back at the trough where it's safe! You understand me?"

Then she heard a sudden *whoosh*, saw a burst of fire right behind Justin.

He screamed, dropped to the ground, and rolled. The back of his jacket was aflame.

Terrified, she gripped the dripping gunnysack in her hands and slapped it against the flames that threatened him, all the while dodging the sparks that teased the hem of her skirt.

Suddenly, the image of her mother desperately dragging her father from the burning bakery flashed through Katrina's mind.

"Don't you die on me, Justin Barrison! Don't you dare!"

19

With fierce determination, Katrina swung and slapped again, her tears evaporating as quickly as they ran down her cheeks.

The minutes blurred. A strange, unreal feeling slowed her motions and dulled her senses. Her cries stretched thin and faded to silence. Justin's groan sounded distant. Everything slowed but the hellish heat.

Dazed, she watched him wriggle free of his charred jacket and kick it aside. Numb to the feel of his hands gripping her shoulders, she stared into his eyes, searching for assurance that he was all right. Finding it, she leaned against his chest, wanting to hear nothing but the sure and steady beating of his heart. Instead, she heard the continuous cry of the bell. Dreams were so hard to fight for.

"You all right?" he asked, his voice raspy from the smoke.

Easing herself from his embrace, she nodded. "*Ja,* I am not harmed. Just scared. And you?"

"I'm scared too. Everyone out here is." He took her hand. "Come on. I want to get you back up to the house."

"No," she said, aware of a quiet, solid strength building inside her. "I can go back by myself. You're needed here." When he hesitated, Katrina squeezed his hand. "I will see you when this is over," she said. "Be careful."

She summoned her strength and went back toward the windmill and the weary bucket brigade. The struggle might be in vain, but she wasn't going to quit.

As she approached the house, five wagons pounded into the yard. Big burly men carrying shovels, women weighted down with gunnysacks and baskets of bread, jumped from the wagons and headed in various directions as though they'd been through this before and knew exactly what to do.

"Boys, you stay to the windward side," one of the men yelled as his sons ran to the fields, sacks in hand.

Just as the entire town of Merriweather had turned out that night to help her family, here too the far-flung prairie community came together to help one of their own.

"How bad is it?" one of the men asked her, as he and another man unloaded a flat wooden sled on which they placed huge barrels of water and more gunnysacks.

From what Justin had told her and what she'd seen herself, she answered. "Mr. Pettibone has good wide firebreaks. The wheat is gone, but the buildings are safe. For now." Her feeling of pride surprised her, but here she was, working side by side with strangers, fighting for people she barely knew.

"If these flames don't jump," another man said. "I seen them once leap across a river like they was pulled by a magnet."

One woman drove up in a wagon and said to the two girls who jumped down, "You go help Mrs. Pettibone on the pump. See if you can pump a hundred."

"We can do it!" they shouted as they raced toward the windmill.

"Don't you leave that windmill!" the woman called after them. "You hear me?"

Several women Katrina had never met gave her friendly but frightened nods as they rushed about, one to the windmill, two to the barn, two to the house. But as grateful as Katrina was to meet them, she didn't hear their names. Instead, she heard the bravery in their words as they shouted instructions to their children and, with voices cracked with fear, cautioned their husbands to be careful.

With time at a premium, Katrina hurried to the windmill where she spelled the little girl pumping water. What kind of hellish place was this? Children should be running for sport and playing ball for fun, not pounding the crackling grass with brooms or bravely stamping the hot ground with their feet.

"Had to be the lightning," the woman next to her said.

Over and over again, Katrina raised the handle and pushed it down till there was no strength left in her arms. "Lightning?"

"Demands at least one sacrifice every fall. About the only thing a body can do is dig good firebreaks, keep sacks and water on hand, and, Lord, whatever you do, don't put all your wheat in one stack."

Wiping her brow on her sleeve, Katrina willed the strength to raise the pump handle one more time.

Suddenly, a tremendous wall of flames reached the freshly turned earth.

Everyone gasped, watched, waited.

The firebreaks held. The fire turned back on itself and died. It was over.

Later, a full harvest moon rose behind swift-moving clouds and the curtain of dust and soot that hung in the air. The moon would be obliterated shortly by the dark heavy cloud bank moving in from the west.

Standing a safe distance from the charred remainders of a year's work, Katrina watched the scene with worry. She could barely make out the shapes of the men still out in the field. They'd be there for hours, checking for embers.

One sacrifice every fall. This time next year Justin might be the one singled out for destruction. This tragedy had to convince him to leave and go back to Merriweather with her. She couldn't bear the thought of living without him.

Lifting her head to the first drops of rain, she walked through the drizzle and into the fields. The scorched earth hissed and spit in reaction. Behind the clouds, a red moon bled on the ravaged land.

Lying in a bed that had felt too cold and too empty for too long, Katrina spoke just as Justin turned down the lamp and headed for his sleeping bag by the door. "Sleep with me, Justin. I don't want to be alone."

Without the benefit of the light, she couldn't tell how he felt about her bold invitation. It had been two days since the Pettibone fire, but Katrina was still exhausted. She imagined Justin was as well. Perhaps he was too tired. Perhaps he wasn't interested. Worse yet, perhaps he'd strengthened the fence around his heart, keeping Katrina just out of bounds so she could leave without hurting him.

Tortured by a silence that seemed to go on forever, she was about to turn away when she heard the smooth slip of leather as Justin removed his belt and the metallic sound as the buckle touched the table.

She heard other sounds, too. The scrape of the kitchen chair as he pulled it out to sit down, the soft grunt as he tugged off his boots, the agonizingly slow shedding of his pants as though he too was questioning the wisdom of what they were about to do.

In the small room, made smaller by all that could not be seen, the air carried his scent and stirred with his movement, ever closer.

Daylight would reveal their differences, for dreams were not easily abandoned. She knew that. But in the dark, in the realm where feelings can be made known by a gentle touch or a powerful embrace, perhaps she could find a way to let him know just how much it meant to her to go back home. But if not—she trembled at the thought of failing—if not, she would have no choice but to find the courage to change her dream, for she didn't want a life without Justin. He was not the reckless, anger-driven man she once knew, the defiant son who would turn his back on security for the sake of pride. He was strong, dependable, committed to putting down roots. Knowing the risk she took, she inched over to give him room, ready to welcome him to her heart.

She felt his weight on the mattress beside her, felt the strength of his arms as he pulled her close, his whispered breath as he kissed her. Along with her willingness to trust him came a dangerous vulnerability. Even as she opened herself to the risks of both passion and love, she pinched a fistful of the soft sheet and held it tight.

A gentle kiss, a sweet caress, hands that cupped and stroked, fingers leaving fire in their wake. Racing hearts, ragged breath, wild abandon, deliverance to a place of peace. So marked their loving in the long dark night.

In the aftermath, nestled safely in Justin's arms, Katrina gave voice to her fears.

"The fire," she whispered, "it brought back memories I thought safely buried. Suddenly, I see myself back at the bakery. Poppa—his skin all blistered and black. Momma—lacking the strength to climb the stairs without resting—there she is, coughing and gasping while she drags Poppa across the floor. And there I am, helping Momma, telling her everything will be all right and all the while knowing from somewhere deep inside that Poppa will die." Katrina closed her eyes and squeezed them tight. "So I try hard to remember my last words with Poppa. But I can't. And now he's gone."

The images continued to haunt her.

"And Momma—she wasn't burned as badly as Poppa so I felt sure she would recover. But she didn't. And she died alone. All alone."

She welcomed Justin's soothing touch as he stroked her cheek and found her tears. The gentle tightening of his embrace told her he understood her pain. For that she was grateful. But he was powerless to change the past and, against the forces of nature, powerless to control the future. Her voice still strained with emotion when she spoke.

"I see her pale yellow hair like a halo on the white satin pillow, the gold coin in her hand for the ferry to the distant shore. Then just as suddenly as the image comes, it changes and I see you on the ground, your jacket in flames—"

"Hush now. It's all right." He cradled her in his arms. "Everything's going to be all right."

All too well, she knew the wishful thinking of his words. She eased back and looked up. She didn't need light to see his singed hair, his blistered cheek, or his loving eyes. "But I could have lost you too," she murmured. Rocked by the terror of what might have been, she reassured herself by tracing the line of his lips. "And I love you so."

Speechless, he drew her close again and held her against his heart. She heard the longed-for happiness in his voice when he finally said, "I love you too."

Eventually she relaxed against the strong wall of his chest, aware of how tenderly his muscled arms enfolded her. His skin smelled of loving and sandalwood soap and still the trace of smoke. She pressed her lips to the hollow at the base of his neck, hoping that tonight she would sleep in peace.

*   *   *

Much later that night, while Katrina slept in Justin's arms, he studied through the window the ink-black sky strewn with stars. Tomorrow would be a good day for threshing. Cool temperatures. No wind. If all went well, this time next year he'd be threshing his own crop. He'd have enough money to buy that piece of bottomland and maybe two or three more quarters, another milk cow, and some pigs. Or he could buy lumber.

Wanting more than anything to be a success in Katrina's eyes, he pictured his four head of cattle growing to fifty, maybe a hundred, the arrow-straight rows of black earth that, come next year, would be filled with pale gold wheat, butter-yellow corn; the hundred and sixty acres that would double and triple and double again.

He pictured Katrina that night in the gazebo. In the midst of her despair she had turned to him for compassion. She trusted him. If she hadn't surrendered to him that night she could have married Richmond. She wouldn't be housekeeping in a sod hut, her eyes keen for bugs and snakes. She wouldn't be scrubbing clothes till her hands were red and cracked.

But she said she loved him.

He played her words over and over in his mind. Filled with pride, he rested his palm against her belly. His baby moved beneath his hand. God had blessed him.

She'd shown him the letter from Gretchen. She said she didn't understand why he didn't want to rush back to see his father. Even though there'd been hard feelings between them, grave illness often made a person face their own mortality and set about to put things in order. She said perhaps Eberhard's heart had softened, as had Gretchen's and Richmond's.

His father's heart hadn't softened. That would never

happen. As for Richmond, he was still young enough to learn from his mistakes, young enough to change. If Richmond's heart had indeed softened, Katrina would have no obstacle in going back to Merriweather. From the sound of Gretchen's letter, he might even send her the fare. It shamed Justin to admit he hadn't offered her the means himself, but that would have been giving up without a fight.

Justin wasn't a quitter. He knew he hadn't been Katrina's first choice, but he'd spend the rest of his life proving he was the *right* choice. Even if it meant buying lumber instead of land, instead of cattle, instead of wheat. Even if it meant risking everything he had to make her happy.

With a clean rag wrapped around her finger, Katrina polished the stove. It wasn't as big or as fancy as Dulcie's, but it had served Katrina well.

Less than an hour ago, she'd fried a breakfast of fresh eggs and diced potatoes, onions, and the last pepper from her small garden. Justin ate heartily and said it was the best meal he'd ever had. He kissed her before he left for the fields, a habit he'd started after the fire, a habit Katrina liked.

Justin. The thought of him gave rise to feelings that were tender and passionate all at the same time. Katrina remembered how he'd held her in his sleep those nights after the fire, how now and then he'd tighten his embrace, protecting her from demons known only to him.

She stooped down to exhale on the nickel-plated medallion. Suddenly short of breath, she gripped the handle on the oven door. Trembling, she stood and splayed her hands high on her midriff. "Easy, little one," she said. She took a deep breath and gently patted her abdomen. "Easy."

Once she was upright, the pressure passed. But her heart still raced. She opened the door and shivered as the

November chill collided with the warmth inside. Fighting the panic that came over her when she least expected it, she searched the endless flat horizon. Which field did Justin say he was going to this morning? How far away was the midwife, Cleophee Yucker?

Mounted on the doorframe, hanging at the ready, was the black bell, its clapper tied to a two-foot length of rope. All she had to do was ring it. Just as neighbors had all rushed to help the Pettibones, Justin would rush home to help Katrina if she rang the bell in that fast and frantic way that meant trouble. Knowing that, she let the bell stay silent and instead took a deep breath and went back inside the soddy.

It was still dark at five in the morning, the air cold and crystal clear. Glittering beads of frost, caught in the light of the lantern, studded the fields, as though the land offered treasures just for the taking. Katrina, however, was not tempted, for by reminding herself of the prairie's hardships she had protected herself from the zealous spirit that bewitched so many.

Sitting in the wagon waiting for Justin, she hunched down into her coat, shivered, and tightened her shawl. Just last night she'd hemmed her new cornflower calico dress. She'd also stitched a long smock of flour sacks to wear over it, to protect it. There just hadn't been time to get to Dulcie's to use her Singer. Over the winter months, Katrina planned to stitch and knit for the baby. As her time grew shorter, her worries increased.

She glanced in the back of the wagon to ensure the safety of the pot of chicken stew, the pan of cornbread, and the basket brimming with warm sticky buns. A pile of gunnysacks was tucked in the back too. Like all the other farmers coming to the threshing, Justin brought along every sack he owned. Filled with grain, the sacks would be needed for only a few days, just enough time for the man who was threshing to get his grain to market. Then the sacks would be sorted and returned to their respective owners. No one farmer owned enough sacks by himself.

In less than a quarter hour they would join the Warbecks, the Peroskys, the Roundtrees, the Scogginses, and the Pettibones, all at the Hemmelers' place, for the first threshing of the year, the most dramatic event of the harvest season.

Justin came out of the soddy carrying their two bed pillows. "Here," he said. "Put these behind your back. They'll cushion the ride."

"*Danke.*" She wedged them behind her lower back.

"Threshing out here is nothing like it is back east," Justin said. "I can't wait to see the machine. I've heard it's huge. Belongs to Big Angus McVee. He and his crew work their way up from Kansas every year. Next year he'll have to spend all his time in the Dakota alone."

Katrina noted his enthusiasm. She too was looking forward to the threshing and the opportunity to get acquainted with her women neighbors, to know that there were others who had survived the childbed on the prairie. There certainly hadn't been time for visiting on the day of the fire. Prairie life being what it was, it could be, most likely would be, long and lonely months between visits.

As they rode along, Justin said, "I hear Big Angus charges five cents a bushel plus board or five dollars for a set job of under a hundred bushels. That's steep but worth every penny. The flat fee is pretty common for most folks the first few years, until they get more land. I plan to be paying by the bushel in another three years, two if I can get that piece of bottomland next year."

"Justin, look. The lanterns." Like strings of flickering fireflies, lanterns attached to wagons and lanterns carried by people walking alongside approached the Hemmelers' place from all directions. It reminded Katrina of the feast of Epiphany and how the village children, the "star singers," would dress in long white gowns, carry lanterns, and parade through the village, stopping at each square or corner to sing a few carols. She was not prepared for the stirring of her heart.

Justin flicked the reins to pick up speed. "I'll bet Big Angus has that team of his moved between the stacks already. I'll bet he's already got power set up. I wish I could have been here to see that."

As they approached the Hemmelers' farm, the cold air carried the sounds of a man's booming voice, coils of heavy chains sliding off the back of a wagon, and a rattling waterfall of sliding metal.

"Listen," Justin said. "That's the sound of progress."

Katrina was looking in the other direction. She could see the outline of the house. "Do my eyes deceive me?" she asked. "A soddy?"

"That's right. They've got a sod barn too."

Smoke curled from the chimney. Katrina inhaled a variety of aromas. Mrs. Hemmeler must have been cooking for days. Katrina knew that if she were to ever host a threshing, she would bake a ham glazed with honey and mustard. She would fix baked beans with onions and molasses, potato salad with vinegar. She would make the flakiest of biscuits, whip honey into the butter—she caught herself, unnerved that she'd pictured herself living here.

The wagon rolled onto the bare hard-packed dirt of the front yard. A white-haired woman of substantial height and substance, wearing a smile from ear to ear, came through the door of the soddy, wiping her hands on the apron about her waist.

She reached up to help Katrina down. "I'm Gussie Hemmeler. My man's the one over yonder trying to tell

Big Angus how to run his own machine. And you must be the new Mrs. Barrison." She gave Katrina a kiss on each cheek. "Welcome, welcome." She took Katrina's hands, held her at arm's length, and looked at her belly. "You look just beautiful," she said. "How are you feeling? I can see you've passed the danger months. I hope the retching passed, too."

"I'm feeling much better," Katrina said, adding as she looked down, "though I'm growing so fast—"

"You come on inside where it's nice and warm," Gussie said. "I've got a dress or two you can borrow. My regular fit ought to do you just fine. I've got some baby items that will come in handy, too. When are you due?"

"March, in the middle."

"Good. By the time the baby is ready to go outside, you'll have the spring to enjoy." Gussie took the pan of cornbread from Katrina's arms, leaving her with the sticky buns. Justin had already taken the stew inside and left to join the men. "Are you feeling like you have to run to the outhouse every ten minutes?"

Embarrassed, Katrina nodded.

"And the skin on your belly is starting to itch?"

Katrina nodded again.

"I want you to meet my sister, Bessie. I went through all this with her last year." She waved her hand excitedly at the other women approaching the soddy. "We'll all have us a nice talk, just the girls."

A tall reed of a woman came out of the soddy and insisted Katrina try the sliver of ham she held between her fingers.

Katrina tasted it. "It's delicious."

"I knew you'd like it. I'm Bessie Warbeck, Gussie's sister. I'm married to that bald behemoth over there, the one chasing kids with a pitchfork. Lord, but that man loves to tease."

They stood outside. It seemed to Katrina that everyone

arrived at once, some in wagons loaded with chairs and tables, some on foot, women with great picnic baskets at their sides, men with pitchforks on their shoulders. Gussie made more introductions: Etta Scoggins and her three daughters, Lily Roundtree and her dog, a gentle golden giant who couldn't wait to frolic with the children. Everyone commented on the devastation of the Pettibones' wheat and the encouraging sign of another baby to be born on the prairie. Katrina felt a little less apprehensive than she had before she came, and a certain kind of loneliness faded away.

As they stood there talking, another woman arrived, driving a wagon by herself. "Howdy," she said to Katrina as she jumped down. "I'm Winona McBride. I'm proving up on a place about six miles east." She easily lifted a large dutch oven from the back of the wagon and headed for the door.

The women drew one another into conversation as they followed Gussie inside. The soddy was much like Justin's, square, but at least twice the size, with separate rooms, wooden planks boarding at least the lower half of the walls, flour sack curtains trimmed with lace at two windows. The hard-packed dirt floor had a sheen to it. Katrina stared in puzzlement.

With a grin, Gussie said, "Sunflower seeds. Pop the shells, eat the seed, and toss the shells on the ground. Leave 'em set overnight, then sweep. They give a little oil to the floor, make it hard and shiny. Helps control the fleas, too."

A parade of children came through the soddy. The women moved quickly, inside and out, carrying chairs and table linens, pleading for their children to be careful and not to get in Big Angus's way.

In no time at all the kitchen was filled with baked hams and roasted ducks, beef roasts brown to the bone, huge pots of veal stew and creamy potato soup, spicy sausage full of garlic and marbled with fat, fried cabbage, pickles, apple slaw, buttermilk pies, and huge blue granite pots of brawny coffee.

Dulcie Pettibone arrived last. "It's a good thing I didn't bring anything but vegetable soup," she said. "You've got enough food here to feed every threshin' crew in the Dakota Territory."

From comments Katrina had heard earlier, Dulcie always brought something elaborate to a threshing. For her to bring only a vegetable soup had to mean something was wrong.

Gussie took the pot from Dulcie and set it on the stove. "I don't know," Gussie said. "We've all been up since three. I made a breakfast of my special vanilla flapjacks, wild berry syrup, ham, and herbed potatoes. Big Angus and that crew of his, Wayland and Roy, why, I've never had the pleasure of seeing men eat so much in all my life. They've all been out there for the better part of two hours setting up power."

Winona spoke up. "I heard he's using a five-pair team."

"You heard right," Gussie said. "I wish you all could have seen it. There was Big Angus, a mountain of a man himself, hoisting himself up on that mammoth wagon of his, easing those ten horses in between the two stacks, just as perfect as you could want."

As though everyone understood that the sight of setting up power was something to see, they all went outside and walked a good quarter mile out into the field where the bundled sheaves of wheat formed two giant stacks, each the height of a two-story building. Katrina gasped at the sight of so much wheat.

For a moment, men and women alike just stood there, mesmerized by the activity, listening to the clash and clang of rods and bars and the chain-gang cadence of the beat of a sledge as Big Angus and his crew drove in the iron stakes that would hold to the ground the mechanical contraption they called the "power."

Reflected from some faraway place below the horizon, the sun washed the darkness from the sky and brought on the morning. A loud ringing hum caught everyone's attention and drew them closer.

Flicking his whip in the air, Big Angus stood on a small wooden platform centered over an assembly of huge cogwheels. Ten steel-shod horses, harnessed to five long metal sweeps radiating from the cogwheels, snorted frosty puffs of air and slowly cut their first circular path on the ground, setting into motion a noisy contraption of cogs and gears and balance wheels.

"We got power!" Big Angus called.

The chorus of claps and whistles that surged through the crowd had Katrina smiling and waving to Justin, as he stood with the other men eagerly waiting for Big Angus to give them an assignment. On the way over he'd explained that Big Angus was the driver, Wayland the feeder, and Roy the tender, and they were the only three men rightfully entitled to be called "threshers," so not to be surprised to see Justin and the other men, even Hemmeler, taking orders from Big Angus. He was the boss today.

Justin had also talked about how he planned to buy more land and have his own crop next year, big enough to warrant hiring a threshing crew. Until now, Justin's dream had seemed no more than that—a dream. But in all likelihood, Justin's dream had once been the Hemmelers' dream too. And here it was, coming true. Now she understood why he said he felt privileged to be part of this territory's foundation, to have a stake in its future. She could see now what he would be giving up by going back to Merriweather.

The children looked in awe at Big Angus. "Now you younguns stay clear, you hear me, or old Mr. Wayland over yonder could mistake you for a sheaf of wheat, spread you on that conveyor belt, and feed you to the machine."

His whiskered jowls shook right along with his finger,

though Katrina suspected he was forcing himself to look stern. From what Gussie had said, all Big Angus talked about at breakfast was his new granddaughter, pink as a prairie rose and just as pretty.

With an exaggerated look of concern, Big Angus waved to Wayland. "What's that you say? Your wheat-eater is hungry and looking for breakfast?"

The girls, wrapped in coats and mufflers, gasped and huddled together. The boys butted one another, proving their bravery. A moment later, however, as though the children could sense the true character of Big Angus, they were singing songs and racing around the yard.

The sight of happy, healthy children frolicking with that big frisky dog pulled at Katrina's heart. Being up so early, the little ones would need a nap soon, that was certain. If she were hosting the threshing, she'd give them all warm milk, fit them sideways on her bed, and cover them with her quilt.

Gussie Hemmeler left the circle of men gathered by the machine and came over to Katrina. "The old men are talking politics, weather, and the price of wheat, as usual, and the others are just itching for Big Angus to assign them to a station. Look at them all, slapping their hands about their arms, every one of them too stubborn to wear a coat."

"My poppa never liked to wear a coat either," Katrina said, surprised to be thinking of her father now. "But, oh, he'd take such delight in a big threshing like this. Momma would have everything in the house just so. And my sister, Gretchen, would be turning out pastries too pretty to eat." The vision choked her.

"Now don't go getting teary-eyed on me," Gussie said as she patted Katrina awkwardly on the shoulder. "I don't know the first thing about fixing soft hearts."

Katrina took in a deep breath of the frosty air and fixed her eyes on the wide streamers of red unfurling in the eastern sky, welcoming her as they did every morning to the prairie.

"You going to be all right?" Gussie asked.

Shaking memories of what was and dreams of what might have been, Katrina said, "I'm fine." *Better than I thought I'd ever be.* She gestured toward the huge metal insect, its mechanical buzz filling the air. "Let's go get a better look."

Katrina, Gussie, and several other women walked closer to the center of attraction. A wide canvas slide had been stretched from the mouth of the wheat-eating machine to the top of a ladder between two stacks. There were ladders on the outsides of each stack as well.

"Hellfire and damnation, will you look there?" Gussie said, pointing to where her son perched, pitchfork in hand, on the top rung of the center ladder. "That's my boy Jack. Wants us to call him 'Shoutin' Jack' during the threshing season."

While the women watched, Shouting Jack saluted Big Angus and gave the order for the other pitchers to climb the stacks. Before the others reached the top, he howled like a coyote and ceremoniously threw down the capsheaf.

Katrina noticed how Etta Scoggins's oldest girl, Lucy, looked on with admiration, clapping and waving at Jack as though he were the star of the day.

Gussie tightened the knot on the thick shawl she wore around her shoulders and nudged Katrina. "To look at that boy, you wouldn't know he's been moping all week. One minute he's lamenting on how it's going to take him a lifetime before he can work himself up to earning the proper title of thresher, and the next he's pounding his chest like he's king of the mountain." She sighed as though seeing her son grow before her eyes. "A smile from a pretty girl can make a man do most anything."

Katrina thought of the angst poor Clifford Pettibone

was going through over Amadee Ducheneaux. She thought of how Pius, always pretending to be such a skin-flint, lavished every luxury on Dulcie. How Karl and Gussie Hemmeler and Bessie and Dutch Warbeck had achieved the companionable state Katrina's own parents had known. She thought of how Lukas Heinz had comforted Gretchen and how he'd encouraged her to keep the bakery because that's what she wanted, even if a woman operating a shop of her own did raise some eyebrows. Katrina thought of Richmond, who had offered her what he valued most—a carefree life of luxury.

Then she thought of Justin. What had he offered her? A life of hardship? A constant battle with the forces of nature? That was all she had seen when she first came here. But now she realized he offered her much more—a place in a closely knit community where warmth grew from shared experiences and the dependence each family had on the others. Though the distance between doors was long, and the path of tough grass was not smooth cobblestone, each door did lead to the home of a friend, just as in the old country. The prairie itself offered her a chance to sink her roots in its fertile soil. But only if she was strong enough.

Just then Big Angus cracked his whip over the heads of the ten horses and shouted, "Let's move!"

The horses increased their speed, causing knuckle-jointed rods to tumble as they carried the power. Wayland cut the straw band on the first sheaf, fanned the wheat on the broad smooth belt, and fed it onto the separator. The metal teeth inside the big cylinder caught and tore the wheat like some primitive monster. The children squealed. The women clapped.

The measureman's helper stood at the side of the separator and governed the amount of wheat allowed to pour into the sacks held by the boys not old enough for the harder work, while the keen-eyed measureman himself watched and counted and worked a series of wooden pegs in a board of gimlet holes to keep track of how many bushels had been threshed, knowing each hundred-pound sack contained nearly two bushels.

With an old needle speared through his battered felt hat as a mark of pride, the sack sewer stitched the sacks with lightning speed, leaving two ears of cloth for carrying.

Other men, those who'd soon be wallowing up to their waists in chaff, stood at the back and pitched the straw away to keep it from clogging up the machine. Roy, oilcan in hand, gave constant close attention to every joint and cog and gear.

The men took a short break at ten, to wolf down the sandwiches and guzzle the water the women brought them. By noon, with a blistering sun right overhead, every man and boy out there had to blink to see through the sweat in their eyes. The horses strained their necks to keep moving at a strong and steady pace. The noise from the cylinder had grown to a howl. And the wheat was rushing out of the separator in a stream big as a stovepipe, straw gushing out the back just as fast.

A bucket brigade of dirt-faced, brawny-armed men and boys panted while they rushed to fill the sacks and haul them to a spot on the ground designated with optimism as "the granary," where the bottom row was stacked on end to minimize the amount of moisture the sacks might soak up from the ground. Every man and boy out there had swirling chaff and wheat beards caught around his neck and down his shirt. Some wore goggles to keep the black soot from their eyes. Some chewed tobacco, the only way to keep their mouths moist.

Gussie checked with the other women to be sure they were ready, then rang the bell for dinner.

There was no mistaking the eagerness of those who answered. Crowding around the water trough, grimy-faced men joked and cuffed each other, all the while jostling for space, sloshing themselves with water, trying to make themselves presentable for the bounty the women had prepared.

Justin, looking like a man who'd just hit a jackpot, washed up, then approached Katrina. He took the bowl of mashed potatoes from her hands and set it on the table. Then he clasped her hands, making no attempt to hide his affection. "So how does it feel, Mrs. Barrison, to be part of your first threshing?"

Mrs. Barrison. Aware of all the tender looks from the women around them, the winks from several men, and the undeniable love in Justin's eyes, Katrina surprised herself by saying loud enough for all to hear, "Wonderful!" She grinned as he gently squeezed her hands.

For a moment she thought he might kiss her. Instead, he squeezed her hands again, then left to find a seat on one of the several long planks stretched between kitchen chairs, all of which, including the tables, had been carted over by the neighbors.

The men ate first, ravenously gobbling food brought from the kitchen by a brigade of laughing apron-clad women. Later, while the men collapsed on blankets in the shade of their wagons, the women and children ate.

The days were too short to allow for a generous nooning, and it wasn't long before Big Angus, Roy, and Wayland had checked the equipment, sewn up a few rips on the belts, taken out three bent teeth in the mouth of the big machine, and called the men back to work.

The afternoon passed quickly. When even the sun could no longer hold itself up and the air had grown cooler, Justin pitched his fork into the stack and shouted they were down to the last of the sheaves.

Eventually, the cylinder took on the empty rattle it had when first fed that morning. Men who could barely move dragged themselves to the water trough and the supper table. The young children, the only ones with any energy left, ran after the rats that were always uncovered at the bottom of a stack.

Even though it was the Hemmelers' wheat that was threshed and not Justin's, Katrina had worked hard and felt the importance of her efforts. She looked with pride at the stack of five hundred cloth bricks bulging with edible gold, enough to warrant holding back some for feed, some for seed, and some for the higher prices that always came in the spring. Here was a glimpse of what it might be like for Justin someday.

Big Angus was tending the horses when Katrina noticed little Merton Pettibone, the eight-year-old, fidgeting while he talked to Etta Scoggins's youngest girl.

"Hey," Merton said, pointing to one of the horses Big Angus had just unhitched, "want to see how fast I can mount that horse?" He raced ahead, jumped in the air, and tried to grab a fistful of the animal's mane. Instead, he fell against the horse's side and landed on the ground.

With far less patience than he'd shown earlier in the day, Big Angus growled at the boy. "That animal has worked hard all day. Now you get away from him this instant or I'll warm your backside with a whip. You hear me?"

Merton walked away, his lower lip drooping. Then he said something to the little Scoggins girl, and the two of them ran off toward the wall of sacks next to the barn. Katrina thought that was the end of the episode until twenty minutes later, when the Scoggins girl came running up to the soddy, screaming.

"Merton said he could fly and he jumped off the sacks. Now he's flat on the ground, dead like. And his arm is all twisted and buckled up."

Dulcie gathered her skirts and ran. Chased by the dark side of life on the prairie, Katrina and the others followed.

20

It was four long days before Justin and Katrina heard the news about Merton. Clifford rode over to return the bed pillows and deliver two items he'd picked up at Rhinedollar's on the way back from Eureka: a package from Gretchen, a letter from Rosamond. Both sat on the table, untouched, while Katrina sat transfixed in a chair by the window and Justin leaned against the door, his arms crossed, braced for bad news. Sitting at the table, Clifford worried his fingers while he relayed all that had happened.

He and his father had driven the horses full speed, taking turns at the reins. They'd had to go all the way to Eureka to find a doctor and would have gone on to Leola if they'd had to. They even had to stay overnight and half the next day. It wasn't the broken arm that had the family so worried. It was the blow to his head that had left the boy unconscious.

Though the news was grim, Justin was particularly concerned about Katrina's reaction. It did not bode well for his plans. He wanted to talk to her about marriage. He wanted to show her his ledger and explain that he had enough money to build her a frame house and that he intended to do just that—if she'd stay. He wanted her to see the facts and figures that, providing nature cooperated, ensured a life of financial security—if she'd stay. She had enjoyed herself at the threshing; he knew it. But Merton's accident made her look at the soddy, the dirt, the dust, and the fabric-covered ceiling with its unsightly bulges, all with that same revulsion she'd shown when she first arrived. This wasn't the time to try to convince her how happy they could be, living on the prairie.

Katrina braced one arm around a large wooden bowl in her lap while she used the back of a wooden spoon to work salt into the kernel-sized granules of butter. Every time Clifford relayed a point of pain or drama, Katrina winced, gripped the handle of the spoon and muttered, "Poor little Merton, poor little Merton." Just as her voice had quivered when she talked about her parents' deaths, it quivered now when she asked, "But he *will* be all right, won't he?"

"He'll live, if that's what you mean," Clifford said, "but it could be awhile before we know if he'll ever be all right in the head." He stood, ready to leave. "But Paw says that whatever happens, we can handle it, as long as we all stick together."

Justin walked over and put his arm on Clifford's shoulder. "Tell your folks we'll be over in a few days."

"Yes, sir." Clifford turned to Katrina. "Afternoon, ma'am."

"Thank you for coming by," she said. "And for bringing the mail. We'll pray for Merton."

"Yes, ma'am."

When Clifford had gone, Justin said, "An accident like that can happen anywhere. You know that, don't you?"

"I know." She took the knife from the shelf and snipped

the twine around the package from Gretchen. "But there is no doctor in Prosperity. There might not have been one in Eureka. Or Leola. And then what would have happened?"

"But there was a doctor."

She shook her head with a look of exasperation. "Justin, in trying to make a home for you, I have tried to love your prairie, and for moments here and there, especially at the threshing, I thought it possible. But it is a dangerous place. Who is to say that the future will bring churches, schools, and doctors? Maybe yes, maybe no. Only the most reckless of gamblers would chance his future on this barren land."

"It's raw," Justin said. "The land is just raw. It won't always be like this. Why, in Eureka alone they've got two churches now, a school, and a doctor. Ever since the railroad came, that town has been growing like a weed."

Katrina gave him a dubious look, but he continued.

"I've never seen so many grain elevators in one place, and all of them full. You know what every farmer around here says: 'Wheat is money and money is wheat.' This country is going to be the wheat capital of the world one of these days. Some are already calling it that."

"No," she said firmly, her hands still on the package that linked her to home and family. "Once our baby is born, so helpless and trusting, you too will see how danger lurks at every turn and you will want safety for our child as much as I do."

"There are some things more important than being safe. Like having opportunity, being able to dream." He gripped the back of the chair and blurted out, "And so is legitimacy. We must get married, Katrina. I don't want my son born a bastard."

"You think I do?"

"I don't know. You haven't mentioned it. Not once."

"I would never willingly bring such a curse to my own

child." She looked him straight in the eye. "Unless it were the lesser of two evils."

"What is that supposed to mean?"

"You know as well as I that if I were your wife I would be bound before God to go where you go." She glanced around the room. "To stay where you stay."

He sized up her strategy quickly and didn't like it. "So unless I agree to go back to Merriweather, you won't marry me. Is that it?"

She held up her hand, displaying Richmond's ring. "These people here think we are married already. When our baby is born, no one here but you and I will know the truth."

"You can accept that?"

"I don't like it. But I can accept it."

He straddled the chair. "Well, I can't."

There was no anger in her voice when she said, "You cannot force me to stay." Just determination.

As though each knew they'd come to an impasse, and neither wanted to weaken the progress they'd made, they said nothing further, letting the package and letter on the table take their attention.

Justin picked up the letter from his mother and held it while Katrina opened the box from Gretchen. She took each sheet of wadded newspaper and pressed it flat with her hands. They would provide hours of reading later. Beneath all the paper was a baby's bread-and-milk set, with the alphabet rimming the plate, cup, and cereal bowl. One by one, she examined them and set them on the table. "The alphabet," she said. "How like Gretchen to want to be sure my baby will learn to read."

"My baby," Justin said.

"What?"

"The baby is mine too."

"*Ja*, I know."

She didn't need to look so concerned. He did have a plan—a big one. It wasn't to force her to stay but to make her want to.

Casually, he asked, "Is there a letter?"

"Yes." She retrieved several folded pages and read aloud.

I hope you are liking the bread-and-milk set. You can use the letters to teach your little one how to read. If you have a boy, I will send a train. If you have a girl, I will send a doll house with fancy cutouts for each room. If you have a girl, don't pierce her ears to trick evil spirits. The *Gazette* says American girls don't have to do this.

My Lukas talks about your baby all the time. He says having children makes a woman tender and sympathetic. He says now you are a gardener with a duty to provide good soil for your baby. And I say that after you have the baby, Merriweather will provide excellent soil. Lukas says you should have no false modesty in walking about freely to get the exercise you need. So, is he right? I told him not even you, a modern woman, would walk about and let your sacred secret show, but maybe the rules are not the same on the prairie. Also, maybe you practice the lullaby for when your garden bears fruit. *Ja*? Write and tell me how it is with you.

Katrina looked up from the letter. Justin recognized the power of Gretchen's words to sway her heart. He had his work cut out for him.

Katrina continued.

At the bottom of my letter is a recipe for the new round pies. This is a popular item which is making for me a nice amount of money. A few more good years and the debt to Richmond Barrison will be paid, though he has not pressured me for it, not once.

Katrina pressed the letter to her chest. "Did you hear that? Business is strong. You don't know how that lightens my heart." Her eyes glistened with unshed tears. "I knew she could do it, my Gretchen." She looked back at the letter and continued to read.

Already I am asked about gingerbread houses for Christmas. Richmond wants one in the image of the fancy new home he is building. He showed it to me and my Lukas. Like a castle on the Rhine, that is how it looks, with windows from floor to ceiling and carved doors throughout. I told him he would have to reach deep into his pockets if he wanted a copy of such a grand house. He said to have what he wanted was worth any cost. So this Christmas I will make not only the little cottages but also a grand house. Do you remember last Christmas when I made too many *Pfefferkuchen* and you had to push the sales? We make a good team, you and me, and I am glad we have made peace.

I think Richmond asks for the gingerbread house so he can make peace with me too. He was keeping company with a new girl, Magda Rammelt, but no more. Now he goes to the *Biergarten* with only his parents, and even at the *Oktoberfest,* when he tapped the first keg, the honor brought no joy to his face. I think his soul is troubled for his ugliness to you and he is willing to accept your choice of his brother.

So tell Justin he can bring you back now and all will be well. Also write and tell me about your wedding, for surely Justin has done right by you. Did you have roses for your hair? Who stood up for you? Tell me also that he is a good husband and then I will know that all is well.

"You told your sister we were married?"
"No, but I didn't say we weren't. I guess she just

assumed . . ." She closed her eyes a moment. "Your brother's heart has truly softened."

"So it appears."

"You don't have to sound so suspicious."

"I know my brother."

"You knew the man he was. But people change, you know. They do. Richmond's actions show his contrition. A person should be willing to forgive."

"Have you?"

She looked uneasy.

He asked again. "Have you forgiven my brother for banishing you? For taking out his anger on your sister?"

"I haven't forgotten."

Frustrated, he said, "Maybe the thought of his floor-to-ceiling windows and his fancy carved doors makes it easier to put the past behind."

"I don't say this to hurt you. I know your home is built with the best this country has to offer, but I don't want to hurt our baby either. Try to understand. It's not just the soddy. It's everything the soddy represents, everything about this land, everything wild and dirty and dangerous. Justin, I do want something your brother has, but it's not his fancy house. I want his safe and secure life. But not with Richmond. With you. If you don't understand that, you don't know me very well."

He forced down the lump in his throat and spit out the words he'd been holding. "I would die before I would let any harm come to our child. If you don't know that, you don't know me very well either."

"I know that no matter what a person desires, simply wanting it never makes it so."

He stood and paced the floor. "Damn it, Katrina. Why can't you be more patient?"

"You want me to be patient while you are as pigheaded as you ever were? I have learned in two months what you will never learn in a lifetime. You cannot control this land. Only God can. And even God gave up on it ages ago."

He slammed his fist on the table, wanting once and for all to make sure she understood how he felt. "God would never give up on this land. And neither will I."

"No," she said sadly. "I suppose you won't."

She took the gifts from the table and set them on the shelf. He knew the point she was making by covering them with a dish towel. She had to protect them from the dust. He had the feeling that time was running out on him and if he didn't do something soon, she would be gone and it would be too late.

Then she came back to the table and sat down. "Are you going to open your letter now? I recognize your mother's hand."

Justin slit the envelope with his thumb and removed the folded sheets. As Katrina had shared her news, he now shared his.

My dearest son,

This envelope is not edged in black, though the next may well be. It is my sad duty to tell you of your father's recent illness, an affliction of his heart. I had the parlor prepared for the deathwatch, but thanks to a merciful God he pulled through. Though I lack the simple childlike faith I long for, I do believe the experience has brought about a change in your father, for he knows now that any day he could be laid again upon a bed of suffering.

My son, this house has never been in so much distress. Nor has there ever been such a distinct possibility that joy might return to these dark rooms. Your father has asked me to tell you that, should you wish to return, he will arrange an equitable sharing of the brewery between you and your brother. At one time I thought peace between you and your brother would be impossible, but Richmond talks now of wanting to make amends with both you and Katrina.

Do your poor mother's heart a good turn and write and tell me the status between you and Katrina. How I miss her. It is my fondest wish to know that the two of you have married and that my grandchild will carry the Barrison name.

Finally, let me know of your decision at the soonest. I will say nothing to sway you in either direction, except to assure you, Katrina, and my dear first grandchild of a warm welcome.

Her eyes sparkling, Katrina said, "You see? Your mother is of the same opinion as Gretchen. Richmond's heart has softened. Better still, your father wants you to come home."

"So?"

"Your father knows he has done wrong by you and is eager to set things right. You have been given a second chance."

"This is my home. I don't want to go back there. I don't want any part of him or his brewery. I don't need a second chance to say no. I meant it the first time."

"Proud and stubborn. You are so like him."

"I am not. I am not like him at all. I never will be." He sat down across from her. "My mother also asks about the status between us. What should I tell her? You would rather have a bastard child than marry me?"

She looked into his eyes. "But I do want to marry you."

"Only if we go back to Merriweather."

Instead of answering him, she turned toward the window. He hated to see her look so sad, but he was angry that she still had no faith in him.

"Everything would be so much easier there."

He reached across the table and took her hand. "I know how you feel about this prairie. But, please. Give me some time. Let me show you how good it can be."

She drew her hand back and placed it on her belly. "I am not about to go anywhere until next summer."

"And then?"

"You know what my plan is."

"Your plan. Oh, yes, your plan to go back to Merriweather without me. Tell me again how you're going to explain the baby."

"I will say that I went to New York—"

"My mother knows you came here. My brother knows it. Your sister knows it. I imagine the whole town knows it at this point."

Undaunted, she continued. "I will say that I married and am now widowed."

"Gretchen thinks you married me. My mother hopes as much. Are you going to tell everyone I died?"

Katrina said nothing.

"You don't understand, do you?" he said. "Unless you're prepared to face a scandal, you can't go back to Merriweather without me. And I'm not leaving."

He stood and took his hat from the nail by the door.

"I'll see you for supper," he said and went outside. It always hurt him to walk away from her, but sometimes it was the only way.

The leaves on the little stand of cottonwoods down in the draw turned gold, shook in the wind, and fell as winter claimed the prairie. Bunches of sage, soft and silver-blue, dotted the land. Katrina saw the changes and worried. Everyone said winters on the prairie were hell.

With only four cows, they didn't have enough to butcher. They couldn't get a pig until next spring, so there'd be no pork other than what neighbors were willing to trade or sell. The hens had stopped laying at the end of summer. Oh, for sure, Katrina had salted down dozens of eggs and they'd keep fine for baking, but unless Justin could shoot a duck or a prairie chicken, they'd live the winter on bread and the provisions stored in the root cellar: a barrel of sauerkraut and another of pickled watermelon, sacks of potatoes, onions, beets, and carrots.

A light, powder-fine mist of snow swirled on a soft late-November breeze the morning Katrina decided to take the wagon and drive over to Dulcie's. Justin gave her the argument she expected.

"You can't drive all the way over there by yourself."

"Why not?"

"It's not safe. Look at you. You're too big to be bouncing around on a road that's nothing more than a wagon rut. What if a wheel breaks? What if something spooks the horse?"

"Now you understand how I worry about our baby."

"Wait till I'm finished plowing," he said. "I'll drive you to see Dulcie."

"And when will that be?"

"Two more weeks."

Katrina shook her head. "I haven't seen her since the accident. I should have gone over long before now." She picked up the basket of biscuits she'd baked that morning and tucked a jar of wild berry jam under the flap of the red-and-white checkered cloth. "Don't worry. There's ham and potatoes in the covered fry pan for your dinner. I'll be back in time to make supper." With that, she lifted her chin in a show of independence and marched outside.

"All right," he said, close behind her. "But you be careful." He helped her into the wagon, then made a quick check of each wheel. He looked at her heavy wool coat. "You going to be warm enough in that?"

"I'll be fine."

"You can't even button it. Katrina."

"I'll be fine."

"It gets dark by four o'clock."

"I'll be back by then."

"The temperature really drops when the sun goes down."

"I know." With that, she flicked the reins, leaving Justin to worry just one small fraction of the way she worried every minute of every day.

The Pettibones' landmark poplar had lost its glittering silver leaves, leaving nothing but gray bone limbs. Frost had snapped all the red geraniums by the front porch. Inside the house, the aromas of food were noticeably absent.

After insisting Katrina sit in the comfortable rocker, Dulcie asked, "Did you bring your sewing?"

"No, I stitched by hand."

"Oh, you shouldn't have."

"It was nice quiet work. Gave me a chance to sit and rest."

"Won't be much longer now, will it?"

"Just over three months." Grateful for the support of the sturdy chair, Katrina pressed her toe to the floor and set the chair to a gentle rock. "Sometimes I wish the time away, until I think of the dangers of this land. And then I want to hold this baby in me as long as I can."

Dulcie stiffened.

Katrina knew both of them were suddenly thinking about Merton. Her voice just above a whisper, she asked, "How is he?"

Dulcie's eyes filled with regret. "His arm is as crooked as a willow, though the doctor says he'll have use of it just the same. 'Course he won't ever be a trick rider, but I suppose that's not the worst calamity in the world." She stepped to the window. Using a wadded corner of her apron, she cleaned a spot on the glass. "It's his head I'm worried about. Oh, he's come a long way since the accident. He can see things clear now and he can talk all right. Most of the time, anyway."

"So he's on the mend, *ja*?"

"I suppose."

"And the other boys?"

"They've been a godsend. The twins cart him around in that hand-pull wagon Mr. Pettibone made for me to truck my gardening. Sometimes Clifford sets him up on a horse 'tween his legs. Says he can't have his little brother forgetting how to ride." Dulcie shook her head, then went on. "Pitt even gives his dessert to Merton—that is, whenever we have dessert, which isn't that often anymore." She pressed her lips into two straight lines, as if to keep herself from saying more.

As gently as she could, Katrina said, "The fire took a heavy toll, didn't it?"

Dulcie eyed Katrina suspiciously, a reaction that took Katrina by surprise. "Nobody's carting us off to the poorhouse, if that's what you're getting at."

Stunned, Katrina said, "No, I didn't mean that at all. I just meant that if recovery is not readily at hand, I'm sure Justin could advise your husband—"

"Mr. Pettibone can do just fine on his own."

Katrina's discomfort grew, as she realized she had wounded Dulcie's pride. Not wanting to bring more irritation to her friend's already painful life, Katrina said, "Don't be angry. All I meant was . . . well, Justin knows a lot about the financial sphere. He says time payments will be the ruin of every farmer."

"We don't need advice from some city folk who can spout a lot of fancy ideas but who can't even tell when a storm's coming."

Katrina stood up. "Now you wait just a minute. Justin is the first to admit his shortcomings in the ways of farming—a sign of maturity by my measure."

"A sign of a soft-handed man, if you ask me."

"How dare you say such a thing about my husband! He's a brave and hard-working man. He gave up a lot to come out here."

"So now you're saying my husband is a coward? Well, I'll have you know back in the Civil War, Mr. Pettibone faced shot and shell without a flinch."

"I'm not saying your husband isn't brave," Katrina said through clenched teeth. "Just pigheaded."

"Mr. Pettibone is a strong, independent man who carved all this out of nothing." Dulcie walked toward the door, signaling it was time for Katrina to leave. "When he tells me it's time to worry, I will, but not a minute before. And when I do, *if* I do, I won't come begging advice from you."

"As you wish." Katrina grabbed her coat from the hook behind the door and slipped it on as quickly as she could. Then she marched outside, climbed into the wagon, and took off, churning up a cloud of sooty dust.

Though it hurt to do so, she relived the incident over and over again as she drove home, with the underbelly of the wagon scraping over the dry grass-covered mounds of the familiar ruts. In trying to explain Dulcie's caustic manner, Katrina remembered something her momma said the day the family left Russia. Katrina had asked what was the real reason Poppa wanted to leave.

"If you would know secrets," Momma had said, "look for them in grief or pleasure."

Justin noticed the look of anguish in Katrina's eyes when she told him about the incident with Dulcie. Poor Katrina. He had a strong feeling the argument reminded her of the split she'd had with Gretchen. No wonder she seemed not only angry but frightened.

"Give it time," he said, as he poured her a mug of hot coffee and gestured for her to sit on the stool at the kitchen table. While she repeated portions of the story, he stood behind her and massaged the knots in her shoulders. "It will all blow over. My guess is Dulcie is trying not to show how upset she is over the boy."

"But that doesn't give her the right to say those awful things about you."

She couldn't see how he smiled at the protectiveness in her words.

She leaned forward, her arms crossed on the table, her head hung low. "That feels so good," she said, as Justin kneaded the tension away. "All I wanted to do was help her. She won't admit it, but they're having hard times over there. It's plain as day."

"I know," Justin said. "I tried to help too."

"You did? When?"

"At Hemmeler's threshing. I told him there was no questioning his skill at either ranching or farming, but he was digging himself a grave with all those time payments."

The small motion of her head told him she didn't agree. "I made mention of your feelings on the subject, but I think I am in agreement with Dulcie. Time payments are the way of the future. Everybody says so. Even Gussie Hemmeler has used them."

"Then sooner or later 'everybody' will be visited by the debt wagon."

He felt her shudder at the mention of the debt collector. And if there was nothing to collect, as was often the case, the collector would enlist the aid of the local sheriff in eviction proceedings and then auction off whatever was left of some poor grubber's dream.

"That's just how it is," Justin added simply, remembering a bleak winter day long ago in Philadelphia when the debt wagon had called on his father.

Katrina, too, seemed lost in her thoughts, probably thinking of how Richmond had nearly foreclosed on the bakery. If Justin could, he'd make her forget every sadness of her young life. He caressed her narrow shoulders. She had more meat on her bones now than she used to, but that was because of the baby. He hoped she'd hold on to at least a little of that extra flesh after the baby was born. He couldn't help but remember what Pius said about the little women not making it on the prairie. The thought of losing his Katrina shook him deep inside. He squeezed her shoulders harder.

"Easy," she mumbled.

"Sorry." He bent down and kissed her neck, silently cursing the sun that had darkened her tender skin. He slid his finger under the collar of her dress. "Loosen a few buttons for me. I want to do this right."

She lifted her head slowly, but before she could summon the energy to move, he slid his arms around her neck and skillfully slipped the buttons from their holes. All the buttons.

He eased the cornflower calico from her shoulders and bunched it up. Her one chemise, the one with the limp ruffles around the deep neck and the strip of calico she'd added at each side, barely contained her breasts. She didn't discourage him when he slipped his hands inside her chemise and cupped the swollen flesh. They were like orbs of white marble, only soft, very soft, with tiny blue veins. He stroked the tips with his thumbs until he felt the tight buds that told him she enjoyed his touch.

As though under a spell, she stood and turned to face him. The gold flecks in her eyes danced against an ever-darkening background. A faint blush colored her cheeks, crept down her neck, and spread across her chest.

His gut felt twisted tighter than new wire on a fence. He saw the tip of her pink tongue and the bashful smile that told him she felt the same powerful urge he did. But whether it was instinctive or deliberate, she held her belly with her arms, spreading her hands across the treasure she carried, and he realized the carelessness of his thinking.

He stepped back and shook his head. "We can't do this. I can't take a chance on hurting you or the baby. It's not safe."

She lowered her eyes, letting her disappointment show. Then she said, "But I could still pleasure you, *ja*?" She sat back on the chair. "Come closer," she said, reaching for his waistband and the bulging row of buttons. "Let me loosen a few of those buttons." Her fingers fumbled as she released the first. "I want to do this right."

21

Justin rose early the next day, invigorated by the night before. Shivering in the cold, he hurried to feed the animals and hauled the empty water bucket to the pump.

He blew on his hands and rubbed them together, then gripped the cold metal handle on the pump. He forced the handle down again and again until he could feel the pressure build against his palm and hear the water bubble up from the ground.

With a smile on his face and snowflakes twirling around him, he carried the bucket of sloshing water into the soddy and set it on the floor. He found Katrina staring out the window and was reminded again that she wanted a world far away from this prairie.

"Justin, do you ever think about what kind of father you will be?"

These changing moods of hers no longer took him by surprise, but this time she spoke as though she envisioned him in the role, as though she were actually considering staying on the prairie. Justin took heart. He hung up his coat, hid his concern behind a smile, and said, "A good one." He poured himself a cup of coffee and sat down to the breakfast Katrina had prepared for him. "My son—"

"Or daughter."

"My son, or daughter, will never go hungry. He'll have a place to live. Clothes on his back."

"What else?"

He'd asked himself the same question a hundred times. "I'll show him how to manage his pennies. I'll teach him how to milk a cow without getting kicked and how to plow a straight furrow. I'll teach him about respecting his neighbors and about how folks out here help one another in every season, not just the harvest." He took a sip of the coffee and set the mug down. "Soon as I learn more about it myself, I'll teach him how to recognize the weather signs."

She turned from the window, and some of that faraway look had left her eyes. "What about discipline?"

"Firm. But kind."

When she nodded he couldn't help but wonder if she'd been thinking about the iron-fisted way he'd been raised.

"Anything else?" he asked, feeling confident of giving the right answers.

"Will you love him? Truly love him?"

"I already do. How can you even think otherwise?"

"What if he doesn't share your dreams? What if he feels like a prisoner in all this open space? What if he wants to leave?"

"I'll make sure that both his trunk and his pockets are filled and send him with my blessing." He could tell just by the way she angled her head that his answer surprised her. "You're asking if I could let him go. Yes, if I had to, I could. He's my son. Not my wife."

Before she could protest, he added, "I couldn't live without my wife."

*   *   *

She took Richmond's ring off the next day. She had to soak her hand in cold water straight from the well first and then smear butter all around the ring, and even then she had to tug to ease it past her sausage-swollen finger. Her feet were just as puffy, her face too. The flesh across her belly, no longer able to resist the swelling, had stretched, leaving her once smooth skin branded with stripes she knew would never totally go away.

Her mother's belly had been scarred that way. Several years after Gretchen was born, Katrina remembered surprising her mother as her mother stood naked at the wash basin. The skin on her belly was covered with those wrinkled white ribbons, her belly itself a loose hanging pouch. At only twelve years old, it frightened Katrina to see her momma so deformed. Momma had told her it was part of the price a woman paid—and paid willingly—to have children.

Momma told her a lot more that day, all about how a husband touches his wife in a special way so she can have a child. Katrina had blanched, as though Momma had been bewitched to come up with such a horrid tale, but they sat on Momma's big feather bed and talked for hours, and when it was over Katrina knew Momma was telling the truth. She eased off Momma's bed, not wanting Momma to see how revolting she thought the whole idea. She never looked at her momma, or her poppa, the same way again.

None of her friends had heard such tales. If a wife wanted a baby, she placed a lump of sugar outside the window on the sill and waited for the stork or sent the midwife to fish a baby out of the milk spring. But even as her friends recited the simple explanations, their eyes showed the fear that kept them from questioning what they'd been told.

It was while making feather pillows that Katrina heard

the whispered stories about babies and birthing, about women spending hours, sometimes days, in excruciating pain, about fevers and convulsions, and about the mothers for whom the bleeding never stopped. Those were the ones who died. She heard tearful stories, too, about the babies who didn't live.

The women all agreed on one thing. Besides having a good midwife, the new mother's best hope of surviving was to have family around: sisters, aunts, and cousins who would care for the other members of the family while the new mother recovered and nursed her child.

The baby kicked, and in that instant Katrina wished with all her heart to have Gretchen at her side. As the movement stilled, she took a settling breath and reminded herself that Cleophee Yucker was said to be a fine midwife and that both Gussie Hemmeler and Bessie Warbeck had offered to help when the baby came. But then, so had Dulcie, and now she wasn't so sure that Dulcie actually would.

She wrapped the ring in a clean hankie and put it in her trunk.

You were supposed to be here too, Momma. You said you longed for the day when you would hold your grandchild. You said not to be frightened by stories of pain and death. You said you would be right beside me. You promised.

Instant tears born of an anger, a grief, and a loneliness she was just beginning to comprehend all but choked her. She cried out loud, feeling the walls of earth absorb her sorrow.

Justin sat at the table examining the secondhand harness sprawled across his lap. Frost had hardened the ground, so plowing was done for the year. Winter was get-ready time. They already had several inches of snow. Folks out here said spring calving makes a body forget a hard winter, but just how bad could a prairie winter be? Not for the first time that week did he review how much food they had, how much fuel. Not for the first time did he estimate how long it would take him to get by wagon or by sled to Cleophee Yucker's place and back. As Pius had warned him, this was Justin's first winter, with his first child by his first wife.

He looked over to where Katrina sat by the window mending his shirt. He wanted her to be his first wife, his last wife, his only wife. But what he wanted and what she wanted were still miles apart.

He rubbed his fingers along the thick leather straps, stopping to examine the depth of the hairline cracks. He squinted. Dry rot. Right where the straps rubbed against the big metal rings on the hame. He pulled up a long length of strap and checked the spot where it hooked to the singletree on the wagon's tongue. Worn there too, but not bad yet. He'd rub linseed oil into every inch of that leather. That ought to coax out a few more years.

He suddenly thought of the provisions box in the rear of the wagon and made a note to check it one more time. He'd already added an extra piece of strap, a rope, and a coil of old wire he could use to hold something together if he had to.

He had to make sure there were enough provisions in the house, too. With winter easing in day by day, he'd have to make another two-day run to dig coal, though he'd just gone a few weeks ago. One of Etta Scoggins's girls came to stay with Katrina while he was gone. Still, he didn't like leaving her alone that long.

He reminded himself to check the wheels, make sure the spokes were tight. It'd been such a hot year, any moisture in the wood had long since dried up and that meant the spokes would be loose. The rims too. They needed a good coat of linseed oil. He made a mental note to take care of that tomorrow. He'd grease the nuts too. When the time came to fetch Cleophee Yucker, he didn't want to have to worry about his horse, his wagon, or his sled.

What could she use for a wreath? Katrina wondered. There were no evergreens. She had no ribbons. She did, however, have four candles. They were for the lantern, but they'd do just fine in an Advent wreath, if she could find something to make an Advent wreath with.

Despite the freezing temperature, Katrina opened the door and stepped outside. Eight inches of snow had fallen the night before, fallen soft and quiet just the way it did in the old country. Old Frau Holle shaking her pillows, that was the story she'd been told as a child. Katrina braced her hands at her lower back and stretched. As far as she could see, the world was a flat white canvas just waiting for her to color its fate.

Later that day she placed in the center of the table the wreath she'd fashioned from the dried sage she'd hung about the house and the cattails she'd gathered last month from the draw. That Sunday and the three following, Justin, as the head of their little family, lit a candle until all four burned with the light of hope and love. She prayed that he would see the wisdom of moving back to the safety of Merriweather. Until he did, she prayed God would forgive her for willingly bringing a bastard child into the world, especially when she so enjoyed pretending to be Justin's wife.

On Christmas Eve, with no church or choir, no tree, no ornaments but a star-strewn sky, and no family but each other, Katrina and Justin sang the hymns both his family and hers had sung for generations. She gave him a pair of socks she'd knitted herself. He said they were the perfect size and just what he needed.

He had covered his gift to her with a tarp. Her eyes

widened when he lifted it. "A cradle," she whispered with awe. She knelt beside it, uttered a prayer, and lovingly ran her hand along the straight, sturdy sides and the carved head and foot.

"It's oak," he said.

She heard the pride in his voice, not just because he'd managed to get such a sturdy piece of fine-grained wood and keep the making a secret, but because he'd pleased her. "The wood of Donar," she said, "god of thunder. It is beautiful."

"I ordered the wood one day on the way to dig coal. I swore Nadine Rhinedollar to secrecy. It's a relief to know she kept the news to herself. You are surprised, aren't you?"

She nodded. "I thought I would have to use a wooden crate."

"I've been working on it since early November. Clifford picked up the wood for me in town. Pius loaned me the tools."

Afraid to harbor ill will in her heart, especially at Christmas, Katrina asked, "How fares Pius? And Dulcie?"

"Hard to say." Justin knelt down beside her and ran his hand along the headboard as though examining it for flaws. "I didn't set foot in the house, and that in itself was odd. Pius saw me coming, met me outside, and took me into the barn where he keeps his tools. He acted so strange."

"He's a strange man. I told you that."

"That's because you don't know his ways yet. No, this time was different. He hardly said a word. Except he did say a body's got to read and accept the signs. Said only a fool wouldn't read the signs. Said a man's very survival depends on it." Justin held his hand steady on the side of the cradle and paused in contemplation.

Katrina stood and nervously rubbed the small of her back. "I never thought I'd see the day I would agree with

Pius Pettibone, but I do." The baby kicked. Katrina arched, wishing she could give her little one more room to move.

She walked to the window, its cold glass webbed with frost, and stared out at the snow and the blackness, out at the eve known for its spirits.

"What is it?" Justin asked.

She turned to him. "When last I visited Dulcie I saw the glass in her cupboard door. It was cracked. You know as well as I what that means."

"It means the glass was cracked. That's all."

"It means something terrible is going to happen to them."

Justin rolled his eyes, though his smile said he had no intention of arguing. He tapped the runners on the cradle.

"Don't!"

Katrina rushed toward him and quickly stayed the gentle motion. "To rock an empty cradle is to give birth to a sleepless baby."

Justin took Katrina's hand. "We'll have a healthy baby, all pink and sweet smelling. A baby who sleeps through the night. And next Christmas we'll have our own *Tannenbaum.*"

"What we need is mistletoe to ward off evil spirits."

"What we need is a tree, covered with glass balls, brown sugar cookies, paper roses, colored ribbons, and lots of white candles."

Katrina wondered if in describing the trees of his own Christmases past, he could be thinking of all he had left behind. She hoped so. Fervently, she prayed that before summer came, he would give her what she wanted most—a wedding band and a life together in Merriweather.

Justin drew both her hands to his lips and kissed them gently, as though she was the woman who owned his heart, as though he would do anything for her. Maybe, in time, he would. He traced the indentation on her swollen finger. It was his ring she wanted to see on her finger. Maybe, in time, she would.

He kissed her hands again, then pressed them to his heart. *"Fröliche Weihnachten!* my Katrina."

"Merry Christmas, my love."

Feeling too heavy and awkward to stand on tiptoes, Katrina slipped her hand around Justin's neck and drew his lips to hers in a sudden need to feel the sureness of his touch, for not only did she love him, she depended on him for survival. He drew her closer, gently, but with unmistakable purpose. For this one small moment, she felt safe as his arms enfolded her, even as she felt the wild beating of his heart.

She knew by the way he pressed his lips to hers, tenderly at first, then with a growing restlessness, that he wanted her. By the way he traced her lips with the tip of his tongue and the way she responded in kind, she knew that heat surged through him just as surely as it did through her, taunting them both with the thoughts of pleasure to come. She could tell by the way he forced himself to ease back, his breath ragged, his eyes dark with desire, his hands firmly on her shoulders, that he was trying to control the passion that threatened to overtake him. She didn't try to change his mind, for she, too, was wary of her pregnancy. But how could a man who so clearly longed for her touch let her walk out of his life? She prayed with all her heart he couldn't.

Momma had said it took courage to marry a man. Now Katrina knew why. Perhaps it took courage on the man's part too. Remembering it was the season of hope, she pushed to a dark corner of her mind the fear that still gnawed deep, deep inside, the fear that she and Justin would never come to a meeting of the minds, the fear that she would have to live without him. Somewhere. Somehow.

Justin tightened her white bedtime shawl, and while his

hands lingered on her shoulders, he murmured, "Everything will be all right. I promise."

"You promise," she said, gently mocking him.

"Yes." He steered her toward the bed. "Now you lie down. I think you're tired." When she didn't argue with him, he added, "You see. I'm already learning to read the signs."

She lay down, stretched out, and slipped her hands under the small of her back to relieve the strain. It would be a while before the effects of Justin's touch would diminish enough to allow her to sleep. In the meantime, she watched him as he fingered the socks she'd made for him, as though he knew and appreciated all the work she'd put into them. He was a good man. But he promised what he couldn't control. What was she going to do?

He could make light all he wanted, but what Pius said was true. Survival depended on the ability to read the signs and accept them. And cracked glass in a cupboard foretold certain disaster.

The new year, 1888, was not ushered in with the customary dancing, feasting, and drinking. There were no church bells at midnight, no group after group of revelers going house to house, knocking on doors, reciting poems in exchange for the New Year's ham and the holiday schnapps, firing shotguns into the air. Katrina remembered the last year before Justin went to Germany. He had been at the forefront of the revelers, laughing and shouting as he led his friends through the streets of Merriweather. He never mentioned Merriweather now. She wondered if he missed it.

Nearly two weeks later, on a clear and balmy Thursday morning, while Justin was making repairs to his wagon and Katrina was hanging laundry on a rope Justin had strung from the chicken coop to the house, the northwest sky suddenly filled with a bank of ominous black clouds, rolling toward them with the speed of a train. Paralyzed by the sight before her, Katrina could only stand still as she heard Justin shout for her to get into the house.

In less than a second, just as surely as the extinguishing of the evening lamp will plunge a room into darkness, the day turned to night. The wind roared like some ravenous beast, swirling blinding snow in every direction. Katrina turned to get the clothes but the wind knocked her down, into the blanket of snow already on the ground.

She managed to get to her feet, but the stinging snow blinded her. She couldn't see a thing. She could hardly breathe. She shielded her eyes with her hands to find the soddy, but there wasn't a trace. She couldn't even see the chicken coop, and it couldn't be more than a few yards away.

Which way should she go?

She screamed for Justin, but her words seemed to freeze in the air.

The snow swirled around her, and she winced as chunks of sleet cut her face. She tried to step forward, but the force of the wind pushed her back.

Which way? Which way?

The temperature plummeted. With knowledge that was both sudden and definite, Katrina knew that if she and Justin didn't get out of this blizzard they would freeze to death. So would her baby.

The rope. It was as though courage dwelt in a place deep inside her and only now, faced with the thought of dying, was she able to reach in and find it. Katrina tried in vain to shield her face from the ruthless wind and snow as she raised her hands over her head, groping for the rope Justin had strung for her.

Seconds raced away.

She felt the rope on the back of her hand first, then clutched it tight. She closed her eyes. Prayed. Hand over hand, she followed the rope till she reached the soddy.

Coughing and sputtering, she fell inside, the wind both pushing the door in and sucking it back out. Racing around in the dark, she found the portable lantern. Her hands trembling, she lit the candle.

She grabbed the longest length of rope Justin had hanging on the wall, tied one end around her, high, under her breasts, and the other end to the leg of the stove. Then she stepped outside, lantern raised high.

"Justin!" She tried to call his name, but the wind snuffed her voice, threatening to steal her breath if she tried again.

The candle sputtered. The flame died. But not before she saw a patch of Justin's red flannel shirt. She fought her way toward him, more terrified than she'd ever been in her life.

There could be no sweeter sensation than the feel of his hand as he gripped her arm.

"Hold on," she tried to say as she picked up the rope tied about her and, hand over hand, led them both back to the soddy.

Inside, Justin fell to his knees, coughing as she had done, gasping to breathe, cringing as his lungs adjusted to the warmer air. Only when he could open his eyes without stinging pain did he look up to see Katrina standing there, a bedraggled angel with a rope for wings. Never had she looked more beautiful.

Wordlessly, he opened his arms and drew her in. While the wind outside lashed about, piling more and more snow all around the soddy, he cupped the back of her head with his hand and kept his lips pressed against her hair.

His breathing finally slowed. When hers did as well, he released her only long enough to light the kerosene lamp and untie the rope about her waist. He looked at the other end, tied to the leg of the stove, and smiled with sweet sadness to know she had risked her life for him.

"Are you all right?" he asked. "The baby?"

She nodded, placing her hands on her belly.

"Still," he said, "I think you should lie down."

"Lie down? It's the middle of the morning."

"I think you should."

"I have no wish to be coddled," she said.

"Katrina, please."

"No!" She went to the stove, stoked the glowing coals, and put on a pot of coffee.

He looked at her with fresh eyes, as though seeing for the first time just how much strength she truly had. While it relieved him to know she was so resourceful, it also reminded him that when the baby was old enough to travel, if she still wanted to leave without him, she could.

With February came *Lichtmess*, Candlemas, the celebration of once again having enough light to eat the evening meal in daylight. It also marked the return of the planting season and the hiring of farm workers. Justin said he planned to hire a worker this year. He wanted to plow and plant a hundred acres at least. Katrina found it hard to show enthusiasm. Not that she expected him to throw his hands up and say he wouldn't do another thing on the farm until the baby was born and all three of them could go back to Merriweather. She just didn't expect him to dig in so much deeper, to risk so much more of his future on the land. Not when everyone for miles around was still talking about the January blizzard.

She prayed the weather in March would be kind.

*   *   *

Cleophee Yucker buckled her satchel and looked straight across the table and into the eyes of the town girl who stayed with her in the winter. "I want you should take the big sled. Hans will fix. Go to the sisters. Say it is time for the Barrison baby. Then come back here and wait for word on the Dorfman baby."

Clearly familiar with the routine, the girl, who appeared twelve or thirteen years old, grabbed her coat and hat and rushed out toward the barn.

"Come on," Justin said as he took Cleophee's wrinkled leather satchel from the table. "We've got to hurry."

"*Ja, ja,*" she said, as though she agreed with the seriousness of his urgency. Still, she moved as slowly as ever, knotting a length of twine around the pile of fresh linens on the chair.

"Here," Justin said, "I'll get that." He put the satchel down, fumbled with the rope, then yanked off his gloves to finish the job. "Her pains are coming fast."

Cleophee wriggled herself into a sheepskin coat two sizes too big for her strawlike body. "Don't be forgettin' the newspapers. Over to the corner." She inclined her head to the pile of papers already neatly stacked and wrapped in twine. "It is hands-in-the-pocket weather we've got out there, *ja*?"

"It's freezing."

"*Ja.* Now don't be frettin'," she said, as she wrapped a thick black shawl around her head. "Your little frau is wonderful heavy but she won't be birthin' soon. Not with the first."

Justin tucked a pile of linens under one arm, the newspapers under the other, and shot her a look that said she'd better know what she was talking about. "She's even bigger than when you saw her last week."

Cleophee gave him a little nod, the kind that wasted no energy. "Is she walkin' about yet?"

"No. I put her in the bed."

"Goot. You spritzen the room with the cleanin' water I give you?"

"Yes."

"Goot. And fresh water? You have plenty?"

"Every pot we own is on the stove, filled to the brim."

Cleophee took her satchel and nodded toward the door. "So, let's go already."

Once outside, Justin helped Cleophee into the sled, a crude box atop a pair of wooden runners, and sat by her side on a narrow bench that spanned the width of the sled. It was a far cry from the gleaming steel-blade cutter his family owned in Merriweather.

"She been restless, *ja?*"

"Yes. Especially at night." He thought of how she paced the darkened room, praying that God would see her through this ordeal. He prayed too. "She woke up in pain," he added, "moaning and shivering."

"*Ja, ja.* The approach to the sufferin'."

Like a yellow crystal frozen in an icy white sky, the sun shot beams of blinding light across the snow. Cleophee shielded her eyes with hands wrapped in thick woolen mittens. Justin wished he were bringing a qualified doctor to Katrina. He gripped the reins and squinted against the sun. There was nothing to cast a relieving shadow on the snow, not even a cloud . . .

Justin never saw the rock.

It caught the wooden runner on Cleophee's side and toppled her out. After making sure Cleophee wasn't hurt, Justin set about to right the sled and reload the newspapers and linens that had fallen in the snow. It took a precious thirty minutes. By the time they could see the soddy, Justin's nerves were frazzled. He cracked the whip over the horse's head, urging the animal to go faster, but the snow was thick and the horse was tired.

They finally pulled up in front. That's when he heard Katrina scream.

Justin jumped out of the sled and burst through the door. Katrina was lying on the bed, her face awash in sweat.

"Justin! The baby! The baby is coming!"

He rushed to the bed and grabbed her hand, feeling helpless, not knowing what to do. "Cleophee Yucker is here. You're going to be all right." She squeezed his hand hard, reminding him of how much strength she would need to get through the hours that lay ahead.

"Vell, vas is dis? The prairie going to get a new homesteader?"

"Help me," Katrina said to Cleophee, who had hung her coat on the hook by the door and was now methodically unbuckling her satchel. "Something is wrong. I know it."

Cleophee stepped over and placed her hand on Katrina's forehead. She spoke in German, telling Katrina to be strong, to have faith. Katrina spoke German in return, breathlessly rattling off her fears as though Cleophee had never heard them before. Cleophee gave a little smile, not full of false promise, not empty of hope.

"You ain't drinking strong spirits, no?" Cleophee said as she scrutinized the kitchen table and, finding it satisfactory, laid out a small leather-cased flask, a pair of scissors, a spool of white thread, and a bottle of herbs. With a dead serious look in her eyes, she crooked her finger to Justin and motioned for him to ready the pile of linens she'd brought with her.

"No," Katrina said between nervous gasps. "No spirits."

"Goot." Cleophee took a long starched white apron from the top of the pile of linens, slipped it over her head and tied it around her waist. To Justin she said, "I wash up now."

As he'd been instructed during Cleophee's surprise visit the week before, Justin filled the washbasin with hot water from the kettle on the stove. He watched as she scrubbed. She had small, weak-looking hands with skinny fingers. Could they do the job? He fisted his own strong, muscled hands, wishing he knew what it was that had to be done.

Katrina screamed again. Justin looked on in panic.

"I examine now." Cleophee's look told him he should leave the room, but where was he supposed to go?

"I'll . . . I'll . . . see to my horse."

"Goot." She gave him a shooing wave and when he'd gone she hooked on her spectacles and examined her patient. When she finished, she wiped Katrina's brow. "How long since the breakin' of the waters?"

"I don't know. An hour. Half an hour. I don't know." Katrina moaned as a pain gripped her, then shivered despite the roaring stove.

"You be doing just fine, little frau. Ain't time for the bearin' pains yet, but considerin' the snow I do think it time for the callin' of the women." She checked the masculine-looking timepiece around her neck and studied Katrina one more time. "*Ja*, you'll be forcin' pretty soon. I'll tell your man to keep his eyes for the sisters. I already give word for them to come." Cleophee stepped outside and closed the door behind her.

A moment later, her belly gripped in a rock hard band, Katrina cried out again, praying Cleophee would bring her and her baby safely through this ordeal.

Gussie and Bessie arrived a short while later. They found Katrina lying atop several thicknesses of newspaper and a bleached white sheet made of flour sacks. She was propped on her elbows, her hair plastered about her face, panting in a kind of panic the sisters recognized.

"Well, well, now," Gussie said as she slipped on the apron she'd brought with her. "Looks like the Dakota Territory's gonna be getting a new citizen any minute now."

"My sister is right," Bessie said to Katrina. "And with eight of her own, she should know. Let's plait that hair of yours out of the way." Bessie slipped a ribbon from her pocket and held it between her teeth as she scooped Katrina's hair from the sides of her face and pulled it back. "Next time you'll know to braid early."

Katrina looked up in horror. "Next time? There's never going to be a next time. Never." Her belly hardened again and she screamed, falling back on the bed. This time she felt Cleophee's small warm hands pushing her knees apart.

"That's it," Cleophee said. "Nice and easy. Bessie, you stay at your place and lever her up to position. Gussie, down this end. I'm needin' the birthin' towel and your big flat hands. Now, little momma, it's time for the bearin' down."

Outside, Justin stood in the windbreak, currying his horse. He stroked with a powerful yearning. He prayed the same way. All the while he kept his gaze fixed on his front door, hating that, at a time like this, when the one person he loved more than life itself could be dying, he wasn't allowed to be with her.

When Gussie finally opened the door, his heart stopped.

Frantically, she waved him over. He dropped the brush and ran.

As soon as he stepped inside he went to Katrina. Propped up with two pillows, she looked deathly pale. But her eyes! They sparkled with a kind of wonder he'd never seen before. And her lips turned up at the corners in a sweet smile of contentment. He bent and kissed her forehead.

Weak from her ordeal, she whispered, "Say hello to your daughter." She lifted the corner of the blanket that hooded the baby's head. "I'm thinking of calling her Tatiana. What do you think?"

"Tatiana? The fairy queen?"

"*Ja*, do you like?"

He crouched down and peeked at the sleeping bundle

nestled by her side. "Tatiana," he murmured, as though not wanting to disturb her slumber yet wanting her to know he was her poppa and he was right here. "Tatiana." As he whispered her name again, he dug his nails into the flesh of his palm, counting on the pain to force down the lump in his throat.

"She has your dark hair," Katrina said, "but I think she has my eyes. And Gretchen's cheeks, that's for sure."

"She's beautiful. Our Tatiana."

He didn't know how long he knelt there, watching Katrina drift into sleep, watching his daughter wrap her tiny pink fingers around his own. Married or not, this was his family. They depended on him.

Cleophee cleared her throat. He turned around to find her buckling her satchel. Bessie and Gussie had their coats on and stood waiting by the door.

"The women, they gonna fetch me home," Cleophee said. "They be back tomorrow, Gussie for the morning, Bessie for the afternoon. Now, your little frau there, you just leave her sleep. For all her sufferin' in the childbed she's looking mighty good in the face. Her eatin' went away, though. She might get it back tonight, maybe not till morning. You knowin' how to cook a little porridge?"

"Yes."

"Goot. Now the babe," Cleophee continued. "You don't want her gettin' the milk fever, so best she's put to the breast early. I don't hold with not lettin' them suck for the first three days." She shook her head as though she'd argued the point many times.

Justin committed the advice to memory while he watched Cleophee disappear into her coat. Her voice rose up through the heavy sheepskin as her small but capable hands poked through the sleeves. "Now I'm tellin' you true here, Poppa. Take care that no mischief gets done. Protect both your frau and your babe from all sharp air and unnatural commotions."

"Don't worry. I will."

"Goot."

"Thank you." The words hardly seemed enough.

"*Ja*." Cleophee sighed with the contentment of a job well done. "You three gonna be wonderful happy."

With that prediction, the women left.

Though Justin longed to stay, there were chores still to do. He would hurry. He didn't want to be gone a moment longer than he had to. He leaned over and kissed Katrina and his child. Katrina opened her heavy-lidded eyes. She did no more than take Justin's hand, but at that moment he vowed to make Cleophee's prediction come true. The three of them were going to be "wonderful happy."

That night, after he'd milked the cow, fed the animals, and fixed himself a pot of beans and Katrina a cup of warm milk and a slice of the bread and jam she'd make earlier in the week, Justin peeked at little Tatiana for the tenth time, then spread his bedroll by the door. This had been a day he'd never forget. Seeing his baby curled up in the cradle he'd made with his own two hands caused his heart to swell.

That was when he realized just how glad he was that his first child had been a girl. Because sometime during the day, sometime while he was busy with mindless chores, memories of his childhood crept in, right along with his own fears. He could show little Tatiana how to gather eggs and how to ride a pony, and he could show her a few weather signs too. And he hoped he could show her he loved her. This business of being a father carried an awesome responsibility.

A few days later Katrina got up. Much as she wanted to, she couldn't spend the customary nine days in bed waiting for her muscles and bones to return to the normal prebirth position. If she were back in Merriweather she could, for she would have Gretchen to help her. But not here. Gussie and Bessie had taken turns coming by each day, but they had families of their own to care for and could never stay long. They did, however, summon Cleophee Yucker.

She came the next day, on the heels of another storm. She brought with her a package of sugar and a tin of coffee. She brought loaves of bread and pots of chicken soup thick with rich egg noodles. She also brought a special egg and pressed it lightly to the baby's lips.

"Touched by the *Schwatzei*, she will go peep-peep-peep like a little chick and learn to talk early," Cleophee said.

"*Danke*," Katrina said, happy to see that not all the old customs were lost on the prairie.

Cleophee also brought a nursing bottle, complete with a strawlike flexible tube attached to a white rubber nipple.

"Bessie, she tells me your milk isn't coming so goot."

Sitting on the edge of the bed, Katrina looked down at her breasts. "Not yet."

"Don't you be frettin'. Sometimes you young mommas need a little help. Everything it's gonna be fine in a few days. But you keep this bottle around anyway and go to the cow if you have to. Your little fairy queen, she ain't gonna starve."

That night Katrina wrote a long letter to Gretchen, telling her about little Tatiana and the nursing bottle. She avoided any mention of wedding Justin.

22

Gussie came the next day and took Katrina's laundry as well as the letter to Gretchen. She returned the laundry two days later, all ironed and neatly folded. She and Bessie repeated the kindness for the next two weeks. It was during that last visit that Katrina heard about the financial troubles of Pius and Dulcie Pettibone.

The following morning Justin, Katrina, and the baby set out in the wagon for the Pettibone ranch. A few nights earlier Justin had pointed to a huge ring around the moon and said there would be a storm. It snowed an inch before dawn, just enough to remind Katrina that winter was not finished with them yet.

Even without the blizzards of January and March, she knew that watching for spring would be difficult. With no trees, there would be no buds on the maples and oaks, no fragrant lilacs and lindens. No leafy canopies to give shade. No strong limbs to hold memories. No roots to ripple along the ground, holding the world together. No robins. Still, the clear yellow sun warmed the waking earth, melting snow filled the gurgling streams. Now and then the April air carried a hint of new grass, the sweet clean smell of a prairie spring. It was impossible not to appreciate it.

What little joy the season brought disappeared when the Pettibone ranch came in sight. Justin stopped the wagon and stared.

Katrina clutched Tatiana close to her heart and looked at the sleek black carriage with its team of matching black horses tethered in front of the house. Dreading the answer, she asked, "Is that it?"

"That's it," he replied in a hoarse voice.

The collection man had never visited her family, not in the old country or the new. Both Momma and Poppa would have died of shame. But Katrina had seen one such man as a child, though he didn't parade his power in a sleek black buggy. From village to village, he walked with a long twisted stick in his hand, a man of imposing height and girth, charged with ferreting out something—a piece of jewelry, a tool, a child's toy, a pot for cooking, the last bucket of coal—something to satisfy a debt made when the future looked brighter.

With a determined set of his jaw, Justin eased their one-horse wagon along the trail of slush and mud until they could read the intimidating gold lettering on the side of the carriage: WENTWORTH COLLECTION. CHICAGO.

Katrina looked toward the corral where the Pettibone boys had gathered. Some leaned against the fence and stared at the ground. Some straddled the fence and sat nose to nose with their pets. Katrina's heart ached for what they must be going through. "It feels as though someone died," she said.

"In a way, someone did."

Just as they reached the house, two men came out the

front door. One was of medium height, muscular, dressed in denim and boots. He carried a piece of paper in his hand and a gun on his hip.

"That must be the sheriff from over in Eureka," Justin said. "The tall one in the black suit, the one who looks like an undertaker, he must be the collection man." Justin reached over and laid his hand on Katrina's knee. "And that," he said, staring at the carriage, "is the debt wagon."

As Justin helped Katrina down from their wagon, Dulcie rushed outside, ranting in desperation at the neatly dressed man in the black suit. "You're not attacking some nobody, I'll have you know. My man once got a ribbon for shooting seven birds in a row! Do you know that? Do you?" She saw Katrina and, just for a second, stared like a startled deer. Then she turned back to the man in the black suit and shouted louder. "You and your heartless kind are bound to depopulate this land, you keep forcin' folks out like this!"

"He's just doing his job, ma'am," the sheriff said, nailing the piece of paper to the front door. "I'm sorry, ma'am. I've got to do my job too."

"For God's sake," Dulcie pleaded as the sheriff mounted his horse. "Please! He didn't commit no penitentiary offense. He just can't pay his debts."

The collection man climbed to the seat of his carriage and took the reins. "I will return tomorrow morning at ten o'clock sharp with the auctioneer. Good day, madam." He tipped his hat, flicked the reins, and left, the sheriff riding by his side.

Katrina stepped up on the porch, hoping to find a way to help.

Fidgeting with her hands, Dulcie said, "How'd you find out?"

"Gussie Hemmeler."

"I'm so ashamed. The collection man was at Rhinedollar's last week askin' after us. Sent the sheriff out here yesterday to serve us with some papers." She looked toward the incriminating notice on the front door. "I'd rip that right off if I thought it would do any good." Her shoulders slumped in defeat. "But I doubt there's a single soul in this whole territory who don't know our shame. And if there is, he'll know for sure come ten tomorrow morning."

"You're with friends now," Katrina said.

Dulcie sighed. Katrina hoped Dulcie took her words to imply apology and forgiveness for her part in their earlier argument. Lifting the edge of the blanket to look at the baby, Dulcie said, "Look at this sleeping angel. She's prettier than a prairie rose. What are you calling her?"

Justin answered. "Tatiana."

"Tatiana," Dulcie repeated, nodding her approval. "I'd ask to hold her, but the way things is flying out of my hands these days, I don't trust myself. Why don't we go on in." She turned and led the way.

Once inside the house, Justin looked around and said what Katrina had been thinking. "Where's Pius?"

At the mention of his name, Pius shuffled into the room. Justin gripped his friend's hand and shook it with fierce determination.

Every feature weighted down with worry, Pius focused on the floor and mumbled, "Good to see you both."

Justin looked around. "How bad is it? Maybe we can help."

Pius shrugged his shoulders. "Too late." He stood in the middle of the cluttered room like a man who has lost his way. He spoke slowly. "You know, I recollect the year when the grasshoppers was so bad they ate holes in the curtains. Then there was the coyotes: when they wasn't gettin' the eggs, they was gettin' the chickens. I remember one winter I had to form me a skinnin' team to salvage the hides of all the cattle killed in a storm."

He walked over to the kitchen table and sat down on the far end of the long bench.

"Then there was the fire. I lost two fine wives. Almost lost Merton." He gazed into emptiness.

"Pius?"

He looked up at Justin and continued. "But I ain't never been up against somethin' like this." He ran his hand through his disheveled hair. "A man knows when he settles out here, Mother Nature calls the shots and there's gonna be times when he faces both God and the devil in the same day. And a man knows he's gonna die. A man knows all that. But he settles out here anyway. Why? So he can leave a legacy to his children." He walked toward the window overlooking the corral.

When he turned around, his eyes had hardened. He glared at Dulcie. "Forty cents a week for a year, and I'm paying twenty dollars for a twelve-dollar sewing machine. A gravy dish going for the ungodly sum of two bits winds up costing me one dollar twenty."

"You told me to go on and get whatever I needed," Dulcie said, though the hurt look on her face took most of the bite out of her words.

"Good lord, woman, what demon possessed you to think I needed a new set of studs and collar buttons? I got the ones my pappy give to me. They're as old as you are, but they still work." He turned to Justin. "One dollar thirty for a dozen collars and eighty cents for a blasted set of pearl buttons. What do I look like, some kind of dandy?"

Dulcie choked back sobs. "You said you'd tell me when to start worryin', but you never did."

"Well, you can start worryin' now because come morning we're gonna lose the farm." He held out his hands, displaying his calloused palms. "And farming is all I know."

Justin looked as anxious as Katrina felt. "We can all pitch in," he said. "The same way you and your boys helped me plow, and Hemmeler lends his tools to those who need them, and Roundtree—"

"I need more than sweat, son. I need cash."

Justin paused a moment and then said, "I've got some money set aside."

Pius gave a sad smile. "Not enough, I'm afraid."

"How do you know?"

"Because I never knew a German to trust his money to a bank. He always puts it into land or stock, and, son, you ain't got enough to brag on either."

"That's not exactly true," Justin said with a genuine smile. "A German might not trust his money to a bank, but he will lend it to a friend."

Pius looked at Justin, then at Katrina, then at little Tatiana, all safe and snug in her mother's arms. He looked at Dulcie, her hands locked in her lap, her leathery skin hidden in the folds of her apron, her head bowed low. Finally, he said, "You got an extra four thousand dollars?"

Justin's jaw dropped. Katrina blanched. Dulcie moaned at hearing the figure out loud. A moment of paralyzing silence hung in the air.

"We don't have near that amount," Justin said.

"I figured as much," Pius said with a shrug. "A few bucks won't do nothing but prolong the agony. Still, I damn sure appreciate the offer."

"What about a bank?" Katrina asked. "They lend money."

"Only to folks who don't need it. Your man can tell you about that." With respect, Pius added, "He knows about money. Make sure you listen to him."

"What about your cattle?" she asked. "You could sell them."

"Couldn't hardly afford to feed them this winter. Had to turn them loose on the prairie to forage. Now they ain't but skin and bone. Don't expect to get more than a few cents to the pound."

Justin spoke up. "What about your harvester? Your big double-bottom plow? They should bring a nice piece of change."

"Well, folks, that's exactly what I'm gonna do come ten o'clock tomorrow morning. I myself won't be selling them. The collection man will. See, I don't outright own any of that equipment. The bank does. Owns all three teams of breaking horses too. Called them collateral. The bank owns those four quarters I bought last year and was fool enough to put into wheat. Could say the bank owns the wheat too, but since there ain't no wheat, not after the fire—" He slammed his fist against the wall. "God damn it!"

Justin walked over to Pius and placed his hand on his shoulder. "There must be something we can do."

"Ain't a damn thing you nor anybody else can do. Except maybe be here tomorrow morning. For the wife, you know."

He looked toward Dulcie, who by now had tears streaming down her face.

"And if you're as smart as you're supposed to be," Pius added, "you'll buy that team of black Belgians. A good work team is mighty hard to come by and you know it. Had to work that young one for a year till she stopped kickin'. Now the two of them set in and pull together and give you the true power of two horses."

"I'd feel like a buzzard," Justin said.

"Son, how much sod can you turn in a day with one horse and that single-bottom of yours? Two acres, if everything—and I mean *everything*—is going your way. I got a double-bottom out there. Takes six horses to pull, which I also got. You use that double-bottom and you can turn five acres a day easy, maybe even six. I bought that plow new from the implement shop. Paid close to one hundred dollars for it. You can get it tomorrow for twenty."

"Twenty?"

"Twenty-five tops. You watch. Ain't nobody out here got

the kind of cash the collection man is looking for. And I'll guarantee you he don't relish the idea of dragging a bunch of animals behind that fancy carriage of his, or having to drive a big old wagon loaded with furniture." He waved his arm across the room. "The rocking chair, the stove, the Singer, the ice-cream freezer—they'll all go cheap."

"And then what?" Katrina asked. "What do you do after the auction?"

Pius seemed surprised she needed to be told outright. "Then we start over."

Katrina breathed a sigh of relief.

"Back east," Pius added. "Can't stay here. Even if I could, I'd be too ashamed."

"Now wait a minute," Justin said. "There's not a homesteader for two hundred miles north or south who hasn't experienced some measure of what's happened here. You don't have to leave. Maybe you could get a smaller place."

This time it was Pius who placed his hand on Justin's shoulder. "For all your fine talk, son, sometimes you ain't too smart. See, I'm already dead. Now it's just a matter of where they lay my bones."

Dulcie jerked her head around, her eyes alive with a kind of defiance. But if she had something to say, she thought better of it and turned away.

After a moment, Justin said, "I think we'd better go now." He held the baby while Katrina slipped on her coat.

She took the baby and said to Dulcie, "Come to supper tonight, all of you."

Dulcie shook her head, clearly too upset to speak.

"Thanks," Pius said, "but no. We still got some things to pack. We get to keep our clothes and such."

Katrina followed Justin to the door. Sensing the final nail in the coffin, she said to Dulcie, "When will you be leaving?"

Through her tears, Dulcie answered. "Tomorrow. Right after the auction."

After Katrina and Justin said their good-byes, the ride home was a long one. Justin noticed how tightly Katrina held the baby.

"You saw all this coming, didn't you?" she asked.

"I knew they were in trouble. I didn't know how bad."

"Do you blame them for being in such a state?"

"A man who spends money for something he doesn't need is just robbing himself." Then he added, "But they didn't go under just because of time payments on hand lotion and gravy boats. That's not what this is all about."

"I know," Katrina said. "It's about everything a farmer has to have to succeed out here—a lot of land, big equipment, bountiful crops. It's about trying as hard as a man or woman can and still being helpless in the face of weather and illness and things a body just can't control."

"It's about survival. For all of us."

Justin couldn't sleep. At three in the morning he rose from the bed, pulled on his shirt and pants, and sat at the table, listening to the stillness, wondering if he would ever be able to conquer the demons that still threatened his dreams.

Katrina stirred and sat up. "Justin? Are you all right?"

"I'm fine," he whispered. "Go back to sleep."

Instead, she got up, wrapped her shawl around her shoulders, and came to the stove. She added a few coals to those banked from the night before and shivered as she lit the lamp. Sitting down across from Justin, she said, "What is it, a bad dream?"

"It's nothing."

"The Pettibones, *ja*?"

He sighed at the thought of what would happen at ten that morning. "I guess."

"Talk to me."

He wasn't sure he wanted to. The memories had been

pent up for years, and for good reason. But he could tell that she was asking not out of curiosity but out of concern.

"We were living in Philadelphia. I was seven, maybe eight. Richmond two or three. My parents had come over from Germany in 1855, when they'd been married barely a month. My father and several other young men had been chosen by their village council to investigate the wild rumors of freedom and free land."

"He must have felt greatly honored to have been selected."

"I suppose he did. From what my mother told me, he couldn't wait to write back that the rumors were all true. He also said that with proper financing he could buy a small hardware factory. He promised that if the council would lend him the funds, he would give jobs to others who wanted to come to America."

"So that's how he got started?"

"Yes, with money scraped together from the family and friends he and my mother had left behind."

"And he was successful, of course."

"For a while, yes. Saying he wanted to give more opportunity to those still at home, he offered to settle his debt by paying the passage of anyone who wanted to come over, whether they worked in his factory or not. The council agreed. Over the next few years, hundreds of others from the village came over. More than anything, he wanted his own father—my Grandfather Heinrich—to come, but he never did."

"My *Grossvatter* wouldn't come with us either. He refused to leave his village."

"That wasn't the case with my grandfather. He and my grandmother wanted very much to come to America to see their successful son."

"Why didn't they? They wanted to and your father would pay their passage."

"Because my grandfather wouldn't take the money. In his eyes, the factory belonged to the village and he said the people there had already done enough in setting up his son. No, Heinrich Barrison insisted on saving the money himself." Justin tilted his head back and closed his eyes. Why was he remembering all this now?

"Did your grandfather ever save enough?"

"Yes, but it was too late. The War Between the States broke out. Like the other Germans who had settled here, my father was proud, very proud, to fight against what he saw as another feudal system complete with black serfs and powerful southern princes. But the war made all travel dangerous. He told his parents to wait. They did.

"In the end, I imagine my father was only too happy his parents never came. The war ruined him. He lost everything. His money. His honor. He told his father not to come. Ever."

"How could he possibly lose everything? He had plenty of work, which means plenty of money, right?"

"He had plenty of work and plenty of customers who couldn't pay their bills. And even after his debt to the council was settled, he still paid the passage for anyone from the village who needed it. Many times he had to choose between paying his personal debts or paying for more ocean passage. He always chose to bring over more of his countrymen."

"Maybe he hoped his father would still come."

"Who knows? But I remember how Richmond and I were taunted by neighborhood kids because our clothes were patched and we didn't have shoes to wear in the summer. I had a hard time understanding it myself. After all, my father was a businessman, not a laborer. He would say, 'Never mind those barbarians. You have what you need.'"

"So what did he do?"

"He borrowed from the bank. He managed to hold on for several years. He had always been a good businessman, practical and clear thinking, except when it came to his homeland."

"What about your mother? How did she manage?"

"Oh, Mother would have understood that with no money coming in, there would be no money to go out. But he thought it was beneath him to discuss money with a woman—even his wife. So he never told her. Fortunately for all of us, she was frugal by nature and never spent unnecessarily to begin with. Poor Mother. She never knew how deep was their loss until the day the debt wagon came to our door."

"No!" Katrina covered her mouth with her hands.

"I don't remember much," he said, though what memories he did have gnawed at his gut. He stood and walked to the window. He would tell her the story because he could no longer hold it in. She might not understand how such a small incident could leave such a deep scar, but it didn't matter. He had to talk about it.

"Mother had finally bought a bed for Richmond and me. My father shouted so loud people on the street heard him. But Mother insisted. We'd been sleeping on blankets on the floor for as long as I could remember. We were always cold. My back was always sore. Finally, one day Richmond was bitten by a rat and Mother said 'Enough.' She had the bed delivered that afternoon.

"Every morning I straightened the blankets. Every night I turned them down. Even Richmond, young as he was, tried to help. We both took care not to mar the wood. I don't think we'd had that bed a whole three months when the collection man came and took it away."

As he sat back down, he saw tears fill Katrina's eyes. He didn't want to make her cry and he definitely didn't want her pity, but now she might understand why it was so important for him to be independent.

She reached over and put her hand on his arm. "Just when you thought the fates had blessed you, your happiness was snatched away."

"Something like that."

"I know the feeling too. That's why it is so important to have the security of family and community."

He took the comfort she offered, but she didn't understand. She never would.

Katrina sat for a moment. Then she said, "Surely you take comfort in knowing that, despite his earlier adversities, your father didn't end up a failure. Far from it."

"He came to Missouri a broken man with nothing left to lose. There's no other way to explain the risky business deals he made. This time, luck was on his side. So, if you mean he didn't end up a failure because he owns a thriving brewery, you're right. But did he ever once bother to ask what either of his sons wanted out of life? No. Did he ever admit that it was his own cold heart and blind ambition that drove the happiness from his wife's eyes? No."

"You see the Pettibone boys, maybe Dulcie too, headed for the same suffering, don't you?"

"Unless someone helps that old cuss, yes. That's exactly what I see."

The black of night had turned to gray and the gray to a fragile blue. Ribbons of pink and yellow shot through the dawn sky as though the day were worthy of celebration.

Justin stood and looked around him, at the house Pius and his boys had helped him build, at the pail of water from the well Pius had helped him dig. It was Pius and Dulcie who had stocked Justin's root cellar for the winter. He had a hundred acres of land plowed for next spring, thanks to the use of that big double-bottom plow of Pius's. Though Justin didn't know for sure whether or not Pius had helped his neighbors in similar fashion, he suspected that was the case. Maybe here was a chance for the neighbors to repay the favor.

He grabbed his boots. "Katrina, can you feed the animals this morning?"

"*Ja*, of course. What is it? Why are you rushing so?"

"I'm going over to the Hemmelers'. I've got a plan."

Later that morning, with Tatiana asleep on a quilt in the corner of the Pettibones' bedroom, Katrina helped Dulcie pack the last of her personal items, all the while keeping her ear to the open window, now and then glancing at the horizon.

"Not much of a crowd out there," Dulcie said, glancing toward the window. "I figured the close-by neighbors would be here first, but they ain't here, not a one of them. I don't even know these folks. Must have come all the way from Eureka, maybe even Leola. Guess they knew there'd be good pickings here today."

"Justin will be here shortly. So will the others; I'm sure of it," Katrina said. She wanted to tell Dulcie that Justin had dropped her off early because he still had to speak to the few families he hadn't managed to see at the crack of dawn. He had a plan to save the Pettibones, but he was quick to admit it might not work. Katrina didn't want to give Dulcie false hope.

Outside, the sheriff stood by while the auctioneer prepared to sell off a dream, and stately Mr. Wentworth, the collection man, waited to count his money.

The auctioneer, a short husky man in a gray flannel shirt and plain black suspenders, hoisted the heavy ice-cream freezer over his head and bellowed to the sparse crowd standing amid puddles and patches of snow, their eyes downcast, their hands in their pockets. Not one of them looked happy to be here. "All right, folks, let's have a history on this fine item. Practically brand new. Just what a family needs for a Sunday picnic or Fourth of Ju-ly celebration. What am I bid?"

No one spoke.

"Folks, this is a big freezer, fourteen gallons. I believe it to be the latest model in the Sears catalogue. You pay full price, and you'd have to part with six dollars and eighty-five cents at least. What am I bid?"

Still nothing.

"Look at this good and hard now, folks. Cast iron on the top, heavy-grade tin on the inside. They don't come better than this and it's hardly used. So what am I bid?"

When still no one spoke, the auctioneer turned to the collection man as if to say, What do you want me to do?

Mr. Wentworth stood on the porch, drumming his fingers on the black felt hat he held in his hands. "Get on with it," he said with a dismissing wave of his hand. "And do it quickly."

"Folks," the auctioneer said to the small crowd, "I don't like this any more than you do. If I didn't need the money so bad myself I wouldn't be working this job, but I'm trying to make a go of it out here same as you."

A few people nodded or whispered to each other.

"So how 'bout it?" He lifted the freezer one more time, held it over his head, and turned left and right. "The Pettibones are good people. We all know that. So come on, let's help them get things squared away."

A woman in a homespun dress that had more patches than cloth nudged her husband. After several shared whispers, he shouted, "Thirty cents!"

"That's a good start. Now who'll go to fifty?"

Katrina heard it all as she carried her baby through the empty hollow-sounding rooms and followed Dulcie outside. At the door, Dulcie turned back for one last look at the place she called home. Though Dulcie didn't say a word, Katrina could guess her thoughts. She'd recall each joy, each sorrow, each wish granted, each promise unfulfilled, just as Katrina had done when she'd left *her* home—not once but twice.

Anxiously, Katrina looked to the horizon. The Pettibones

truly loved the prairie. She hated the thought that they'd have to leave.

The two women stood on the far side of the porch for what seemed like an hour, sniffing and blinking back tears as, one by one, the smaller household items and farm implements were loaded into the backs of empty wagons.

Sounding more encouraged now, the auctioneer stepped over to the sewing machine. "All right now, ladies. This is the item I know all of you have been waiting for. A genuine Singer."

"I can't bear to watch," Dulcie said as she turned away.

Where was Justin? Only now, as the minutes ticked away, did Katrina realize how much faith she'd placed in him, how swept up she'd been in listening to his plan, how certain she was that he could perform the miracle so desperately needed here today. Where was he?

The auctioneer pushed. "Come on, folks, look at this cabinet. That's solid cherry. A work of art. A genuine Singer in a cherry cabinet. Who'll start the bidding at two dollars?"

There was no cloud of dust on the horizon to draw Katrina's attention, because the ground was still too wet. And yet suddenly there was a change in the air, a gathering of hope from the groaning of wheels under heavy loads.

She prayed that Justin had been able to persuade the others and, if so, that they would make it in time. He'd asked for her approval of his own role in the plan, but she had given neither, saying she had no right. It was his own hard-earned money he was talking about, not hers, not theirs.

The sound grew louder. Several people at the auction turned around. The auctioneer stood still. Katrina saw the curiosity on Dulcie's face, then the fragile hope, then the excitement she couldn't contain.

One by one, like pop-ups in a children's book, the wagons of the close-by neighbors came in sight. Though each one carried husband, wife, and children, these were not the regular family wagons. No. These were the long flatbeds used to haul sacks of wheat to market. Pulled by six- and eight-horse teams, each flatbed was stacked front to rear, five stacks long, three stacks high, with wheat, the money of the prairie.

The wagons pulled into the yard and crowded the area around the auction as though daring the proceedings to continue.

Pius, who'd been in the barn with his boys all this time, came over, his eyes red and swollen. Justin jumped down from his wagon, as did Karl and Gussie Hemmeler, Dutch and Bessie Warbeck, the Peroskys, the Scogginses, Lily Roundtree and her big dog, and Winona McBride. They gathered around Pius, waving for Dulcie and Katrina to join them, leaving the auctioneer speechless and Mr. Wentworth highly annoyed.

After several moments of intense conversation, protests on Pius's part, insistence on the part of his neighbors, a grateful-looking Pius shook each man's hand. Standing taller than he had in a long time, he called the sheriff over.

The sheriff nodded, as he listened to what Pius had to say, and beckoned to Mr. Wentworth.

"What is the holdup?" Mr. Wentworth said as he pulled his gold watch from the pocket of his vest.

Pius could barely restrain the grin that lit up his eyes. "I'm paying you off. In full. This minute."

Justin interrupted. "Less what you've already collected, of course."

"With what, wheat?" Mr. Wentworth asked indignantly.

Pius nodded. "That's right."

The sheriff broke in. "It's as good as gold. I'll vouch for that. Some places it's legal tender, at least for court fines and such."

"Not to me, it isn't. I have the right to demand at least twenty-five percent of what's due in cash."

Pius withdrew from his pocket a stack of bills wrapped

in twine, money Justin had given him only moments before. His hand shook as he handed it over. "Here you go. Eleven hundred dollars."

Mr. Wentworth crossed his arms. "I have no intention of accepting that. I want the entire amount in cash, or the auction continues as scheduled."

"Sorry," the sheriff said. "You don't have a choice in the matter anymore. Mr. Pettibone here is offering to pay you what he owes, and you're obliged to accept."

"And just what in the name of God am I going to do with all that wheat?"

The sheriff shrugged. "Haul it to Eureka and sell it, just like everyone else does."

Wentworth smirked. "If I have to pay transportation, I am within my rights to increase the amount of the debt."

Earl Hemmeler stepped forward. "We'll take it into Eureka for you, Wentworth. We'll have it at the warehouse tomorrow afternoon."

Not waiting for any further argument, the sheriff went over to where the auctioneer stood, a Singer instruction manual in his hand and a look of relief on his face. "Auction's over," the sheriff told him. He turned to the crowd. "You folks can go on home now. The Pettibones will be staying on with us."

"You did it!" Katrina cried as she kissed Justin on the cheek. "I knew you could!"

Beaming in the light of her praise, he said, "*We* did it." He shook hands with each of his neighbors and gave Pius a hearty slap on the back. He put his arm around Katrina's shoulder, holding the three of them together. "We *all* did it."

One evening a couple of weeks later, with Tatiana safely asleep in her cradle, Katrina headed for the corral and pig-pen Justin was building with a jug of cool water in her hands. For several weeks now he'd gone off in search of cottonwoods to use for fencing. He had far less than a wagonload, but it was enough for a small enclosure. He said he planned to buy pigs soon, but not before he had the pen ready. She thought of the day he'd impulsively bought Gilbert Bodine's chickens when he had no coop in which to keep them. He'd learned a lot in a short time.

She found him working away. It was warm for the end of April. He'd taken off his shirt and flung it on a pile of straw he'd hauled from the Hemmelers'. He said he'd have his own wheat next year, his own threshing party, his own mountain of straw. She believed him. Walking toward him now, she actually considered staying around to see it, to be part of it.

Two weeks ago his skin had been milky white, in strong contrast to the dark hair on his chest. Now, as he worked in the spring sunshine, it was growing darker with each day. He stood even taller than he had before, and walked with purpose in his steps. He'd always cut a fine figure, but now . . . now there was something more compelling about him. More times than Katrina cared to admit, she found herself staring at him, as familiar longings reawakened.

He stopped working when he saw her and gave a smile that told her he was not only glad to see her but glad she was nearby. She suspected that he shared the same longing to touch again, to kiss deeply and not have to stop.

Wordlessly, she handed him the jug and watched as he drank till he was satisfied. With her finger, she reached to wipe the single drop of water that clung to his chin. He took her hand, pressed it to his face, and slowly dragged her palm along the stubble of his cheek.

Her own cheeks burned in a blatant display of the shameless desire in her heart and the pleasure of knowing he shared her thoughts. She could look nowhere but in his eyes.

He dropped the jug and bent to kiss her, a prelude of soft fluttery kisses that served only to arouse her all the more. She slipped her arms around his neck and deepened the kiss. He enfolded her as though there was no sweeter toil, pressing her against the hardened proof that he, too, had longed for this day.

To keep satisfaction at bay only heightened the pleasure and so she turned her head, only to find him insistent to draw her back, his wild and hungry kiss almost painful in its need.

"It's time," she murmured and glanced toward the pile of straw.

Moments later, lying on her back, her breasts bared, her skirt bunched about her waist, she moaned with pleasure as he thrust deep inside her, again and again. Then she clutched his shoulders and cried out in satisfaction as he lay spent across her chest.

Satisfied, she looked up at the bright blue sky, smelled the clear spring air and the fresh sweet hay. The prairie was beautiful today.

23

Eureka grew by the minute. Wide enough to accommodate six wagons and teams abreast, the main thoroughfare groaned as frisky horses, slow-moving oxen, optimistic shopkeepers, determined citizens, and wide-eyed newcomers crisscrossed the street, churning up dust along the way.

Easing his wagon down the street, Justin pointed to the hotels, restaurants, saloons, livery stables, and warehouses. "Look around, Katrina. This is the picture of confidence. Hemmeler told me that before the railroad came, this place was nothing more than three or four shacks. Now it's the end of the track and look at it!"

Excited by all she saw, Katrina looked left and right as Justin slowly maneuvered their wagon down the street. She'd grown so accustomed to the silence of the prairie that the shouts and whistles, the creaking of wheels, and the bellowing of tired oxen confused her. She'd seen New York and knew the look of a big city. Eureka wasn't as big as New York, but it was as busy. Surprised, she gazed at men in clean canvas suits, leather chaps, or denim overalls, and women in straw hats, calico bonnets, and thick black scarves. She strained to catch the familiar German words carried on the breeze.

"Wheat, *Weizen. Weizen,* wheat!"

She turned to hear who had spoken the language so dear to her heart, but the hubbub around her made that impossible. She understood the message, however. One look at the countless grain elevators under construction, and the memory of one auction, made translation unnecessary. Wheat was money, and money was wheat.

No wonder Pius had gambled on putting all his land into wheat. No wonder Justin wanted to buy more land for that purpose. No wonder farmers took on debt to buy the machinery needed to harvest their fields of gold. Justin was right. Subsistence farming as she'd known it in the old country was on the way out. Here in the Dakota Territory, farming, particularly wheat farming, was big business.

From the inspired look on Justin's face, Katrina knew he was thinking the same thing. Maybe one day this wheat would feed the world.

Justin didn't have the luxury of time. His better judgment had cautioned him not to go to Eureka yet. But for the first time since she'd come to the prairie, Katrina could see its beauty. If he didn't make a move now, he might never have another chance.

He gave her some money and dropped her off at Hezel, Hepperle & Sauter, a general merchandise store that dwarfed the Rhinedollar establishment. He told her to meet him back there in an hour. He had some business to tend to. They'd have dinner in town, spend the night at the new hotel, and head back in the morning.

His first stop was the bank exchange. He listened carefully as the terms were described. He had to wipe his hands on his pants before he could hold the pen to sign the loan.

His second stop was the lumberyard.

Back at the soddy, Katrina opened the box they'd picked up in Prosperity.

"A dollhouse! Oh, Justin, isn't it beautiful?"

Katrina examined the structure in the center of her kitchen table: a white villa, two feet high, trimmed with pink gingerbread, with bay windows, turrets, and rooms full of miniature furniture and real lace curtains. "I'm so glad we stopped in Prosperity on the way back. Gretchen's gift might have sat there for weeks."

He nodded. "It's pretty, all right."

Puzzled by his reserve, she said, "Is something troubling you?"

"No. Why?"

"You've been awfully quiet. You've hardly said a word since we've been back. You didn't say much along the way either."

"Everything's fine."

"Then why the worry lines across your brow?"

"It's nothing." He went to the box he kept in the corner and took out his ledger.

Katrina looked at the supplies she'd unloaded and arranged on the shelf: cocoa, dried figs, fresh oranges. With a railroad, Eureka could bring in anything. "Oh, but wasn't Eureka grand?" she said, the excitement of the trip still in her voice. "You were right. It has all the makings of a new metropolis, like New York or Philadelphia."

Then it dawned on her. "It was the extra miles it took to go to Prosperity, *ja*?"

"No." Justin studied the pages like a man distracted. A few moments later, he closed the ledger and put it away. As he walked to where his saddlebags hung on the wall, he said, "Get the baby and come outside with me. Please." He turned around. "I almost forgot. I need the hammer. And rope."

Twenty minutes later, down by the small creek that ran across Justin's land, Katrina studied the square he'd outlined with rope and a bunch of stakes, pieces of red bandanna fluttering from the tips of each.

"Well?" he said. "What do you think?"

She shrugged. "What is it?"

"The plan for your new house."

He couldn't have predicted the look of panic on her face. His whole world depended on her approval.

"With what did you pay? After helping Pius, you had next to nothing left. That's what you said. Was it not the truth?"

"It was true." He laughed nervously. "I have even less now."

She swallowed hard. "Then how—"

"I took out a loan."

Her eyes widened. "You borrowed?"

"Eight hundred dollars, including interest. Three dollars and eighty-five cents a week for four years."

She covered her mouth with her hand, as though the staggering amount had taken her breath away. He'd had a similar reaction at the bank.

He knew by the look on her face that she was about to ask why but thank God she didn't. With her less than enthusiastic reaction, what was he supposed to say? Because I don't want you to leave? Because I'm willing to risk everything I have to make you want to stay? Because my life would be nothing without you?

He was too proud to admit now that he would never

have built something like this for himself, so he pretended to be enthusiastic, a task that grew harder by the second.

"Over here is the sitting room, over here the kitchen, with a fireplace open to both rooms. Over here the pantry. The bedroom."

In an impersonal voice, as though she were speaking to a friend, a neighbor, she said, "I think it will be a fine house. One story or two?"

"Two. With a sturdy loft." He didn't say the loft was meant for children. He couldn't get the words out.

Late that afternoon, sitting with Tatiana on a blanket by the garden she was tending, Katrina abandoned the tender new shoots of cucumbers and radishes and retrieved from her apron pocket the letter that had come with the dollhouse. She read it again.

Gretchen and Lukas were getting married.

Justin had said he would lend Katrina the fare when it was time for her to leave, but that was last summer and much had happened since then. He had no more money to lend. Katrina would have to find another way to get back to Merriweather, or else she would not be there to see her sister get married. Someone else would be Gretchen's bridesmaid. Someone else would remove Gretchen's veil and crown. Someone else would slip the simple white bonnet onto Gretchen's head and loosely tie the white satin ribbons. Someone else would see Lukas gently squeeze Gretchen's hand.

Katrina read it all again.

Dear Katrina, my sister,

I hope you and little Tatiana are liking the dollhouse. This is the style so many Americans are fond of.

Every day is baking day for me. I do all the usual

breads and such, and now I also do cracklin' buns and nobby buns, some butter horn rolls, some prune kolacky, and sometimes I fry up some humbug cakes. The kids, they just love my humbug cakes. I am exceedingly glad to hear that your friends enjoy my sticky buns. Try the humbug cakes. Write and tell me if you do.

And now I will tell you of the wedding plans. It will be a morning wedding and it will be eight Wednesdays next, July 25, because Wednesdays are lucky days for weddings, but that you already know. My dress it is pink, not too fancy, but I will wear lots of ribbons. Everyone will wear lots of ribbons, all colors. Lukas's house, too, will be decorated with ribbons.

After the wedding I have plenty of cooks who will serve the dinner. We will have soup, nice and thick with egg noodles and home-grown hens. For supper, more chicken soup, some sausage, and baked ham. Plenty of kuchen. And, of course, at midnight the rice, cooked in milk with cinnamon, sugar, and raisins. All I am still needing is for you to stand by me. Write and tell me that you can come and when. I hear that all wheat farmers are rich. I am glad, because I have no funds to send for passage. Every coin must go to the Barrisons' loan. So I will meet you at the dock.

One more thing. Richmond has truly lost his anger. You are free to say the truth of your marriage to Justin, which you have yet to detail and which many, especially Frau Epple, have already guessed. Write and tell me.

I am loving you every day.

> Your only sister,
> Gretchen, soon to be Frau Heinz

Katrina sighed and closed her eyes. After lending nearly all his money to the Pettibones, how could Justin have done something so foolish as take out a loan, and such a big one? He, of all people, knew the danger lurking in time payments. Katrina did too. Perhaps he was more like his father than he realized, for hadn't Eberhard sacrificed his own comfort and that of his family so he could play the big man to his countrymen? Wasn't that what Justin had done for the Pettibones?

Tatiana began to fuss, and Katrina adjusted the basket she'd brought with her to provide shade. She leaned over and kissed her baby's apple cheeks and ever so gently touched the short dark curls on her head. Then she read the last page of Gretchen's letter, the one marked *For your eyes only.*

You must write to me at the soonest and tell me about the wedding night. Frau Epple knocked on the door one morning, very early, even before I opened to customers. She said that with both you and Momma gone, she worried that there would be no one to instruct me in my wifely duties. She shook her finger at my face and said I must submit and let my husband do whatever he wishes, no matter how shameful I might feel.

Lukas and I have kissed deeply, and I have found nothing but pleasure in his kiss. I thought to tell Frau Epple this but decided against it for she said that in the dark all men are beasts. And then she spit on the floor. She has been widowed a long time, and the lines on her face are not from smiles. I'm thinking that maybe she was married to a beast, but what if her lot had been to marry a kind man? A man like my Lukas or your Justin. Would she still feel the same?

So write on the very next mail and tell me if Justin, too, is a beast. Then I will know if my Lukas will change in the dark. I pray Frau Epple is wrong. For your sake and for mine.

Frau Epple. Katrina didn't know whether to be angry at the woman for worrying Gretchen so or to pity her for being given the kind of life that left her so bitter.

She slipped the letter in her apron pocket, picked up Tatiana, the basket, and the blanket, and went inside to fix supper. She would write to Gretchen tonight, right after she did the dishes. All men were not beasts. Justin might be impulsive, and he might do foolish things like take a loan for lumber, but he was definitely not a beast. That glorious evening in the haystack just three days ago reminded her of that.

Justin tossed and turned in the bed.

He'd sunk every last cent into a house. Not a barn that would protect the animals a family needed for survival. Not more land that would enable him to feed his animals and prosper as a wheat farmer. No, he hadn't invested in anything that sensible. He'd gambled everything on a house.

It would be a fine house, there was no argument there. It wouldn't be as large or as fancy as the one Richmond was building. Justin didn't need to see Richmond's house to know that. But it would still be a fine house. A fine, expensive house. He just wished Katrina liked it.

Now their survival truly depended on a good crop. What if there wasn't enough rain this year? What if there was too much? What if the grasshoppers came? What if, God forbid, there was another fire?

Katrina was right. He was reckless.

And he was scared.

His mind racing with plans to conquer every disaster he could imagine, he looked at her lying next to him. Moonlight peeked through the blue calico curtains she'd made by hand and danced across the quilt that covered her long legs, her back, the gentle swell of her hip as she rolled to face him. He looked across her naked shoulder, up the narrow column of her neck, and into her eyes.

She reached over and stroked his cheek. "I do love you."

Driven by a need to possess the woman who possessed his soul, Justin flung the quilt to the floor. As though she burned with the same need, Katrina reached for him.

In an instant, their bodies joined. His hands worked feverishly to unbraid her hair, to sift through the silky tresses and squeeze them in his hands. Katrina sighed with pleasure as she entwined her legs with his and pressed her breasts against his chest. God help him, any restraint he had hoped to have was lost.

There were no firebreaks to contain his passion. He entered her, vowing with each thrust to do everything in his power to keep her with him.

Katrina wore gloves to ward off the splinters, but the handle of the hoe was dry, and no matter how carefully she cultivated the rows of corn she always came home with a sliver of wood under her skin.

Every day for weeks now, she'd packed food and water and the baby's cradle into the back of the wagon, and she and Tatiana went into the fields with Justin. With the baby safe in the shade of the wagon, Katrina bent her back to the sun, turning the soil, weeding out the sunflowers that somehow managed to take hold.

She had to admit it pleased her to see the tender green shoots break the soil and reach for the sun. They'd grown three inches in a week. Sometimes she was sure they'd grown a foot overnight.

Tatiana enjoyed the outdoors. The fresh air gave her a healthy appetite and made her sleepy. Justin certainly liked having Tatiana with him. After eating his lunch, he'd lift her high in the air. "Take a good look, little princess, at your kingdom of prairie and sky, at the golden wheat and golden corn growing just for you."

Katrina couldn't help but notice how Tatiana always reacted to the sound of her poppa's voice, how she reached for him as soon as he came into view, how she grabbed his dark hair with her tiny fingers, how her eyes followed his every move.

Sometimes, in the evening, Katrina and Justin would hold hands and walk out into the prairie, with Tatiana snug in a pouch on Justin's back. Each would look quietly on the golden destiny that stretched before them, growing with each ray of sun, each drop of rain, each ounce of sweat.

Katrina realized now that she would need more than money to be able to leave. She would need the courage of her convictions—the courage to leave or the courage to stay.

The pitter-patter of midnight rain against the new windows sounded like music. Tired but happy, Katrina lay between the fresh sheets of her bed, a bed that sat on the planks of a sturdy wooden floor, beneath a ceiling that didn't leak, in a room where freshly planed boards gave the walls a soft yellow hue. She thought of all the evenings during the past few weeks when she and Justin, already exhausted from a hard day's work, had gathered stones, mixed concrete, and dug out the foundation of their new home. He had told her not to worry. When the time came to actually build the house, their neighbors would be there to help.

He was right. They'd arrived that morning with their hammers and their saws, their food and their recipes, their news and their gossip. Dulcie and Pius were doing well. Little Merton had recovered. Cleophee Yucker couldn't stop talking about her relatives who would be arriving from Hamburg any day. Lily Roundtree said her dog would be having a litter next month. Some of the men teased Justin for not having the brains to build a barn first, but he had taken it all good-naturedly. The women seemed to understand and looked at Katrina with that kind of soft sentiment always seen at weddings. They'd all gone home that evening, fed from the bounty of hearts and hands joined in a single purpose: to make this prairie their home.

Gussie had asked her how long it would be before they got the inside squared away. Katrina said she didn't know. She and Justin spent so many hours in the fields, it was hard to find the extra time. He'd plowed over a hundred acres and together they'd planted wheat, corn, potatoes, and pumpkins—but mostly wheat.

Even now, lying in bed, she could close her eyes and picture the sea of pale yellow wheat waving in the wind and see the orderly rows of dark green corn and their glistening golden tassels. She'd been out there every day, weeding, hoeing, watching it all grow. To look at it gave her a sense of satisfaction like nothing she'd ever known before. Now and then, she'd stand in the middle of a freshly turned field, inhale the richness of the land, and tell herself it wouldn't be so bad to live out here. That's what she thought now, too. Just before sleep overtook her, she wondered if she was only trying to convince herself because she had no other option.

Katrina shaded her eyes from the sun. "Justin, look. Isn't that one of Etta Scoggins's girls?" She tamped the soil around the prairie rose cuttings she'd just planted on the side of the house and stood to get a better look.

"Yes," he said, resting on the handle of his shovel. "The little one. Amy."

On a horizon shimmering with heat, a tiny slip of a girl bounced on the bare back of a work-weary horse. As she drew closer, it wasn't her stringy brown hair or her dirty bare feet or the furrow of her brow that both Justin and Katrina noticed. It was the black-edged envelope she clutched in her hand.

"Oh, no," Katrina said, biting her lip.

"Maw just come back from town. She said to fetch this out to you right away. She said to say she's real sorry."

"Thanks," Justin said, taking the envelope. He studied the return address. His own fears slowed his words. "It's from my mother."

With her heart pounding in her chest, Katrina barely heard herself offer Amy a drink of water for herself and her horse. By the time Amy rode away, the pounding had reached Katrina's ears and squeezed her throat.

Justin had waited until the girl was gone. He slit the envelope with his finger, unfolded the paper, and read. His voice sounded hollow when he said, "It's my father."

"Oh, no," Katrina said, placing her hand on his arm. "Oh, no." He shrugged. Katrina knew Justin well enough to know that he was upset, despite the lack of expression on his face. "How did it happen?"

"His heart."

Katrina took the letter and read the feathery black script. "Your mother says he collapsed after some verbal altercation—"

"With a boy at the brewery. My father died screaming at a boy no more than eight years old. A child!"

"But why? Something must have happened. Something serious."

Justin bent over and picked up his shovel. "No. He didn't need any one incident to get himself all lathered up like that. He had years of anger stored inside him. That's what killed him. Anger, pure and simple."

He searched the horizon and squeezed his eyes shut in pain.

"He hated the strength that let me leave. He hated the weakness that made Richmond stay. Sometimes I think he even hated my mother for finding her own way to endure." He paused, as though waiting to digest a sudden bitterness, and then jammed the shovel into the ground.

Katrina longed to put her arms around him and soothe his pain, but some things had to be dealt with alone. As she watched him dig, she knew he'd work through his grief in his own way. Just as she had.

She picked up the baby and went inside. Later she would talk to him about his mother's request, for in the midst of sorrow they'd been given an opportunity to go home. Rosamond wanted Justin to return and take over the brewery, with Richmond as his assistant. No longer would Justin be in his father's shadow.

The day started out as one of the prettiest Katrina had ever seen: soft blue skies, butter-yellow sun, just a hint of warm summer breeze. By noon the sky looked more gray than blue, the sun scorched the ground, and the air hung heavy with moisture.

Two hours later, after working over a hot stove, Katrina knelt at the edge of her garden, fighting the weeds that threatened to overtake her cucumber patch. She pinched the collar of her dress and tugged it away from her itchy skin. She unbuttoned her cuffs and rolled her sleeves back, but nothing helped. She lifted her face, seeking even the slightest movement of air, but all was still. Deathly still.

It had been several days since Justin received the letter from his mother. He still hadn't talked about it, and Katrina hadn't wanted to pressure him. But if he was going to go back and take over the brewery, Katrina wanted it to be soon, so she could be there for Gretchen's wedding. He had, however, mentioned that Richmond was far smarter than people gave him credit for and that, given time, he could do a fine job with the brewery.

Katrina prepared herself for the worst, that he wouldn't want to go back. Living out here was no longer as frightening as it had once been. She had good neighbors and a house of quality.

At three o'clock she heard the lumbering sound of animals and looked up to see the cows coming in from the prairie and heading for the corral. She'd learned from Justin that when animals sense bad weather they seek shelter.

"Everything will be all right," she said to Tatiana, who squirmed on a blanket at the edge of the garden. "It's just a little summer storm."

She shaded her eyes with her hand and scanned the wide horizon. Giant thunderheads, only their tops shot with sunlight, their thickening middles gray, their heavy bottoms shaded purple to ominous black, gathered in the western sky. "Maybe this time we'll get some rain instead of just wind and dust."

She picked up the baby and cradled her in one arm while she shook the blanket. "We'd better go inside."

The air crackled, and a blue-white bolt of lightning slashed the sky. Katrina clutched the baby tight. "Justin!" she shouted to the tiny figure in the distance, knowing he couldn't possibly hear her.

The clouds darkened. Suddenly brought to life, they inhaled and grew, rose higher, and clustered like some menacing evil blotting out the sun. A sheet of heat lightning flashed against the sky. Another bolt stabbed the ground. "Justin!" she shouted again.

Pellets of hard-driven rain slapped her face. She ran to the house, rushed inside, and closed the door, all the while repeating to Tatiana what she sensed wasn't true: "Everything's all right. Everything's all right."

She put the baby in the cradle and went back to the door.

Spikes of lightning popped and cracked in all directions. "Hurry!" she cried as Justin grew closer. "It's going to pour!" She caught her breath as a gust of wind swirled her dress about her ankles and sent the strings of her bonnet flying.

"Let's hope so!" Justin called as he hurried his horse to the corral. A clap of thunder quickened both his and the horse's steps.

Katrina held the door open and frantically waved. Suddenly, the sky broke open and rain fell in torrents. Justin hunched his head down between his shoulders and raced across the yard.

Katrina stepped back to give him entry. "Good thing I came inside when I did," he said. "That ground is so dry I don't want to waste any of those big drops on me."

"This is no time for foolery."

"You're right," he said, as he wiped his face on a towel in the small room off the kitchen. He went back to the window, but with the heavy rain pounding against the glass, he couldn't see much.

"Don't open that door again," Katrina said. "The wind will rip it off its hinges."

"We'll be lucky if that's all it takes."

He inched the door open and squinted at the driving rain. With dread in his voice, he looked at Katrina and said, "Dear God almighty, not this."

Katrina tensed. "How bad does it look?" She peered over his shoulder as he forced the door shut.

"Bad. I'll get the baby. We're going to the root cellar."

"Why? What is it?"

"A tornado."

The bone-white trunks of two spindly cottonwoods supported a slanted roof that was nothing more than a crisscross frame of even smaller limbs, all thatched with twists of hay for insulation and buried under two feet of earth. Katrina scurried down the three steep steps into the cool, musty room dug in the ground where huge chunks of ice Justin had taken from the river months ago still slept under thick blankets of hay. On the crude plank shelves ahead of her sat two small wheels of cheese, a tin-lined box of butter she'd churned the day before, and a few dusty jars of pickled watermelon rind that she'd managed to save from last year. A clap of thunder made them tremble.

Justin inched a crock of sauerkraut in front of the door to keep it from blowing in. Plunged into darkness, Katrina winced at the whistling wind and patted her baby's back, far too scared to say that everything would be all right.

The next minute blurred as Justin forced her to the floor, sheltering her and their child with his body. The howling wind descended, deafening the baby's cries and Katrina's scream.

24

All was silent. They were safe.

With Tatiana clutched to her bosom, Katrina knelt in the dark and thanked God for deliverance.

Justin hesitated before climbing the steps. "Just remember," he said, "no matter what we find out there, we're lucky. All three of us are alive and unharmed." She nodded and he added, "If any damage has been done, we can fix it."

"Be careful," she said, as he opened the door.

Blinded by the sunlight, Katrina shielded her eyes. The sudden sweet clean smell of wet grass and the rich aroma of a just-watered garden helped calm her fears.

Justin stepped up to ground level and for a moment just stood there, his broad back blocking the sun. When he spoke, it was to groan. When he moved, it was to drop to his knees.

"Justin?"

Katrina rushed up behind him and gasped at the destruction. Like so many wooden bones all fractured and broken, her house, her beautiful new house, lay in a pile of rubble. She looked to the clear blue cloud-free heavens and cried, "How could you do this to us? How could you be so cruel?"

Justin looked not at the heavens but at the ground. "I know it looks bad, but—"

"It *is* bad!"

"I know. I know."

Hearing the strain in his voice only heightened her own fears. "What are we going to do?"

He stood and looked around, but there was no starting point for the disaster. It was everywhere. "I don't know," he said. He reached down to pick up the tin mug he'd used that morning at breakfast, the mug he'd rinsed and left on the kitchen table. "It's dented."

Katrina scrutinized the mug too. It was easier than looking at anything else. Easier and safer, for she was terrified to recognize the true extent of their loss. The house—her beautiful safe house with its wooden walls and wooden floors—was gone, as were her few treasured mementos of the past.

"I'll leave it right here." He placed the mug next to the entrance of the root cellar. "That way we'll know where it is." Shaking his head in disbelief, he said, "I've got to check the animals."

Katrina followed him to the corral and waited while Justin stepped inside. Mud, wads of grass, and unrecognizable debris had collected around the posts of the corral. The animals were splattered with mud. "At least they're all standing," she said, though the horse was skittish and Blossom, now a yearling, wouldn't leave her mother's side.

Justin put his arm around Katrina's shoulder and looked down at Tatiana cradled in her arms. Just for an instant Katrina thought he felt as truly devastated as she did. Quickly, however, the confidence he usually displayed returned to his voice and he said, "Everything's going to be just as good as it was. Even better. You'll see."

She didn't believe him. Looking left and right, she felt an overwhelming need to restore the order she'd lost, but equally overwhelming was the sense of alarm that no matter what they did, no matter how hard they worked, the land had finally defeated them.

"Look," he said. "The wagon. It's still standing."

The wagon. Yes. They could salvage a few things, load them in the wagon, and leave. They could go far, far away. Back to Merriweather.

"And, thank God, so is the soddy," he added.

"Thank God?" A lump of betrayal formed in her throat. "If this had been God's doing, it would be the house that was left standing, not the soddy."

"At least we'll have a roof over our heads."

She was about to say that she couldn't go back to living like a rodent, but she knew that would be cruel. Justin hadn't done anything to deserve this disaster. But he couldn't have prevented it either. That was what was so frightening.

His eyes darted left and right as though he were seeing—or thinking—about something else. "It won't be forever," he said.

"Don't try to convince me we're going to rebuild. I know better. You haven't even paid for this yet, and it's gone."

Katrina walked closer to the rubble, all the while choking back tears. A scrap of blue calico caught her eye. Trapped in a jumble of lumber, it fluttered in the gentle breeze that now floated over the prairie. As she watched, a piece of lumber shifted and the blue calico disappeared, just as easily as her dreams.

It was so hard to comprehend. Just moments before, she'd had so much and the idea that she could be happy living out here seemed possible. But not now. Now more than ever she wanted to get away.

Katrina held Tatiana and stared off in the distance, hoping that at least an aftermath of silence would quiet the trembling deep inside her. But she heard the chickens squawking as they ran riot, their coop destroyed. She heard the horse, the cows. Tatiana cried. "There, there," she said as she swayed from side to side.

As she stood amid the rubble, she tightened her hold on her fidgeting baby. She remembered the day she'd made her first gingerbread house. Oh, how Momma had praised her, saying that though she was only ten it was clear she already had the gift in her hands. She remembered how awful she had felt when her carelessness sent the brown confection tumbling to the floor. Now costly planks of lumber had crumbled just as easily as those walls of gingerbread, sweet and dark brown with molasses.

In every direction lay jagged pieces of glass, cracked and shattered like windowpanes of candy, sparkling under a mocking sun. In a burst of anger, she kicked one of a thousand stones strewn about like rock candy freed from a hard frosting foundation. Her outburst didn't change a thing. Her garden, so full of promise, still lay buried under a roof of licorice shingles. And where her chimney once stood, there was nothing but a pile of gumdrop bricks.

She raised her arm and wiped her tears on her sleeve. "Hush now," she murmured to the baby—and to herself. She didn't dare say everything would be all right. For such a deliberate lie, God would surely strike her dead.

Justin came up behind her, the confidence he'd managed to gather already gone. "I should have built on a safer spot," he said. "Maybe over there." He gestured. "Or over there."

"There is no such thing as a safe spot out here. You couldn't have known."

"Sure." He said it as though he suspected her of holding back her true feelings, and maybe he was right. She couldn't blame him for the tornado. That would be foolish. But she could, and she did, blame him for insisting on staying.

He started to say something, then turned and walked away. Just as well. The way his jaw was clenched, his words were bound to be hard.

With the hem of her skirt dragging in the mud, Katrina tried to sidestep the puddles left by the rain, but that soon proved useless. With each step, all hope of controlling her situation slipped further and further away.

What should she do first? She looked around, trying to find a fry pan, a kettle. Somewhere, somehow, she would have to make supper. After all, they still had to eat. She felt a rising panic. What if she couldn't find any food? Oh, but they had butter and cheese in the root cellar. And eggs. She could cook eggs—if she could just find a pan—if the chicken coop hadn't been totally destroyed. What about laundry? How was she to do the laundry? The baby needed diapers. The baby. Where was the baby going to sleep?

Tatiana cried at being held so tightly.

"Justin!" Everything was slipping away. "Justin, I can't find the cradle."

Fierce, like some mythic hero engaged in battle—that's how he looked to her as he came marching from the corral.

"I can't find the cradle," she said again. "It's gone."

"For God's sake, Katrina, the *house* is gone!"

"Do you think I'm blind?" she screamed back. "Everything is gone. *Everything!*"

With his eyes wide and wild, he looked as desperate as she felt. In a voice that, if not at all tender, was at least steady, he said, "Then put the baby in the wagon and help me."

"I'm not putting her down anywhere—certainly not in this ruin."

Stifling an oath, Justin picked up a board, its edges

waterlogged and black. With the determination only a fool would summon, he clenched his teeth, wiped off the mud with his bare hands, and carried the board to a clear spot a few yards away. He went back, picked up another board and did the same thing.

"What do you think you're doing?" she said.

"Rebuilding." He tossed aside a piece of wood too splintered for anything but fuel, then took a deep breath and wedged another piece from the pile. "Homesteading."

"You're fighting an invisible force." He was just as foolhardy as ever. Just as wild. Just as much a dreamer. "You're crazy!"

But he kept on working.

The air turned cool. She shivered and held Tatiana even closer.

"It's going to get even colder," Justin said as though he delighted in her discomfort. "Usually does after a twister passes."

"If you know so much about them, why didn't you see it coming?"

He rolled his eyes in exasperation. In a surly voice he said, "I'm not perfect, but then you know that. I wish I were. But I'm not."

"You're just pigheaded. None of this would have happened if we'd gone back—"

"God damn it, Katrina, not again!" He raked his hand through his hair, streaking his forehead with mud. "I'm going to rebuild this house. The corral too. Then I'm going to add a barn. A big one." He glared at her.

"Then I'll have to leave without you!"

"So go!" He stomped through the mud to what used to be the other side of their house. With his back to her, he raised a piece of lumber over his head and slammed it to the ground.

His words stung, but that pain was nothing compared

to the pain of being forced to stay here, for he knew as well as she that without him she had no way to leave. Not yet.

She wandered through the hopeless mess, all the while watching Justin vent his anger and grapple with his own demons. He'd been betrayed by this precious land of his. Why couldn't he see that?

Over by her trunk, its domed lid hanging like a broken limb, she found one of the pillowcases her mother had embroidered, the ones Katrina had just washed and starched. Using the toe of her shoe, she lifted the mangled fabric from where it lay stomped in the mud. Its white satin-stitch hearts, broken and brown, hung limp and lifeless. The sentimental value alone was enough to warrant keeping it, but no amount of scrubbing would restore its beauty.

She found her Poppa's flag too, already faded, frayed and battle-scarred, now mired in mud. She would wash it and store it away, though she doubted the white stars would ever look white again. Poppa said those were the stars under which dreams were born. Poppa was wrong.

She draped the flag and the pillow case over a section of wire ripped from the chicken coop. She looked over at Justin again. He was climbing a pile of giant toothpicks, wobbling on countless loose planks.

"I can see the cradle down here," he shouted, his breathing labored from exhaustion. "I think I can get it."

Katrina hurried over, thanking God for this small miracle.

Justin grunted as he wedged another board free. He didn't move as quickly as before. He didn't hold his head as high.

With a few more moves, he lifted the cradle from the pile and emptied the debris that had claimed it. For a moment he stood there, staring at the little bed he'd made with his own two hands, then brought it to the clearing and set it down.

"Look in the provisions box in the back of the wagon," he said. "There's an old blanket in there. It's nothing fancy, but it's clean and it'll keep her warm." He looked at his daughter. His voice softened. "She'll be all right, Katrina. I promise."

It was so arrogant of him to attempt the impossible, so foolishly optimistic, so blind. And yet, when it came to Tatiana, he always sounded so hopeful, so tender.

How many times had she wondered what would happen when this wild and unforgiving land finally beat him down so hard he'd have to admit defeat? Now the time had come, and she ached to see his pain.

Tears are for those who have no hope. Katrina looked around the empty soddy knowing this would once again be their home. Although the afternoon sunlight poured in from the gaping hole in the ceiling where the stove had been vented, the walls looked darker than before. What was left of the ceiling sagged with small clumps of dirt, seeking the earth from which they'd been ripped. The floor, slick in places from the rain, felt harder beneath her feet. Already a musty odor clung to her skin.

"Ssh," she whispered to Tatiana, squirming in her arms. "At least we will be sheltered from the wind." Standing in the center of an ugly room made all the uglier by the lack of curtains, the lack of glass at the window, the lack of so much as a bit of lace or a coffee can of flowers, Katrina rocked from side to side, all the while rubbing and patting her baby's back. "Your poppa will put your cradle in the corner where you will be safe. The ground, it is too wet for the snakes, and the coyotes will not come this close. We will be safe. Your poppa promised."

Tatiana began to cry. Though her tiny pink face scrunched up as tightly as her wails were loud, there were no tears. She was but a hungry baby and knew nothing of despair.

"I know, little one, I know." Tenderly, Katrina pressed her lips to her baby's head. Fighting to hold back her own tears, she admonished herself to abstain from the sorrow and anger that could trouble her milk even as she decided on the driest corner of the room in which to nurse.

She sank to the floor and leaned against the wall, feeling the cold hard earth assault her bones. For her baby's sake she had to be of cheery countenance. She unbuttoned her bodice and slipped it off one shoulder. She pictured the sweet-smelling bakery back in Merriweather, Gretchen's apple-cheek smile, the graves of her parents united in eternity. She shunned the grief that overwhelmed her as she lifted her breast from her chemise and suckled her child.

It would do only harm to think of Justin now, for thoughts of passion could corrupt the milk as easily as strong ale. Yet in this moment, as in all other moments, he was in her thoughts as surely as he was in her heart.

How she longed for her momma's counsel. For sometime during this past year, despite her dislike of the prairie and her misgivings about Justin's ways, she'd come to love him. There was even a time when she'd thought she could be happy living here. She wondered now if that was only her practical mind at work, telling her that because she had no means to go home she must make the best of a bad situation.

No. It was because she loved Justin so deeply, so desperately, that the thought of living without him saddened her already grieving heart. But Eberhard's death and Rosamond's request that Justin come home changed all that, rekindling Katrina's hope—until Justin, more adamant than ever—said he refused to go. Only the fact that he had yet to answer his mother's letter gave her reason to think he might still change his mind.

If she still had hope, then why, she asked herself as she sat on the cold hard floor, her trusting babe asleep at her breast, why did the tears fall so quickly?

*   *   *

Justin couldn't sleep. Stars close enough to touch provided only a faint light, but it was far more than he needed to see the truth of his life. Sitting on the floor in the corner of the soddy, he leaned against the wall and shifted his position slightly, not wanting to disturb Katrina, who had fallen asleep sitting between his spread legs, the back of her head against his chest. One arm rested around her waist; the other across the cradle next to him where his baby slept, too young to know how selfish a man her poppa was. Here, in a hovel of dirt, on a bare floor, he'd made his child and the woman he loved sleep.

He hated himself. His baby should have soft blankets, a nursery filled with toys, and a noisy loving family to dote on her. Katrina should have a feather bed with plump down pillows and lace-trimmed sheets and all the other fancy things a woman like her deserved. She should have new dresses, pretty bonnets, and shoes without holes. She should have an elegant house with a grand lawn and library windows in every room.

How many times had he dreamed of the day when Katrina would embrace his love for this wild prairie and share in his determination to conquer it? But it was never to be. His acceptance came not simply because he'd come to understand her with his heart, but because he'd come to see that she was right. What kind of fool was he to think he could do everything, protect everyone? He was no better than his father, sacrificing his family for his own selfish need to be a hero.

He looked up at the stars and sighed. How clearly now he understood his father's drive to prove himself. Had the old man been blind all along to his family's feelings? Had he assumed just because he gave them a fine house and a well-stocked larder, that they would give him more than obedience, gratitude, and begrudging respect? Or was that all he wanted?

Justin wanted much more than that from his family.

The way he saw it, he had a choice to make. He could borrow more money and send Katrina home. He'd still have his prairie but he'd have only memories of the woman he loved. Or he could sell out, go back with her, and take over the brewery. He'd lose something of his soul, but he'd have the woman who owned his heart.

His baby started to whimper. As he gently rocked the cradle, he whispered in the dark. "Don't cry, little one. Everything will be all right. Poppa is going to take you home."

Nadine Rhinedollar gave a low whistle when she saw the devastation. She hopped down from her wagon and retrieved a ledger from the back of her wagon. "Looks like you folks got hit pretty hard."

"You should have seen it yesterday," Katrina said as she wiped her brow. "At least today we have a clear sky."

As Katrina and Nadine spoke, Justin tucked his hammer in his pocket and came over to them. All morning, while Katrina had cleaned out her garden, grateful to find tender peas and fragile lettuce buried under a protective layer of wet hay, Justin had acted strangely, tearing through pile after pile of rubble until he found his ledger and the coffee can that held his homestead papers. Only then did he set about repairing the chicken coop.

"Morning," he said to Nadine. "What brings you out this way?" He sounded apprehensive.

Nadine surveyed the damage and shook her head as though she'd never seen anything so bad. "Just wanted to see what you folks needed is all. No one's been able to get in to town. I'd say of the folks out this way you got the worst building damage by far, except the Roundtrees got the roof of their barn blowed clean off. I ordered them a sizable load of lumber and shingles."

"Was anybody hurt?" Katrina asked.

"No. But they did lose three pigs. Hemmelers lost a cow and God knows how many acres of wheat to the hail. Toppled the windmill at the Scogginses' place. I've ordered new parts. Tore up the Pettibones' barn somewhat, but not too bad. When I left they was all working each by side the other to shore it up. I guess the good Lord determined they'd had their share of trouble." She opened her ledger to a clean page with the name Barrison printed boldly across the top. "Now, tell me what all you folks need."

Katrina looked at Justin. They needed everything.

"We aren't buying anything right now," Justin said. "We'll let you know."

"But Justin—"

"Now, Mr. Barrison, I know your way isn't to take advantage of time payments, specifically after that business with the Pettibones—you can rest assured I was saddened by it—but under the circumstances, if you don't have cash, you'd be plain foolish not to reconsider."

"Wouldn't be the first time I'd done something foolish."

Nadine looked undaunted. "You got enough lumber?"

Justin waved his arm in the direction of the salvage. "We'll make do," he said.

"What about food? I can't believe you don't need food."

Something about the way Nadine looked at Justin made Katrina think of the way Richmond, his father, and the banker had glared at her, demanding she do what they wanted. Katrina linked her arm with Justin's. She didn't agree with what he was doing, but she knew he needed her show of support, just as she'd needed Gretchen's that awful day. "My garden survived," she said to Nadine. "And we have a supply of items in the root cellar. We'll be all right."

"What about that sweet babe of yours?"

"It's kind of you to ask," Katrina said, "but she's fine as well."

Nadine frowned. "Guess there's no need in my staying then. You folks sure you don't want me to order anything?"

"We're sure," Justin said.

Katrina knew Justin wasn't overly fond of Nadine, but he didn't have to shoo her away like a bluebottle fly. "You're welcome to stay awhile and rest your horses," she said.

Nadine closed her ledger, tucked it under her arm, and climbed back into her wagon. "Don't have time. Thanks just the same."

She picked up the reins but stopped abruptly; looking distraught. "Mercy. In my zeal to see to my customers' needs, I clean forgot to tell you. Mr. Richmond Barrison is in Prosperity."

"Richmond?" Justin and Katrina said together.

"Arrived late yesterday on the riverboat. Took a room in town. I recommended the Royal Roost. Includes a bath and breakfast. Anyway, seeing as he's your kin, I took him over to the livery myself and saw to it he was treated right. What a charming man he is. Simply charming. And so well dressed."

Katrina looked at the destruction that would be impossible to set right in a month, much less a few hours. Richmond certainly wouldn't be content to sleep on the floor of a soddy. "Why now?" she said, more to herself than anyone else.

"Oh, I told him a twister had touched down in these parts and you could well have been ruined," Nadine said. "Funny thing is, he didn't look all that sad at the prospect. I suppose that's because he's a man of substantial finances and knew he'd be able to remedy your loss. At least that's how he looked. Is he? A man of substantial finances, I mean?"

Justin turned and walked away without a word.

Nadine grunted. "Sure is a persnickety one, that man of yours."

"It's just the surprise. We haven't seen Richmond in—well, nearly a year."

"You suppose his visit has anything to do with that black-edged letter you folks got a short while back? Who was it passed on anyway?"

"Their father," Katrina replied, trying not to show her annoyance that Nadine always tried make everyone else's business her own.

Nadine nodded. Watching Justin's retreating figure, she said, "I'll wager his mood is gonna be a heap different when he sees his kin. What do you think?"

"I think you're right."

"Well, I'd best be going. I'm needed just about everywhere these days. Be seein' you." With that, she left.

Katrina walked straight to where Justin was hammering away at the chicken coop, pounding hard as though determined to fix the structure for all eternity.

"What do you think is going on?" she asked. "Why would he come all this way?"

Justin smiled grimly and wiped the sweat from his brow. "Because he wants something."

"Maybe what he wants is to make amends."

"My guess is it has something to do with the brewery."

"I still can't imagine why he'd have to come all this way."

Justin stopped hammering and paused. "Katrina, I know this isn't the best time, but I need to talk with you about something."

An awareness of motion on the still horizon drew both Katrina and Justin to the direction from which Nadine had just come. The image of a horse and buggy came in view.

Katrina smoothed her hair and straightened her apron. "Whatever it is," she said, "it will have to wait. We have company."

25

Justin accepted Richmond's extended hand, which encouraged Katrina to think that the visit would go without argument. Then Richmond kissed her cheek and, after groping for the right word, told her she looked lovely, which she knew was far from the truth. Cradling Tatiana in her arms, she positioned the baby so Richmond could see what a beautiful angel she was. He simply nodded, leaving her to wonder if saying a kind word about her child was asking too much of him. Open mind or not, if he couldn't acknowledge her child, she decided she had no use for him.

"How dreadful," Richmond said as he stood by the wagon he'd rented and looked around. "Simply dreadful."

"We had a beautiful house," Katrina said, ashamed to be stammering as though he still held power over her. "Two floors, all wood. Windows with real glass."

"We live in that sod house now," Justin said, pointing to the squat brown structure with its gaping holes in the side and roof. "Dirt floor, dirt walls, dirt ceiling. Not a lick of furniture. I doubt you'll want to stay the night."

Richmond winced. "Under other circumstances," he said, "I would welcome your hospitality, but perhaps it's best I keep the room I've taken in town."

"Thought you might feel that way," Justin said. "Bring your horse up to the corral," he added, as though he were obliged to be civil. "You can water it, then I'll show you around."

Richmond hesitated. The fussy look on his face reminded Katrina that he was unaccustomed to caring for his animals himself. Perhaps he was also afraid that stepping into the debris would somehow taint him beyond mussing his polished boots.

"Never mind," Justin said, hopping up into the wagon and taking the reins. "I'll take care of it." As he headed for the corral, he looked over his shoulder. "A word of caution, brother. Keep your head down."

"Why?"

Katrina set out for the soddy. "Rattlesnakes," she called over her shoulder, feeling pleasantly superior.

"Wait for me," he said, as he stepped cautiously behind her, looking in all four directions between each step. It took awhile for them to reach the yard.

"Are you thirsty?" Katrina asked.

"Yes, as a matter of fact, I am, though I don't suppose you've a glass of wine."

"No." She led him to the windmill. "But we do have the coldest, clearest water you'll ever find." When they reached the windmill, Katrina looked up at the huge fanned wheel clicking softly in the breeze, effortlessly pumping the spurts of water that collected in the redwood tub beneath the faucet. "Justin dug this well all by himself. Our neighbors helped, of course, but Justin did all the hard work."

She settled the baby on one hip, and unhooked the ladle from the hook. "Help yourself," she said, offering him the ladle. When he didn't reach for it, she added, "Or you can cup your hands."

He gave a nervous laugh as though the idea of drinking from his hands was far too unseemly. He took the ladle, examined it quickly, then held it under the faucet. He sipped, then drank the contents in one long draw. "You were right," he said, holding the ladle for a refill. "It is delicious."

When he'd had his fill, Katrina led him to the edge of the wheat field. "That's our wheat," she said, inclining her head toward the new blanket of soft green and an early hint of yellow that covered the land. "And over there is our corn. Justin plowed every row and I planted every kernel."

There'd been many a day when she'd stood in this very spot and gazed out at these same fields, watching the miracle happen. Working beside Justin had made her appreciate not only his efforts but her own as well. The feeling of pride that now caused her to straighten her shoulders was not new, but never had it felt this good.

"That's my vegetable garden over there. Already I have the sweetest peas. Soon I will have the firmest heads of cabbage, the reddest beets, and watermelons big as barrels. Come, I'll show you the root cellar and then the chicken coop. And our cows. You must see our cows."

"Katrina, wait."

She stood on the edge of Justin's dream, feeling it become her own, with all its threat of failure and its lure of success. "What is it?" she asked.

Richmond's pause lent emphasis to his words. "You plan to stay here?"

"Why do you ask?"

He shrugged and turned at the sound of Justin's approach. "You've done a lot out here, brother. I'm impressed."

"No need," Justin said. He put his arm around Katrina.

Katrina looked at him as though he were a stranger. Even if the tornado had destroyed the house, how could he not be proud of all the other things he'd done to make the farm a success?

"Still," Richmond said, "I can see the possibilities. During the whole trip up here I heard nothing but talk about all the rich wheat farmers on the plains. You'll be one of them one day. I'm sure of it."

"Why?" Justin asked.

"Why?" Richmond echoed. "Because you've always had an intensity about you, a push to excel. You're bound to be a success at whatever you do. That's why."

"But why a wheat farmer?" Justin persisted. "Why do you find it so easy to see me as a wheat farmer?"

"I don't know. I suppose because that's what you want."

"Could it be because you don't want me to want to do something else—something like run a brewery?"

With eyes suddenly too wide to be honest, Richmond fumbled. "Well, as a matter of fact, yes. I did assume you wanted nothing to do with the brewery. If you recall, that's what you told Father."

"Father is dead."

"Yes, and once again I had to deal with catastrophe by myself, no thanks to you."

Justin considered Richmond's words. "You're right. I'm sorry I wasn't there to help with the arrangements, especially for Mother's sake. How is she?"

"As well as can be expected. She mentioned several times how glad she was that Father's heart had softened toward the end. I can't say I saw it, but if she wants to think he had some kind of epiphany, who am I to argue with her?" With a look of exasperation, he added, "I didn't come all this way to argue with you either."

"Then why did you come?"

"Yes," Katrina added, "why did you come?"

Richmond's nervous laughter only made Katrina suspicious, a feeling she knew Justin shared.

"Well," Richmond said, "I suppose I should get right to the point. It's clear the two of you have more important things to do than stand around and visit." When neither Justin nor Katrina contradicted him, he cleared his throat and looked at Justin. "I came for your signature."

"On what?" Justin said.

Richmond's hand shook as he reached into the inside pocket of his suit coat. He withdrew an envelope and handed it to Justin. "This is a release Mother had drawn up. Father left the brewery to her, a move I find perfectly ridiculous. However, as she explained it to me, Father didn't want to stand in judgment before almighty God knowing his actions had torn his two sons apart."

He brushed the dust from his jacket, then nonchalantly added, "I certainly don't consider us torn apart. Quite the contrary. I've always thought we had, if not deep affection, then certainly abiding respect for each other. My feelings, however, are not relevant to the issue at hand." He paused. "I know Mother wrote you, asking you to come back to take over the brewery. I assured her you had no interest in it, a fact you made clear before Father passed on. I also told her I was perfectly capable of managing the business, but she would have her way, as usual."

Without comment, Justin opened the letter and read, holding the document so Katrina could read it as well.

"As you can see," Richmond continued, picking at a piece of dried grass that clung to his sleeve, "Mother will not turn over full control of the brewery to me until she is convinced, by your own hand, that you still want no part of it."

"She could have mailed this," Justin said, folding the letter and tucking it inside his shirt.

"And you could have put it in a drawer," Richmond answered, staring at Justin's pocket.

"So what if I did? You're there. I'm here. Whether I sign this or not, as long as I stay away from Merriweather you'll be the one to run the brewery."

"But I won't own it," Richmond said, his voice rising. "Don't you see? Unless you sign off, we are forced to share. I can't go on until you formally relinquish what we all know you never wanted. I came out here myself to speed the process. Admittedly, I'm eager to be about my own business." He withdrew a gleaming new fountain pen from the pocket in which he'd kept the letter and offered it to Justin.

"I can see that," Justin said, leaving the pen untouched. He tapped his chest where the letter now rested. "I've got to get back to work now."

"Wait a minute! Aren't you going to sign it?"

With an innocent look as wide-eyed as Richmond's, Justin said, "Not this minute. I need time to think."

Richmond blanched. "You mean you would actually consider *not* signing it?"

As startled as Richmond appeared to be, Katrina said to Justin, "You would go back?"

"I might."

Go back to Merriweather! Katrina blinked back instant tears, not only for herself, but for the struggle she saw in Justin's eyes, for this sudden change in his thinking overwhelmed her, bringing joy within her reach. After enduring all these months of hardship, of defying the land to break him, would he truly give up and walk away? Would he sacrifice his dream for hers?

Even as she felt the lifting of one burden, she felt the weight of another. Suddenly, that place in her heart she thought would be filled with happiness felt strangely empty. She too would be giving up a dream, one she'd only begun to have.

Now, of all times, she wanted to look into his eyes, to see if his thoughts of going home came freely or if, as she suspected, he was ready to give up the land he loved because he loved her even more.

But Justin looked away. "Richmond, I know you've come a long distance, but as you can see I've got a lot to do. How long do you plan to stay? In town, I mean."

Looking deflated, Richmond said, "I took the room for four days. I planned to take the next boat back. It leaves on Monday."

"You might want to extend your stay awhile."

"How long?"

"Hard to say."

Richmond pressed his lips together. "I think I'll stay here," he said, "if it's all the same to you."

"Here?" Katrina asked, knowing there was no place for him to sleep except in the soddy and knowing the pleasure he'd take in showing his disgust. Why couldn't he have come before the tornado, when Justin could have shown off the results of his hard work?

More important, with Richmond here there would be no opportunity for her to be alone with Justin, to talk in private about going back to Merriweather, to let him know how much it meant to her that he would. Tonight, more than ever, she wanted to show him how much she loved him.

"Yes, here," Richmond said, taking off his coat. "I can help you." He turned to Katrina. "You needn't look so surprised. I'm not a stranger to manual labor. I just don't prefer it."

She turned to Justin to gauge his reaction. His brow furrowed, an indication that he wasn't at all pleased to have Richmond stay. Yet all he said was, "I've got an extra pair of overalls hanging just inside the door. Why don't you put them on?"

"Overalls?" Richmond's nose twitched. "Well," he said, "I suppose it would be prudent of me to protect my suit."

"Then meet me over there by the lumber."

"Splendid." His head down, his eyes keen for danger lurking in the grass, Richmond walked to the soddy.

While Richmond was inside, Katrina and Justin walked over to her garden. She put Tatiana in the cradle on the blanket. "It is true?" she asked, concern creeping into her voice. "You are thinking of going back?"

He nodded. "I thought you'd be happy with the idea."

Katrina glanced at Tatiana, at the soddy, at Justin. "Yes, I'm happy," she said, though she didn't feel it in her heart.

"Good. Then we can get married in any of a dozen towns along the way. That way no one here or back home will have to know that we haven't been married all along. I mean, if that's what you want, of course."

She nodded. "That would be best." She'd miss the chance to have a wedding celebration with friends around, most importantly with Gretchen. But she'd been deprived of a woman's customary joy on finding she was pregnant, too. Why should her wedding day be any different? Who was Katrina Swann, the poor immigrant, the unwed mother, that she should expect more of life?

Even as the bitter thoughts crossed her mind, she rebelled. She was Katrina Swann. A good mother. Soon she would be a good wife. One day she would be a good American citizen. She hadn't crossed an ocean to settle for crumbs. She had as much right as anyone else to expect all that life had to offer. All of it!

When Justin leaned close to kiss her cheek, she grabbed the front of his shirt and kissed him hard. A year ago she might have enjoyed a beautiful wedding ceremony, but she would have been marrying Richmond. It was Justin she loved.

Reluctantly, he pulled away, with a quick glance at the soddy. "What are you doing?"

"I am exercising my rights."

The smile on his lips was pleasant enough, but the fire in his eyes thrilled her. "And just what rights are you exercising?"

"Those of an American woman."

Just then, Richmond came out of the soddy, the sleeves of his starched shirt neatly rolled to the elbows, the legs of the overalls rolled several times over. "Well, brother, where shall we begin?"

It pleased Katrina to see that Justin had a hard time clearing his thoughts after their embrace. Finally, he said to Richmond, "If I do decide to go back, one of the first things I'll want to do is sell all this lumber. So let's tackle that first. Separate the building material from the kindling. Stack it up. I need to see what I've got."

"If that's what you want," Richmond said, a little too readily for Katrina to believe he truly wanted to help.

She watched the two brothers walk away before returning to her garden. If she were to leave, who would water, who would weed? Who would pick the green waxy cucumbers, the slender green beans? Who would dig the bright orange carrots, round red radishes, and deep red beets?

Three times that day she boiled eggs in a dented pot over a fire in a pit dug in the ground. Breakfast, dinner, supper. She still hadn't found the plates. The stove had fallen into the gaping hole that had been the basement. It would take a lot of work to get it out. If she could find the fry pan she could set it on the hot coals and make griddle cakes, assuming, of course, that she could find the sack of cornmeal and it wasn't soaked. All day long, as she improvised ways to return life to normal, she did so knowing that her life could change any day; the dream she'd carried for nearly a year could come true.

Slashing through all these thoughts was the memory of how Richmond had forced her out of town, how he'd lied to Justin, how he'd threatened to destroy the bakery, Gretchen's only livelihood. Eberhard's death may have softened Richmond's heart, but Katrina didn't trust him. There was still something oily about him, something wrong. Maybe it was the quick way he'd offered to work. Death may have softened Richmond's heart, but she knew it would never make him eager to soil his hands.

Katrina spent most of the afternoon gathering up hay and spreading it on the soddy floor. At least that way they could lie down. Poor Justin. Last night he'd had to sleep sitting up, all to give Katrina a little comfort. But he hadn't complained. He never complained.

Tatiana fussed all through supper. After eating his dinner, Justin held her against his chest. He walked the floor, patting her back, gently bouncing her with each step. Still she cried. It wasn't until Richmond left the soddy, saying he needed a walk, that she calmed down and fell asleep.

Later that night, when they'd all settled down, Richmond said to Justin, "I don't know when I've worked as hard as I did today. My muscles will be sore tomorrow, of that I'm certain, but I must admit to feeling invigorated. I suppose life out here will do that for a person."

Justin settled down next to Katrina and closed his eyes. "Not for long. Sooner or later it will break your spirit as well as your back."

Katrina couldn't understand why he'd turned so quickly, so definitely, against the life he loved. She spoke to Richmond, though it was Justin she wanted to listen. "The prairie offers opportunity to both men and women. Out here a man in rags is as good as a man in whole cloth, as long as he proves himself a man. Out here a man works in no one's shadow but his own." Even as the words poured out, she asked herself why she was trying to convince Justin of what he'd been telling her since the day she arrived.

Richmond fidgeted with the jacket he'd rolled as a pillow. "I know if I'd put this much hard work into a place, I couldn't just pack up and walk away. Not when it looks like the wheel of fortune is about to turn in my favor." He spoke to Katrina, but she couldn't help but wonder if his words, too, were meant for Justin. All day long her thoughts were divided. Could Justin truly walk away? Did she want him to?

She settled herself on the bed of hay and waited for the sound of deep breathing, assuring her that Richmond had fallen asleep. Only then, when the darkness of night gave her cover, did she turn toward Justin. As though he too had been waiting for this moment, he quietly slipped his arm around her and drew her close.

Just the nearness of him soothed her worried mind. Just to touch him restored her faith that life had something more than hardship in store for her.

She ran her hands over his bare shoulders and felt the taut muscles of a man weighted down with responsibility. With her finger, she stroked the stubble on his cheek and traced his lips and was reminded that he never complained when life worked against him. He just tried harder.

He kissed her finger, then her lips, slowly, tenderly, as though he wanted not to arouse her passion but to touch her heart. And he did.

Nestled against him, she closed her eyes. Wherever their home turned out to be, there she would plant a patch of periwinkle, the assurance of a long and happy life, and there it would thrive, assuring happy memories for both of them, for she knew beyond a doubt that her fate was entwined with his.

*　　*　　*

The following day and the day after that, Richmond worked beside Justin to salvage the lumber. It surprised Katrina to see how much there was. She realized that they could rebuild if they wanted to. They might have to do without a loft for several years, but they could rebuild the ground floor.

The next day all three of them worked to haul the stove from the basement and set it up in the soddy. While Justin repaired the hole in the roof in case it rained, Katrina scoured the prairie, looking for far-flung items. She found the laundry tub, the fry pan, most of the plates, a can of cocoa, a can of figs, and a tin of coffee. Her winter coat had been all but buried in mud. It would take a lot of work to return it to wearable condition.

Just after the noon meal, she put the coat to soak in the laundry tub she'd set up by the windmill. She had already washed the flag and the pillowcase. Poor Momma and Poppa. They had been gone a year now. How they would have loved to see the prairie and to know she and Justin had found the lasting love Momma and Poppa had shared!

Her thoughts were interrupted when Richmond came up. She assumed it was for a drink of water.

He took the ladle, filled it, and quenched his thirst. "You know, I've worked alongside my brother for three days now without an argument. I can't say I ever thought that possible. But working out here and working at the brewery are two different things."

She wiped her forehead on her sleeve. "What do you mean?"

"Only that Justin would be a fool to think we could get along like this forever. Truth is, I can't take much more of this. I'm not used to all this hard work and I'm not ashamed to admit it. I'd much rather spend my days in a nice clean office. And my nights in a nice clean feather bed." He took another sip and looked at Katrina over the rim of the ladle. "A warm bed."

She ignored his innuendo.

"How can you possibly stand living out here? If the sun and wind don't get you, the snakes will." He looked around at the remaining evidence of the tornado. "Or nature itself."

"But it was a flood that nearly destroyed the bakery and a fire that did."

"Meaning?"

"Only that there is no safe place in this world. You must accept the prairie for what it is, not hate it for what it is not."

"Maybe so, but I for one can't wait to get home."

She couldn't wait for him to go either. The sooner he left, the sooner Justin's fighting spirit would return. She was sure of it.

Richmond shook his head. "If I could just get Justin to sign off on that letter, I'd be on my way."

"Why should he give up the brewery?"

"Because he doesn't want it. You know that as well as I do."

"Maybe yes, maybe no. But if he gave it up for you, what would you give him in return?"

"In return? What are you talking about?"

"Look around you. The tornado has all but ruined him. His finances are little to none. Rebuilding will be hard. And expensive."

"Oh, I see. You think Justin would sign off on the brewery if I gave him some sort of enticement."

She nodded. "I think that would be fair."

"Well I've got a surprise for you. I've already offered him an enticement, a cash enticement of two thousand dollars. He turned it down. He didn't tell you?"

"No." Katrina couldn't believe it. If Justin had turned down that much money, it could mean only that he truly intended to go back to Merriweather!

Though her head told her to be happy, her heart urged her to change his mind. Just as Momma had said it would happen, Katrina listened now only to her heart.

"What if he could be persuaded?" she asked, an idea forming quickly.

"By you? Of course, why haven't I thought of that? He still seems quite taken with you. Maybe you could persuade him to give up the brewery."

"I know I could. But I would expect the two thousand dollar enticement."

His mocking laugh irritated her. "Oh, you would?" he said. "Now why doesn't that surprise me?"

She bristled. His attempt to humiliate her wouldn't work. Not this time. This time, as Poppa would say, she held the winning cards. "Whether you are surprised or not, that is my offer. My influence to get Justin's signature on the release in exchange for your two thousand dollars. Do we have a deal?"

"It sounds too easy. However, I'd planned to leave Prosperity—God! what a name—tomorrow. If I have the signed release in my hand before the boat leaves at noon, you'll have your money."

"You'll have the release. But you must go back to town now. This afternoon. I'll meet you there tomorrow."

"Now just a minute. I don't want to leave your beautiful home and hang around that excuse for a town, only to have to come back out here and start all over currying favor with my brother because you weren't able to get him to sign."

"But I will succeed," she said, knowing her own happiness and Justin's depended on it.

She thought he wanted to shake her hand to seal the deal, the way people did on the prairie, so when he reached for her hand, she let him take it.

Instead he held her arm out, so he could eye her figure,

which was still trim but made rounder and more voluptuous by the baby. "So you can still work your charms, is that it, Katrina? You plan to trick him the way you tried to trick me?"

She jerked her hand away. "You swine. Get out of here. Go. Now."

"He wouldn't marry you either, would he?" Laughing, he turned and walked away.

She balled her fists, digging her nails into her palms. It would do no good for her to go up to Justin now, to tell him of Richmond's words, for then Justin would never sign the release, Katrina would never get the two thousand dollars, and she and Justin would never climb out of debt. They would never get that piece of bottomland.

She willed herself to calm down, to stay where she was and watch. Richmond stopped and talked to Justin. They didn't talk long. Justin didn't hand Richmond any paper. Good. They didn't shake hands. Even better. Justin did, however, help Richmond hitch up his horse. He shaded his eyes as he watched his brother drive away.

Katrina walked up to him. "You didn't sign the paper, did you?"

"No. I'm not going to."

"You are sure?"

Without hesitation, he said, "I think I've kept you on this prairie long enough. It's time I took you home."

"Oh, Justin," she murmured, knowing as she never had before just how much he truly loved her. "You don't want to go back. I know that."

"Things might be different now. Father is dead. Not that I'm glad, but maybe now Richmond and I can work together after all. We did all right here for a few days, though I'll admit there were several times when I nearly thrashed him. I haven't forgotten how he lied about you when we were back in Merriweather."

"Why didn't you?"

"Thrash him? I don't know. I guess I don't like thinking of myself as a violent man." He paused. "Or would you rather I'd blackened his eye?"

"Oh, no. Fists are for those who lack a brain for finding solutions. You have a good brain."

"You think so, do you?"

"Oh, *ja*. And you are a kind and gentle man."

He smiled at her praise. "Well, there's a good chance things would be different back there now. I think we should go. This lumber will fetch a good sum. So will the land. The livestock."

"Selling all this will let you walk away without debt hovering above you?"

"No. I can't say things are that good, but once I'm back to work at the brewery, I'll have money to settle our accounts. Until then, we'll manage."

"I think it is your head that says we should go back. Not your heart."

"What are you trying to do? Talk me into staying here?"

She swallowed hard, for she had to be absolutely sure before she committed herself to a life on the prairie. It would be the utmost cruelty to tell him she wanted to stay, have him plant his heart and soul in this land, and then change her mind. She looked him in the eye and spoke with conviction. "I want to stay here."

"What?"

She gave a sigh of relief at having said the words aloud. "You heard me. I want to stay here."

"No, you don't."

"I know my own mind, Justin Barrison. I want to stay here. I don't want anyone else harvesting our wheat, or picking our vegetables, or living in the new house we will build again."

Silently, he looked in her eyes. She knew exactly what he

would find there—love and determination—for those were the qualities filling her soul. "You're certain?" he asked.

"*Ja*. I am certain."

He looked ready to sweep her into his arms, but he stopped. "Why?"

She wasn't unprepared. She'd asked herself the same question. "I have come to love the prairie, more than Neudorf, more than Merriweather. Here is where I want to sink my roots."

"But why?"

How could she explain in a few words what had taken her almost a year to realize? That she'd made friends here, that traditions from all countries could thrive in this fertile soil. "You once told me that on the prairie you can be significant. I can be significant here too. Tatiana also. When she grows up she will know that the prairie thrives on the dreams of its women and children as well as of its men."

He lifted his chin and straightened his shoulders. His eyes shone with the power to make dreams come true. She thrilled at seeing his spirit build inside him, restoring him to the man of confidence she'd come to love. Grinning, he said, "I never thought I'd see this day."

She grinned back at him, awed by how she too had become stronger by the power to dream.

"Oh, I do love you," he said and lifted her in his arms.

She woke with boundless energy. Fixing breakfast and brewing a pot of coffee took on new meaning. She was cooking in her home. It might be nothing but a soddy now, but one day she would have a nice wooden house again.

When Justin came in from tending the animals, she said, "Before you go out to the field, be sure to sign the release. There's no sense in delaying."

"I suppose you're right." He retrieved the old coffee

can from the corner and pulled out the paper.

"I will drive into town this morning and give it to Richmond before the boat leaves," Katrina said.

Justin balked. "I don't think that's necessary. We can go into town together in a few weeks. I'll mail it then."

"But I want him to take my letter to Gretchen. She still holds the thought that I will be there for her wedding. I must break the truth to her at the very soonest so she can get over her heartbreak and make plans. To make her wait would be unfair."

Shaking his head, Justin said, "Don't ask me to explain it, but I just don't have a good feeling about your going in to town by yourself. Maybe one of the Pettibone boys can take your letter in."

"I couldn't ask. They too have suffered from the storm and are no doubt repairing. I can go. The sky is clear. If I leave right after breakfast, Tatiana and I will be back by supper." When Justin said nothing, she added, "Please understand. This is something I must do."

"I can't stop you, if that's what you mean." He took out the cigar box that held his pen and ink and signed the release. "Here," he said, handing the paper to her. "Just be careful." He took his hat from the peg by the door, stepped outside, then turned around. "I'd feel a lot better about this if you'd plan to stay in town tonight."

"But the expense—"

"We'll manage. I just don't like the idea of your driving all the way into town and back by yourself, not in one day. It's too much."

"I would enjoy the chance to shop for a few things. Maybe Nadine will put me and Tatiana up for the night."

"That's not a bad idea."

"She's a nice woman," Katrina said as she removed her apron, "just eager to see the country grow. As you are. As I am."

"You're right." He smiled suggestively as Katrina hung her apron on one of the pegs.

"I see the wild look in your eyes, Justin Barrison. But you have much to do this morning. And so do I."

He stepped back inside and kissed her. "So hurry back."

With the boat ready to leave, Katrina stood on the dock, watching Richmond slip the signed release into the pocket of his suit coat. Driving into town, she'd pictured how happy Justin would be to have the two thousand dollars. He could pay off the loan for the lumber and buy that piece of bottomland and still have money left over.

The whistle blew. "Well," Richmond said, "this has been a profitable trip after all. Tell me, Katrina, what did you have to do to get my stubborn brother to sign this? Let him mount you like a dog?"

She would not allow him to anger her. In a few moments he would be gone and she would have the means to fasten her future. She held out her hand. "The money, please."

"Yes, of course." Richmond slipped his hand in the pocket of his trousers, took out a shiny twenty-dollar gold piece, twirled it between his fingers, and handed it to her.

Katrina took it and held out her hand for the balance. Instead, Richmond turned away, headed for the gangplank.

"Wait!" she cried, running after him. "You owe me two *thousand* dollars, not twenty."

He looked at her with disgust. "Consider yourself paid, Katrina, for you are nothing but a twenty-dollar whore."

26

"*Mrs. Barrison, ma'am,* are you all right?"

Katrina turned to find Clifford Pettibone standing behind her, his hat in his hand, a worried look on his face. How long had she been standing on the bank watching the riverboat glide downstream, staring dumbfounded as Richmond waved triumphantly? How long would it take her to find the courage to go back and tell Justin what she'd done? For she'd convinced him to sign away the only thing of value he had left. He had relinquished it willingly, true enough, but he had done so at her urging. All because she dared to dream that she could provide the funds to pay their debt and buy the land that would ensure their future. Now she would have to go back empty-handed.

"Mrs. Barrison? Ma'am?"

She knew her silence was rude, but it took so much effort to speak. Finally, she looked into the young man's eyes, still innocent, still trusting, and said, "I have had a shock, that's all. But I will be all right."

"You look a little peaked. You want to sit a spell?"

She shook her head. "I will be all right."

"We came to bring some pieces to the harness shop for repair—Woolsey, Maw, and me. I don't know as I've ever seen so many people in Prosperity, have you?"

Until then, Katrina had been only dimly aware of the people who had gotten off the boat: women with familiar black shawls carrying a clumsy featherbed and a satchel filled, no doubt, with Old World keepsakes. Men wearing heavy sheepskin jackets, carrying the treasured sacks of seed wheat. They looked left and right, unsure of where to go and what to expect. But all the while they held their heads high, daring the summer sun to beat them down. Their faces reflected what she couldn't see in their eyes, the recognition of opportunity.

Clifford looked about. "Homesteaders. Much as I love to see them, I'll wager that come sunup they'll all be heading for the land office in Aberdeen to stake their claims. That's why I'm heading out this afternoon. On horseback. I can go faster that way. A wagon would just slow me down. As it is, we'll be gone most of two weeks."

One of these strangers would file on that piece of bottomland Justin had his heart set on. Katrina felt sick at the thought.

"Did I tell you that Miss Amadee is going with me? She intends to file a claim too."

"Miss Amadee?" Katrina said, with little interest. "But she's a woman."

"Don't matter. The law says the head of a household can file, so even a widow woman could come out here and stake a claim. Or a spinster like Miss McBride. Long as she's of legal age, unmarried, and in possession of fourteen dollars, that is. The government knows a woman who owns her own land has a real good chance of attracting a man and getting him to settle down out here. 'Course I'd want to keep company with Miss Amadee even if she had nothing but a smile. Still, if she files on one quarter and I file on the quarter next to hers, we can build us a soddy that stretches over both and each say we proved up. Then we can get hitched and start out with two quarters instead of one. That's what my paw did with each of his wives, and it's all legal."

A woman? Head of household? "Wait a minute. What did you say?"

"Oh, nothing. I was just rambling. I do that sometimes."

"No, please. Tell me again—the part about a woman being able to file her own claim. Is that what Winona McBride did?"

"Sure is."

"I always thought she was a widow."

"No, she ain't decided on a man yet, but with the spread she's got, she can have her pick."

"So tell me again, the part about a woman filing a claim."

"Well, she has to be of legal age, unmarried, and in possession of fourteen dollars."

"Does she have to be an American citizen?"

"No, but she has to swear her intent to be."

Katrina opened her palm and stared at the twenty-dollar gold piece, gleaming in the sun like a flaming disk. Suddenly, she remembered the old woman on the riverboat and her prediction that Katrina's life would be changed by a different kind of fire.

A new idea took hold—a bolder plan, a bigger dream. A trip to Aberdeen could make it all come true. It was all within her grasp.

Katrina gave her baby a kiss, then handed the cradle and sack of diapers up to Dulcie, who was standing in the back of Justin's wagon. "The nursing bottle is in the sack.

I know you'll take good care of her," Katrina said. "If getting that piece of land weren't so important, I would never leave her. You know that, don't you?"

"'Course I do, but don't you think you ought to wait until Mr. Barrison can accompany you?"

"He can't come." Richmond had reminded Katrina of how hurtful words could be. She didn't want to give Dulcie any more details than she had do.

"Well, I'll take good care of your little one." Dulcie positioned the cradle to keep the sun out of the baby's eyes. "And I'll have Woolsey drive your wagon home in the morning."

"*Danke*. I don't want to leave Justin without a horse or wagon for two weeks. I asked Clifford if there was a land office closer than Aberdeen, but he said no."

"He's right. There's only eight or nine offices in the whole territory, and Aberdeen is a long way from Prosperity. Still, I'd feel a heap better if Mr. Barrison was going with you."

Growing more impatient by the second, Katrina said, "But this is June. Justin can't get away for at least two more weeks. If we wait till then, we'll never get that quarter, not with all these new people looking for land. This time tomorrow they'll all be out with a land scout to see what's available. When that happens, we'll lose that piece of bottomland, I just know it."

"I guess I can't argue with you on that. Just this morning two scouts rented out space at Rhinedollar's."

Katrina looked over at the store and noticed the new sign nailed to the door: *land scouts open for business.* She felt an increased urgency to her mission.

"You're right, of course," Dulcie went on. "If we hadn't been hit so hard by the tornado ourselves, I'd send one of the boys over, but Mr. Pettibone, he's powerful concerned about doing good so he can make his paybacks."

Katrina understood all about the determination to be debt-free.

The two women looked down the street toward the livery, where Clifford and Amadee stood waiting with three horses. Dulcie placed her hand on Katrina's arm. "Seein' as you're determined to go, I have to admit that knowing you'll be traveling with Clifford and Miss Amadee like a chaperone does make me feel a bit easier. You know how folks talk."

"*Ja*, I know all about that."

"You ride horseback, do you?"

"I used to."

"It's a long way to Aberdeen."

"Clifford has it all planned. The first two days we ride hard to Eureka, where we change horses. Then two more days to Leola. Change horses again. A day and a half more to Aberdeen."

"Then you got to make the trip back. You up to all that? Bedding on the ground and all?"

"I can do it."

"You got a glint in those brown eyes of yours tells me you can do just about anything. Still, I ain't all that comfortable with seeing you go off like this."

"I will be all right."

"But what will Mr. Barrison say? Won't he be worried?"

Katrina stepped to the front of the wagon, where Woolsey sat patiently holding the reins. She knew Justin would be worried, but she hoped—she prayed—he would understand why she had to do this. "Woolsey, you understand, don't you, that there is no time for me to explain to Mr. Barrison? That's why you must do it for me. Can you do it?"

His blond bangs fell into his eyes as he nodded. "I sure can."

"Good. Now, please, repeat for me one more time what you are to tell Mr. Barrison. This time go nice and slow."

Squinting his little gray eyes in concentration, Woolsey repeated for the third time, "Mr. Barrison, Mrs. Barrison says you ain't to worry. She met the boat on time but now— I forget."

"Take your time." Maybe it was too much to expect a young boy to deliver such an important message. Still, she had no choice. With Clifford and Amadee waiting, there was no time to find someone who had both paper and pen. Besides, once Justin talked to Dulcie, he would understand everything. "Try again, Woolsey. You're doing fine."

He stared at his fingers and mumbled the first part of the message, the part he'd already delivered. Then he said, "She's gone to Aberdeen with Clifford and Miss Amadee. She'll explain everything when she comes back in two weeks."

"Wait. Don't tell him about the boat. That will only confuse things. Just tell him the other part. And be sure to tell him that your momma has Tatiana, 'cause Mr. Barrison can't be taking care of a baby and working the fields. And be sure to tell him not to worry."

"I will."

"*Danke*. You are a fine young man."

Woolsey beamed.

Katrina peered over the side of the wagon to see her baby one more time. As she did, Dulcie said, "I'll bet that piece of land is going to set you back at least three hundred dollars."

"Only fourteen." She pulled out the gold piece and showed it to Dulcie. "I am going to file a homestead."

Dulcie laughed. "Lord, I'm glad you told me that now before you set out. You can't file a homestead claim. You're already married."

Katrina felt the sudden weight of a scandal heavy on her heart, but if she proceeded with her plan, the truth would have to come out. It hadn't occurred to her until now that by finding a way to give Justin the land he wanted she might also be destroying her place in the community she'd come to love. If she hadn't left Merriweather when she did, Richmond would have poisoned the minds of all her neighbors. It could happen here, and it would be her own fault.

Knowing the risk she took, she took a deep breath to steady herself and said, "I have something important to tell you. I pray it will not poison your heart to me and Justin."

"Surely nothing can be that bad," Dulcie said.

"Justin and I are not married."

Justin gripped the hoe with white knuckles and glared at the stammering child in front of him. "What do you mean she's gone?"

Standing on the edge of the cornfield, Woolsey, no taller than the waist-high stalks, looked down at the ever-moving knot of his fingers. "She said to tell you she met the boat. And she had to leave. They all left. She said to tell you she had to go and she would explain and you had to understand."

"She left on the boat?"

"Yes, I mean no. She left on a horse. And she said for you not to worry about her."

"How did she get a horse?"

"She had a gold piece. She showed it to Ma. I saw it."

She hadn't had any money when she left. The only person who could have given her any—especially gold—was Richmond. But she couldn't have gone away with him. She just couldn't have. Yet even as he assured himself of Katrina's love, old insecurities crept in.

"You must be missing something, boy. Now what else did she say? Think hard."

Woolsey narrowed his eyes and gnawed his lower lip as though the outward gestures would prove his efforts. "She told Ma she couldn't wait for you to go with her. She had to go right then or it would be too late."

Justin's mind raced. Maybe she did go with Richmond. Maybe he gave her the money for passage. Maybe she couldn't stand not being with Gretchen for her wedding and didn't want to wait for next week's boat. "Woolsey, think. Did she or didn't she go on the boat?"

"I ain't supposed to tell you about the boat. I'm to tell you she left on a horse with Miss Amadee." Woolsey looked over his shoulder as though he couldn't wait to get away.

Towering over the child, Justin shouted, "That's the craziest thing I've ever heard of. If you're lying to me—"

"I ain't lying! No, sir! I heard her tell Ma she was never married to you, and Ma said, 'Then you might as well go.'"

No! Justin felt the pain as surely as if someone had reached into his chest and yanked his heart out. How could he have been such a fool? Why hadn't he seen it coming? He was ready to sell the farm and take her back to Merriweather, but she said she didn't want to go. The truth was she didn't want to go back with him. She wanted Richmond. She still wanted Richmond.

"Oh," Woolsey added, "and she said it wasn't right to leave you high and dry so that's why she wanted me to fetch your wagon back to you."

His baby was gone too. His little girl.

"I gotta go. Ma told me to hurry back."

Pain humbled him. "Your mother knows all about this?"

Nodding his head, Woolsey stammered, "Your missus, I mean your—I mean her—she couldn't have gone without Ma's help. She expects you'll want to come and talk about it. See—"

"I see, all right." With a dismissing wave of his hand, Justin turned his face and struggled to keep his voice steady. "Go on, get out of here."

Woolsey ran.

Justin stood alone in the middle of his empire, a field of bright green corn rustling behind him, a sea of pale golden wheat waving before him. He took out his handkerchief and wiped the moisture from his eyes. How quickly the acceptable feeling of being alone could become the pain of being lonely.

He kept himself busy. Days passed. At least once a day he thought about going over to the Pettibones to talk to Dulcie, to ask her to tell him exactly what happened, but he just wasn't strong enough yet to hear it. He didn't want to hear "I told you so" from Pius either.

The days turned into a week. One week stretched toward two. He didn't remember which day was the first that he didn't sit by the door after supper and chores and stare at the horizon, watching for her. It hadn't been her idea to tell people they were married, but his. He recalled her words with cutting clarity. "If you tell people we are married, what will you tell them when I am gone?"

But she'd also talked about "our wheat" and "our vegetables" and "our house." She'd said she wanted to stay on the prairie. If he closed his eyes, he could hear her voice, see her smile, feel the warmth of her welcoming embrace when he came in for the evening.

He fell asleep that night thinking about all they'd been through together and how many times she had urged him to read the signs. Until she left, the signs had all said she loved him. So what should he do? Stay out here and feel sorry for himself or go after her, find out what went wrong, and set it right?

The next day Justin woke early. He fed the animals and packed his bag. He planned to stop on his way to town and ask Pius to take the animals to his place while he was gone. If he didn't come back, Pius could keep them. Then he would take the riverboat down to Merriweather. He wasn't about to let Katrina walk out of his life without an explanation. No. Absolutely not.

Eager to get home, Katrina's heart quickened at the sight of the familiar windmill, its metal blades whirling in the breeze, their soft click growing louder as her horse approached the soddy.

She couldn't see Justin yet. He was probably out in the cornfield. For two weeks she'd dreamed of the look on his face when she told him the land he wanted would soon be theirs.

She tethered the horse by the corral and glanced toward her garden. It didn't appear to have been tended, but it certainly had grown. She couldn't very well complain. She'd left Justin having to cook his own meals and wash his own clothes in addition to all his own chores. She could hardly expect him to tend her garden. She didn't mind. In fact, she liked knowing that later today she'd be out there watering, pulling up weeds, and cultivating the soil. Just the thought of digging her hands into that rich black earth, warm on the surface, cool deeper down, added to her eagerness.

She looked at the soddy. She was home.

She reached the door just in time to meet Justin coming out, bag in hand. Arms open wide, she ran to him.

"Katrina!"

He looked stunned, as though he never expected to see her. Then, grinning ear to ear, he dropped his bag and gathered her in his arms.

She expected—she longed for—the passion in his kiss. But he held her so tightly, kissed her so hard, she felt a sense of desperation. She pulled back. "Justin, has something happened? Why is your bag packed? Where are you going?"

He looked confused. "I was going to find you. Where have you been?"

"You didn't know?" Distressed to think of the agony she had put him through, she blurted out, "Woolsey didn't tell you? I went to Aberdeen with Clifford and Amadee. Dulcie kept Tatiana for me. I met her in town the day I went in to give the release and the letter to Richmond." She searched his eyes for comprehension. "Didn't Woolsey tell you?"

"You didn't go back to Merriweather with Richmond?"

She drew back. "With Richmond? That low-bellied snake? Is that what you thought? Oh, Justin, have you so little faith in me? In us?"

"I—I don't know," he stammered. "I thought maybe you decided you wanted to see Gretchen."

"Of course I want to see Gretchen, but I wouldn't just up and leave without telling you."

"That's exactly what you did!"

"But I had good reason and no time for explanations."

He kept looking at her as though he didn't believe she was there. "So it's true? You rode all the way to Aberdeen? With Clifford and Amadee?"

"*Ja*. All the way."

"Why? And whatever the reason, why didn't you come back here and get me first?"

"There was no time. The land agents had already set up shop at Rhinedollar's." She hated thinking he'd gone through two weeks of torture not knowing where she was. "Poor Justin. Why didn't you go over to the Pettibones and talk to Dulcie? She knew I'd gone to Aberdeen."

"I was going to, but every time I started out, I remembered that Woolsey said Dulcie had been the one to help you leave. I didn't know he meant by taking care of the baby. I'm sure he would have explained if I'd given him a chance, but I was so upset . . ."

Katrina hid a smile, for while she hated to see how much pain her absence had caused Justin, she couldn't wait to see his expression of joy.

"So you really did go to Aberdeen?" he asked.

"*Ja*, that's where I went."

"What for? The only thing Aberdeen has that Eureka or Prosperity doesn't have is the federal land office."

"I know. Come with me," she said, slipping her hand in his.

He drew her hand to his lips. "Why don't we stay here for a while?" he said, a gleam in his eye.

"Later. First, I have something of the highest importance to show you. A surprise. Come. Let's take the wagon."

He set his bag inside and gestured for her to lead the way.

"You can drive," she said. "I have had my fill."

He helped her into the wagon, joined her, and took the reins. "Which way?"

"Toward the bottomland."

They rode slowly, the prairie stretching beyond what their eyes could see. She told him about the trip, about how much she'd missed him and Tatiana. He told her about the long lonely nights when he thought she was never coming back and about how he came to decide to go after her.

"What caused you to make that decision?" she asked.

"I read the signs. They all said you loved me."

She placed her hand on his arm. "You read true, for I do love you."

They continued to ride. Katrina directed him until he came to the section marker at the edge of his quarter. Just beyond, a blanket of soft green prairie grass covered the flat-land all the way down to the creek, where a stand of cotton-woods offered shade. Justin stopped the wagon and, as he always did when he came out here, he whistled in admiration at the prime quarter that stretched out in front of them.

"Keep going," she said, "down to the trees."

Shaking his head, he said, "I don't think that's a good idea. It's a dangerous thing to want something you know you can't have."

Katrina stepped down from the wagon and walked a few yards onto the new quarter. Using the heel of her boot, she kicked up a chunk of dirt. She picked it up, examined it, smelled it, rubbed it between her hands. "It is as you said," she called to him, "black and rich, with a hint of moisture." She looked all around her. "Flat, not rocky. No washouts. It would be easy to plow, *ja*?"

Justin hopped down from the wagon. "Excellent farmland, water for cows, water for a garden. A few trees. Excellent. But it's not mine."

Katrina started walking toward the trees.

"What are you doing?" he said as he hurried to catch up to her.

"I would like to build our house here."

"So would I, but I don't own this land."

"I would like one half of the house on your land and one half on this land."

"Like I said, I don't own this land."

She pulled an envelope from the pocket of her skirt and handed it to him. "But I do."

He stood dumbfounded. He opened the envelope and read the contents. "This is a homestead application. It has your name on it."

"*Ja*, that is what it is. A homestead application in the name of Katrina Swann."

"I don't understand."

She explained the bargain she'd made with Richmond and how he'd refused to keep his half, giving her not two thousand dollars, but twenty. "I wanted the money so you could buy this land. When Richmond cheated me, I felt *I* had cheated you. And then suddenly—like a kind spirit—there was Clifford, telling me about how he and Amadee were going to Aberdeen, each to file a homestead claim, their quarters side by side. They planned to build a house stretched across the boundary line and then get married, their holdings doubled from the start."

Justin nodded. "That's what Pius did. Three times."

"Clifford told me that even a woman can file a homestead claim as long as she is of legal age, which I am; as long as she has fourteen dollars, which I did; as long as she is an American citizen or swears intent to be, which I did; and"—she hesitated—"as long as she is the unmarried head of her own household."

Eyebrows raised in surprise and apprehension, Justin said, "You confessed that we aren't married?"

"It was the only way to get the land."

"Katrina, I love you for what you've done for me, but even though Prosperity stretches for many miles, it's still a small town. People will find out the truth soon enough. They'll talk."

"People know the truth now. I told Dulcie that we are not married. I said it right on Main Street. I'm sure others know as well." She wasn't sorry for what she'd done, but her confidence in the future did weaken a bit as she said it.

Justin took her hands. "I don't care if the community accepts me or not, but that sort of thing is important to you. I know it is."

"You are even more important."

"So what shall we do?"

"Erect a soddy. A tiny one will do, but it must be completed by the Fourth of July."

"That only gives us ten days. Why so soon?"

"So I can honestly say I proved up on my homestead before I got married."

"You're getting married?"

"*Ja*. On the way back from Aberdeen, we stopped in Eureka. I bought a few supplies and arranged for the preacher to come here on the Fourth of July. Tatiana will at last be christened and we will at last be married. It will be a Wednesday, the luckiest day for a wedding."

He grinned. "You sure are making a lot of decisions these days."

"That is what American women do."

"Who did you have in mind to stand up for us?"

"I thought to ask Dulcie and Pius."

"And if no one else comes?"

"I can't say I will not be sad, but I know in my heart that wedding you here and now is the right thing to do."

He kissed her quickly. "Let's go talk to the Pettibones. And bring our baby home."

Thirty-eight white stars on a field of blue. Seven red stripes, six white. While Justin and the preacher talked outside, Katrina knelt on the floor of the new soddy she and Justin and the Pettibones had built. With great reverence, she unfolded the flag her father had bought when he came to this country. Word was out that next year, 1889, four more states would join the Union, one of them South Dakota. She, Katrina Swann, soon to be Katrina Barrison, a woman, an immigrant, owned one hundred and sixty acres of it.

She understood now why her father had willingly risked so much to come to America. The streets were not paved with gold but there were golden opportunities, as long as a person worked hard and dared to dream. She thought of how proud her parents would have been to see this day.

Justin had cut a branch from one of the cottonwoods and mounted it on the front of the soddy. Katrina had fashioned a series of loops and ties to fasten the flag to the branch. Even if she and Justin were joined by no one else today but the Pettibones and the preacher, Katrina wanted to fly the flag. It was, after all, the Fourth of July.

She stood and straightened the lace collar that her mother had worn on her wedding day. Her cornflower-blue calico had already been mended in several places but was clean and starched. Justin had picked a bouquet of wild violets. They waited for her in a can of water on the floor by the door. This was her wedding day. All her life she'd thought that she and Gretchen would stand up for each other, but she realized now that some dreams were meant to die in order that others might live.

She didn't expect a crowd today but the Pettibone boys were big eaters, so she'd fried ten chickens, filled her biggest bowl with potato salad, baked a dozen loaves of bread and as many kuchen, and, for the traditional wedding celebration, cooked a big pot of rice and raisins.

She gathered the flag in her arms and went outside.

Justin looked both handsome and nervous. He was dressed in his gray suit and white shirt, his hair combed, his boots polished, his hands in and out of his pockets. "You look beautiful," he said.

"*Danke*. You look handsome."

He tugged at his jacket. "This suit doesn't fit me anymore."

"The prairie has broadened your chest and given you more muscles."

He smiled sheepishly. "And besides making you even more beautiful than ever, what has it done for you?"

Without hesitation, she said, "It has given me roots."

They looked at each other for a long moment. Katrina wondered just how hard it would be to sink roots in soil unnourished by the support of the community, but she'd made her decision. She had Justin's love. They had their land. She had no regrets.

"Let me hold her," she said as she took the baby from Justin and gave him the flag. She kissed Tatiana's forehead. "You are an American," she said, "a true American."

She watched while Justin affixed the flag to the pole, letting it unfurl in the soft prairie breeze.

"That's a handsome flag," the preacher said.

"*Ja*, it was my Poppa's. It was the first thing he bought in this country—even before food."

"All the more reason to fly it."

Justin stepped back to admire the flag, then took Tatiana from Katrina's arms. "The Pettibones should be here any minute now."

Drawn by the faint sound of horses and wagons, Katrina turned to the direction from which they would come. "Justin, look!"

Balloons of dust rose from the wheels. "There's the Pettibones!" Katrina cried. "And the Scogginses. The Roundtrees—"

"The Peroskys, the Warbecks, the Hemmelers—"

"Cleophee Yucker and Winona McBride. Even the Rhinedollars. Oh, Justin! They're all coming!"

Tears sprang to her eyes as the parade rolled toward them, each man, woman, and child waving a smaller version of the flag that fluttered over the Barrison soddy. Katrina felt Justin's joy as he put his arm around her and gently squeezed her shoulder.

"I hope you fixed enough food," he said. "Looks like we're going to have a big wedding after all."

Epilogue

Prosperity, South Dakota, 1892

Katrina pointed with pride to the loft, where a colorful quilt of appliquéd hearts and flowers hung over a protective railing and a sleepy, four-year old Tatiana and three-year-old Nikolas napped beside each other on a plump feather bed. At the foot of the bed curled an ever-vigilant dog, his big brown eyes fixed with curiosity on the newcomer. "And this is Strudel," she said. "He was a wedding gift."

"Another Strudel . . . a wedding gift . . . Oh, Katrina, my heart warms to see you so happy." Gretchen drew a handkerchief from the pocket of the apron that covered her swollen belly. Dabbing her eyes, she said, "All those years I feared I would never see you again."

"I feared the same. But here you are—you and Lukas and your babe to come."

"Your letter said that someday Prosperity will be big enough to need its own apothecary. In the meantime, we will homestead and Lukas can set up a small shop in our house."

"Your baking will be appreciated out here, too." Katrina looked at her sister, with her pale yellow braids, her round apple cheeks, and the swelling that said she would have a harvest baby. "Though I wished it every day, I never believed you would really come."

"Why not? What did Merriweather hold for me but graves?" Gretchen patted her heart. "Here is where I carry the memory of Momma and Poppa. Right here."

Katrina gave her sister a hug, one of a dozen they'd shared since she and Lukas had arrived that afternoon. Choked with emotion, she said, "I touch you and I still can't believe you are truly here."

"We would have come sooner, but we had to sell both the bakery and the apothecary. Now when my little Inga or Stefan is born, you will be close beside me, *ja*?"

"I promise."

"And as soon as we find some land, you will help us build a house?"

"Oh, yes, and so will our neighbors—your neighbors. They're kind, big-hearted people. I can't wait for you to meet them and for them to finally meet you. I've talked about you for years."

"Your friend Dulcie. She is the one I want to meet first."

"Oh, you will. And wait till you see her little girls. Twins. She's a grandmother now, too. Her oldest boy, Clifford, married a pretty little French girl and they have three daughters."

Katrina recognized the anxiety as Gretchen placed her hands on her belly. "We have a wonderful midwife. Cleophee Yucker. She knows all the new ways as well as the old."

"Good," Gretchen said and seemed to relax. She walked to one of the two windows in the large kitchen. "You will help me plant trees? I know they do not grow so easy here, but I see you have found a way."

"Those are just cottonwoods." Katrina joined her at the window. "I don't know that we will ever coax a giant oak to take root here. But look at the wheat. It thrives in this land. See the corn? Whole flocks of blackbirds sleep beneath the rustling leaves. Then in the morning they flutter to the heavens like a sheet flapping in the wind. Come, let's go outside."

As Katrina and Gretchen stepped out into the summer sun, they saw Justin and Lukas riding in from the north. Gretched waved with exuberance. As always, Katrina's heart skipped at the sight of her husband, the man whose love had given her the security to put down roots and the courage to dream.

A few minutes later, all four of them stood by the corral. Justin looked particularly pleased with himself when he said, "I took Lukas up to see that quarter Pius wants to sell."

Lukas turned to Gretchen and beamed. "It's a fine piece of land," he said. "Wait till you see it. The rocks have all been cleared, the sod busted."

Katrina suspected Justin's hand in this, for Pius wouldn't readily sell a quarter he'd already cleared and turned.

Lukas continued, "We'll have to build a soddy and a corral. Dig a well. Buy at least one cow, some chickens, some pigs. And, of course, plant wheat. Justin has been telling me all about it. I know you and I have talked about all this before, but . . . well, it might be harder than we thought to make a go of it out here, though I still think we can do it."

Gretchen's smile stayed just as bright as ever when she said, "We will manage. You'll see." It was only when she took a pinch of her apron and squeezed it tight that Katrina knew just how worried her sister was.

"Where is this piece of land, Justin? I didn't know Pius planned to sell any."

"He didn't exactly say he wanted to sell, he said he

would. I talked to him about it last week. He named a fair price, too."

Katrina noticed the twinkle in her husband's eye. The first time she'd seen it was the Christmas he gave her the cradle. She'd seen it several times since then, when he told her they'd saved enough to rebuild the house, when he insisted they leave Tatiana with Dulcie for a few hours so he could take her on an anniversary picnic. Nikolas was born nine months later.

She took her sister's hand, freeing the wad of cloth locked between her fingers. Anticipating her husband's answer, she smiled and asked, "So tell us, Justin. This piece of land, where exactly is it?"

"Just north," he said, pointing to small clump of cotton-woods visible on the flat horizon. "No more than two miles."

Tame the Wildest Heart by **Parris Afton Bonds**

In her most passionate romance yet, Parris Afton Bonds tells the tale of two lonely hearts forever changed by an adventure in the Wild West. It was a match made in heaven . . . and hell. Mattie McAlister was looking for her half-Apache son and Gordon Halpern was looking for his missing wife. Neither realized that they would find the trail to New Mexico Territory was the way to each other's hearts.

First and Forever by **Zita Christian**

Katrina Swann was content with her peaceful, steady life in the close-knit immigrant community of Merriweather, Missouri. Then the reckless Justin Barrison swept her off her feet in a night of passion. Before she knew it she was following him to the Dakota Territory. Through trials and tribulations on the prairie, they learned the strength of love in the face of adversity.

Gambler's Gold by **Barbara Keller**

When Charlotte Bell headed out on a wagon train from Massachusetts to California, she had one goal in mind—finding her father, who had disappeared while prospecting for gold. The last thing she was looking for was love, but when fate turned against her, she turned to the dashing Reade Elliot to save her.

Queen by **Sharon Sala**

The Gambler's Daughters Trilogy continues with Diamond Houston's older sister, Queen, and the ready-made family she discovers, complete with laughter and tears. Queen Houston always had to act as a mother to her two younger sisters when they were growing up. After they part ways as young women, each to pursue her own dream, Queen reluctantly ends up in the mother role again—except this time there's a father involved.

A Winter Ballad by **Barbara Samuel**

When Anya of Winterbourne rescued a near-dead knight she found in the forest around her manor, she never thought he was the champion she'd been waiting for. "A truly lovely book. A warm, passionate tale of love and redemption, it lingers in the hearts of readers. . . . Barbara Samuel is one of the best, most original writers in romantic fiction today."—Anne Stuart

Shadow Prince by **Terri Lynn Wilhelm**

A plastic surgeon falls in love with a mysterious patient in this powerful retelling of *The Beauty and the Beast* fable. Ariel Denham, an ambitious plastic surgeon, resentfully puts her career on hold for a year in order to work at an exclusive, isolated clinic high in the Smoky Mountains. There she meets and falls in love with a mysterious man who stays in the shadows, a man she knows only as Jonah.

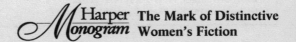